PLAYING THE GAME

Other fiction by Alan Lelchuk:

American Mischief

Miriam at Thirty-Four

Shrinking

Miriam in Her Forties

Brooklyn Boy

PLAYING
THE GAME

A NOVEL BY

ALAN LELCHUK

BASKERVILLE
PUBLISHERS INC.
DALLAS • NEW YORK • DUBLIN

This book is a work of fiction. Names, characters, places and incidents are either the product of the author's imagination or are used fictitiously. Any resemblance to actual events or locales or persons, living or dead, is entirely coincidental.

BASKERVILLE Publishers, Inc.
7616 LBJ Freeway, Suite 220, Dallas, TX 75251-1008

Library of Congress Cataloging-in-Publication Data

Lelchuk, Alan.
    Playing the game: a novel / by Alan Lelchuk.
        p. cm.
    ISBN 1-880909-32-4
    I. Title.
    PS3562.E464P57 1995   95-5384
    813'.54--dc20   CIP

All rights reserved
Manufactured in the United States of America
First Printing, 1995

Dedicated to old friends, the living and the dead:

Charlotte and William Irvine

Arthur Krasinsky

George Lichtheim

Page Stegner

Judith and Michael Walzer

With special thanks to
J. Laurie Snell and Peter Fox Smith

CONTENTS

But sternly discarding, shutting our eyes to the glow and grandeur of the general superficial effect, coming down to what is the only real importance, Personalities, and examining minutely, we question, we ask, Are there, indeed men here worthy the name? Are there athletes? Are there perfect women, to match the beautiful manners? Are there crops of fine youths, and majestic old persons? Are there arts worthy freedom and a rich people? Is there a great moral and religious civilization—the only justification of a great material one? Confess that to severe eyes, using the moral microscope upon humanity, a sort of dry and flat Sahara appears, these cities, crowded with petty grotesques, malformations, phantoms, splaying meaningless antics. Confess that everywhere, in shop, street, church, theatre, barroom, official chair, are pervading flippancy and vulgarity, low cunning infidelity—everywhere the youth puny, impudent, foppish, prematurely ripe—everywhere in abnormal libidinousness, unhealthy forms male, female, painted, padded, dyed, chignon'd, muddy complexions, bad blood, the capacity for good motherhood decreasing or deceas'd, shallow notions of beauty, with a range of manners, or rather lack of manners (considering the advantages enjoy'd), probably the meanest to be seen in the world...

Walt Whitman, *Democratic Vistas* (1871)

Basketball is almost an addiction to an athlete. It's what makes you what you are, and it's what got you where you are. Even 10 or 20 years from now, he'll probably still think he can play the game. That's what makes you good at what you do, and it's the mentality of an athlete.

Isiah Thomas, player (1991)

You are what you are. Bill Parcells is a football coach. I miss the camaraderie. The fighting and bleeding and sweating on Sunday is special. It's something you don't get anywhere else in life. I know it can't last forever, but I'm trying to prolong it as long as I can. It's like going to the schoolyard when you're a kid. Sometime, you have to grow up. But thankfully, I haven't had to.

Bill Parcells, coach (1993)

Man's chief difference from the brutes lies in the exuberant excess of his subjective propensities—his pre-eminence over them simply and solely in the number and in the fantastic and unnecessary character of his wants, physical, moral, aesthetic, and intellectual. Had his whole life not been a quest for the superfluous, he never would have established himself as inexpugnably as he has done in the necessary.

William James, *The Will To Believe* (1897)

PREGAME TALK

Coaching kids in America at the end of the 20th century turns out to be a kind of religious experience, native style. One that William James—and Hank Iba—might have found of interest. Strange terms. But the total experience so lends itself to irrational impulses and demands, to inward pulls and calls, to modern mystery and a sense of divine transcendence, that reason and secularism fall gradually by the wayside. Along the way one is reduced—or lifted—to faith, prayer, babbling recitation, higher callings (beyond, say, ESPN, CNN). Let me put it another way. A coach today, in college basketball—my recent beat—is part teacher, part therapist, part priest, part father. Who would have dreamed it? Not Dr. Naismith, that inventive Canadian.

Healing and saving, not X-ing and O-ing, is the name of the game today. Misguided or overheated nomenclature? Anyone who believes that a coach nowadays is defined mainly by qualities like game strategy, or recruitment ability, is still living in the ancient era of the Jazz Age, the Great Depression, World War II. Not the age of 240-meg hard-drive Dehumanism or Crack Rehabilitation Centers or $4,000,000 Final Four Holy Grail Games. No way.

The boys are his flock, his crew, pure and complex. Coach

needs first to find them, banged up in the ghetto ditches and alleyways or lying bruised in the working class gutters and ravines, then pick them up and guide them into the modern houses of worship—our high school and college gymnasiums—and there nurse and nurture them, until graduation if possible, and after that too, if necessary. The boys are his flock, no matter what they do or how they sin, how little they know or what they desire. For it falls on Coach to educate them when the professors scorn or overlook them, guide them when the Deans and Counselors write them off, raise them up when the fans and media use and abuse them. Coach, as the crew calls him, needs no article to augment his power. The boys are his flock, and Coach and Gym are their true sanctuary; that is his covenant and he must not forget it. It's been my credo, too, which has been both a blessing and an undoing. In the great epic movie called Amerika, where Coach has been thrust into a starring role, surrounded by college profs, perks, and glamour, that covenant keeps one grounded in the real.

Yet those thoughts were the bane of my daily existence, the albatross hanging around my "thin-skinned liberal neck," as the Colonel put it, my former boss and ex-coach of Conway's hoop squad, who never tired of mocking me. But that was all right with me; I was too old at fifty-one to learn new tricks, let alone new philosophy. An Assistant's role was a fate accepted by me, after modest gains and key losses in the trade. A checkered career, sure; but I've always thought that such a career prepared one well for the vicissitudes of life. And while down and out in our native land was not a very respectable position, as we know, nevertheless it had this virtue: it allowed you the bunker of obscurity necessary to view things clearly, accurately. That is no small plus in a country of smokescreens, a territory of ambiguity and deception, where seeing reality is a major breakthrough. So too with the elements of my field: hungry young athletes set amidst genteel students and professors, big money dreams and empty pockets, gyms and manicured lawns instead of hovels and gunfighter streets. Scramble them together and what do you get? A rich but scrambled map, demanding interpretation, judgment.

That's why, amid the sound and fury of contemporary noise and educated static, I repeat to myself: remember your allegiance, your flock. In the crunch, as the boys say, it's them and you. I know, I've been there, in the crunch, as you'll hear.

Do I sound ornery, skeptical, preacherly? Well, why not? Throw in a touch of wit and a bit of bile, a learned pipe and a totebag of bookish pipedreams, a poignant belief in pointguards and perverse view of higher education and you've got a pretty fair fix on yours truly, Sydney Berger. (How about tormented will, bent on winning, self-destructing?)

Oh yes, one other item. Why in the world does an intelligent man, an intellectual no less, go into the unseemly profession of coaching? (Especially if his parents have raised him in a peculiar incubator, forcefed a European diet of Kropotkin and Gigli, Emma Goldman and Titta Ruffo, Bakunin and Caruso?)

Well, look at it this way: if at 32 or so you awake one morning from a lifelong sleepwalk to look up and around at the world of your life, to consider the job you're laboring at day in day out, and you're hit with the urgent sense that something is missing, some part of your soul is starving, and you're propelled back, way back, to an age when you really felt a surge of body and mind at the prospect of doing something, and that age was 12 or 14, and that something was play on the court or green field, why then it's simple. The source of full gratification has been located. Now, the switching of the tracks, the hitching up of the new profession and the transference of feeling from adolescence to adulthood, is up to you.

Sure, in Europe I might have become a cosmopolitan novelist, a postmodern filmmaker, a New Renaissance man; you know, a Serious Fellow, adored in the New York Review of Books (my old dream). Here, however, it's the roundball and hardwood game that has my attention. Here, my reading lens is focused on zone defenses and half-court offenses, rather than only texts; here reading means seeing games and video reruns in order to assess individual talent and team strategy. For a Ph.D. in History (Stanford), it was a sea-change to learn new ways of interpreting reading and selecting from the past, a learning experience to study classic playmakers (Davies, Cousy, McGuire) rather than classic historians (Burke, Parkman or Macauley).

Getting back to a turf of love, beginning in your mid-thirties and working itself up through your forties, refreshes one like warm sun and April rain after a long winter of adult illness; it nourishes the spirit, lightens the step. A new life in mid-life. No matter if pals (and family) think you've gone a bit bonkers, colleagues (in teaching) glance at you with derisive smiles, spouse stays politely silent. Small slaps on the return route to pleasure. So what if the slaps become blows later on?

After all, if you're the kind who happens to believe, as I do, that all divergent lines in one's life are ultimately connected, meeting up at some unlikely mysterious juncture, then other lines of development are not wasted, by any means. If for example the idea of the full-court trapping zone intrigues as much as the myth of the virgin land, or the ramifications of the Oversoul extend like those of the weave-pick-and-cut offense, if ideas of how to play the game by Wooden, Iba or Newell inspire like reflections on how to conduct one's life by Emerson, Thoreau or Whitman, then it's obvious that excitement can be discovered anywhere, if you dig at the bare ground hard enough, scratch long enough. For more than fifteen years I've played that sort of chicken, digging and scratching, and it's been as much a labor of love as an act of survival, my redemption and my downfall.

1   BOUNCE OF THE BALL

Down and out in America is not the way you want to be, or appear to be, for everyone's sake. When everything looks grey to you, the morning sky, "All Things Considered" and Lurtzema, the day's work, your favorite team's chances, you best hide it or hibernate. Otherwise you begin to feel that everyone senses your interior growing morbid, a greasy slide from respectability, and smirks behind your back. Of course the paranoia comes from one's own slipping self-respect as much as anything out there.

Thus, when the phone call came through from Dick Porter, the A.D., asking me to come in that late morning for a chat, I had it figured immediately. I mean, I slid the request into the bad news slot. "That's it, fella, nice knowing you, but you see, the team's not doing well, and the Colonel feels that a change can only be for the good. Of course you're entitled to a letter of recommendation on your way out." And so on.

I played that adieu over and over through the bright September morning, while cleaning out my office. My odd mix of favorite hoop text and history books, two certificates of excellence (the last one ten years ago, pal) and a hodge-podge of files and 5 x 8 note cards, yellow and pink for offense, blue and green for defense. And the old photographs, of the kid and ex-country house. Going on the road again, after three years at Ivy Conway, was not going to be a journey of ease. If I were coming from Duke or Indiana or even Penn, that would be one thing. But from little Conway and its small-time hoop program? The next step was down a notch, I feared, below NCAA Division I. A drop into full oblivion, from which there's hardly a rescue. Naturally I'd be dropped from the History Department too, though I could probably hang on as adjunct for a term or two, and face the daily indignities. Oh well.

"Sit down, Sydney, won't you?" Porter motioned with his usual hospitality. He was a Redford type, a tad older, but with the same pale, cool imperturbable handsomeness.

I hadn't known the man too well in my three years, having been cordoned off from him by the shrewd Colonel, but he had always been cordial when we met. So why not now, at the end, right?

He wore a short-sleeved shirt and yellow linen necktie, and offered me coffee from his machine. Krupps, not Mr. Coffee. I looked around the swell office, lined by photographs of winners and a shelf of trophies, with the view of sloping lawn, and figured he belonged here, the lucky son of a gun.

He handed me the beige mug with the Conway logo on it, and took one himself. He sat on the edge of the desk, sipped, and spoke softly. "Well, I'll lay it out to you straight, okay?"

"Sure, Dick." Getting fired had its privileges, I figured, like first names.

He nodded at that and said, "We'd like you to be the new Head Coach of the team, starting immediately. Strickland informed us *yesterday morning* that he was leaving for Kansas State, where the job suddenly opened up. His alma mater, too good to pass up, he claims. After talking with some people and assessing the situation I feel you're the best man to take over right now. For the season, I mean."

I circled the mug with my hand, studying the small shield of the college for the first time, a pastoral portrait of a white colonial with trees, a book in the upper left corner, and two students approaching. The date was 1769, the motto *Vox Clamantis in Deserto*. Cute, that Latin, like aphoristic wisdom on bikini briefs.

"I know it's a surprise, Sydney. Think it over. If you can give us an answer in 24 hours, though, it will help matters. In eighteen days school begins and it would be good to have our man in place as soon as possible, as you can imagine."

"Well, I'm flattered as well as surprised. And you know," I said, fingering my beard, "I've had just enough time. I accept."

A beat. He smiled widely, stood up and put out his hand.

"Congratulations. And welcome aboard."

I stood too, and took his hand, firmly.

"We'll announce the news today. And can you stand a small press conference tomorrow morning?"

I had stood far worse. "Sure."

He walked around the desk and took something from the drawer. "Now give me the lowdown—is the team as bad as it looks on paper? And is that really why the Colonel took a flyer?"

He was thrusting a narrow box of cigars toward me. "Havanas."

I took one and slipped off the cellophane just as I had done in childhood with my father's Dutch Masters. Dick lit it for me.

"Thanks. Well, it is pretty bad, I guess. On paper, that is. And for now, on the floor too."

"Hmm. What do you mean, 'for now?'"

"Well, there are several names crossed off the Colonel's player's list whom I think may be salvageable. For this year."

"Oh?"

"Yeah, well. A kid in New York, a Prop 48 with some medical problems. And a local lad, from down in Brattleboro, who quit the team last spring. And a Maine Indian, whose family supposedly—"

"Hold on a minute, I'm impressed. You do keep up, don't

you?"

Sipping the fine coffee, I put "Colombian?"

"Colombian Supremo, there's a difference."

I smiled. "Oh, they're my kids. My recruits, I mean."

"I see." He puffed. "Is the high attrition rate common?"

I shrugged. Why indict the Colonel and his arrogant, errant ways, now that he was gone?

"Do you think you can get the missing ones back in school and suited up for this season?"

"I don't know. But I can give it a try."

He nodded, reflecting. "Let me know if I can help with the Registrar, or Admissions. I think I can get the scholarships reinstated, and maybe get you another one or two. But we're still talking a weak club, right?"

I nodded and considered the matter. "Yeah, it's pretty weak as of now. But it has some potential."

"Well, we won ten last season, lost fifteen, plus three regulars. So I'm not expecting miracles. Nor are the alumni. But if you can make the games competitive at least, that would be a victory. At the end of last season matters got worse as I recall, not better."

"Yes, it was pretty tough at the end. By midseason anyway, with some breaks, I think we can be competitive." One of the magical words of the place, like "productive," "big time."

He walked over to his bookcase, selected a book and brought it over to me.

A basketball primer, I figured.

"You might have a look at this in the next week or so. A history of the college. Skim it anyway. You see," he said, sitting down in a college Windsor armchair, "here at Conway the school counts for more than the sport. In other words it's *how you play the game*, on and off the court, that finally matters the most. The conduct of the coach, the players. You've been around here long enough to understand what I mean, I think?"

"Yes, I think I do," I responded, keeping to myself my

ambivalence on the subject. "I will have a look at it. Thanks."

"Sometimes the Colonel didn't quite understand that, I fear. And even maybe resented it. The nature of Conway and its strong belief in tradition and character, more than winning, even. I hope I don't sound too corny."

What else to do but shake my head? "I understand, I think."

He smiled now, breaking up his formal pitch. "Of course we appreciate winning too."

"But Conway comes first."

"You got it. Conway comes first. Now," and he sprang to his feet, "I've got a tennis match at one. Do you play?"

"A little," I said.

"Well, we'll have to get you out on the court. Oh, one other thing. Salary. I haven't mentioned it. Let me see here, what you've been making." He picked up a printout sheet and studied it. "My, you've not been getting a fair share, have you? Too bad you didn't mention it to me."

I smiled weakly. Twenty-nine five had been enough to eat, sleep, keep the ancient Saab running, see a movie and buy a few Legos for the boy. Not much more in the expensive Upper Valley.

"Let's say we move you up to... forty-five for the year? How's that?"

If he had said, "Let's lower you by five G's" that would have been fine, too, in order to have my own club. "That's fine. Really fine, thanks."

He jotted a note down with his gold pen and said, "Now, any sort of help you need, let me hear it. I know how rough it'll be, especially at the beginning. So I'm here if you need me, okay?"

"Okay."

He licked his fingers twice. "And we'd like you to come over for dinner this weekend. Well, no—but next week, say? I'll let you know, all right?"

"Sure."

He checked his watch. "Well, I can't tell you how pleased I am that this has been settled so quickly. I'll see you then at

9

11 a.m. tomorrow, and let's have a little lunch right after that? If you're free?"

"I'm free. And thanks again."

"Let's see, Sydney, if you feel the same way in January." He smiled. "You may be hating me by then for kicking you upstairs."

"I'll remember that."

Afterwards I took a leak in the john and splashed water on my face, observing it. Curly hair, arched eyebrows, aquiline nose, firm cheekbones, high forehead, and a look of grave inquiry with a dash of skepticism in the brown eyes. Not quite a head coach's mug, as the Colonel had noted: "Did you ever consider, Berger, that you look and dress and act more like a Soviet cellist than a coach?"

Outside the sunshine splashed down on the sloping Conway lawns and buildings in ways that made me perceive the place differently. I walked along tree-lined Wheelock and up to the spacious Green. On the Wimbledon-neat grass kids were tossing Frisbees, others kicking a soccerball. The season was youth. At the far end of the green rose white-towered Butler Hall, one of the oldest college libraries. On the hillside overlooking the green, the three white colonial buildings, Wentworth, Madison, Conway, were perched like three Puritan judges. I felt rather curious standing there, now that I was supposed to be a part of this ordinary scene. My outsider bones tingled.

The tower bells chimed noon and I figured I deserved a decent lunch. Why not the Faculty Club, where I hardly ever ventured, though I joined dutifully ever year?

Lodged in a charming old wooden building, the Club allowed you to have a lunch in relative anonymity—at the unreserved open table, if you got lucky. Privacy was a reward for the elite. On the way upstairs, of course, you might have to endure a snub or two.

I took an end seat at the long table, which held one other person only, and filled out my lunchcard with the short yellow pencil. Half a salmon sandwich and a cup of cold asparagus soup seemed a proper way to celebrate my elevation. Plus a beer. An import.

On my long narrow pad, I began writing down the names of my players, both present and absent, with an asterisk by the missing. And as I took note of the three key people missing and saw what I did have in hand, I realized the obvious. I was being kicked upstairs in order to be thrown to the dogs. I mean, I was going to be the patsy of the year, once the full results were in. With this club I'd be very lucky to win three or four conference games and maybe scratch around enough to defeat another half-dozen clubs—*if* I were lucky. The down side could be worse. And then you could see my letter of goodbye: "Though Mr. Berger only managed five victories in 1989-90, he did show..." Fat chance for another job. The squeeze was subtle.

Along with the cup of asparagus soup and half-sandwich I received a tug on the shoulder.

"What are you doing around these parts? I thought you hung out in dank cellars or pizza parlors, on the lookout for talent, of course."

It was lanky Wim Haarhus, a tenured member of the History Department and a full professor of cynicism.

"Oh, seeing how the upper half lives," I responded.

"We live the same as you." He took a seat across the table. "Only a tad better. But remember, we work harder."

Just what I needed to accompany my dry salmon and tart beer, a little local kibitzing.

"Made up your reading list yet, Sydney? Any more Wobblies or radical trade unionists who have composed their memoirs or made home movies?"

Strangely, he was in his way good to have around, this thin-shouldered, sardonic Dutchman with the mysterious past. Kept me on my toes. Allergic to the straight academic life. He and my big brother Robeson—that big rat amidst all the Harvard cheese.

"I'm not teaching till the winter quarter, Wim. So you'll have to hold onto your humor for a while."

11

"Just warming up, Syd. See me at a department meeting. I forget now, are you invited to those things as an 'adjunct'?" The way he said it the word could have described an insect. "Was that a Ph.D. in American Studies, or A.B.D.?"

"You don't seem to like me, Wim. How come?"

A narrow smile creased his long pallid face, seeing my fast ball down the middle of the plate. "Truth is, I disdain impostors and hangers-on. If you receive my meaning. If it weren't for being some sort of hanger-on in the Athletic Department you'd never be associated with the History Department."

For the time being I'd keep my new athletic job to myself. As for my opinion of the History Department, well... "You know, Wim, I read that one monograph you wrote, maybe twenty years ago, to get your tenure. Where have you been since then?" I stood up, watched him color, and felt a bit guilty. Hard for me to believe he hadn't been a collaborator at the end of the War.

Anyway, he had ruined the rest of my lunch, so he had won the battle.

Outside in the svelte autumnal air I walked around the corner and took a seat on the porch of a deserted fraternity. I jotted down the names of the four towns I was going to be visiting right off. Brooklyn, Brattleboro, Olde Towne, Boston. Less than pleasing prospects. I would have to re-recruit a few and rehabilitate a few others. And then I had to go to work with—or on—Admissions. No, it wasn't going to be an easy three weeks or more.

"Hey, Mr. B, nice surprise. How goes it?"

A bulky fellow from the football team who had made the basketball squad because he was clean-cut and personable in addition to having linebacker shoulders. Just the wrong reasons for keeping him aboard, unfortunately.

"Fine, Kevin, just fine."

"I guess you heard about the Colonel by now? They sure are losing a fine coach."

I nodded, feigning sympathy.

"I don't really envy the new guy they pull in, however. With what we got this year we'll be lucky to finish in the basement."

I nodded again, with some self-mourning now.

"At this late stage they'll probably fill the slot with a bottom-of-the-barrel type for one year, then go out and get themselves a real coach. Hey," he patted my shoulder and sauntered toward the front door, "at least football'll be a blast, huh?"

I waved, wanly. And squirmed just a bit trying not to scrape the bottom.

The news conference was the first I had ever conducted and I was more nervous than I had expected. It was held in the athletic office and all of eight people showed up. A pair of stringers from the Boston papers, a college kid and local newspaper journalist, a college publicity woman, and three students. Not enough for a *minyan*, as my mother might joke, right?

I wore a sport jacket and tie, had trimmed my nails and beard for Dick's sake (and Conway's?), and adopted my full diplomatic tone. Pocketed the pipe.

The A.D. handed out a publicity announcement, which included some résumé data, and it didn't look too bad.

"Are you a lame-duck coach for a year and that's it?"

"I hope not." I smiled. "But you better ask Mr. Porter that." I turned to Dick.

Dick was cordial, shaking his head and saying, "Syd Berger is the best man for the job, and that's why he was hired, period."

Was it true that I had been fired a half dozen years ago from a Miami of Ohio position? If so, for what reason?

I fiddled with papers. "My contract was not renewed, if that's what you mean. And if you want to know why, I didn't get along well with the administration or athletic staff." Enough said.

A pause, and then: "Did you not get along with George

Strickland? What did you think of him as a coach?"

"Got along well. And I respected him as a coach. Look where he's heading." Ah, the lies; they piled up like small stones on your grave.

"With the kind of checkered career you've had," put the apple-cheeked student reporter, tapping his pencil impatiently, "Do you think you'll be able to cope with Conway ways and pressures?"

"Well, I take exception to your phrase about my career. But that aside, I've been here three years now and 'coped' just fine."

"Are you going to have full say in the choice of assistants?"

Before I could answer Dick Porter said, "Absolutely. No question."

"Is it true, Mr. Berger?" asked a Globe stringer, "that your best ballhandler is down and out on coke somewhere?"

How'd he hear? "Well, there is a young man who is having some sort of personal problem, as I understand it. I'm certainly going to check into it." The usual formula: no names, no specifics, no incriminations—if you could get away with it.

"How many will you win, sir?" asked the young lady from the college paper. "Can you give us your sense, or a prediction?"

"I'll give you that next season."

A few laughs.

"Who are your favorite coaches," asked the Valley News reporter, "and what philosophy of coaching will you follow?"

Kant's or Locke's, I wanted to say. "Oh, I've always admired gentlemen like Nat Holman, Clair Bee, Hank Iba. And John Wooden."

They looked at each other. "What about Bobby Knight? John Thompson? Tarkanian at UNLV?"

"Excellent coaches," I allowed, not wishing to discriminate aloud between recruiters and true strategists, "but it certainly helps if you have the talent."

14

"Do you? I mean, does Conway?"

"We'll find out. Though places like Indiana, Georgetown and UNLV do live a few notches above us in the recruiting zones."

"Sir, realistically speaking, does an Ivy ever have a chance of going a long way?"

"Sure," I answered, "look at Princeton with Bradley, back in the mid-sixties. Or Penn in '72. Went to the Final Four. But the odds get longer and longer, it's true."

At that point Dick Porter stepped forward and said, "Thanks everyone. See you all in Seattle, huh?" And everyone smiled at the reference to the Final Four site.

We had lunch at the Ivy Grill in the Inn and Dick, after complimenting me on my comportment at the conference, asked me about the assistants. "There's Billy Calloway, Roscoe Grumman, Percy Grimes. And old Duddy Hamsun, who's recovered and wants back in. You can have two. Which do you prefer?" He sipped his beer.

"Well, that's not easy," I admitted, taking out my small spiral pad and removing a page. "Here, you write down two choices and I'll write down mine and we'll see if we can come up with two names."

He smiled and nodded. "Sure."

I ate my grilled ham and cheese and assessed personalities. Calloway had the basketball smarts, but could be abrasive and surly with the players. Grumman was a good straight guy, a Conway athlete, a so-so hoop man. Grimes was an ex-player, enthusiastic and the right color. Duddy was an old-timer who, before his triple bypass, hollered a lot and motivated guys to dive for loose balls. Also, he had become a keen outdoorsman, and that could be useful.

I wrote down my two names and we matched pieces of paper.

"Hey, pretty good, Sydney." Dick smiled at our mutual choices.

We had taken Grumman and Grimes.

15

"I hate to leave out Duddy, though," I added, "especially given the circumstances. Can I get two and a half? You know, a special assistant for recruitment or travel, whatever?"

He nodded and jotted down the idea. "Let me see what I can do. Meanwhile, any immediate requests? Your office should be ready by Monday, by the way. The painters are just finishing up."

"Thanks, Dick. No SOS's just now. But give me a week or two on the road and you may be hearing from me."

"I'm here. Though..." and he searched his pocket calendar. "I'm off to Maine next week to get a little September sailing in. Want to come over to York Harbor for a day?"

"Thanks, I'd love to. But I've just taken on this new job and there are a few loose ends to take care of."

A little laugh. "I understand. But wait, Nellie says the weekend after this is good for a dinner date. How about the 15th?"

"Sounds fine, boss."

He marked the date. "I certainly admire the way you make decisions without having to consult calendars or datebooks. Just like that."

"My dance card is empty," I acknowledged. "That makes it easy. Except for little Daniel on weekends."

He nibbled at his chef's salad. "How old is he?"

"Six plus."

"And he's local, I take it?"

"Yes."

"That's a better situation than mine was, after my first divorce. He was some fifteen hundred miles away, and we had to fly him, or me, back and forth. It was trying. How long you been axed?"

"About nine months now."

"Divorce go through yet?"

"Still just separated."

"Rough going?"

"Yeah, I guess so."

"It takes a year or so to move ahead, I found. The second

time is a bit shorter, actually. Anyway, we do have this good divorcee friend, and Nell is planning to invite her over, unless you'd prefer not?"

"Swedish, of course."

"Half, I think."

I drank my club soda. "I look forward to the half," and glanced up at a bulky fellow, standing above us, saying, "Well, Dick, how about an intro to the new coach?"

"Hey, Sib, how are you? Sydney, say hello to Sather 'Sibby' Coldwell, Conway '46 and maybe its greatest pulling guard."

His hand was firm for sixtyish, and as he chattered on, in a booming voice, about the virtues of the college sporting tradition, I made a point of taking note of the busy room and engaging atmosphere and his bright green tie. In a few days I'd be elsewhere, and maybe pinching myself that all this was a dream.

"So remember, Syd, anything you need from the Alumni Club, you let us know. We can come in handy sometimes." He winked broadly. "Sometimes more than any old A.D."

An empty gymnasium is surely one of the dream palaces of this world. For me, a city boy, it was like a farm field, a baseball diamond, an old movie theater. Alumni Gym had been built two years before, and the fact that it was only high-schoolish in its seating capacity only added to my goose bumps as I walked alone in there. Removing my shoes I strolled back and forth on the shining hardwood floor—conjuring up all the dirty tricks that sly coaches played with wax on such a floor, depending on the opponent—and felt something like a general surveying the battlefield before combat. Looking for an edge here or there.

But what I saw were clean rectangular lines, the red paint of foul lanes and the yellow half-circles for three-point goals, the two glass backboards with their net baskets, like oval faces with white goatees. Within that 110 by 60 feet I'd soon be witnessing splendid athletic feats and also hard defeats, clever plans for attack thwarted by smart defenses. I would be the director/writer, all right, but how foolish or bad would my scripts look when the performers failed me? Or how foolish would *they* look, if I failed them by not understanding their talents and limits?

Instinctively I paced off the length and width of the court, checking the distances. And glancing up at the audience-to-be. How very different the game was up there in the stands, where you cheered on your team like safari-tourists observing the lush lions and sleek panthers, oohing and aahing from the comfort of Land Rovers. Down here you slugged it out and fought for survival by means of body, brain, eye, heart, luck, ref's calls, conditioning, fingertip delicacy, shrewd repetitions, and sometimes a coach's wisdom. (Or was *that* folly?)

If survival was one name of the game, another was beauty. You aimed for it, aspired towards it, though mostly you got the plain, the mediocre. But when the movement was going well, when five youngsters suddenly became one team and the ball moved almost by itself, when the variations and repetitions became like a piano sonata, then you felt a little different about the sport, and yourself. Uplifted. Spirited. In a world elsewhere. Well, dream on, Sydney boy, but not this year, not with this club. Unless miracles descended.

I paced back and forth, eyeing the angles, the baselines, the foul lanes, sniffing a mix of resin and wax. What would Mom and Dad, my passionate anarchists, think of their son now? As for brother Robeson, professor of English in Cambridge, I knew well.

"'Scuse me, sir, do you have permission to be walking around here just now?" the janitor wondered, standing there with his broom.

"I'm the new coach," I murmured modestly, "but maybe I shouldn't be here?"

"Oh no, sir, you can do whatever you want, whenever. Pardon me." He began to back off.

Signalling him to go on, I walked over to the gaunt black man wearing a green Conway cap and put out my hand.

"Sydney Berger."

He put out his hand, uneasily. "Roosevelt Stallings, sir. Call me Rosey. If you would need anything, just yell."

"Thanks. Just some luck."

He stared, then beamed. "I'll rub my rabbit's foot for you, Mister Berger. That should do it."

"Thanks, Mr. Stallings. You wouldn't happen to have a six-foot eight-inch rabbit son or nephew around, would you?"

The grin spread. "Sure not, otherwise I'd loan him out to you."

"Well, Mr. Stallings, if you should hear of one, let me know."

"Rosey, sir. It's more comfortable."

"Sydney, then. That's better too."

I couldn't help wandering over to my future domicile and, finding the door ajar, entering. Obviously the painters were waiting for the Colonel to clear his things out; boxes were piled up; the desk was piled with files and manila envelopes; the walls still contained his framed credentials and exaggerated credits. You know, the gilt-edged bachelor's and master's degrees in Phys. Ed., Various nominations to NCAA committees, awards from Booster and Alumni Clubs, summer basketball camp citations and signed celebrity photos with the old pros (Tom Gola, John Havlicek, Jerry Lucas). At least a dozen of these success-by-association displays were up there, visually ablaze with official seals and handsome calligraphy, making him look like Dr. Schweitzer or Adolph Rupp. The man had a pair, didn't he?

But there was one citation that truly ripped me, as I stood there. A Coach of the Year award from the Mid-American Conference. The Colonel, coach of the year? Which year, 1258? That guy couldn't coach a junior high team, and any colony of ants or bees would toss his ass out. I had watched this character up close for the better part of two years and the SOB didn't know the game, didn't like kids or know how to organize them, preferred podiums and cameras to gymnasiums. He had tongued enough behinds to wiggle his way up, and conned enough A.D.s with his phony jocularity. Just put the guy inside a game situation and watch him rant and rave and then go for his cup of water while the little matter of strategy was left to the assistant to take in hand. In other words, he resembled about half the well-known coaches in the country: a public relations figure, made up of PR dossier, sawdust, media sucking and a smart assistant, with a megaphone for bluster and bullshit.

I went over to the oversized desk (to be shipped out) and took a seat behind it, swiveling about. In my bones, I knew that one of the reasons why I took the job right off was to get mine back, to take a run with this season at least, against all the phonies, boobs and bullies who were out there running the shows, winning the awards, taking the big bows and knowing nada about the game. Those sorts had kicked my ass for a long time, at places like Humboldt State, Long Beach Community College, Miami of Ohio. To use the vernacular of the kids, this job was going to be my "comeback sauce," no matter how much of an ordeal it was, or how short. Now, I was going to get mine. For me, a gym rat from childhood, it would be sweet, Sicilian revenge to be on top.

More, I knew, unwrapping one of the A.D.'s Havana cigarillos which I had saved for private celebration. I suppose too I wanted to get back at older brother, show him a thing or two. Dearest Robeson, the P. Miller Professor of Literary Pomposity at Harvard, had been pretending for years that I was the slob and he the gem, the true heir of mother and father, the full-fledged intellectual they had wanted to be. But Belle and Giorgio were passionate creatures, even if they were naifs of the left, failed and frustrated in their lives. Brother Robey, acting as though he had been named for some Presbyterian minister and not for Paul Robeson, one of their heroes, had won his spurs as a model of Scholarly Objectivity, distancing himself from anything touching radicalism, Wobblies, immigrants (both parents), anarchism. Anything passionate, period. An ostrich in the sands of Puritan history, looking up only to mock me—kid brother, kid failure. "Basketball coach?" He looked at me with his puckered lips and mischievous grin when I first told him of my change in careers. He rather liked condescending to me as high school teacher and perennial grad student. But condescending to a hoop coach? The role was beneath condescension, right?

The Havana drifted pungently through me and I rolled it around my palate. Faintly it reminded me of my few days down in Cuba with the Venceremos Brigade, helping to harvest the sugar. But the dark señoritas and wonderful cigars dazzled my imagination more than sugar cane and socialism. My last attempt at leftist politics was cured. I swivelled and observed yellow grosbeaks on a nearby maple. Yes, I wanted mine back at him now, one way or another. As head coach I had a shot at respectability at least. Maybe at fame, too, something that dear Robey craved, while appearing a pure ascetic devoted to high literature.

But you don't coach on vengeance alone. (Oh, why not?) You do it out of love too, a passion for form, an aesthetic consideration. Odd, but true. At least for me. There is something so splendid, so right, about the game, when it's played well and played true—it deserves the language of art. Only here the form is a game, not a poem or picture; a swiftly moving play, not still-form art or a set piece repeated the same way again and again (see drama). Indeed it was the novel (19th century) and great historical narrative (Parkman, Trotsky) that gave me some of the basic ways I perceived the game, or my private metaphors for it. And I couldn't resist writing down, for the umpteenth time, my favorite notations for the team: I needed a fine narrator, a rich texture, a progressing story, a group of real characters. Narrator, texture, story, character/characters. A nomenclature that seemed to fit the game as I saw it, hoped for it; one that inspired and intoxicated me too. And one that I kept to myself, obviously, so as not to appear Looney-Tunes to the rest of the profession.

A knock on the ajar door startled me from my rumination

and I quickly stood and nodded guiltily to Rosey Stallings, who apologized for the interruption. "No, no, it's my fault. It's not quite my office yet." I patted him on the arm and departed.

2 THE RECRUITING OFFICER

The small plane ride down to LaGuardia on Saturday morning was like a rollercoaster to hell, the only consolation being that the Dornier 320 was built by the Germans. Didn't know they could engineer a machine that bumped and jangled like any old American Cessna. I figured it this way: in the jungles of Ecuador or Peru I'd be a Catholic missionary on my way to save some primitive souls. Here, in the gran' ole opry of USA, I was a college hoop coach on his way to save some burnt-out bodies and heal wounded recruits. We had this habit hereabouts of banging our kids black and blue and then cradling them in our arms and telling them to forgive us. Or better, that we forgive them.

Anyway, it wasn't me but the Colonel who had bruised and insulted my players. Straight Colonel Strickland and his dogged, biased ways. I would bring them in and by midseason or so he had carried them out. Sure, some were "problems," but who wasn't a problem who had a degree of excellence? Each kid just needed a little extra caring, a little tending, then watch him bloom. As it was my kids either languished on the bench, dropped out, or quit in quiet desperation. The subtle Colonel, who'd eye me and say, "Another one of your teen-age case studies, Berger? Save him for the social worker, corporal." Team behavior and school decorum was what mattered for the old boy. "We're going to have team discipline and Conway dignity, come hell or high water!"

I'd stare at the old Georgia dinosaur and he'd add: "Just tell me, son, how'd an egghead like you ever wander into this field?"

I'd smile, shrug and walk off to console some player (and myself).

"Where to, mahn?" asked the Caribbean cabbie.

"Do you know Brooklyn? Brownsville, East New York, Crown Heights?"

He shook his head from side to side. "You direct me, mahn, and I get you there, all right?"

Okay, I'd navigate. Would he stick around in a pinch? "Take the Belt Parkway and get off at Linden Boulevard. I'll show you."

We took off, curving around the highway and the sweep of ocean before heading inland for the bushes. (Inland? Like Burton or Speke...) Some thirty years ago I had played some ball back there when we lived in East Flatbush, and the place was a basketball hive. On a given day you could pick up a team on the playground who could stay with most college squads. So here I was, returning, trying to find and glue together my star playmaker, *if* he was salvageable. And maybe trying to find myself, too, and put my pieces together—but that story was not for now.

I recalled when I had first recruited this kid, Nurlan Waterford Reeves, and knew I had a fifties playmaker, not merely a 1990 pointguard. Ten minutes in I watched him control the game for Jefferson High, setting up his players, threading the passes unselfishly, never losing his dribble. But I didn't know how special the kid really was until later that night when, after a bite to eat, we went over to the Brownsville Boys Club to shoot around a bit and meet with a few pals. I watched as they played a few halfcourt pickup games; what caught my attention was his dribbling ability and the pleasure he took in it. The kid loved to dribble, beamed while he did it, and you couldn't take the ball (or smile) away from him. The real sport in those games was for his opponents to double-team him and try to steal the dribble. Nurlan had mastered the art too well—had become too agile with his fingertips and his feet, too smart with his thin body, too peripheral with his vision. At one point I stopped play and asked two kids to go up against him just to steal the ball, with no screens or shooting, and for three or four minutes they tried, but it was no contest; every time he slithered right through them to the basket, laughing like someone skydiving or sailing. The kid was a Cousy at age 17, with his big hands and flashing smile and superb instincts. Not jumpshooting, not dunking, just that dribbling, and his ardor for passing, made his game a perfect little art form.

Now after an hour we made the first pit stop, a longshot at the old asphalt courts at Lincoln Terrace. Once upon a time here Sid Tannenbaum and Max Zaslofsky (and even Don Forman) pumped in two-hand set shot after set shot from 25 feet away, shooters of needle-point accuracy. The old steel poles and netless hoops were now crooked and mangled, as though awaiting a hanging. A few halfcourt games were in progress on the cracking asphalt surface. One or two stray white folk, balding Rabbits in their forties, were huffing and puffing alongside the younger black kids. I walked over to a sideline and asked two dribblers if they had seen my man.

"Not for years, Mista."

"Who you with, mothafucka, the fuzz or the schools?"

When I announced Conway, they shook their heads and wondered, "Where's that, Colorado?"

Should I tell the A.D. or Sibby?

At the schoolyards of PS 189 and 210, no luck either.

"The man's wasted, I hear," a fellow told me in the latter, dribbling a ball like a chainsmoker with his cig. "Too bad, huh?"

We plunged deeper into the Brooklyn bush with my cabbie growing antsy. "Glad it's daylight, mahn, or you wouldn't catch me out here just waitin' 'round to get picked off."

At Betsy Head Park in the heart of East New York, a territory like the West Bank or Mozambique, I got out again. The day had grown warmer.

"You betta pay me the seventy-four-fifty now," my driver said, "just in case anything happens."

"Inside or outside?"

"Either, mahn."

I handed him two fifties and said, "Don't cut out on me now, Jimmie." Then I took a receipt and his cab number for my account and his viewing.

He widened his eyes at his name and the tip as I walked off. On the way in I passed two clusters of teenagers who scoped me out with surprise. At the door to the gym a fellow with a fedora and a toothpick curled me over and propositioned, "Yo, sport, wanna handle some fine crack, real pure? Direct from Colombia. I can letcha have it cheap, real cheap!"

He started to lay his hand on my jacket lapel and I took it away casually, shaking my head. Heart beginning to quaver I moved on to the door.

The old gymnasium hadn't changed much, Saturday morning was still basketball time, still Show Time, the way it had been for forty-odd years. The smallish dark gym was all grey steel, like a cage, with stone floor and netless baskets with rims bent from hanging and dunking. The slants of sun entering created a grid of stippled grey, like a prison gym, not a park place. A game was in progress, four on four fullcourt, that was all the tiny floor could accommodate. On the sidelines were groups of kids, waiting to form teams to challenge the winner. A boombox was blasting rap. On the court down-and-out kids, brown and ebony-hued, were choreographing suspended leaps and dancing moves of athletic grace, forming The Betsy Head Ballet Company. Teenage orphans, junior high dropouts, apprentice druggies and porters-to-be exhibited their anger, spite and desire via the stutter step, the behind-the-back pass, the monster dunk.

I had dressed carefully for the occasion, wearing a muted yellow sport jacket and white shirt without tie. I had to look official, but ambiguous; an authority of some sort, yet not a narc or mere cop. Here, I was the only white face in the place.

The players were racing, leaping, jumpshooting, dunking; any three would start immediately for Conway. But most of these gents had sixth-grade reading skills, fourth-grade math skills. Most, but not all. A good recruiter, if he had the time and instinct, could scan for the buried brain talent as well as the physical.

"You heah for somebody in particular?" A fellow had sidled up to me. Wore dark shades and a red beret.

"Yeah, Nurlan, Nurlan Waterford Reeves."

He eyed me, sideways. "Whatcha got with him?"

"He knows me. Old friend."

"You D.E.A.? Or new detective from the 73rd?"

I shook my head, facing him squarely.

"You be the Nike man? Or Reebok?"

"Coach."

"Oh yeah? Where?"

"Conway College. Up north."

His taut brown face eased up. Several others had joined him now, circling us. "You a recruitin' officer, right?"

Yeah, like Farquhar. "Head coach. Was Nurlan's recruiter, though. Is he around?"

"I'll check it out. Who should I tell him is callin'?"

"Sydney. Sydney Berger."

"You got I.D.?"

It was a little like trying to get through to a Resistance friend in Holland or France. Why not? Wasn't it War down here? Wasn't this the combat zone? Had Nam been more menacing? I took out my Conway I.D.

He studied it, checking out the photo and me, and passed the card to his buddies. "Hold on right heah fuh now."

"Hey, where you going with that?"

"Just want to ver-i-fy you are who you say you are, 'coach.'"

I stood there surrounded by a huddle of menacing youngsters and kept my eyes on the court. In this Fourth-World zone you could be taken out anonymously and your nametag(s) sold for junk.

"What's it like up there, man, trees 'n stuff?"

I nodded to the questioner, in black headband. "Yeah, it's in the hills."

"Any black dudes go there?"

"Oh, maybe three hundred or so."

"Hey, James, catch that?"

"Can ya get me in, Coach? I got a wicked jumpa!" He showed it.

The fellow with the red beret returned now and took my arm. "Come on, and here's your I.D. back."

As if entering a mountain guerrilla camp he led me single-file across the narrow path between court and stands, teams of dark figures staring at the stray white wanderer. I stood out like an albino in the sea of dark faces, making me feel ghostly, strange. At the far end of the floor, in the dimness beyond the court, huddled on a torn easy chair, was an obscure creature, holding himself around and rocking. Some ancient Brownsville Oracle who'd ask me the Nurlan riddle?

The small head, buried within a baseball cap, raised up as I approached, and a low soft voice murmured, "Hey... Coach."

Approaching I hesitated, disbelieving.

The creature smiled wanly. "What you doin' down here?"

I curbed my emotion. "Coming to take you back to college."

A weak laugh, interrupted by a moan. Then, hard as he could, he hugged himself tight! My dim sense was that he was some twenty pounds lighter from last spring, when he carried about 145 pounds on his 5' 10" frame. The light chocolate matte color was streaked with yellowing stains, odd patches.

He took several deep breaths, after the convulsion had left him. "I ain't gonna make no college, ya know that."

"Sure you are. You're my playmaker."

A pause while he caught up his breaths. "Head Man'll never accept it, ya know that Mista B. No use kiddin'."

"He's gone. I'm the Man now."

He looked up at me, the head shrunken, a kind of skull on a stick. Kurtz in Betsy Head. A feeble smile spread. "Ain't that somethin'. A salute to yuh, Mista B."

"And good for you too, Water. Now let me give you a hand. Come on." I leaned down and started to lift him, taken aback by his weight, or weightlessness.

"Yuh need help?" Red Beret asked.

"Yeah, thanks."

The two of us began to move him on out, a wounded figure in torn t-shirt and frayed sweatpants, supported easily on our shoulders. We marched step by step through the small crowed gathering, the smells of sweat mingling with garbage stench and pot, and I had the sense of lifting a hostage out of Beirut. He kept breathing hard, snorting for air. Come on, Jimmie; be there, pal, or we're in some trouble.

The sunlight was too striking for Nurlan, I saw immediately, and I turned his baseball cap around so the visor would afford protection. He coughed steadily, low, and perspired. The cab was waiting, motor running, and we lowered him into the back seat.

"Thanks," I said to the driver, and asked Red Beret, "Do you know where he's been living? At his mother's, on Hopkinson, or...?"

The slender voice in the seat whispered, "Not there, Mista B. Not... like this."

I turned back to the beret and asked, "Is there a drying-out place around here? A Methadone center?"

The beret shook his head. "You *get* the habit here, man, not give it back."

I paused, perplexed, trying to think fast and stay cool.

"Heah, take him uptown," and the aide handed me a card with a Manhattan address. "They'll tuck him in fuh you fuh tonight."

"We gotta move," urged my driver, "while our luck is holdin'."

I thanked Nurlan's cunning pal and asked his name.

29

"Abdul Mohammed, man. Abdul Mohammed Moses Johnson."

I nearly smiled. "When he's better and playing again, come on up and watch him—on me."

I waved and slid in, just as a 73rd Precinct squad car passed us slowly, eyeing the goings-on, me.

"Jes' might do that, man. Here, take this for bro, he'll want it later." He handed me a crumpled brown paper bag.

I gave him my card and nodded, figuring I'd dispose of the bag at a trash can. To the driver I gave the card with the uptown address. "And take it easy, for godssake." Just in case that squad car was prowling.

"Everyone spend like you, gov', and I'd only need one fare a day."

I held Nurlan around just as he was seized by a fresh wave of convulsions. The cab drove off and I felt the sweat pour off my forehead, and my muscles suddenly ease up, as though I had been in hand-to-hand combat for the past hour. Soon I was cradling and rocking him as though he were a sleepysick baby, and my mind shifted to his other escape route from all this: his meticulous drawings and pasted-over collages of aerial citystreets and uneven rooftops, organized with lucid serenity. A junior Utrillo...

Before disposing of the bag I peeked inside: an assortment of Baby Ruths, Mars Bars, Three Musketeers. Always learning, right?

On my flight back the next day I got off at Keene for my second pit stop of the weekend. Brattleboro was a far cry from East New York, though it was seedy enough. The Konepskis lived in a poor part of the old woolen mill town, in a peeling Cape that was closer to a ramshackle bungalow. It was Sunday afternoon, after Church, when I knocked and asked where I might find Edward? His father, a Schlitz and Parade Magazine in his hand, looked me over and asked if I was a cop. When I said no he told me Eddie was out shooting baskets, probably in the local playground.

"Hey, you're that recruiter guy, right? Forget him, he ain't goin' back to that crummy place and friggin' coach, forget him! He shouldn't have gone in the first place, like I told him!" The door flew shut.

Who could blame the piece of granite named Walter Konepski, I thought, walking over to the playground. After all, his kid had been called a "gutless Polack" by the coach in front of the team in practice one day; and in his second game, jerked out peremptorily and mocked at the bench, "You slow light bulb!" Neither adjective described the Eddie I had known, recruited, fought to get in.

However, in ten minutes I saw the old Eddie, hustling out there on the scrubby court. Large-boned, raw-featured, the six-foot five-inch Eddie K. was a born rebounder, a boy who loved to bang the boards and backed down from no one. Now in sleeveless undershirt and jean cutoffs he moved with his old purpose. Once the roundball went off the basket, off the backboard, the outcome was not in doubt. Though it was a pickup game, there were some decent older players, a few muscular, taller bruisers too. I watched them race up and down the court for a half-dozen missed shots, and Eddie didn't miss a rebound. His body would get planted, his hips and elbows out and ready, his sense of the opponent's position sure. Good, smart, tough as ever. This lovely kid, the next Rudy LaRusso at Conway, was forced to quit the squad, and school, because of the Colonel's misjudgment and prejudice. Because working class ethnics made him bristle. Well, Eddie Konepski was one of my two cornerstones, and I wasn't going to lose him now.

At last I let myself be revealed on the sideline, and on one of his trips down, called out to him.

Stopping in midtrack, he took a double glance. "Mr. Berger? Is it really you? Wow. What's up?"

"C'mon, Eddie, play ball, huh?"

"Three more baskets, sir, and I'll be with you." And he took off downcourt.

Leaning by my tree, I looked over at the nearby Church,

Sacred Heart of Jesus/Our Lady of Perpetual Help, where I had once attended a Sunday mass to ingratiate myself. I winked up at her now.

At fifteen they called a halt and Eddie came over, sweating profusely, his short reddish hair and freckles glistening, on fire in the sun.

"God, I never thought I'd see you again after I let you down that way." He shook his head. "I'm really... sorry, sir."

Sacrificial Eddie, the victim feeling guilty; it was we who owed him the apology. "Not at all, Ed. Look, I'd like you to come back."

He grabbed a sweatshirt and began toweling off his forehead. He laughed nervously. "Ah, you know it wouldn't work. The Colonel and me, well, we never hit it off, you know. It got real bad there. There's no point."

"He's out. I'm in."

The news swept his innocent face. "Whatdayaknow!... Really?"

"Were you passing everything when you left?" Students in good standing always got a year of grace, I knew, before they lost their official standing and had to be readmitted.

"Oh yeah, I was okay. Freshman English was a downer, but nothing drastic, you understand."

"Not an F?"

"Nah, nothin' like that. How's the team this year, Mr. B?" Is the Water comin' back? Or The Chief? Vargas?"

"Those are precisely my pre-school projects. Along with you."

Towering above me, he backed off and sat down on the stone bench. "Even if I wanted to, Dad'd never let me go back. The Colonel sort of insulted him, he felt, the one time he went up there to watch me." He shrugged. "He's kind of sensitive, you know, about that Polish stuff. He's got me workin' on the roads with him now. Maybe that's for the best, huh?"

The poor kid didn't even know enough to get angry at a bigot. His look read, "What do you think, Mr. B?"

"What's for the best is what you want, Eddie. But if you want it, I think you can do it. As a player and a student. Come on, let's walk and talk a bit. Then maybe I can help convince your Dad to give you, and us, another chance."

Oh, Eddie wanted it all right, badly, but convincing father Konepski was no bed of roses. (Would I have to rely on Father Meyers again?)

Soon enough we were sitting in the Konepski living room, a dark narrow room, on thick Mediterranean-style furniture, eyed by two huge crucifixes at both ends. While an NFL game played on the Sears TV I was served Polish sausage and home-made sauerkraut, and a full dose of the old man's college anger, much of which had fine justification. When he came up with an anti-Semitic slur about a professor at the college I had to call him on it, mentioning that I myself was half-Jewish. He nodded and changed tracks.

"I tell ya, the boy don't need no 'higher' education. What the hell's he goin' to do with it, 'cept go to work for the nuclear reactor down the road? Ya know what he's earnin' right now, on my crew? Go on, take a guess, why doncha? Well, how does $7.50 an hour sound for starters, huh? That's a little better than shellin' out some eight thousand bucks a year—"

"Six, Dad, with my job at the library, and not counting summer—"

"You shut up when I'm talking. Helen, give the coach 'nother beer and kiebaski, go on. As I was sayin', what the hell's he goin' to get out of it all, 'cept some more frustration?" He leaned forward, his pallid face reddish from three beers, to whisper more wisdom. "Ya don't really think a white kid like Eddie got a chance in hell up at yer joint? C'mon, the fix is in at good colleges for poor white workingclass slobs like my kid. *They're* the real minority at your fancy schools, not the coddled blacks or spics. You throw a Polack from Brattleboro or a Mick from Boston at those admissions offices and you're throwin' fifty bucks down the drain. And the same goes for his treatment by those liberal profs. Who they kiddin'? I may be illiterate, but I'm not stupid!" He smiled, delighted by his distinction. "And as for—"

"Hold on, Walter, hold on," I interrupted. "Let the boy speak for a minute. How were the classes, Eddie, the profs? And peers? And what about the team, how'd you like playing with them?"

While bullied Eddie murmured a few sentences of shy hope I planned my strategy. As soon as Walter cut off his son, I cut him off, and made my pitch about ethnic pride. "He'd be the *first Polish player* to start up there, Walter. And maybe the first all-Ivy player from Brattleboro. Picture that, Mr. Konepski..."

Thus I played Kissinger to that Vermont-peasant Sadat, and after two hours I managed to convince the hulking man, inflamed by pride, to give the kid, and Conway, a second chance. And me, of course. (At one point indeed he brandished his fist and threatened, "If you disappoint the kid again, I won't look easy on it, I'll tell ya!")

We shook hands at the end and I said, "Let me know when you want to come up and watch your son. He'll be worth it, even if the team won't quite be up to par for a while." To Eddie I said, "Now get that pre-registration stuff in first thing Monday, okay? Any questions, call me, right?" I realized that on Monday I had yet another date out of town, so I added, "Or speak to Mary Jo, my assistant, and see if she can help. On Monday I go to work on Roberto..."

"Hey!" Eddie's face lit up. "That would be somethin'— toughest offensive rebounder I ever went against. Get him back, Mr. B, and we'll sweep both boards clean for you, I promise!"

He was right, too, I thought.

I hooked up with Vargas in the Courtside Restaurant in East Cambridge, the old A and S Deli dump. He was working as a waiter and I sat at a table in his station.

He brought a glass of water and asked for my order without once looking up from his pad.

"Make sure the corned beef is lean, Roberto; otherwise

no go."

He looked down at me startled, his dark face lightening, and a narrow smile creased his sensual mouth. He wore an open-necked white shirt, sleeves rolled up, and looked handsome enough to fit right into a daytime soap or *L.A. Law.* Soft skin, sleepy bedroom eyes, Brando lips.

"Came in for lunch. And to see you."

He nodded. "I'll make sure it's lean. It's sure decent of you."

"I'd like you back—to Prescott, to Conway, to the team."

He stared at me and did that little clicking motion with his neck when he was suddenly pressed and unsure. "A drink with your sandwich?"

"I'll take a beer. Sam Adams or Heineken Dark."

He shook his head, named what he had, and I chose a Molson. He went to get it and put the order in.

They had put dough into remodeling the seedy place, but dough didn't mean taste. The new lighting was motel invasive, and the old wooden booths had become like molded shower stalls laid horizontal. Vargas's situation made him one of my hardest cases. He was a sensitive, quiet kid whose itinerant stepfather—an off-season, Puerto-Rican migrant picker in Concord—beat up on the mother and got sent to the clink, dropping the kid into a ditch of despair. He lost his will, his poise. The Colonel's reaction was standard ex-Marine hardline: mourning and puzzlement were no more than a sissy's self-pity. When I tried to counsel the kid, since he wouldn't go over to Dick's house for the professional stuff, I was told to lay off. So, in mid-season, the young man went down the drain. My two stellar rebounders were off the team by February 1 and out of the college to boot. So much for recruiting.

"Lean, I promise," he says, setting the sandwich down with those large delicate hands that could handle a guitar pretty well and work wonders around the offensive basket.

"Can you sit a minute?"

He checked his watch. "Give me ten or fifteen minutes, okay?"

I eyed him pursuing his tasks, a thin-hipped, broad-shouldered hawk who reminded me of the legendary hawk, Connie Hawkins.

In fifteen he sat, stirring chocolate into a tall Coke glass of milk.

"How's it going?" I ask.

"Oh, not too bad. Job's steady. Movies are okay."

"Playing any ball?"

"Oh, I play now and then at the Y or over at the Ebony/Ivory Summer League in Roxbury. Some good competition."

"I'll bet. Any guitar?"

"Oh, some."

"How's your Mom?"

He clicked and rolled his neck. "Recovering. Back to work. She'll be okay. How's the team? The guys?"

I gave him the news and he looked at me disbelieving. "You, the Man at the Top? Really?"

"Look, I, we, need you, and you need Conway. You got to move on in your life despite the bad news, the setbacks. You can't give up your own best potential. You know that. I remember when I first talked to you, over at Rindge and Latin in the schoolyard, and you said something like, 'No one's gonna pull me down, only myself, and I'm not gonna let that happen. And if I'm the only Puerto Rican up at Conway, that's cool. So long as there's a moviehouse around.' And maybe a guitar freak or two." He laughed now, his first radiating smile, revealing the youthfulness beneath the overburdened soul. "Well, that's what I'm coming down here to remind you of—your own words. Your family stuff is rough, sure, but you can't let your life go down the drain because of it. Or him."

He finished his milk and glanced up at me from beneath those dark, glamorous eyebrows. The kid's life was at stake here and now; basketball was his way out and up, his ego-opening.

"Look, I want you to come up this week and feel it out again. Walk around with me, visit the old dorm, see some of the guys. All right? Then, if you decide to drop it, fine. Is that fair?"

"I don't know... I don't know if I can even take off a day here, you know. The money's important to my mom now, see."

Of course he was right. "Come up for the day, here's bus-fare, and I'll make up for the day's tips and wages. Okay?" Stuff the NCAA and its absurd, trivial rules, I thought. "A loan, that's all."

"Gotta cover your ass, right?" He smiled.

I hit his arm. "You talk too much. Pick a day, come on."

"Just for the day, right? Well, Wednesday, I suppose. Maybe I can come up after lunch so Mrs. Martino won't be bummed out, and I can return on the morning bus, huh?"

"Absolutely. Call me with the time... No, I'll call you. Give me your number."

He wagged his head. "We were unplugged back in July."

"I'll call you here, then."

"Okay." He paused and wondered, "You believe in this club?"

"Well, I believe in you. You're my Paul Silas."

He shook his head. "Who's that again?"

"A great Celtic rebounder who was always there when you needed him, and a genius on the offensive board. The best."

He blushed at the comparison.

Back from the nether world, up on the serene green campus, I felt rather proud of my recruiting trip until I hit the Admissions office on Tuesday morning and tried to work out the details. Even though each of my kids had a particular field of interest—Nurlan his drawing, Eddie regional history, Vargas music—that meant little. It didn't take me too long to figure out that I was in an Old Boys network, though it had been revised by current liberal trendiness, and that my recruits, like me, were beyond the respectable pale. My kids did not have parents who were Conway alumni or who, on paper, looked to be "the future leaders of our society." (A big

PR line at the college, referring probably to future leaders of Paine Webber, etc.) Nor were their SAT scores very convincing, hovering around 1000 at best, and their Academic Index quite low. Finally, they were not middle-class—i.e., good, clean—minority kids, sons of college grads, the Desirable Sort. No, my boys were borderline cases, street kids with specific talents but handicapped by poor schools, bad homes, disaster streets. Knowing that beforehand, I had handpicked my athletes, seeking out the hungry ones, those still alive at 17 with curiosity and wonder, primitively trained but motivated, each with a quiet capacity, a small accomplishment. My one thousand hours of recruitment sorties had included discussions with school counselors, teachers, and the recruits themselves, to make sure of my selection. I knew my boys, their flaws and potential, and was not about to let administrative paper-shufflers or School of Education knuckleheads close the gates now.

As the two officers looked over my priority list I made the case for Vargas, explaining the disturbing family situation and emphasizing the self-taught classical guitar ability, which had produced a Berklee College of Music recommendation letter.

"Technically he's eligible to be reinstated," said Dak Walker, "but a kid who's quit in spring term should stay out till midyear at least, to make sure he's here to stay this time."

"As for this next kid, this uh Nurlan Waterford Reeves—cheez, where do they get these names, huh?" Rick Jamison winked.

"His mom named him for the Waterford Crystal," I replied needlessly, "that she cleans in her doctors' and dentists' homes."

Mistake, I saw immediately.

A stocky fiftyish man who wore a Conway ring, Jamison nodded, not happily. "You're really asking for trouble with this kid. What were his grades, 2.1 or so? And everyone's heard the rumors of his other problems. Do you really want that sort back?"

"And bring back that kind of problem to this campus?" Dak.

Drugs. If Betsy Head and Brattleboro were sleazy stops, Conway was a turf of polite arrogance and hypocrisy. "Don't you think that 'problem' is here already, in various forms? Isn't alcohol a rampant problem with our well-bred prep-school fraternity boys? And do you think it's difficult to get some grass or coke? Last year, for example, didn't we have a hushed-up cocaine case involving half a dozen students, boys *and* girls? With me around all the time, Nurlan'll stay clean. And as for his art abilities, call Professor Burghesian in the Art Department."

"Look, Coach, a few bad apples exist here and there, sure."

Jamison, all blue eyes and Caesar haircut, appealed to reason. "I'm all for the new policy of increasing the minority enrollment, and we've added some splendid ones. A preacher's son and a doctor's daughter, for example. But kids like this Waterford or Vargas? You had four of them on the preferred list last year and their GPAs were borderline. Why not take them out to the 'Big Sky' or 'Big Eight,'" he mocked, "an Iowa State or Oklahoma, maybe even a 'Big Ten,' a Michigan State? Decent schools, only less... fussy academically."

Heating up, I replied, "*Because I'm here,* and *these boys* deserve a shot at a real education, not simply indentured service in a sport bootcamp, to be tossed aside when they're no longer useful. Look, SAT scores, high school grades or family backgrounds don't tell the full truth about these kids. *I know them.* Why shouldn't Conway take a real risk and make a commitment when—"

"Oh, come on, Berger," ripped Jamison, having had enough. "Don't play Lincoln just because you've become head coach by a freakish accident. We've been meeting our quota of 'need' scholarship kids."

"You know something else, wiseguy?" added Dak, turning back to his Mac. "The Colonel may have been a stiff guy who played by the rules, but at least he knew the rules and didn't try to bend them. And he knew a *good kid* from a *bad risk."*

Of course I should have just kept quiet, sucked it in and tactfully pleaded for mercy. But I knew, from my own dumb experience (and Papa's), that once you begged instead of fighting with these types you were in for the full snobbish ride. I was not only a *mere substitute coach*, but an *outsider*. Not *Conway*. Also, I was hot-tempered (from mother). I counted to five—son Daniel had ordered ten—before letting loose: "He knew *bubkas*, fellas. And he acted against the spirit of the rules—against fair play, hospitality, real support. These kinds of kids never stood a chance with him, he didn't respect them on or off the court. Necessary scum, that's all. And they knew it, could feel it." I stood up, burning. "Well, here's the morning news, they're as good or bad as the next bunch of kids, only they're exploited more, and have less of a real opportunity. We mock them privately, tacitly, as baboons on loan from the zoo, their talent of use for the good name, the visibility, and the coffers of the college. One solid PR sell, for Conway sports alum, boosters, federal regs, and everyone's conscience. If the baboons win, they're *of use*. And *we're good guys*. Well, as long as I'm around, we're going to give these kids the benefit of the doubt," I concluded, trembling, sensing my folly but unable to check it, "or you'll have a stink around here you won't easily get rid of. After all, Conway is not exactly a Harvard or Yale, on the lookout for a Jude Fawley or two."

Rick Jamison reddened. "I don't remember any Jude Fawley case. And your angry little outburst will be remembered, Coach."

"Especially in January," Dak added, "when losing streaks sometimes inspire resignations, forced or otherwise."

"In fact, Coach, we'll keep a sharp eye on their grades for you," Jamison was smiling narrowly, "and let you know if anything goes wrong, horribly wrong, so you can help them out if need be. Fair enough, *Coach?* I'll let the Director know you've been in." And he too showed me his back.

On that note I departed, out into the overcast day. Had I

done myself more harm than good? Naturally. Acted from the gut instead of the head. Why didn't I just shut up and take it? Or hand over one or two to dropout city, Nurlan to the dope hustlers and early doom? Who the hell would ever know that there was another dark mote of ghetto dust in the local sewer? Did I have to tweak their noses about Harvard or Yale? Stupid, stupid! And I still had Jack, Eddie and who knew who else for them to reinstate or shoot down? I was too old to change from a hot-headed shmuck to a slick diplomat. What could you expect from the red-blooded son of black-flag anarchists, right? The rebel genie had to pop out in some form, I rationalized, crossing the lovely green.

In my office I cooled down with a coffee and a cheese Danish and made a damage control call to Dick Porter, who was out on an errand. I removed my shoes, set my legs up on the desk and gazed around. Having one's own office calmed one's nerves, I thought. Especially a freshly painted one, with fresh lettering on the door announcing who's boss, who has power, and it's you. That helps. ("Power is the first good," Emerson had noted.) Even if you sensed that the tenancy might be shortlived.

I wrote down my list of urgent tasks in the next few days, trying to fit in the necessary social commitments—an alum get-together, a President's lunch for the athletic coaches, my own coaches' meeting—with the heavy stuff of my visit to Water's rehab place near Glens Falls, New York. Plus my Wednesday propaganda date with Roberto V. And I still had to check in with Jack Lightfoot way up yonder in Maine. How the hell was I going to do it all?

The telephone rang and I heard the A.D.'s pleasant voice. "What can I do for you, Syd? Before you speak, we're on for Saturday night, don't forget now. It's all set up. Now shoot."

Oops. "Oh yes, I'm looking forward to it." I hesitated, then said, "Anyway, it's Admissions. I'm afraid I had a little trouble there, put my foot in it." My first SOS.

"Probably nothing more than a misunderstanding," he offered casually at the end of my briefing. "Let me look into it.

I'll speak to Webb Smith, the new Director."

"Thanks."

How nice when you had cool skippers like Dick around to help out in rough waters, I reflected. How about in major storms?

Now, for wall decorations: My academic degrees? My photos of Mom and Dad at the Lincoln Brigade Reunion or the Sacco and Vanzetti Club? Yeah, sure, Sonny Boy, as Mama would say, just what Conway visitors would want to see. How about a certificate of inheritance of the operatic temperament?

I decided for starters on black and white photographs of Earl the Pearl faking an opponent into the air, and CCNY '54, with Ed Warner, Irwin Dambrot and Floyd Lane running the fast break. Plus Angelo "Hank" Luisetti throwing up the one-handed shot in '38-'39 and changing the game. My own grownup cave. Would Mom and Dad be proud, or laugh and wonder at what the hell I—or America—was up to?

On the bookshelf I set my first volumes: *Pinocchio, The American Boys' Handy Book, The Jungle Book* and *Two Years Before The Mast.*

Elbow on shelf, I remembered how, as a child, I had been a nervous boy, always in motion, twitching my legs or scratching my hair or picking my lip. Not to mention, from an early age, thinking and worrying in overdrive. To calm me, soothe me, Mama told and read me stories. I'd sit on her lap or she'd sit by my side and read to me. (For a few years I would eat dinners only if I got a story.) I remembered her low clear voice mesmerizing me with *Peter Rabbit* and *Jeremy Fisher, Babar, The Wind in the Willows,* scary *Hansel and Gretel, Rumpelstiltskin, The Snow Queen,* and *Pinocchio.* (Though I had many versions of *Pinocchio,* picture books and modern abridgments, my favorite was the original Italian story from 1883 by Carlo Collodi that Papa had found, where the little wooden wayward boy was stabbed and hanged before he reformed himself. Italian realism. Aloud to myself and Papa now I recited the opening epigraph from forty odd years ago: *Come andò che Maestro Ciliega, falegname, trovò un pezzo di legno, che piangeva è rideva come un bambino.*)

As Mama read I'd reach under her sleeve to rub her smooth skin while staring into the distance, and immediately her soft, lyrical voice transported me to a land of spellbinding enchantment! Along with Papa's operatic arias from Verdi or Ponchielli or Leoncavallo, those stories formed the happiest minutes and hours of my childhood, her silken voice hollowing out a private cave of intimacy and pleasure.

3   CITIZEN BERGER

Coaching in season must be like writing a serious novel or having a real illness; it affords little time for living. If you worked it seriously, from the inside out—on the court and not on the outside as a diplomat or politician—it absorbed your hours, revved your brain, scrambled your guts. It distorted, at times enchanted, your reality-sense. Like art or illness, it became your most demanding mistress at the same time that it gave order and meaning to everyday experience. I had sensed this before, and now, as head coach, knew it more and more. Well, thank god for the boy then, who was real and enchanting himself.

One late afternoon he played with Legos while I leafed through old notes, old mentors. At six and a half, Daniel was devoted to these little plastic building blocks from Denmark; they calmed and exhilarated him. I had just finished constructing a knight's castle, and then conducted a major war with him, one of his favorite pastimes. This released me for an hour or so of doing my own work, while he played on the rug in the modest living room. Periodically he talked to himself, using his best bass or soprano voices for his different parts: the dangerous Black Knight versus the good Silver Knight, Lancelot, Merlin, King Arthur. Our weekends together were savored hours; he was an articulate, independent boy, richly imaginative, and having him at age 45 came upon me like getting a fresh skin. Precociously mature, he understood that there was no return between me and his mother, though who knows what it cost him. For me, during the nine months of our separate ways, missing him had stabbed me once or twice a day, especially around 7 to 8 p.m., our appointed story time.

I had out my laptop desk, my four stenography spiral pads, 5 x 8 color-coded cards, and several felt and rolling point pens. My homework. For defense I went back to Clair Bee and Hank Iba; for fast breaks, Nat Holman and the old 1954 CCNY clubs (I had the videos of their twin victories over Rupp's Kentucky squad); for all-court play and pressuring zone defenses, Pete Newell and John Wooden. Oh, there were other fellows, like the Redheads (Auerbach and Holtzman), Phog Allen, Dean Smith, Jack Ramsey, and the crafty Pete Carril right in my own backyard, down at Princeton, who also contributed ideas, notions, fragments. These fellows were the Drydens, Popes and Austens of the game.

Basically, of course, I had to figure out what I could do with my own ragtag material, which was essentially two teams: with Nurlan (Water) and without him. If, as the Docs said at the upstate New York Rehab Center, he'd be back by early December, approximately, then I'd have to tread water for a month or more, before kicking in my real offense. In the interim I'd go conservative, and concentrate on a slowdown strategy, using the 45-second clock, a pressing defense, and the passing game. With luck and work and maybe a surprise walk-on, I might be able to get away with that. With Roberto and Eddie at the forwards I'd get my share of rebounds, and the Chief was a hell of a defensive disrupter. But who was going to score? Or set us up? How would we score more than 55 in a game?

Daniel was standing and shouting with passion, "And now we'll cut your arm off, Silver Knight, and teach you a lesson you won't forget easily!" Swish! From 7 a.m. till he went to sleep at night he nattered on in long formal sentences. Brown-haired, blue-eyed, firmly built, he had developed a sense of delicacy and justice, and had chastised me many a time in my domestic battles with Becka.

...Defense meant humiliation and cruel punishment—offense, glamour and narcissism. If your defense was smart enough, irksome enough, disruptive enough, you could slowly twist and torture an opponent, force him into stupidity and clumsy panic, and, if he were playing at home, take away the home crowd advantage (and therefore the ref advantage, too). Nothing insulted and injured a team more than stealing a ball and driving the other way. But you needed quick hands, anticipatory instinct, positioning, the guts of a burglar. Just now, except for Jack Lightfoot, the Chief, my boys were not up to this. As for offense, we'd build that once Nurlan returned, build on his playmaker's peacock beauties—his feathery passes, intricate dribbling, his court smarts and the cocksure strut which seemed to say *"You can't touch me, man, and you know it."* A self-projection made real.

Playing without a center was either going to make me and the team or break us, I figured. But what were you going to do when you didn't have a real center, but a pair of six-foot ten-inch suburban stiffs who couldn't jump four inches off the floor, and who could only shoot when no one was in their face? Put them in against a couple of the long-legged springy ghetto leapers from Penn, Yale or Brown and they'd be stuffed and cooked; so much for the morale of the team. I saw that happen last year in the very first two games. No, I'd give it a shot with my three six-five, six-sixers and let them bang and crash. Now, if that lanky black freshman from the Vermont prep school came on, or that high school principal's raw kid, or the unsuspected walk-on, well, things could be interesting.

"Papa, why do you have to go out tonight? It's not fair!"

"Hey, I thought we had that cleared up. You know Karen, she's coming all the way over here to be with you."

"Will you tell me my story before you go off?"

"W-e-l-l," I said, in my false voice of doubt, "I just might."

What good in the world were all the game strategies if you couldn't motivate the kids, make them believe in their teammates, and even con them about their talent? Did we or Washington know what kind of general he'd be until he was in the hot seat? Didn't he need a defeat or two, Battles of Long Island and White Plains and even a long retreat across Jersey to reveal his full mettle? The same went for Lincoln as a Commander in Chief. So too my young men had to be cajoled, disciplined, encouraged, promised, provoked, scolded, tempted, cared for, conned. Beneath it all there had to be the safety net of affection that they believed in, even if it was invisible. Trusting, maybe they'd try to ascend to the higher regions. Question was, when they started falling, as the team would do in the beginning, would they hit the net or go straight to the hard ground and never bounce back?

I glanced at the local *Valley News,* and saw a picture of our college president smiling widely and shaking hands with a five-million dollar donor for the new med school. The glamour stuff... Did outsiders, like administrators, professors, fans, know what a college coach was up to these days? Christ no. A thousand times no. Early on, you had to spot those kids whom you could drag out of the subcultural swamp, out of the refugee-camp shanties and incendiary ghettos where they were housed—in Bridgeport and Roxbury, East St. Louis and Fort Greene, Newark and Watts—and give them a sense of belonging in a land that was ivycovered and lilywhite. Shelter and nourish them after their abortive starts in life, the three-furlong handicap of third-grade education and one-parent (or orphaned) family life, and television- or drug-doped pals. Squeeze them through the brutal competition with the richest, brightest, most tutored and most pampered adolescents in the land. Easy, you think?... Like the ancient Romans, we spoiled natives wanted our gladiator entertainment, and so for four years my boys were fed to the English, History, and Science profs, while they performed athletic feats for the elite citizenry. And who cared for the boys? Educators, college presidents, NCAA officials, intellectuals? Maybe a

47

Newell or a Wooden. A McGuire. Or a Berger.

And even caring wasn't enough in many cases. You had to do more than care, you had to fight for them, be in on the dirty deals and deceptive practices that entrapped them, you had to dirty your hands, as Sartre might say, in their cause. Love by itself, as Bettelheim noted about his autistics, was simply not enough. You had to put in the nitty-gritty dirty labor. A matter of trust, you in them, and soon, they in you. Emotional trust funds, not the capital stuff. And still, how many made it through, up to the "clean" air of civilized life? One in three, one in four, one in six or ten? Well, it was up to Coach to get them through. And even then, afterward, what?

The doorbell rang me from my obsessive reverie. Teenage Karen had arrived, the boy's regular babysitter, and I got dressed. Before leaving, I sat down and read to him from "The Red Dog" tale in Kipling's *Jungle Book*, and then added a mini-version of our ongoing narrative. "Tomorrow morning the rest, okay?"

"*If* I'm good," he cautioned me, and added the new idiom he had learned, "that goes without saying, right?"

"Yes, that goes without saying," and I kissed his boyish skin and received a tight kiss on the lips in return, one of the fine fragrant moments of middle age.

The Porters lived in a modern house on Wheelock Street, a short walk from the campus. Nellie Porter was a hearty athletic woman about forty-five with a jutting jaw and short hairstyle. "Glad to meet you," she said at the door, "I've heard a lot about you these past few weeks and seasons."

I said hello, wondering if she had ever heard my name before this week.

The Bromleys were the second couple there, a broad-shouldered, genial ex-Tuck faculty fellow and his bird-like wife.

Over drinks, I sat in the armchair, listened to the banter and was glad I had worn a tie. The room was studied modern Scandinavian, leathery and tweedy, with a postmodern painting or two.

Five minutes later my arranged date arrived and she wasn't bad at all. Trim-waisted, light-brown hair, pale complexion with just a touch of makeup and lipstick. Claire Clarkson was a Julie Andrews lookalike, it struck me; wearing a black crêpe dress, she shook my hand and accepted a glass of white wine.

Fortunately the Bromleys were garrulous, especially Janet, and they and Nellie kept the conversation flapping, since it was obvious that Claire and I were rather quiet guests.

"I've always wanted to know," Janet Bromley asked at the dinner table, over early crisp salad, "is it exciting to be a head coach?"

"Too early for me to tell," I responded.

"Whatever you do," Chip Bromley defended, "don't ask him in January, if it's twenty below and Penn or Princeton is in. Give the man a break, hon! This is not even his squad."

"Well, actually, it might be half my squad," I explained, trying to crunch quietly, "so ask me how my half is doing."

"Well, I personally think it's terrific that you're getting a chance," Nellie Porter declared. "From what I hear you were easily the first choice of the players themselves." To her husband she said, "It's one of the best damn decisions *you've* ever made."

"You wouldn't know that I'm popular elsewhere," Dick retorted amiably.

"Just answer me one thing: why the hell has the basketball been so dull around here," Janet said, with force, "why? Because we're a hockey and football school first? But it's not as if we're winning any championships in those sports lately!"

"Well," Dick answered, "Penn gets the inner city boys, and Princeton has Carril and a Bradley tradition of winning. And so on. And I guess too that the Colonel was a conservative-type coach. What do you think, Syd?"

"Oh, I think you've touched the bases," I said, trying to keep the answer gracious, and to restrain my thoughts about the recent misguided past. "You play the hand you have," I added, "though there are various ways of playing it."

"You're not kidding," Chip said heartily. "I remember during the grand old days on the gridiron around here, when Conway was king of the hill, and Blackmon was coaching the football team. You had as many variations on the running game as Walsh has with the Forty-Niner passing game. Afterwards, the running game became dull as dishwater."

"You do keep up with the coaches and teams, don't you?" I noted.

"Well, to tell you the god's honest truth," he leaned over, slightly redfaced, "what else is there besides family and Conway? We raised three boys, not a one of them became a big-time college player, but they loved sports and it made them gentlemen, darn it!"

"Now come on," Janet corrected, "let's not have the 'Bromley cheering squad' right here at dinner." She made a face at her husband. "And would you call Keith or Denny 'gentlemen?' *Please.* "

Laughter tinkled, while the main course was brought in, a rack of lamb with rosemary, and small red potatoes.

"My oh my, what will you do for an encore after this sort of meal?" were Claire's first words.

"This is it, folks," responded Nellie, "for the season. The rest will be cocktail invitations only, thank you. Unless," she turned to me, "we have a championship, of course."

"In that case," I rejoined, "I'll do it with you."

"Oh, do you cook?"

"Soft-boiled, hard-boiled or scrambled."

The lamb was excellent, though a bit rare for primitive me, and I managed a bit of private chat with Claire. Soft-spoken and plain-pretty, she had a cheery manner and spoke intelligently of her clinical work with adolescents. When I asked who was prominent up here in the Valley, she laughed it off. "No one. This is the sticks. You have to go to Boston for someone of quality."

When she turned to accept a demitasse of coffee I couldn't help take an interest in her small well-rounded fanny and fine legs.

I felt an arm drape my shoulders and Chip Bromley said, "You know, I want to take you around a little and show you *my* Conway, if you don't mind. The Conway I've known and loved for forty years."

The fellow had it bad, didn't he? "Sure. Whenever you say."

"Doggone it," he offered, in his cups, "how 'bout tonight?"

"Let's wait for some daylight."

He laughed broadly. "Yes, you'd see more. But I'd go right now, if you wanted. That's what this school means to me, Syd!"

"Sydney," I corrected gently. "We'll do it this week, okay?"

Janet Bromley rescued me and chatted me up with a perfectly irrelevant anecdote.

"Okay," Nellie announced, sipping cognac, "now that we've all been good little boys and girls, give us a rundown about that brouhaha over in Admissions. You've been called *confrontational*. Ooh la la. Two weeks on the job, and he's taking on the Establishment. Good for you, the place needs shaking up. Give us the scoop!"

Embarrassed, I drained my espresso and tried to pass it over. "Well, it was a matter of different... definitions of education, I think. Judging student potential."

"How so?" Janet wondered.

"Really?" I glanced over at Dick, for a sign.

"Sure, really," reasserted Nell, cultivating her naughty side.

Okay, just go easy, Sydney boy. "Oh, I think Admissions goes by Who's Been Who in Conway, prep school recognition, and what the latest hip trend in Administration is, liberal or conservative. Right now they seem to be in a transition to politically correct turf. Of course they play the numbers game: SAT's, high school grades, any set of stats. And that's okay for a certain number, and kind, of qualified student. But what about my kids, the ghetto athletes who've had little time or encouragement to develop their academic side? Don't they deserve a shot at big-time education? Kids who spend their boyhoods playing ball, who see or hear nothing bookish in their environments, but who happen to be eager to learn, to change, to find out what's happening out there, *and* who have some specific talent, what about them? The best are hungry to learn. Why should they be penalized for being good on the court, when the court is their only route for escape? Why should they be shipped out to Iowa State or UTEP or a JUCO?"

"Whoa, hold on, what the hell is UTEP?" asked Janet. "Or JUCO?"

"The University of Texas at El Paso, a regular dumping ground for south Bronx or south Chicago kids. JUCO is a junior college where the hotshots can pump up their grades by dunking the ball." I drained my second cup. "What's education mean, how do you measure it? By college grades or SAT scores? Come now. All sorts of well-trained chimps wind up with A-'s or B+'s by learning the tricks of the trade, just as their parents paid for them to learn how to handle the SAT Q and A's, and earn their way into Shearson Lehman or Coldwell Banker or top Wall Street law firms. Would you really call a high percentage of business leaders or corporate lawyers *educated?*... Rich and successful does not mean you've read Edith Wharton or Dreiser, studied Parkman's view of history or Emerson's notions of the self."

"Well, without insulting present company," Nell said, only half-mischievous, "go on, what then?"

"To be educated doesn't mean that you now belong to the Book Clubs and read the bestsellers, buy theater series tickets and visit museums three times a year. No; that just defines you as a culture consumer. My sense of education is for a student to have been put in touch with certain books and people, certain ideas and events in history and to absorb them, somehow, into his sensibility. Like remembering the Triangle Shirtwaist Factory Fire in 1911 where Jewish immigrants watched their daughters leap to their death on the East Side, or the Sacco and Vanzetti case in Massachusetts, or the

'Ludlow Massacre,' when police killed eleven children and two women to break the strike against the Rockefellers' Colorado Fuel and Iron Company. Remembering those stories is one measure of education. Not smooth dinner chat about this movie, that bestseller or stock. Maybe that student's education will be reflected in a moral decision later on. Some unlikely act on the job, or small gesture with a friend, something where the previous conventional wisdom or ignorance is replaced maybe by a memory of a Thoreau essay, by how Huck acts on the raft with Jim, by the moral courage of a Harriet Tubman. You want to be on the lookout for kids who *show the potential to take learning to heart,* rather than only for students who are at college because they've been programmed since age twelve to use schooling as a union card for successful careers in profitmaking, prestige, public esteem.

"In other words, what I'm saying is that the majority of actual educating that goes on, maybe especially at the better colleges, is a matter of a gentleman's agreement, a kind of high hypocrisy, where the exams have certified the genteel negotiation that has gone on, and where four years of A-'s have been more or less guaranteed, right? So why keep my boys out? Why not give them a shot at getting *semi-educated* like the majority of middle-class kids? Wouldn't the results ultimately be the same, five or ten percent serious?"

I realized I had been walking about, up and back, sort of like teaching, and pulled up short, embarrassed, aware of my lengthy heated lecture. By the tall rubber tree I smiled sheepishly, aware that I had probably gone too far, yet again. I had an impulse to do a quick change with the shrewd, silent plant, and sprout my own large and glossy, leathery leaves!

Dick, arms folded, remarked, "That's the best argument I know of for athletic scholarships at the Ivies. Sometime you'll have to make it to the President."

"My, my, you certainly have traveled a different path as a coach, I'll say that for you," Nell observed merrily. "Didn't know that coaches could be eggheads too. Just one question:

can you coach half as well as you speak?"

Everyone laughed and I breathed easier, like a man with a reprieve. "We'll see, but don't give me too early a report card."

"You're not also teaching this year, are you?"

I shook my head. "No, I'm relieved of that, thanks to Dick."

"Unless it's in classes like these," said Janet. "Informal sessions for the laymen."

I nodded, and found a smile, too.

As we said our goodbyes Dick took me aside and murmured, "By the way, I've straightened out the Admissions people about your cases. More of a misunderstanding, I think, than anything else. Especially with Webb Smith missing. He's the most tolerant of the crew."

"I'm sure that's all it was," I said, privately decoding the language now.

I thanked our hosts, said goodbye to the Bromleys, and escorted Claire to her sleek white car. On the way she offered, "You were interesting in there. And passionate, driven. That's unusual for these parts. Watch out, or you'll get a *reputation.*"

I nodded. "As a 'character,' right? Driven, huh? Was I *showing?*"

"Well, maybe."

Code word for *outsider*, I thought. Well, you are that, Sydney, aren't you, in this community of collegial gentility?

At her hatchback Saab, I said, "Yours is about six years and sixty thousand miles younger than mine."

"Oh, do you have one too?"

I indicated my battered 99 across the way. "Problem is service around here," I remarked, gazing at her green eyes.

"Dean Hill Motors, in Claremont," she said authoritatively, and tapped my chest with her forefinger. "The only way to go."

That forefinger signalled me, and I nodded. "I'll call you and you can give me the details. By the way, I have to confess that I was observing you in there, and admiring what I saw. Does that make me a full-blown sexist?"

"Probably. But I was looking you over, too. Does that make me... feminist, or coarse?"

"Just modern," I responded, flattered. "Now tell me where that occasional voice inflection comes from. Sweden?"

She laughed. "Not quite. Montana."

"Close enough," I said, and closed the door for her.

"Grandmother was Swedish, though. Middle name is Ulla, after her. How'd you know?"

Should I explain how I was promised an Ingrid Bergman lookalike? But then I'd have to explain that Julie Andrews was good enough. "Cheekbones. Saab. Welfare state concerns."

She laughed and half-pouted. "Is that what I sound like? You call me, and I'll straighten out *all* your misperceptions."

The next morning the boy was in bed with me at 7:10 a.m., his standard waking hour.

"Could you finish the story now, Papa?" He leaned into me, his smell sleepy-delicious, wearing his red and black striped devil-pajamas, purchased in Canada for their 100% cotton fibers.

Groggy, I pleaded for ten minutes more of sleep and he said, "Sure, Papa." He began chattering to himself while I dozed off.

About twenty minutes and a quick nightmare about brother Robey later, he intruded. "Is it ten minutes yet?" Sleepily, I began narrating about Saint Hospice, the undersea dragon who spit out fire when tickled by the young boy Sheltie, and the attempt by the evil Dr. Emil Noxious to steal the dragon's treasure trove...

Having the boy alone with me on weekends was delicious, and afterwards, by Wednesday, his absence was punishing. The weekends were a clear frame of limits on my time with the boy, a stabbing reminder of my old summer afternoons with him, and the slow, long evenings. At four he had already become an interesting companion, a boy of long precise sentences and free-for-all imagination. At six he displayed more poise and discrimination than Becka and I, adjudicating our stormy fights with a referee's calm judgments: "Now, Papa, don't say another word. I'll speak to her." His finger at his lips. "Mom, you were wrong, he wasn't yelling at you, his voice was *accusing,* but he wasn't yelling." Then, turning to me, "You mustn't *accuse* Mom, even if she did lose the paper you wanted, you see she didn't *mean* to..." But the pressure on him to be our daily Solomon was too constant, I figured, too unfair.

Did I miss Becka, the marriage? Sure, I had invested eight years of energy in that partnership. And on her own, she was a fine woman, intelligent, warm, uncorrupted; but her ways in thinking, feeling and needs—*to be a good person*—were not mine at all. The differences drove me crazy. She needed a form of fathering, to salve the wounds from adolescent battles against a tyrant Dad, and I was not up for that. On my side I probably wanted a bit of mothering, a set not for her. One of only 57 varieties of incompatibility, I reckoned. But towards this little creature beside me, she was an excellent mother, her maternal feelings of warmth balanced by a firm sense of restraints and boundaries. She was literary and sporting, too, and could talk a new Bellow or last night's game, getting you through many a dinner. Losing her, losing the house in the country and my country life, losing the treasured boy for most of the week, a boy who had splashed my forty-five years of bachelorhood with a fresh wave of exhilaration, all that had placed a shroud around my spirit. (On top of the Strickland shroud, the first layer.) So the new job had come at an opportune time.

"But Papa, how can Noxious stay so long at the bottom of the sea with only *one* oxygen tank?" He had caught me up short, as usual. "And does he have *waterproof* lasers?"

On Sunday evening Robeson called me from Cambridge. "Hey, is it really true, you've been hoisted upward? How's it feel, kid?"

"Not bad," I replied. "How'd you hear?"

"Hey, I got spies everywhere, you know that," and he gave off his number one little laugh, the sardonic. "Especially in the Ivies. So how goes it, honestly?"

"Goes well, thus far. Just fine. And you?"

"Oh, okay. Okay. Look, I'm off to Warsaw for a little conference and then maybe I can jump up there and watch your team play. How's that sound?"

"When we're watchable, I'll let you know. That's Warsaw as in Poland, right?"

He gave his stutter laugh, number two, acknowledging my attempt at irony. "That's right, Syddie. Poland, not Maine."

"You're delivering a paper?"

"Well, actually, they're giving a little conference in my honor. They asked me to respond to several of their papers."

"Didn't know they followed American Puritans that closely."

"Sure. Everyone does. Nowadays. Anyway, I just called to congratulate you. It must be pretty nice to come in from the cold, so to speak."

"I get your point. I'll let you know later on, if it's warmer on the inside."

"Or boiling, huh?" Number three, the mirthful laugh. "You take care now, Syddie. And I'll drop you a card from Warsaw."

"Yeah, that'd be fun," I said.

"Now don't go and hoist yourself on your own petard, remember."

"See you, Robey."

Older brother was older brother, I figured. Liked you best when you were down and out, or down and *almost* out. First son of anarchist revolutionaries, now a conservative chief of his own Puritan court down at Harvard. Standard native evolution. Too bad Mom wasn't alive to laugh over it. Or over her younger son's folly...?

Bright and early on Monday morning I got a call from Chip Bromley, who asked if I was still interested in coming along with him for a personal Conway tour? Sure, I declared, with about 49% sincerity. After all, you had to learn what made other creatures tick, like Big Green Lifers, acolytes, Eagle scouts.

That afternoon at 2 p.m. he was escorting me around the campus, periodically erupting with bursts of boyish enthusiasm. Big Bear Bromley didn't need any alcohol for his Conway possession to show. Mention the word and the 66-year-old became 16.

"You know how many times I walked this trail and wound up here at the boathouse and Ledyard? Hundreds, thousands during my four years. I was captain of the crew, so I spent many a day down here, at the river. Oh, we weren't great, never did beat the great Crimson shells or Yale for any championship, but we gave it everything we had and we were close," he took my shoulder, "real close. Bonded for life, you might say."

Next stop, up at the Butler library, he took me into the "1902 Room," and I said, "Otherwise known as the 19-0-Jew Room, yes?"

"Yeah, that was the ugly humor of certain types. No offense now, I hope. I loved it here, it was my real study home, and look at it, still the coziest place around, and relatively empty except at exam time. Just the tables and chairs and these pictures of the old deans gone up to Indian Heaven." He managed a hearty laugh. "And you could sneak your feet up on the chairs without feeling too guilty, 'cause they're all wooden, unlike upstairs."

Next on the tour he showed me the Tower, with its dark walnut woods and stuffed wing chairs. "I used to come up here to snooze a bit, I'll fess up. And to check out this character, come on." He dragged me to the center of the room, where, perched on a table, sat a bronze sculpture of an Indian on a horse, surveying the scene. "I always liked to check on him, for some reason."

But it was outside, after forcing me into Webster Hall and then standing on the grassy green in front of the library, that his excessive piety and chauvinism burst forth. Locking my arm and looking up at the clock tower of Butler, he shook his head. "Nothing like it, is there—the feelings of serenity and pleasure and order this gives off." Adjusting his large arm around me like a protective flag, he said, "Corny, but it's true. Do you feel any of what I'm saying? Give it a few years, you will, Syd. You will."

Last stop was his fraternity house, Sigma Alpha Epsilon. "Oh, I had great years there, but I'll tell you something. I've come to believe that maybe they should be changed after all. I mean, you can't have prejudice or discriminations any more, that crap has got to be a thing of the past. Like Tri Kap not changing its name to get rid of those initials." He nodded sympathetically. "I've tried to be flexible about this stuff, and if it injures students' feelings, enough students, then maybe the Greek system should be changed no matter how many fond memories I have of it. Conway has to evolve like the country, no doubt, while remaining *true to itself.*"

We strolled along and he indicated that we take a seat on the hill overlooking the green. By Conway Hall we sat, and in the warm autumnal sunshine he reflected: "Look at it, Syd, I know it by heart. I walk up here by the Bema, or down by the river, or over to Sanborn and Webster once a week at least, just to behold the felicity of it all. Is there anything more beautiful in the world than one's alma mater, where you spent the finest four years of life? I doubt it. Campus, and family, that's what it's all about. Toss in a childhood baseball club, sure. Oh, don't get me wrong, I love our country too. But this is a private thing, a family matter.

"And that's what disturbs me about this new president. Oh, he's a bright enough fellow, and he means well in his way, I think, but it's just that he's trying to change the place radically, without even realizing what he's got here. We're not a *university,* Syd, we're unique, a *family college.* This is perfection, Sydney, a kind of Platonic ideal of a school, and he's trying to tell us that we need to change this or that? I don't buy it. Oh, you can fix something up, sure; bolster a department, change a curriculum, fund a new building, alter the tenure procedure. Sure. But don't tamper with the underpinning, not the basic structure of the place. No sir. That's not the way to go.

"Look, I've been out there in the big world, in big business in New York and Atlanta, and I know what it's like *down there.*" He shook his head. "Down and dirty, Syd. Eat your neighbor and spit him out. The guy has a wife and family? Tough titty. Betray your friend if it advances your cause. Sell him out to the opposition, all for the big buck and the career. It's dog eat dog. But here, in the land of Conway? Uh uh. *I have friends from forty-four years ago that I made right here, on that green.* None better or truer. Oh, you can be a cutup or SOB here for a little while, till people size you up. But once it's known and you keep it up, you don't get much farther. And always, Conway stays clean. Ready to protect you. You see, the crummy behavior of the few doesn't stain or corrupt Conway. The institution stays true to its history and traditions. And that means friendship, honesty, loyalty, civility. That's Conway, Sydney. And I welcome you to it." He put out his hand, his eyes teary. "Welcome. Anything my friends or I can do to help you preserve all of this, just call. I don't care if you're 0 and 15, you do your part to keep Conway intact, and I'm here, the Friends of Conway are here, a phone call away. Kapish?"

What could I say to all this heartfelt Boy Scout stuff? Thoroughly exhausted, I nodded, knowing that his piety and sincerity were matched only by his devoted naiveté and mushy emotions.

Or was I the one whose vision had become astigmatic, from past experience, cynicism? Maybe I *was* "too hard," as Dick P had noted?

I took his hand and shook it, figuring maybe a little awry sentiment might season me anew, and also, you never knew when you might have to make a call to a scout. Besides, I sort of liked this fellow, he was like some maudlin bear in Goldilocks, dressed in green and gushing over her tresses.

"I'll do my best, Chip, to keep the trust."

A darker, more curious world was the Nils Peterson Rehabilitation House over on the Vermont/New York border. When I arrived there, and first sighted Nurlan through a narrow window, my heart sank. "Don't worry how it looks," Dr. Barnett said as we entered that odd room, "it's been working well. Eighty percent rehab success rate with acupuncture is about the best in the country right now. Go ahead over, you can talk to him right now."

Along with a half-dozen other patients who eyed me, Nurlan was sitting in a high chair like that found in a hair salon. His head was positioned high, and from his ears protruded a halo of silver pins, two or three inches long, stuck there like hatpins by some precise sadist. He and the others looked like inhabitants of a foreign planet, or medical guinea pigs; the atmosphere was eerie.

When he caught sight of me approaching, he smiled. "Hi, Coach. Don't look too pretty, do it?"

I shook my head. "Not quite a television ad just yet. How's it going?" I patted his thin wrist.

"Well, you know, it ain't too bad. I mean, it don't really hurt, that's the thing. Ya jes don't want to look in the mirror," he smiled weakly.

"Yes, don't. But the doc says you're coming along. True?"

He nodded slowly. "Yeah, I think so. I'm eatin' again, and gainin' back some pounds. This place is weird, real weird, but okay. They gonna fix me up swell, I got a feelin'."

"I'm waiting, Nurlan. And the team is going to be waiting."

His pale face grew slightly mobile. "How's it goin', Mister B? Vargas comin' around? Eddie?"

"Got both of them back."

"Thass real news. Those boys ain't afraid to mix it up with no one. And the Chief?"

"My next task."

"The man's a player," he drawled, "and one tough dude

to drive past."

"I noticed. And if we can pick up one or two more players, well, we might have something. Until Water comes back, though, it might be rough going."

He smiled, then suddenly grimaced. "Don't worry, ain't nothin'." Perspiration beaded his forehead. He breathed deeply. "Maybe call the doc, huh? I still get... uh, one a these every few days."

I got up and, at the desk in the corridor, found the doctor.

The lean Scotsman came along with me. "He's right, nothing to worry about. Aftereffects of the withdrawal. Maybe you better finish up your visit now? Oh, by the way, Mr. Reeves has been drawing lately, and has left a packet for you to take home."

Surprised, I accepted the envelope from Dr. Barnett, and presently said to Nurlan, "Hey, thanks for the pics. Glad you have leisure time again. Now listen to the doctor, here, and practice your foul shooting form in your head. You'll be shooting many this winter."

His smile was feeble, his eyes watery, but they followed me. "No sweat... Thanks, Coach. Keep a... place open for me, huh?"

Leaning real close, I whispered, "I got one, running the club. You're my pointguard, with or without pins sticking out of you," and I squeezed his arm gently. A skinny twelve-year-old's. "Catch you in a week or so."

I watched his dappled brown face crease with pain, and his anguished face haunted me all the way back on winding Route 4, through the pretty hills and perfect towns of Vermont, with the white steeples and red schoolhouses.

Getting to the Chief's house in Washington County, Maine, was like driving to some remote site in Central America. It took me seven hours of driving to get to Olde Towne, the quaint home territory of the Penobscot Indians. First I checked out the high school, to see if he might be hanging out and playing ball. No luck, though I was impressed all over by the class photographs, dating back to 1927, placed front and center in the corridor. The Olde Towne H.S. treasured its boys and girls. From there I had to travel another fifteen miles on a rather gutted dirt road, where the landscape was rolling and dreary, and the houses were pink ranches and plain Capes. If I hadn't been in the area about 18 months ago, and wasted a full day trying to find the place, I wouldn't have found it now. Few signs, few streets, few clues.

Jack was inside the house, and his smoky black eyes widened when he saw me at the door. He asked me in, polite as ever, and I saw that he had been watching television in the tiny kitchen while eating a white-bread sandwich.

"How's the family?" I asked, meaning his two kids and wife.

"Okay," he said.

He went to the color TV, set beneath a photograph of Jack Kennedy, and an autographed one of Robert Parrish, the Celtics center, and turned it off. "What are you doing way up here?"

"Coming to get you back," I answered.

He didn't smile or protest, as he put the milk carton, butter tub and American cheese into the refrigerator.

I talked about the Colonel's departure and my ascendancy, and he listened quietly while wiping the plastic tablecloth.

Seeing the improvised halfcourt setup behind the house, I suggested we go outside and shoot around. Sure. A basketball was lying on the ground, near the two garbage barrels, and I picked it up. The basket was set on a painted, cracking white board which was attached to a telephone pole.

"So here's where you practice," I said, tossing up a short set shot.

He skied for the rebound, took three dribbles out into the corner and threw in a jumper. He was smallish, maybe 5' 8", but strong, fast and smart. Very smart. I remembered when I first watched him play, in the high school regional championship, where his defensive wits and quick hands frustrated the star shooter of the other team, and stole the victory for his

Olde Towne club.

In the hazy warm day we took turns shooting and rebounding, while I did the talking, explaining how now, with me, he was to be a starter in the back court, and how the family situation could be improved. I said I'd try hard to get him extra money so his family could come down to live on or near campus. I knew from last year how arduous the drive back and forth had become for him, and how the Colonel couldn't be bothered. ("Why the hell did you bring that midget Redskin down here in the first place, huh?")

"Why would they want to help me out there?" He stopped on a dime and banked in his angled jumper. "I'm nothin' to them."

"To begin with, you did well last year, you're in perfectly good standing." He had managed a 2.9 average, after a year in the ABC program. "And secondly, I want to read you something." I proceeded to take out a xeroxed copy of the original Conway Charter, from the Earl of Conway, which declared, back in 1764, that Conway College was "committed to fostering the education of our Native (American) Indians, and no one of them shall be deprived of a complete education at the college because of financial or otherwise reasons, should they wish to attend." I didn't need to read on, about the desire of the college to make "good Christian gentlemen" out of the natives, since Jack Lightfoot was already a Christian and a gentleman.

His eyes narrowed. "You make all that up?"

"I copied it yesterday. Here."

Cradling the basketball, he read the xeroxed evidence, while I looked around at the thick forest background broken by his green garden, and by the black mesh satellite dish.

When he looked up I asked about that dish. "When and why did you get that?"

"Two years ago, when the Tribe got its payment for our land from the Federal Government, and handed out its distributions. I get to watch the Celtics, and my man The Chief." Why was Parrish so favored? Big smile. "The Chief is the leader, by example, like the other chief, old Joseph, of the Nez Percé.

A truck was rumbling in, a dusty once-red Ranger pickup, holding his wife and kids.

He swished one last jumper, set the ball down and invited me in for a cold drink.

By the time I was shaking hands with Jeanette Lightfoot, I was already planning a two-on-two trap defense for the last few minutes of tight games, with my Chief my freewheeling rover in the middle. This was not some wild little Indian out of the nursery rhyme stereotype, but a shrewd poised fellow who knew that defense was the best revenge.

"You know, Coach B, I never knew that Conway was founded with that kind of interest in Native Americans. Seems as though they always wanted to bury that side of their past or hide that motive, huh?"

I shrugged, thinking how maybe Big Green Bromley should get to know Jack, and maybe also get a copy of his alma mater's original charter.

"Eleazar Wheelock began the school down in Connecticut in 1769," I told him, "and only moved it north a year later. There's a nice picture of the original wooden schoolhouse in Butler Library. You know, its origins would make a pretty good essay topic, wouldn't they?"

His eyes lit up for a second. "Yeah, that's a thought."

No one anticipated a lazy pass like this kid, I was thinking, already picturing it in my mind.

4   HARD FACTS

Man wasn't meant for Administration, at least not this man. (Remember, I was raised by a mother who couldn't care less about grocery lists and school appointments, but who never lost her place in books like *Grapes of Wrath, Jude the Obscure, Tale of Two Cities.* (Hence the "Y" in Sydney. I had been named for Sydney Carton.)

September came and went in a flurry of meetings and tasks, beyond the re-recruiting, that had left me little time for thinking, reading, conversing, idling. (Tasks like assigning extra tickets, signing chits, meeting my assistants.) The A.D. remained steady at the helm in helping me out, making sure that every one of my boys got in, admitted under the legal gun, in time for the season. (Not Nurlan, of course, who wouldn't be available until after the quarter break in December.) Finally in mid-October we were allowed officially into the gym, and I got to see up close the *hard facts*. I had little height, little experience, little cohesiveness, little speed, little firepower. In other words, the ship was leaking badly before even starting out.

But just being inside the gym was, for me, like being a whale lifted out of captivity and returned to the sea. Back in my necessary medium, my beloved wooden aquarium, where

I could breathe and function. Golden hardwood floor, glass backboards and goatee baskets, the thuds and echoes of a round ball bouncing, the squeaking of sneakers and the slants of amber light falling in the late afternoon. The resiny oxygen of gymnasium mingling with memories of youthful ritual. Dr. Naismith's peachbasket bliss. I felt renewed, primed, ready to go despite the obstacles. A basketball gym was the test site where duty and pleasure merged, where rectitude and play, devotion and delight were one. A holy place, though nowhere described or imagined in the King James or William James texts.

In the first weeks I set the 15-18 kids in a series of simple drills, running and dribbling the court, two- and three-man passing, blocking out and setting picks, a basic weave-and-cut, a zone defense and man-to-man switching. The fundamentals. Before focusing on my repetitions, I let them scrimmage too, wanting to see what I had to work with... Was there a more cherished word in the lexicon of the game than repetition? In the chemistry of basketball, I theorized, the pursuit of my "High Flow" had to be injected into the team's brain cells, and then transferred to the individual physical act and team instinct; this process could take a year or more. With Nurlan aboard, it might take much less.

I say this because the pointguard was the key to the game, like the narrator of a splendid story. I confess, I saw the game through the prism of a literary tale, as an art form; not a mere chart of X's and O's. Its ideal form, its Plutonic essence, if you will, I called High Flow. So I looked for texture—interior passing and inside defense; character—how the team did when losing or missing shots; circumstance—when injuries, refs, shots, conspired against them; and plotting—the force of third quarter momentum, after the necessary adjustments of the first half. All this to go along with the linchpin, the narrator (pointguard), whose job it was to run the show and prove credibility—to control tempo, to judge flows, to determine shooters and to perform with a style or signature.

The art of passing was crucial to my desires. Every day I

set aside thirty minutes to an hour practicing that lost art: the basic two-hand chest pass, the curling bounce pass into the pivot or cutter (and back-door layup), the long outlet pass for the fast break (either the one-hand throw or the two-handed toss over the head), the short accurate bounce pass on the break, the firm long passes for ball rotation around the court (against the zone or to work the 45-second shot clock), the four-corner looping passes for endgame delay. This emphasis seemed excessive to some—"Christ, Coach, REALLY, how many times do I have to throw an eight-footer?" "Until you get it right, Eddie, and can do it blindfolded." (Yes, I tried it that way, too, which irritated the boys.) For my club, the excessive was essential. I didn't have a chance against the big, talent-laden clubs without a fluid, patient passing system, handled as well by the forwards as the back court. "Pass first, shoot second," was my bulletin board motto; we'd applaud the good pass ahead of the good shot.

Passing had become a lost art, like radio listening. Why? Because the jumpshot and dunk were more glamorous and easier to acquire; because speed and jumping had grown in importance, creating the illusion that passing was less important. However a superior passing game made good shots that much easier to get; the extra pass often cut half the distance to the basket. And if you could teach your forwards how to pass, you had a serious, nearly indefensible, advantage. (That was what made big men like Debusschere, Bird, Magic and Walton doubly dangerous, and so unique for a team.) To showcase the art I found some old Knick-Celtic footage featuring Bob Cousy versus Dick McGuire, wherein the pass was the thing to catch the love and loyalty of the crowd; the two of them dueled as if the subtle pass, leading to the simple shot, was the valuable score. Look one way, flick it the other way, to a streaking player for a layup. The Cooz and Tricky Dick Show was a thing of beauty, a true joy forever. ("Come on, Coach, you can't expect us to move up to that level now?") Well, not quite, though Nurlan already knew the secret; it would take us a while, weeks, months, a season perhaps, for the art to kick in, to become part of their instinctive game; but once it did, we would be playing with an invisible sixth man on the court—legal, too. What a nice little advantage, that extra presence. So I drilled them in twos and threes with the whole bag of passes, filled their heads with the passing soul of the game, worked on their anticipation, timing and peripheral vision, interior and top-of-the-circle passes, one-hand, off-the-dribble, two-hand chest, long and looping, scooping and feathery, fast break and half-court cutting, until it became part of the daily grind. Thus the idea was inserted into their nervous system that a pass was better than a shot, that a pass could open up a game and enlarge a horizon, that a pass could be as lonely and stubborn as that thistle in Tolstoy's *Hadji Murad*, and just as lovely too. (Sure, they glanced at each other and shook their heads when I gave that comparison. A kook? I'd have to watch that, yes.)

Anyway, was it boring, this constant daily drilling and practicing, like doing conjugations? Sure, the way any work is boring that is yours for life. Boring, yet the way things were; boring, yet the nature of necessary hoop matter; boring, yet nutritious and filling. Like learning the formal art of the sonnet, or the trick sport of dressage. If you didn't drill, if you didn't get used to the labor of daily rehearsing, if you didn't insert dull drill into the loose gaps of free mornings and afternoons of your life, you'd never shine in anything. And remember something else: what went on behind the scenes was frequently more stimulating than the actual show. Ask the actors, dancers, singers, writers. Weren't certain rehearsals supposed to be more exhilarating than the actual productions? Or some manuscripts, when discovered posthumously, much more fascinating than the published books? So too with the stuff of give-and-goes, half-court traps, zone defenses, all-out scrimmages. *With no audience around to show off for and mess up for*, you might suddenly launch into that high zone of basketball transcendence.

For another reason I was in a curious position that season, choosing to flipflop the starters of last year with the reserves,

washouts. And without my pointguard on hand, who continued to gain weight slowly and welcome his unorthodox
healing, my green shirt regulars didn't look so good against
the more veteran white shirt leftovers of the Colonel. His fellows were tall, slow, mostly suburban players; they were not
terrible, and would only lose games by 10 points or so.
Whereas my boys, young, green, hungry were liable to lose
by 20, at the start. But with Water they might get good fast,
real good real fast. So it wasn't surprising when the players
from last year began to grumble and resent me. Why shouldn't
they? I occasionally began to spot the sly glance, and over-
hear the locker room remark "Who the fuck does he think he
is, Bobby Knight?" And, "Bringing in a down and out recruiter to coach here, now, is an insult to the seniors!" They
had a point.

All except the one I could use, a blue-eyed Irish lad named
Dennis Healey. Son of a Windsor, Vermont, high school principal he was here on an academic scholarship, played football,
and was a Rhodes Scholar candidate. On last year's squad he
was a backup forward who would come in and toss up hook
shots as though he were Houbergs, Mikan or Abdul-Jabbar,
except he couldn't hit. But I saw something else: a bull—or
bullvan, as my mother would say—for my front court. Like
Vargas and Konepski he was in the vicinity of 6' 5" and
weighed about 220, no fat. "You're going to be my center,
Dennis, but you're going to be a non-shooting center. Want
the job?"

He looked at me with a little impish grin, a handsome
fellow with a light, ruddy face and soprano voice. "*Never* shoot
it?"

"Well," I allowed, "if you get a rebound you can put it
back up, sure."

He nodded, smiling. "What am I supposed to do in the
meantime?"

"Set picks. Block out. Stuff the middle. Play defense. Or,"
I smiled amiably and tapped his backside, "you can sit on the
bench."

His blue eyes twinkled. "That's some choice you're giving me, Coach. Like my English prof, who says I can write my honors thesis on Chaucer's *Troilus*—*if* I focus on the secular. Can I think on it?"

"Sure. Take till tomorrow."

There were also a few surprises: first, a walk-on kid who could pop them in regularly with defenders all over him. This boy, an Avram Ivan Twersky—he'd need a nickname, quick—would get the ball in the corners, turn, and flick it in, with the oddest of shots, one hand practically twisted around his neck, a little corkscrew like "Silky" Wilkes's (UCLA). He didn't know a thing about defense or passing, and dribbled poorly. But he could knock home the jumper, time after time, arcing the ball as though sending it into orbit the way Vince Boryla used to bomb them in the old Garden.

After the third or fourth practice I became a believer.

"Where you from?" I asked.

He rearranged his angular frame and swung his kinky, black-haired head. "When?"

"What do you mean, when?"

"From now I'm from Brookline, Mass."

"And before?"

"From Kibbutz Ma'agan Michael."

I nodded.

"And before, from the Ukraine. Kiev."

"I see. Your father's a traveling minstrel?"

"A Jew. And engineer. Lincoln Labs. You know?"

"No. But why Conway? How come here?"

"High school counselor say Conway is excellent for math, if I not get in Harvard."

"Is it?"

"Excellent. Kemeny, Snell, Baumgarten, Snapper, all very high notch."

"Do you have a specialty?" I asked, not believing two eggheads, Dennis and this fellow, on one squad.

He shrugged. "Probability theory. But I also publish a paper on Ring Theory. Very specialized, you know?"

Life in the Ivies. "Where'd you learn the peculiar jumper?"

"First cousin in Kiev show me. Coach in kibbutz want to change me, but... One question for you, please. Jews have played hoop ball before?"

I smiled, observing his alert brown eyes and eager face. "One of the greatest teams ever was the Philadelphia Sphas, or the Hebrews, in the 20s. Called Hebes for short. Founded by Eddie Gottlieb, who became owner and general manager of Wilt Chamberlain's 76ers. The Sphas were all Jews except for one Gentile. So there's a native tradition. Maybe you'll add to it?"

With the team so short of scorers, he was worth a shot. I paired him with Dennis, for picks, and explored those points on the floor where he felt most comfortable with his shot.

Another young walk-on who surprised was a skinny 6' 3" leaper from the Governor Dummer Academy in Byfield. Son of a minister, Jarrod Stalleybrass wore glasses, studied religion, listened to jazz and stayed poised. He did a lot of things pretty well, if nothing outstanding. (Except dressing; J. Press and Brooks Brothers were *de rigueur*.) I had little idea how to use this kid yet, but he was unusually mature for a freshman and I marked him for a place. It would be interesting to see how Nurlan would help this kid's game out—not to mention how they'd get along, black kids from different worlds. I also picked up Tony Scalese for his nostalgic two-hand set shot, and one Antoine Johnson, an imposing, mysterious fellow. Strong, sullen and unskillful, he seemed to be right for the role of court bodyguard.

In any case it wasn't long, two weeks in fact, before I had a mutiny on my hands. Three regulars and two subs from last year's squad came to my office and complained about their backup roles. Why, they demanded, had they been demoted?

"The others are better. Or will be shortly."

"You can't do this to us," said a lanky kid from Exeter. "We're seniors and have played here for four years."

"You're showing favoritism because those players are your recruits," remarked another preppie forward, from Greenwich,

Connecticut, and the Kent School. "Let's face it, you're biased on behalf of minority kids."

"I'm biased on behalf of excellence."

"Look, why are you trying to make your one year as head coach such a pain in the ass for the rest of us?" observed a slow-footed guard whose father had been a famous skier at Conway. "Everyone knows you're a goner after the season."

"You may be right, Tim. But for this season, I call the shots."

"We'll see about that."

They took their revolt over my head to the A.D. himself. But Dick Porter held up his end, he didn't budge an inch. In fact he asked me if I wished to cut or discipline the dissident players.

"Nah, no need for that. Let's see if this makes them madder on the court."

The trouble was that my recruits, plus Dennis, were much tougher. Once Vargas and Konepski were around the boards those other kids couldn't touch the ball and frequently got banged around trying to get their hands on it. Basketball as a bruising contact sport on the inside was new to them, though not to Eddie and Roberto, and now, Dennis. These were hardhat bodies in any league. Come January and that front line could harden into basketball concrete. Drive down the lane and your body would feel the impact.

Four players quit and wrote letters to the newspaper and the Deans.

But my real problem was that, as yet, I had no one to run the show, to give the four other starters lubrication and fluid direction, as Cousy had done at the Cross or Andy Phillip at Illinois, or K.C. Jones at San Francisco, Guy Rodgers at Temple, Ernie DiGregorio at Providence. Playmakers made college teams, playmakers and defensive rebounders. So, until Nurlan, I'd have to play a defensive hand, and run my offense by deception. But defense would take a while, maybe a long while, to develop a rhythm, a cohesiveness. And the good teams would learn soon enough in a game that I was trying to get by with smoke and mirrors offensively. They'd shoot me right out of the water. Or, let me shoot myself out of the water.

I saw that in our first scrimmages, in late October, against two small Division 1-AA teams from the area. We scrimmaged with Norwich University, and with St. Michael's, and it was rough going. The results didn't really matter to me—won one and lost one—but the signs were there: early disaster against anyone reasonable to good. Against Norwich we got tons of rebounds and wound up with 54 points. Against St. Mike's and their matchup zone we managed 49. And by the third scrimmage, against little Middlebury, our trouble was double, offense *and* defense.

I sought counsel from our assistant coaches.

Roscoe Grumman advised, "Spread the offense, work the clock, one shot per forty-five seconds."

Percy Grimes concurred. "Yeah, play it Princeton style. And mix up the zone defenses."

"Keep the score inside the 50- to 55-point perimeter," Duddy Hamsun chipped in, "and we got a shot."

"Parameter, you mean? I'm afraid," I said, "we'll be stuck on 55 while the other team speeds right by us."

And when, on the way to the tennis court, Dick Porter asked me how was it going, I replied: "'Time's winged chariot'—it's against me. If I play the few experienced guys, the team will lose competitively in the early part of the season and stay just as weak. If I gamble with my rookies, hoping that my playmaker makes it back *and* is as good as I think he is, then I'll have a shot in the latter part. But it could be pretty bad early on."

He smiled amiably. "Can you stand the heat?"

"I hope so, but who knows? How 'bout you?"

"Oh, no problem for me."

"That'll make it a lot cooler for me, I think."

"That's the spirit. Now, when will I get you on the tennis court?"

"Well, I'm a little busy these days, you know."

He nodded and paused. "I know how. Mixed doubles, this Sunday morning. You and Claire Clarkson against me and Nell. No ifs, ands or buts. Nine-thirty a.m., say? Meet you here." He waved and walked off.

Good. He understood my gamble. Good, too, he figured out the right partner for me. On my own I had not yet had the time to call the woman; too busy, too anxious, too...?

Hey, what about the boy? I suddenly realized.

Mixed doubles was a mixed blessing, usually, but in this case the blessing was whole. Dick Porter was clearly a better player than I, so I didn't have to worry about holding back or beating the boss. And Claire was no match for Nellie. In short, we made perfect fodder for them, which sat well with me. My ego had other competitions to run with. I found myself relaxing, kidding with Claire, and considering, in passing, the upcoming season. (My penchant for doing one thing, but being in mind elsewhere.) Furthermore I could watch my manners nicely on this sunfilled Sunday morning. No cause for temper to flare or competitive side to make me mulish— two of my more inconvenient character flaws.

"Doesn't look good," I said to Claire after losing the first set 6-1. "Should we start the heavy hitting?"

She laughed, charming in her tennis duds. Indeed, when I was serving and she had her backside propped back toward me, she proved to be a slight distraction.

"Sure," she said, "let's."

I felt her biceps and said, "You need your spinach."

"Have a can handy, Popeye?"

Just then the boy and his babysitter, Nell's teenage daughter, sauntered by. "Who's winning, Papa?"

"Dick and Nellie."

"Want a sticker for luck?"

"Oh yes."

He proceeded to paste a dinosaur on my shorts. "There. Do you like it?"

"It may work."

"Know who it is?"

"Tyrannosaurus rex?"

"Nope. Allosaurus. He was a meat-eater, too, and maybe an 'an-cestor' of Tyrannosaurus."

"Oh, I see."

"Okay, I'll see ya," and he skipped away with babysitter.

Claire said quietly, "Does he usually speak that way? With that vocabulary?"

I nodded, shading my eyes.

"Where'd he get that accent?"

"Montana?"

She punched me and we returned to the match.

Waiting in the receiver's end, I reflected. Did I want a woman in my life just now? For what, a passing affair, an intense romance, a longterm relationship? Oddly, I felt inadequate to all intentful situations, not up to much of anything beyond the evening's whim. In fairness, I'd inform Claire of my present emotional infirmity. My head and feelings were too consumed by the boy, the team, 4 a.m. middle-age anxieties.

"You guys ready?" Nell called from across the net.

"Sure. But watch out this set, you got our dander up."

Dick smiled, raised his racket and hit a smooth spin serve with surprising pace that I just barely got my racket on.

Walking to the service line I called over, "So you're forced to raise your game this set, huh?" For a change I felt free and easy on the losing side; was I fast turning into a Conway gentleman?

Less easy, later on, during the first few real games in mid-late November. Yes, we were in for a cruel month. I mean, we didn't look too bad yet, to the unseeing crowd, anyway. Just a conventional, dull, mediocre team, losing one and eking out a winner. But I knew better, I saw the real state of things. Less interested in the outcomes, I was looking for subtextual signals, such as how the boys were learning their passing lanes, moving to their positions, executing picks and blockouts. At the same time I was trying to imagine how Nurlan might fill in the gaps and holes, and spackle over weaknesses. Well, pre-season had accomplished one thing at least—created nicknames to go along with The Chief and Water (also Merlin): Dennis the Menace, Eddie the Red, ChaCha or Lover-boy (Roberto), The Kiev Gunner (Twersky), and Jarrod the Reverend, Antoine the Enforcer. Not classics, but they fit my motley crew.

While Germany broke open and loose, and the wall came tumbling down, we lost to Hartford at their house and sneaked by a crippled UNH squad in Durham. I took notes like an undergraduate. "Dennis: improve inside moves, on D and O." "Vargas: speed up the outlet pass; *look downcourt*." "Eddie: run the break better, practice laps." "Chief: patience, save steals for crucial moments." "Avram: 2 dribbles and out— pass or shoot!" "Jarrod: box out, get back on D." For the team: practice shifting from 3-2 to 2-1-2 zone, and more man-to-man; on offense, work on motion weave and handling the ball, and cutting off screens. Too many basics in too short a time. Gradually I was starting to have doubts about our innate talent; was it good enough finally to make things really entertaining later on? Or had I overvalued it? And was *I good enough* to bring them along, to instill in them the cunning confidence to lift and soar beyond their individual talent? A confidence that was built on victories, not losses. Look at me, did I have it any longer?

Meanwhile, for the alumni magazine, I was asked to do a lengthy interview/profile. Sitting in my ample office, off-white and off-limits, I pieced together my odd path to coaching for the pleasant young reporter. First the struggle to get the Ph.D. (History, Stanford, 1966), and then three years of undergrad teaching at Humboldt State, U. C. Santa Cruz and Miami of Ohio.

"Where is that, by the way?" the interviewer asked. "And what kind of school?" She took notes by laptop.

"Oxford, Ohio, maybe 60 miles from Cincinnati. What kind of school? Well, a decent second-rate place. But its claim to fame is not academics, but coaches. It's a breeding ground for some of the great coaches, especially football coaches. Red Blaik of Army, Ara Parseghian of Notre Dame, Bo Schembechler of Michigan, among many."

She asked for the spellings and then inquired, "How'd you get from American history teaching to...uh...coaching?"

How to answer this with a measure of truthfulness? "After three years of survey courses I realized I needed a little more pleasure in life, so I returned to boyhood and an early fondness for basketball. In high school I had been a fair half-court player. So I made a breakout, found an assistant's job for a girls' high school team in upstate New York, and then took over the boys' team when the coach suddenly took ill. Somehow we won a state title. Then, by fluke really, I became an assistant back at Miami, handling the recruiting. But coaches with doctorates in subjects outside Phys. Ed. are looked at askance in my profession, you understand."

She tapped away on her NEC, and I observed a family of yellow warblers, thinking how Mom used to read aloud Emma Goldman or Hardy while I read sports mags.

"Wasn't there some sort of incident that happened then?"

"Oh yes." I smiled and offered Paula a slice of Danish, making light of that heavy scene: "I just took a kid's side at Miami, a recruit of mine, against the coach at the time. I forget his name. So they said goodbye to me." No need to go into the sordid affair with old McLaughery, or later, where I was trapped in a triple squeeze in the middle of the NCAA, the provost, and the coach. Privately, I replayed the coach's vivid words of adieu: "You moralistic asshole, you'll never get another job in the big time again! They'll ship your ass back to the egghead mines after this!"

Aloud I casually said, "It happens to most assistants not to be renewed at one time or another. As it does to many assistant professors."

But egghead mines were better than coaches' ditches, I knew, those grimy beds of corruption, self-promotion, and player exploitation. You know, the common stuff. You take the kid along for the ride, keep him in the college farm system and, if/when he flunks out, you have never heard of him. *And your hands look clean.* After all, the money for the apartments, gifts, cars and "sweets"—the euphemism for the crack and coke—most of that came from the alumni via a secret slush fund. (You know, if the Contras and HUD had them, why not the Wolfpack or Runnin' Rebels?) Plus the occasional five- and ten-thousand-dollar cash-drop commissions from the agents and pro scouts if you sent them a kid who hit big. Oh, college ball is a sleazy region, secretive fiefdoms of profit and greed protected by a network of bodyguards from university administrators to unsuspecting profs to hired thugs. A kind of Conradian Kurtz U., cordoned off and kept clandestine, and girded well by the enormous money up front and down the pike, from the television stations to the big winners. So when I blew the whistle because of Jake Jackson, ghetto kid from Dayton—later busted up and in jail—I was a "naughty boy." A spy to be shipped back out into the cold, into Division II exile. And—

"But then how'd you come to Conway, Mr. Berger?"

I slowed down with coffee. "Oh yes. Out of the blue, I received a call from Conway and Coach Strickland's staff, who wanted a more... 'professional' recruiter. They had heard I had done well in that area." I began to give the young reporter a description of the sunny side of the recruiting street, the poignant meetings with the poorest families, the lift of seeing a kid graduating whose grandparents were slaves, the sustained friendships with the special few.

No need to tell her the other side. Besides, the Ivy League was an island off by itself, an asterisk by the side of its NCAA Division I designation. No one took it very seriously in the big time; therefore my *persona non gratis* label didn't count for much. Could I enter some of the major local war zones—Roxbury, Bed-Stuy, Hartford, Bridgeport—and bring 'em back alive and leaping?

Well, Frank Buck-Berger did just that, as well as recruiting my north country misfits. But then the Colonel would have his hard time communicating with those boys, and sit them on the pine, building up their confidence with splinters up their asses. And when they did get on the court for three minutes of playing time, they were terrified of making mistakes and looking like incompetent high schoolers. And yours truly of looking like he'd recruited a bunch of overmatched stiffs. Naturally all this would remain for my Memoirs.

"So that's what it's like, huh?"

"A bit. There's a little more to it in the bigger places."

"One last question. How long will it take you to turn the Program around here at Conway? Three years or so?"

Should I disabuse her of her optimism for my tenure? No need.

"I'll take it one year at a time."

After several personal questions, to which I responded as blandly as possible, she thanked me for the "fascinating hour," and departed.

I kept my fingers crossed that I had kept anything and everything fascinating in my head.

After the reporter left I tried to put my desktop in some order, and began to separate the personal items from the video tapes of games and notes. I came across pictures of the old recent home life, over in rural Orange. Rebecca and the boy. My losses there included the post and beam house, the six fine acres, the comfort of real dinners. (Not Mrs. Paul's fish sticks or takeout pizza.) I felt that familiar creasing in my chest, and my hands began to get clammy. I had worked so hard to get the place and fix it up. All that lost! Missed. All that hit me anew when I viewed the photographs.

I had done a pretty fair job of messing up all the way round, I figured, setting my feet up on the desk and staring out at the tennis courts and students hitting. I even had a variety of colors associated with my various guilts. Blue guilt for the marriage. Red guilt for the jobs. Black guilt for the dead mother. Yellow guilt for the boy. White guilt for the half-dozen deserving teenagers I had let down by not finagling them into a college. Color-coded this way I could simply press the color button and pop the scene into place, the figure, the situation. A quicker route to my recessed pain.

And now, here, I had suddenly been slipped a second—or was it third or fourth?—chance, whichever. A native chameleon. Even given my first adult office to contemplate what life is like on the other side. Well, it wasn't bad. A taste of the good life before I went under again? Let go of the fatalism, Sydney boy, and do your job.

I got up, closed my blinds, popped the Ivy hoop videos into the VCR and settled into my homework.

Waves of cold air hit in mid-November, bearing a beautiful surprise; Nurlan in town for the first time. He wore his old easy smile with a navy beret, his clothes fit reasonably again, and he no longer looked like a bag of wired bones. The face wore its flesh again and the ears were free of their odd ornaments.

"Are you in to stay or out on a furlough?" I asked, excited.

"Ah'm sposed to check back in for weekends still."

"Good," I said, walking with him to the gym. "We'll get you some tutoring during the week to prep you for winter term. Come on."

When I brought him out on the court, and the kids saw *what* I had brought, they raced over and lifted him up into the air, their exclamations of welcome floating a festive aura around the gymnasium. For me it was a true Thanksgiving gift and I felt a little like an original Pilgrim, surprised by benevolent natives with maize and four wild turkeys.

Oh, I didn't even mind much when my turkey looked quickly fatigued and stale running the court, and pooped out soon. That was to be expected. I would take it oh so easy with Nurlan, whose heart was there, though his legs and lungs were not—his stamina was missing. Which made it difficult to assess his skills, or his precise skill with this team. But my boys in green were overjoyed to have him around, in the flesh, come back from the house of the living dead.

They ringed him with protective promises.

"We're gonna fatten you up, man," said Vargas. "Take you for double-scoop Ben 'n Jerry's every night, *after* double cheeseburgers at The Hop."

"And hire ourselves as bodyguards to see that you get your forty winks every night," added Jack. "No wild parties, no late night dates."

"An' write papers for me man? Sheet," Nurlan grinned, "you three up front be my bodyguards, on those backboards, man, and I'll be tucked in, with my milk and cookies, by nine every night."

Cookies without crack, I found myself cautioning. I'd speak to the boys about really guarding him, if certain types were spotted hanging around.

Still, December was at hand, with no Nurlan on the court. Fortunately, in the baby Ivies, there are only a few games, and no league games. Just a Christmas tourney. So I had a whole month to lose easy—for free, so to speak—and that was a winter boon.

I had taken Ms. Claire Clarkson out once, to a chamber music concert and Chinese dinner, and it was playful, okay. A hands-off date, except for an embrace and kiss at the end of the evening, a minute or two of pointed energy that augured well.

The second evening was a candlelight dinner at her apartment with a delicate lemon sole and light easy talk, nothing to do with past lives, past marriages. She wore a white blouse and embroidered vest and when I put my handmade cap on her head she looked a little Bonnie-ish, as in "Bonnie and Clyde."

Laughing, she said, "Do you always dress up your dates for your amusement?"

"Not always."

Later, when she was washing lettuce, I stood behind her, free-spirited with wine, and slipped my arms around her. She responded, pressing me to her. I liked that press, that firm backside and beckoning grasp, and felt my desire rise for the first time in a long while. Coaching, and losing, had taken more out of me than I had realized.

A new friend, a strange body—heady stuff, especially when you've been down and out and your confidence has been sliding. Meaning: I had once upon a time been a pretty good man in the courting game, rough and tumble with affection, loose and easy on the sex draw, but near-total fidelity in marriage had made me rusty.

We fit well together for a first time, proceeding slowly there at the kitchen sink with the water running on the green salad. I caressed Claire's back and ass while we explored each other's mouths. Raising her blouse I felt her breasts; lifted that tender pair outside her bra, and played. Flushed and embarrassed, she was defeated by her own growing passion and slipped her hand inside my shirt, and below, holding me. Losing ground, she managed, "Can't we go inside?" "In a minute," I said, raising her skirt and running my hand along the inside slope of her full thigh. She kissed me harder and breathed in my ear. Heating up, I nevertheless lassoed my desire carefully, wanting to make sure that she, along with me, had time enough to spiral toward satisfaction.

The phone startled us both. It rang and rang.

"I should answer it," she said, "just in case it's Heather." She pecked me and went to speak with her daughter.

I heard her talk briefly, and she returned.

"It's for you," she said, showing an odd smile.

"Huh?" I couldn't believe it. "My babysitter?"

She shook her head. "The police."

My god, the kid! It had to be serious for the babysitter not to call me first. I hurried to the kitchen phone, and identified myself.

"The Coach, right? Well, this is Captain Jennings, sir, and we've got a little problem down here at the Prescott station, with three of your boys. A Mr. Vargas, Mr. Healey and Mr. Konepski? And we thought it would be best, sir, if you could come down and try to straighten things out before they go any further. Very sorry to interrupt you about this on a Saturday night. You're probably in the middle of something important, but I hate to see the boys spend the night in jail. And they all felt pretty strong about seeing you first..."

"Thanks, Officer. I'll be there in ten minutes."

I returned to Claire, whose clothes were no longer in disarray.

"Is it serious?"

"I don't know."

"Does this occur often?"

"First time. Here, anyway. I am sorry."

She nodded sympathetically. "I understand. They're like your adopted sons, yes?"

"For a few years." I hugged her, saying "Right, just right. The whole evening. Sorry for it being shortened suddenly. Ring you soon."

"Promise?"

"Promise."

The station was five minutes away on the main street of the cozy downtown. When I got there the captain was waiting with the reporting officer and, in the pleasant anteroom, they explained what had happened. A brawl in A and S pizza parlor.

"Your boys were mixing it up pretty good," said the officer. "By the time we got there a few things were broken and they were going up against a half-dozen or more fellows."

"Can I see them?"

"Oh, sure, sir," he said, with the politeness reserved for upright citizens. "We can sign them out on your recognizance, and have the case continued till next week in the local court. Thought you might want that."

"Thanks. But if we can get the damages paid for, and get the owner of the place to drop any charges, do you think we can avoid the courtroom?"

"Don't see why not."

"Thanks, Captain. I'll see the boys now."

Roberto had a black eye, Dennis a bloodstained, swelling nose, and Eddie looked like his nickname, his face as red as his hair.

"What's going on, are you guys crazy?"

They looked pretty downtrodden.

"Go on, tell me what happened."

They sat on the wooden bench at the long table and Dennis narrated: "Ah, a couple of redneck townies couldn't hold their beers and muttered something about Vargas's ethnic heritage." Here his impish smile took over. "And I guess I took exception to that."

I shook my head. "Christ. What'd they say?"

"Oh, something about how Prescott shouldn't be home to spics."

"And for that you got yourselves all banged up and in jail? Are you nuts?"

Vargas shook his head, gesturing in awe at Dennis. "The man has a temper."

I looked at Dennis. "Won't look too good to the Rhodes judges."

He turned serious. "You think they'll find out about this?"

I shrugged. "And you, Eddie, what the hell did you do?"

Eddie was confused and shocked. "What could I do? They started jumping in from all sides, two of them ganging up on Denny, and—"

"Okay, okay," I held up my hand, "just what we need for publicity. My whole front court banging away in the pizza joint. Save it for the backboards, will you?" I shook my head, trying not to imagine the public fuss if the news got out, with college folk, local citizens, alumni, the Ivy League.

In the car driving them back to their dorm, I thought of where I had been an hour ago, and how quickly the scene had shifted from sensual leisuring to jailhouse lecturing. Were we coaches the only GPs of the modern era, ready to make house calls on a Saturday night in order to tend to our young and hurting? Or running across state lines to check in on our cocaine wounded? Shit. We should get honored like the grand old doctors, then. Memorialized with plaques and movies, à la Paul Muni. Fêted by the whole community.

"Sorry, Coach, it was dumb," said Vargas, getting out.

"My doing, Mr. B, my doing," acknowledged Dennis. "My apologies."

"I hope you won't get in dutch for any of this, Coach," Konepski offered meekly.

There they stood, a shamefaced, tattered trio.

"Maybe it'll get you going on the court. Meanwhile, if guys ask you what happened, say... say..." What could they say?

"We'll tell them it was a fight over honor," figured Dennis. "That's worth fighting over, isn't it? Look at the Green Knight. Or Achilles."

"Yeah. Tell 'em that Achilles was the cause. That'll go over big. Just keep your mouths shut. You can do that till next week at least, can't you?"

Driving home I wondered whether the college lawyers were the right fellows to bring in on this. Whether the hoop program should foot the bill for damages. And when I'd find time to learn all the Coach's Rules and Regs...

5 THE LONG MARCH

In the late fall I learned something else about poor kids: they had poor vision. Flawed vision. No vision. Whereas on the court they had a wide perspective and peripheral vision, here on a pretty campus and in a college town, they wore blinders. They didn't see autumn or colors, missed the rivers and mountains, dimly saw the college itself. All things of subtlety, rural shadings of beauty, were obscure or invisible to them. It was as if the school took these kids into the new land, then dropped them off on a conductorless Underground Railroad for four years.

My lesson occurred in mid-November. After a practice session we had a sandwich and soup dinner at Peter Christian's and were strolling lazily back to campus along petite Main Street. In the early warm evening the small expensive shops and polite expensive citizens seemed haloed by the spreading copper light. Two coeds in baggy shorts and colorful down vests, laughing and shouting, jumped into a red soft-top Wrangler. One waved to Eddie, who exclaimed, "Boy, I wouldn't mind owning that, huh?" Prompting Jack to tease his shy mate, "The Wrangler or Raquel?" "The jeep, jerk!" And I looked on as the freckle-faced lad, in his Brattleboro H.S. State Champ windbreaker, was kidded by the apple-cheeked laughing student in her Jeep perch with its Wellesley and Conway stickers.

Presently the boys stopped at Bennett's Sports Shop and gazed at the stylish Patagonia display of fleece warmup jackets and cotton fatigue shirts, and the latest series of Vasque hikers and sneakers by Nike and New Balance. "Cool stuff, man," oohed Nurlan. "And hot prices," returned Roberto, pointing to a $149.95 tag for a jacket. "Jes you wait till I make the Knicks," Nurlan fantasized. "Ah'm gonna cruise on in and buy a whole window full a that shit, jes like that. And you, Vargas, Eddie, being mah men, can pick yer window." He tapped my arm. "Right, Coach?"

Well, I thought, who knows, maybe the kid would make it. But if not, as was probable, what then? And what then for the other half-dozen lumpenproletariat who were being tantalized into a longing approaching lust for these fancy jackets, hi-tech sneakers, 150-watt stereos and turbo dreams, and hadn't a hope?

"C'mon guys," I said, enjoying the outing. "It's early. Let's take a walk down by the river."

We ambled along, an odd-looking unmistakable group of colonized giraffes heading west, down the sharp incline of Wheelock.

A few blocks down we passed the clandestine winding path leading up to the Packer School. "Look, some of you birds might wind up here, at the business school."

"Which?" asked Jarrod.

"Where is it?" Eddie. The others craned their necks too.

"You've not heard of Packer, or walked up here?"

They shook their heads.

"Okay, let's go, platoon."

Nestled away in the hillside stood the small group of redbrick buildings housing the business school for the elite 250. We walked about the tidy grounds, where young men in sweaters dangling around their necks, or joggers with logo-sweats on, passed and nodded courteously. Did my boys realize that they were eyeing the future Leader Class of the country (according to their own propaganda), maybe even, if the boys were lucky, their employers-to-be?

"What do they learn here?" mused Jack.

"Business techniques, I assume," I said.

"Do you have to *learn* that?" asked Eddie. "Couldn't you just open a business, or go in with your father, like?"

"Sure. But maybe big businesses. Takeovers."

"IBM, Raytheon, yes?" Avram noted.

I nodded.

"It's sorta like a secret club up here," noted Nurlan, walking and nearly sniffing. "Set off outa the way like this."

"This is a bit of *all right,*" confirmed Roberto, nodding slowly. "I'd like to join this sort of club."

"Yeah, sure." Eddie hit him with his Celtics cap. "They're just about gonna let you join, a real live Puerto Rican!"

"Well," I said, "they just might be looking for a Hispanic or two to give a scholarship to. You'd have to get through Conway first, of course. With a few decent grades."

"Coach," wondered Vargas, "would they really let in someone *like me*?"

"Maybe," I said, not really knowing myself. "Just maybe. C'mon, let's make the river before it gets dark. But remember this place, and take a walk around, even sit in on a class if you can get the professor's permission."

Soon we were strolling through the arching majestic irongate entrance leading to the rolling Connecticut. Beneath giant evergreens we crossed manicured grounds.

"Is this *all* Conway's?" asked Jarrod, his awe echoed by the others.

"And yours, now that you're a bona fide student."

Presently, along the riverfront, we stopped by the boathouse and moseyed about the dock, seeing two shells coming in.

"Hey, that's pretty neat, huh? I wouldn't mind trying that stuff," said Konepski, standing on the floating rubber deck. "You think they'd let me try out, Coach?"

"Don't see why not, Eddie."

The crews rowed in, eyeing in surprise my scraggly crew, I saw, until they realized from our size and green jackets who we were. Then they waved and called out.

We ambled on, stopping next at the charming Ledyard Canoe Club, where we were welcomed by three Conway undergrads, sitting on the porch, sunset watching and sipping drinks. Attired in chinos and (sockless) in boat shoes a blond young man explained the services and rules of the club, how you took out the canoes and kayaks and got lessons. As "Rick" mentioned in passing the $35 fee, I smiled to myself, knowing that was like asking my kids for $350. But Nurlan and Roberto nodded politely and soon enough a girl in a Bean's jacket was asking about the team's chances this year. The boys answered modestly, smiling and sneaking glances all about, like deer still unsure of the turf. Finally Vargas mumbled, "Uh, what is a kayak? What's it do?"

Afterwards we continued our meandering through the maze of giant pines and quaint buildings until we hit the Webster Log Cabin, site of department parties or special retreats. The boys couldn't get over the fact that all this too was part of the campus, and open to them to wander about freely. For our return I chose the back trail up the sharp hill, leading to Packer Drive and the Chace School and the campus they knew.

"Man, this is like having your own wild nature preserve or something, isn't it?" cooed Eddie.

Climbing up I was struck by their estimable innocence. "Look, guys, this whole place is Conway, and you're full-fledged members of the community. These grounds are *yours*, understand?"

They nodded doubtfully, climbing too, glancing about. And I made a decision, just then. "You know what, gentlemen? From now on, every Tuesday—after practice, and a little team dinner—we're going to tour the campus, and other Conway territory. Either myself, or Dennis, if I can get him away from the books, will be tour guide."

And so, for the next month, on good days, I took them on

a guided tour each week to the glass and brick buildings of Chace School of Engineering and Fairchild Science; to the twin towers of the Med School and its laboratories; to the sundry reading rooms of Butler; to the hallowed computer center, underground like a Nuclear Command Post. The questions flowed, some surprising, perplexing. "What do these galvanometers and anemometers actually do, Coach?" "How's that scanner gonna tell me if ah have a tumor or not, how's it work?" "Come on, Mr. B, 'splain this Hypercard thing, and what's this 'window' stuff?" And Eddie, observing the Orozco mural in the library basement, asked, "Why all the Antichrists in this mural, sir? What's the man getting at?" Sullen Antoine simply stared; thinking what?

On one brilliant Saturday morning, just after New England seemed cemented solid in grey (a week's worth), I took the bunch and Duddy, my outdoors maven, on a mountain hike, climbing Moosilauke. A traditional Conway hike, where none of these kids had yet wandered, or, judging from their comments, dreamed of going.

"Gosh, Coach, this heah's a long way from the Big Apple," exclaimed Nurlan at the top, breathing hard.

"Man, we must be ten thousand feet high or something, huh?"

"Nah, just about thirty-four hundred or so," Duddy adjusted.

"Now, don't jump off, Vargas, just 'cause your life's fucked up!" advised Jarrod coolly.

"Hey, look, there's the library tower!" Roberto.

"You're in shape, Coach," offered Dennis. "I didn't hear any huffing or puffing from you. Of course you're not Duddy just yet."

"Let me have my triple bypass first."

"You know, I haven't been here since freshman year," added Dennis. "The view holds up. And the boys are appreciating it, too."

Yes, they were, like city kids on their first mountain. And while Duddy delivered an environmental lesson on forest preservation showing off his Appalachian Guide and *A Sand Castle Almanac,* I gradually realized that it wasn't a tour I had been taking them on, in the past month, it was a march, a long march, as long perhaps as General Mao's taking his Communist troops to the northern province of Yenan in another October, some 65 years ago. For my poor boys from the other side of the tracks the journey from the primitive outback of America to the civilized oases and grand natural sites was just as long as the five-thousand-mile trek of the Chairman and his peasants. This understanding startled me, and I promised myself it would stay with me like a Constitutional truth. Meanwhile my lanky mountain goats and dark urban lynx continued to jostle and tease each other, in between their gasps of awe and wonder.

The air was invigorating and clear. A single-engine Cessna flew by, and, dipping down, was cheered. These boys of mine were strangers in our land, real strangers to the land of purple mountains of majesty known to most Americans and even to many foreigners.

During that fall I also realized the obvious: my boys needed a bit of outfitting for their college life. Looking closely at them for the first time, I saw that Nurlan, Jack, Eddie, Roberto, Antoine wore the same jeans, sweatshirts and sneakers every day. That was their wardrobe. They deserved better. So I took five hundred from my paycheck and drove them over to Billick's discount store at the local mall, where we picked out chinos, sweaters, socks, hats and mufflers ("You ain't serious, Coach, 'bout us sportin' these!"), one button-down dress shirt and one chamois shirt apiece; then at Dexter and Bass outlet stores we found oxford walking shoes and insulated winter boots. A good haul, but costing $820.00. Eddie: "Coach, you looking to turn us preppy?" Roberto: "Hey, sir, d'ya think you're sending us off to summer camp?" Pretty close to it, I thought. And for the sake of the all-seeing Judges of the NCAAs I handed them individual bills for $136.50 apiece, saying, "You have two years to pay these loans back. Sign the chits, gents."

At that time, too, roughly midway through the fall quarter, while the Czechs were forging their revolution, I discovered something else. How was school coming, I asked the boys? Sagging faces. Gloomy stares.

"It's hard, man, real hard," Roberto moaned.

"Yeah, there's a lotta stuff that ah can barely read," said Nurlan, who had begun sitting in on classes, "let alone understan."

Eddie nodded in agreement. "Even stuff that you think you should know, like, it isn't the same when it's in the books, and you're doing it for college. Here anyway."

"Such as which subject?"

"Like in sociology, 'The Delinquent Adolescent.'" He shook his head. "I thought I knew this stuff from home, the streets, but the professor... and his texts, they treat it like a different world."

"Yeah," Jack smiled wryly, "you have to know *concepts*."

So they—and I—were in trouble if I didn't act fast, real fast. After inquiring at the Remedial Tutorial Office and meeting with several of the boys' regular senior tutors I figured we needed a crash course program, something like the U.S. Army Language School in Monterey. The simplest, speediest way to do it, I decided, was to match up the weak kids on the block with teammates, to work in buddy pairs and in tutorials. I sat down with each kid, located the most pressing vulnerable area, and then sat with my tutors and assigned partners. For Humanities (Hums for Dumbs) I put Dennis with Eddie, Nurlan and Vargas; for math and basic (earth) sciences ("Rocks for Jocks") I put Avram with Roberto, Jarrod and Chief; for general reading and writing I assigned Marianne A, a friend in Anthropology.

At a small introductory briefing I explained that this was a customized SOS course in the basics and it was probably going to be frustrating, but they, we, had to do it. "Or we'll have some of you missing-in-action come January."

Little did I know *how* frustrating, however. Have you ever sat for a few hours at a clip with twenty-year-olds who read and write slowly, without easy confidence? For whom complicated sentences were like boulders to be moved uphill, painfully, one at a time, before understanding sets in, and the ordeal begins again? Where had they been during high school? And where had the high schools been? Why had they gotten passing grades? Yet there was a fine irony, too; once they did get the meaning of the sentence or paragraph they lit up with pleasure. And with surprising insight. You see, they could decipher meanings and offer critical opinions once the secret sacramental codes of serious reading and writing had been broken.

For fiction I worked on *Huckleberry Finn*, going through the first pages carefully, making sure of their comprehension. Oh, it was slow and arduous. Phrases like "without you have read a book," or "It was an awful sight of money," or "considering how dismal regular and decent the widow was," had to be parsed and interpreted like a Hamlet soliloquy. And I had to talk to them about the tone and irony in Huck's voice. But the surprising thing was, the boys took to Huck quickly, pegged him as a cutup and good guy at the same time. (When we got to the phrase, "they fetched the niggers" on the third page, Nurlan asked, "Was the author a racist, or was he sorta using that like they usta use 'coloreds' or Negroes?" I answered, "Well, I don't think he was, at all, rather the contrary, but you judge for yourself as we go along, okay?") Reading I'd instruct them in but interpretation was theirs.

To show them the dramatic possibilities of a contrasting rhetoric or high style I read to them from *Moby Dick*, a piece of a chapter here and there.

For expository prose I tried a bit of Western adventure, crafted in a vigorous style. "The Colorado River is formed by the junction of the Grand and Green," begins John Wesley Powell's *The Exploration of the Colorado River and its Canyons*. My Penguin paperback had the added benefit of the photographs of the splendid woodcut illustrations used in the original Scribner's Magazine publication of the work. The players really took to those grainy illustrations of the steep canyons and snaking river, leaning way over to view them closeup the way boys and girls take to pictures in their first books. Indeed, for these boys, it was their first real reading, it seemed to me; something of substance written with an eye on the way words sounded when put together. A few pages per day was our schedule, with the boys taking turns reading the text aloud like Yeshivah boys studying Torah. On the first page alone, of course, there were enough puzzles and difficulties to pull them up short and make them ask, ask, ask. How to pronounce this, what did that word mean, where was that place, and was it still around, America?

"'The Grand River has its source in the Rocky Mountains, five or six miles west of Long's Peak,'" began Roberto, reading slowly. "'A group of little alpine lakes'—what's that alpine?" I told him to go on, we'd answer that later. "'—that receive their waters directly from per-pet-ual snowbanks, discharge into a common reservoir known as Grand Lake, a beautiful sheet of water. Its quiet surface reflects towering cliffs and 'crags?' of granite on its eastern shore, and stately pines and firs stand on its western margin.' Whew!"

"What does he mean, 'sheet of water'?"

"What's 'crags' of granite?"

"And what's 'firs' or that 'western margin'?"

"Hey, where is the Colorado, Coach? All of it in Colorado?"

Of course Roberto was right, and I had to go out and find a map before proceeding. Stupid of me. And once I did that I naturally saw the obvious: how ignorant they were of geography, and of the simplest operations, like the location of states, mountain ranges, major rivers. I was shocked and forlorn. How could I get all this stuff in, now, in their lives? Where would you start, and how'd you ever end? Years and years of basic education had been missed.

And a paragraph later, the cliffs of learning grew higher.

"'The mouth of the Colorado is in latitude 31° 53' and longitude 115'.'" Eddie looked up at me dumbly. I signalled him to continue. "'The source of the Grand River is in latitude 40°

17' and longitude 105° 43' approximately. The source of the Green River is in latitude 43° 15' and longitude 109° 54' approximately.'"

"What is this stuff, man? What gives?"

I could have ducked out on that or simply skipped the science; but they deserved, I guess, the full unexpurgated story of Powell, and the scientific end of his expedition. So I had to show and tell my explanation, and find a globe. Then, I saw from their gaping faces, the news hit home about the Equator, angular distances, prime meridian, Greenwich, England.

"Coach, maybe it's just too... much, all this?" wondered Eddie.

"Yeah, maybe we should jes start easier like?"

I nodded. "Maybe you're right. But let's stick it out and see what happens. If you can cut it with Powell's journey and Huckleberry Finn's and Ahab's, you'll do fine in school. Or at least you won't feel too lost. And besides, this material is going to get interesting. Darned interesting, I think."

Make that: hoped and prayed.

Thus my office became, three or four times a week in the early morning hour before classes began, our private reading retreat. We'd have corn flakes, sliced banana and milk, I'd sip my coffee and put on FM classical low, and we'd dig in; enunciating aloud, reading, writing, reckoning figures. A serious prepping. The first few weeks were pure torture as the boys, in sweatshirts or old flannels, practiced their first hesitant steps into civilized life. Sitting in our semi-circle, our children's class went over and over words, sounds, places, zones, numbers, names, maps, pictures. The repetitions of simple survival in the modern world, in higher education. Nearly every other day I reached the point of no return, ready to throw in the towel, and call it a TKO for ignorance and illiteracy. Let the college handle it, flunk them out with Ivy gentility, sweep them out quietly. But what kept me going were those daily embers of comprehension which would flare suddenly into revelation, some dim, some bright.

"Man, I didn't know that Time was sort of, well, two

clocks like—one made up by us, and the other well out there somewhere."

"Ya mean that we can still raft down that same Green River like Powell did and see no houses or developments or nothin'? Jes plain wilderness still?"

Revelation emerged also about language, and it actually sent a shiver up my spine when one of them would ask if he could read a sentence again because he liked the *sound* of it?

Hence Konepski, reading aloud from *Huckleberry*: "'Well, all at once here comes a canoe; just a beauty, too, about thirteen or fourteen feet long, riding high like a duck.'" He shakes his head. "Seeing that canoe as a duck really gets me, you know."

Or Nurlan, after the third or fourth repetition, reciting softly, "'The land-scape of veg-e-tal life is weird—no forests, no meadows, no green hills, no fol-i-age, but club-like stems of plants a-r-m-e-d with sti-lettos.'" He beams and looks around. "If that ain't a sentence, man."

Well, Major Powell would have beamed too, I think.

And if that stuff wasn't something, Dennis came up with another idea. Why not bring a few computers in, make use of those too? Especially since Conway was a regular Apple haven, wired in every niche and cranny for Macs and laser printers as Lebanon was with mines and bombs. Therefore it was easy enough to order, for the basketball program, a half dozen of the little sleek boxed minds, with their white window-faces and beige-handpress mouses, and set them up in an adjoining room. Needless to say the boys took to these like new toys once they had their first elementary lessons from their Russian-Jewish mentor and saw that they could operate them by themselves pretty easily. So from working on their penmanship they moved on to the new world powers of Word 4.0, a leap of some ease, actually, and a lift of spirit, too.

These Little Macs became as familiar to the boys as the Big Macs, surprisingly. They tinkered and toyed with them, making diagrams, writing papers, charting graphs, as much from the pleasure of play as from the responsibility of classes.

At odd times one or another of them would be in there, Eddie the Red, or The Chief, or Water, Prettyboy, the Enforcer. The Minister or the Kiev Gunner, pecking away, working on who knows what? When I briefly looked over Roberto's shoulder one day, for example, I saw that he was writing gibberish more or less. "Briefly" because he asked if I minded giving him his privacy?

I must say, though, that the entire enterprise was like having a parallel class or even a counter-school to regular Conway. In other words, a kind of morning mini-college, a Berger University of the basics, with yours truly as Dean. Soon enough it grew cozy and familial. All we lacked, I suppose, were degrees, coeds, epigraphs in Latin, and our own pennants and colors. Even Janine Wilder, our wily secretary or "administrative assistant," appreciated our setup. "I don't believe I've ever seen such studious young men in the athletic program, Mr. Berger," she twinkled, upon entering in the morning and spotting the boys already at work. "It really is such a surprise."

A surprise indeed. "One that we should sort of keep private, I guess, Ms. Wilder." For all sorts of reasons, I figured.

Periodically while they rehearsed their repetitions (which swept over me like waves of boredom), my mind floated and I wondered about my motives, and more. Why was I doing this? Why promote this sort of ridiculous venture, this sunrise semester (quarter actually) of kiddie learning? Just to keep the team intact? Or my career? To satisfy my own misguided zeal and ego? What would it lead to, and what did it signal about me? Did I really need the extra hours and burden upon my shoulders?

All right, maybe it was in keeping with my quirky ways down the line. The ways that I had taught history (only from sources), shifted professions (downward), mishandled personal affairs, and the perennially inconvenient ways my skepticism ran. Early on I had laid down the law to myself: go at things your own way, and when you find yourself in step with the majority—teachers, coaches, citizens, pundits—

know that something was wrong. For down deep, in my gut, I felt that I had a mission of some sort, a project to fulfill, and though I was unsure of its nature or final shape, I sensed it would be amorphous, unnamed—more like a crazy unpredictable cell than a fixed healthy one—but that was all right since it would be mine. And because of that it would be redemptive for me—redemptive, no matter what the external circumstances looked like.

Was this out-of-step gene no more than an inheritance from my eccentric, anarchist parents, an inheritance I had tried my best to resist for years? Then so be it.

Monotonously first Roberto then Nurlan rehearsed, then Jarrod, Eddie and Chief, even lumbering Antoine, and I began to wonder if I was hallucinating all this? Like the old stage direction given in *Hamlet* and applied here: enter Sydney B, Hallucinating.

Truth was, I suppose I preferred that state to the reasoning one. What was reasoning going to get you in our times? Order? Resolution? Justice? Decency? Please. Quietly, privately, I was in a rage against the leaders, the government, for what it was doing: selling the country down the drain, sodomizing the underclass and drugging the middle-class. And I was furious at the schools, too: at the public high schools for their increasing ineptness and the good colleges for their evolution into institutions of commerce. Did businessmen called trustees really have to run the places? Did Harvard or Yale really have to be landlords? Did Presidents have to be fundraisers first—rather than educators pure and simple? And alumni, were they to be used as backslappers and cash-cows principally? When I looked around and heeded the news my heart would beat fast, my head swirl. No, reasoning was futile, the situation too entangled, too extreme, too out of whack. Forget it.

As for using reasoning as a weapon in personal affairs, that was like taking a butter knife to battle. I had taken many, so I knew. Better to be a knight-errant with a bony nag and a big-bellied short pal and tilt with windmills than trust in Reason in the U. S. of A. That's why I believed in the hoop game so much; there, within the rules of the game, you could deploy reason in terms of strategy, and see it pay off. (Or fail.)

Tilting at windmills; sure, that was the thing. In my case, tilting at backboards; same sport. And the right sport for the middle-aged gentlemen who have had a full taste of the world and come away with the hue of disappointment in their sagging cheeks and gaunt faces, and the feel of melancholy in their stomachs. So why not tilt, and pursue the Final Four Dulcinea, come what may? For example—

"Coach, are you really with us? Or dozin' off?"

Caught idling, I wagged my forefinger. "Don't be a busybody, Nurlan. I'm right here, listening to your every sentence and pronunciation, and even planning a new wrinkle on the 2-1-2 zone."

For strategy reading I had the choice of two turfs, courtesy of Chip B. At night, the Tower Room in the library; by day, the basement rooms surrounded by the fantastic Orozco murals, and the 1902 room; in between, the stuffy, charming library of the English department at Sanborn. Upstairs in the Tower, ensconced in wing chair, feet on ottoman, I went over my Clair Bee and Pete Newell texts, and the techniques of the original Celtics, the great pro team of the twenties and thirties. (The Big Green starting five of Nat Holman, Joe Lapchick, Johnny Beckman, Dutch Dehnert, Pete Barry stressed the team unit and mastery of defense; the two chief goals for my Little Green.) I browsed too in Dr. Naismith's original ideas, the rise of the college game in the 1930s via Ned Irish and the Madison Square Garden doubleheaders, and the one-handed shooting revolution of Stanford's Hank Luisetti (December, 1936), the last great revolution before the advent of the jump shot. (Yes, Mama, I realize that Kropotkin, Goldman and John Reed had other revolts in mind, but Angelo "Hank" Luisetti was also the son of an Italian immigrant, you know.) I made notes, looking for an edge to rediscover in the old sources.

Different spaces compelled different directions. The Tower, a mini-version of the New York Public Library with its dark woods and pull-chain lamps, was the place for firming up my personalized defenses, which called for looseness out front and congestion down inside. Downstairs, in the basement, I felt astir with the revolutionary zeal of Orozco's Mexican Revolution and tended to work on all-court presses and all-out fast breaks. In the 1902 Room, beneath the portraits of past Deans, I sketched in the practice schedule, the halfcourt offense, the reliable weave. And in Sanborn, in a sly alcove up on the balcony, I'd stare out at the large maples and lawn, spiral in hand, and wait for the right wild idea to float by me like a stray Nat Holman or Ossie Cowles cloud.

I couldn't resist taking the boys around these rooms too, to complete their long march. To give them the feel of libraries, books, stacks, solitary dreaming. Wasn't that more important after all than dorms, lawns, bonfires, most classes? I took them in pairs to the sites, so it wouldn't quite be like a tall Mongol invasion. One night I sat down Jack and Eddie in the Tower, and insisted they read there; feeling that I was hovering, I left. When I returned, unfortunately, they had left. Another day I took Nurlan and Jarrod to the 4:30 tea and biscuit hour at Sanborn. I left them alone in a private alcove, books open, and departed. But when I returned in half an hour they were fidgeting badly, talking, kidding around, bothering other students. "Hey, what's going on," I whispered. "Don't you get it, quiet, ssshh!"

Nurlan shook his head, looking pained. "Hey, Coach, can we split? It's awful *cramped* in here."

I turned to the somber Minister. "For you too, Jarrod?"

He grinned with bemused disdain, as though I were the biggest idiot around.

I released them and sat there, alone, feeling foolish. Peering out the mullioned window toward the sweep of green, I realized that library beauties were not for everyone. Then, sitting upright in my curved settee, I tried to imagine Shensi, Yenan, and the various hidden setbacks and difficulties encountered there.

Minutes passed.

Slowly it dawned on me that *they* had something else to contemplate, if they wished: varieties of basketball beauty.

And late that afternoon, in the sacred gymnasium, while sneakers squeaked and balls glanced off rims, I focused on a few of those moments. One, in Nurlan's stop-and-go dribble, and sudden suspended flight through two players for the basket. A second in Avram's resplendent high-arc shot from his baseline spot, where he'd stop on a dime, turn, and put up his behind-the-neck corkscrew jumper softly through the net. A third, in the Chief's exquisitely timed anticipation of an offensive pass, feinting one way and flicking out his hand to steal the ball, and immediately flinging it downcourt. With the sun's late rays falling in amber slants and patches on the waxed wood floor, the game was framed with the necessary elements of light and shadow to make a unique interior—if not exactly a Vermeer, maybe a Berger.

So these boys had their own visions, all right: it was I who had been shortsighted early on. Mountains, rivers, reading rooms, rowing shells had their aesthetic surfaces and solid virtues, no doubt; but the game here, the swift sport, the five-in-one-force floating back and forth now, how could this not be called a compelling art?

Or was I dreaming again, projecting a future?

I proved to be wrong again on the library thing. For when I took them, *en masse,* into Special Collections, they were fascinated. These historical sources ignited the boys' interest and imagination. The eight handwritten letters of Francis Parkman on obtaining books shipped from Spain. The Journal of John Sargent, a missionary to American Indians. The cracked, annotated Bible of Captain Valentine Pease, Melville's Ahab, used on the Acushnet in 1841, when Melville had sailed on it. Family letters and diaries from the Civil War. The prodigious papers of Samson Occum, the first Native American student at the old college, and a major scholar. Finally the original charter of Conway, on two large chunks of parchment, complete with the King's Seal and the Royal Governor's signature.

"Real parchment, this? Whadayaknow, Coach," said the amazed Nurlan, staring. "Look at that script. Ain't that *purty?*"

"Man oh man, this place is *that* old?" noted Eddie, "to have a real king's seal on it? Holy Cow!"

Jack nodded his approval. "Mr. Occum certainly knew a lot of languages, didn't he?" referring to the gentleman scholar's annotated Bible and speeches, composed variously in Hebrew, Latin and Greek. "One smart Indian, wasn't he? Set a dangerous example for the rest of us, though." Jack smiled.

And Dennis remarked, "I can't believe this Collection is right here, across from the '02 Room, and I've never stepped inside it. Gosh, makes you feel stupid. Provincial."

"Just what I've been trying to get across to you, man," observed Jarrod, slapping his arm.

As the group huddled about each new box of materials and lit up with surprise and questions over its contents, I felt a certain tapping in the heart, too.

Even the Collection's Director nodded to me at one point and commented, "Your boys show more interest than most of the students here, let alone faculty. And to think they're athletes! We're flattered."

So was I.

6 WINTER BLUES

Inevitably the word had leaked out about the pizza parlor fracas and people were in a huff about the incident. Though no one "blamed" me, it didn't exactly help out my reputation for control of my players. I had a genial discussion with Dick Porter, who readily understood the situation. And Chip Bromley was nice enough to call and express his encouragement once he discovered what had started it. Of course beneath the liberal sentiments of the progressive citizens, there was underlying anxiety; what was a Puerto Rican doing up here in the snow-white castle of North Country, except that he had been smuggled in by the maverick coach and was now littering the place? And had the talented and honorable Irish senior perhaps had his Rhodes scholarship chances endangered by the stupid incident? And so on.

The talk buzzed on mainly because we continued to fall flat on the court. The Christmas tourney was an out-and-out disaster. Instead of some holiday cheer, there were winter blues. We lost both games, at home, by rather lopsided scores. Our lack of direction, consistency, showed in the latter parts of games. We'd play a few minutes of decent ball, then have a lapse here and there, and poof, the rhythm and game were gone. At the crucial moments we had no composure, no glue.

My vaunted frontcourt of Vargas, Dennis, Eddie, looked like lost road warriors, roaming wild. Three limbs in search of a head. And since the head was sitting beside me, watching, we'd fall apart at the seams at the slightest opponent pressure, like a nervous breakdown after a touch of stress. As with most sports, basketball was a matter of moments, inches.

Things got worse in January when we lost our opening games against our first Ivy opponents, Brown and Columbia. Ordinary clubs at best, they beat us in the second halves of each game, pulling away when the games were still in contention. The odd thing was, everyone was doing his part more or less; but together, as a team, we were nowhere. Vargas rebounded okay, Chief played fair enough, and so on, but it didn't add up to cohesiveness, or victory. As for beauty—not close.

And I had to suffer doubly: watching the video reruns.

We finally got Nurlan into our January games for eight to ten minutes. But he wasn't himself yet. His fabulous dribbling rhythms, like jazz riffs from the Duke or Monk, were not there yet, so that his off-the-dribble offense, especially on the fast break, was missing. And without the improvised, cadenced rhythm of the dribble he was a handicapped artist, unable to toss those leisurely passes or drive the basket in his unstoppable Frazier-glide. Part of it was legs and stamina, part timing. A ton of frustration.

When I pulled him out he'd sit and shake his head. "Sheet, ah'm nowhere, Coach. Jes nowhere. I jes can't get it down yet." And he'd be breathing hard, real hard; his trademark, that pearly smile, was not to be found. "Sorry," he'd moan, and look doomed.

And for the first time I began to wonder seriously whether I had made the whole thing up: a bubble of optimism by a clownish coach? A bubble of overvaluation by a dejected, romantic recruiter?

By January 10, on the eve of a trip down to Worcester to play the tough boys at the Cross, I was pretty down about the whole thing. We had one victory and seven losses, and I began to wonder if we'd win another game all season. All fucking season.

Just the perfect occasion to run into my colleague from history, at Lou's, having a quick sandwich. To my tuna salad he would add pepper, I figured, but there was no avoiding him.

"Doesn't look too good, old man, does it?" he said, sliding onto the next stool.

"Season's young, so far as the Ivies go." I chewed fast.

"Might be long for you, I fear. I actually caught the game against Brown the other night." He smiled narrowly, his thin hair parted neatly on the smooth forehead. "You've not only got a losing team of essentially non-Conway types, but a dull team to boot. I'm afraid your own Italo-Judaic roots are beginning to show, and make quite a mess of things, Mowgli."

I faced him down. "Why do you persist in calling me that name, Wim?"

He nibbled at his carrot sticks. "Because I think of you in that light—half-wolf, half-boy, Sydney. You have that lean hungry look as though you've been searching for a home, or a tasty grandma."

He eyed me with pleased disdain on his long, pallid face.

I left the last bites and edged out from the counter. "Always a pleasure to bump into you for lunch, Wim." I moved off as he was speaking.

In the cold clear Main Street, with shoppers busily pursuing the post-Christmas season I thought that maybe Wim was right in his bitchy way. Maybe I should toss the whole thing in, a coaching Chapter 11....

Later at the practice the kids shot around wearily, waiting for the usual lecture and scrimmage, and I realized I had to rally their interest. I decided to spend a little extra time with each one of them, coaching their physical talent and catching up on their personal life.

With Konepski, I passed him the ball, watched him take his shot and asked how things were.

"Well, ya know, okay, I guess."

"Really okay?"

"Well, I guess Pop's putting pressure on me. Says all I'm here for is rebounding and I never get to score anything."

"I see," I said. "What do you think?"

"Well, gee, Coach, it's your team."

I ran through his point totals in my head and realized he had broken double figures only once. "You know what, Eddie? Maybe Pop's right, maybe you should be scoring more. Tell you what, against Holy Cross on Wednesday, look for the shot. And I'll tell the backcourt guys to look for you more. How's that?"

"Well, sir, I don't want to hog it or anything."

"You won't be. But start looking for the basket more on offense. A drive here or there, a jumper, whatever. Okay?"

His freckled face lit up. "I sure will, Coach. Thanks. Pop'll be glad to hear the news, to tell you the truth."

"Twelve, fourteen points from you,"—for Pop of course—"how's that?"

"You got it, Coach." He took two dribbles from left to right and tossed in a little running hook.

Feeling dumb, I looked around and spotted Vargas, shooting fouls on a side basket. Was something quietly awry there too? I replaced the undergrad manager who had been retrieving Roberto's ball.

"Everything all right?"

He nodded and shot.

I noticed that his old arc was missing and told him about it.

"Yeah. Thanks." He shot again, this time with a higher arc.

"'Berto, what is it?"

He shook his head and focused on his foul shooting.

"That's better. Hey, what's up? You don't seem... yourself, somehow. What is it?"

He looked at me, started to speak, took his shot.

"Come on, Vargas, talk to me. No one's listening."

In a moment he glanced around and said, low, "I'd rather

be alone with you, Coach."

"After practice and shower, meet you right here."

He nodded solemnly.

Christ, I had been amiss, hadn't I? Too caught up in coaching, no understanding, fathering, head-shrinking.

Who else was playing okay, but maybe just okay? At the foul circle I watched a small group popping jumpers and motioned to the Chief. On the pretense of working on his jumper we walked to a side basket. I told him to throw a few up.

"Family well?"

He nodded and took his jumper.

"You depressed about the team losing?"

"Nah, that's okay. We just started the real season."

Wrong intuition then? "School. How's it going?"

"Well..."

"What do you mean, 'well?' What's the problem?"

"I'm flunking English, I think."

I was shocked. "How come?"

He shrugged his narrow shoulders. "Professor doesn't like my papers. Doesn't think my style is *correct*, or my material 'legitimate' or something."

"Is it the grammar or what you're writing about?"

"I dunno really," he said, shooting. "But whatever I write comes back with red scribbling all over it, telling me to forget all this 'reservation talk.'"

I took out my pad and asked the prof's name, and also to see Jack's essays "quickly."

He nodded.

"Bring them around to me tomorrow, by lunchtime, okay?"

"Sure. But... he won't listen to you, Coach. Besides, maybe he's right. It's a freshman seminar thing, and required, and I'm taking it a year late, you know."

"Tomorrow morning, okay?" I started to walk off. "Oh yeah, during the scrimmage today, let's get the ball to Eddie more. We're going to get him more involved in the offense."

"Sure," he said. "Good move. You know what? If I can pass that course, I'm home free."

I nodded. "Get me those papers, pronto."

I had opened a hornet's nest of problems. Fair enough. Now, hoop time. I walked over to Nurlan and told him about Eddie's increased role. And added, "Stay out there longer today and let's see you really run the show. Stretch it out—you've become a bit timid about taking full charge."

Frail still from his rehab days he bounced the ball between his legs back and forth, back and forth, listening. "Sure, Mr. B, sure."

"Just relax and go get it, okay?"

I blew the whistle, gathered the green shirts and the white shirts and told them to go all out. "3-2 zone defense against my first team, green shirt fast break offense. Let's go!

But after two or three runs on the court, during which I stopped play three times to critique a player, I saw they were playing uptight, afraid to make mistakes, wary of more criticism.

What could I do? *Let go, but how?* I blew the whistle to halt things, called them around, and saw their gloomy faces as they approached. My beautiful gymnasium was turning into a twilight torture chamber. I wanted to cry, it was all so bad.

I picked up my notebooks from the table and opened the first one. But I had grabbed the wrong pad, the black one containing my history essay notes ("Emerson, Thoreau and Melville: Our First Anarchists"). Damn! But maybe a bit of anarchy would help?

"All right, gentlemen, sit down for a minute and just listen carefully. It may not make much sense to you at first, but let it sink in, all right? Here goes, from 'Self-Reliance':

"'A man is relieved and gay when he has put his heart into his work and done his best, but what he has said and done otherwise shall give him no peace. It is a deliverance which does not deliver. In the attempt his genius deserts him; no muse befriends; no invention, no hope.'"

I glanced up. The boys looked stunned, or perhaps appalled? Well, what did I expect them to make of "a deliverance which does not deliver?" I smiled at them. What did it matter, right?

I continued from my notes. "'Trust thyself; every heart vibrates to that iron string. Accept the place the divine providence has found for you, the society of your contemporaries, the connection of events. Great men have always done so, and confided themselves childlike to the genius of their age, betraying their perception that the absolutely trustworthy was seated at their heart, working through their hands, predominating in all their being. And we are now men, and must accept in the highest mind the same transcendent destiny...'"

Nurlan began rotating the ball and I was surprised to see that he was smiling, nodding to himself a little, eyes on the basketball. Were they actually getting any of this? I went on.

"'Society everywhere is in conspiracy against the manhood of every one of its members. Society is a joint-stock company, in which the members agree, for the better securing of his bread to each shareholder, to surrender the liberty and culture of the eater. The virtue in most request is conformity. Self-reliance is its aversion. It loves not realities and creators, but names and customs.'"

"Coach," mused Roberto, "is that really a fact, about society in conspiracy against my manhood?"

What could I say?

"Tolstoyan," said Avram, nodding.

"'Whoso would be a man must be a nonconformist. He who would gather immortal palms must not be hindered by the name of goodness, but must explore if it be goodness. Nothing is at last sacred but the integrity of your own mind. Absolve you to yourself and you shall have the suffrage of the world.'"

I stopped and looked around the circle of them. No snickers; their eyes were intent.

Eddie wondered if non-conforming applied to the court too.

The Chief corrected him, suggesting "the man was talking about society."

The Reverend added that it was "good stuff, worth thinking on."

The Chief was probably right. Nonconformity was too much to hope for on the court, but maybe their tightness had been defused, their minds taken off the game for five minutes. What were they babbling about? "All right, let's go!" Flushed and confused, I hustled them back onto the court.

It took about six or eight runs up and back on the court before it became apparent that Nurlan had a little more sparkle out there this afternoon and that the ball was more like his old yo-yo. Wherever he went, it followed. And the team followed, and sparkled too. He ran the break with his old ease and confidence, laying off perfect bounce passes to the lane-runners, Chief, Jarrod, Eddie, and in the halfcourt game he set up Dennis or Vargas inside, or Jack and Twersky for jumpers. After one lovely bounce pass zipped right under the arms of a defender, Dennis looked at me and gave off that impish grin. *Something was happening out there.* On the set offense I called out for Eddie to look for the basket, and when he got the ball on the left side of the basket, face up, he took three dribbles in on the right and muscled in a layup à la Dolph Schayes. "Atta way," I called out, excited by the move. Maybe Mr. Konepski was right after all, the kid could score more and I had been the fool? When he did it again, led by a Waterford pass, going in with undeniable cunning force, I advised myself: you shmuck, you dumb shmuck.

After the scrimmage the kids left the gym, here and there passing a comment on to me. "It felt different out there, Coach," said Dennis. "I'm not sure if it was Emerson or Nurlan."

"The ghost came alive today," noted Chief. "The *man's* playing again."

"Yeah, looks like it. Remember those essays first thing."

Eddie was high. "Boy, Coach, something was different today, huh? What do you think?"

"We'll see for sure Wednesday night. Keep it going."

Nurlan came by wearing his oversized coat and navy beret.

"Looked good."

"Felt good, Coach. At last." He smiled. "Hey, ya know what? Ya nevah hold us that cat's name who wrote that stuff."

"Oh yeah," I said. "Emerson. Ralph Waldo."

He nodded, pleased, and repeated the name slowly to himself.

I hung around, pretending to attend to various details, waiting for Vargas to emerge.

The janitor came, asked if he could get started, and I told him, fine. He put out the big lights and when Roberto came forth I took him to a far corner, where we sat on the bench in the dim light. He sat there gripping his gym bag and it took me some minutes of pushing to pry him open.

"She's let him back in the house. I couldn't believe it, Coach. His lawyer got him out of jail somehow and she took him back in. I can't believe it. And I know he's gonna beat on her again and my little brother, and there's nothin' I can do 'bout it." He curled his neck round and round, creaking the muscles and hurting me. "It's a bad deal, Coach."

What could I do? Old Rosey was sweeping, the radiators were clanging, and the boy before me was in pain.

"Couldn't you call the social worker?" I said, buying time. "Or a parole officer?"

"You know what it's like to deal with them? I mean, man, they let him out and back into the house, with Mom's okay of course. It's been killin' me, Mr B. I went down there last weekend and almost stayed down. Oh, he's on good behavior when I'm there, you know." He shook his head and looked at me, big brown eyes moistening. "What should I do, Coach, huh?" He cranked his neck from side to side and resembled an AWOL sailor in his old pea-jacket.

I took hold of his forearm. "I'll look into it, I promise."

His vulnerable soft face turned now into a taut mask that I had not seen before. "I'm afraid, Coach, I may do something stupid, real stupid, if he's not gotten out of there."

"Studies," I intoned, "and the team. Give me your wallet."

Dazed, he obeyed, and I took from it the photo of his idol, his saint and his namesake, Roberto Clemente. On the back was written the date of the great right-fielder's fatal accident, December 31, 1972. I held it up to him. "Okay?"

The mask dissolved.

"'Nothing is at last sacred,'" I recalled to him, "'but the integrity of your own mind.'"

He nodded. "The man knows where it's at."

At Worcester on Wednesday we were met by a hostile crowd at the Holy Cross gymnasium. As we took pre-game practice the catcalls were vituperative and plentiful. "C'mon you Ivy faggots, are you going to moon instead of dunk?" and "Hey, Big Green, Tiddlywinks, Scrabble?" and "We're gonna stuff it to you, Conway, stuff it down and twist it around!" I tried to have this last genial fellow removed from a few rows behind our bench, but no luck.

I gave the boys a little pep talk, explaining that it was an important game to test where we were and to see if that practice was for real or not, and to play hard. The canned-fruit talk.

They went out and played hard, all right—too hard. And got creamed. The Crusaders were at home in Hart Center; a veteran team, they knew how to work the refs and make my kids pay for every mistake, and even took to baiting and cheapshotting my boys. Avram they called "Rooskie" and banged his ribs on every jumper; they railed at Jack: "Scalp 'em, Geronimo, scalp 'em!" and held his shirt. Vargas was teased with "Roberta dear..." and just before the end of the half he took a split lip and needed three stitches. Seeing what was happening I pulled out Nurlan halfway, for safety, and inserted Antoine, Tony and the other subs. By the half I had a headache and we were down 19.

"Suck it up, Green," roared my favorite fan as we left the court, "and fart it out all the way back to Prescott."

In the locker room at half-time my head was spinning, I didn't know what to say. I was flustered and furious at myself, at the kids, and at the Cross coach for allowing that sort of atmosphere to develop. I gathered them around me and, in front of the blackboard, paced back and forth, tongue-tied, bewildered.

In the painful silence Dennis offered, "Maybe it's just our fate to get blown away down here. It happens every time, sir."

"Fate?" I said. "Fate?" repeating the word like some call to arms. "Listen: 'In short, there ought to be no such thing as Fate. As long as we use this word it is a sign of our impotence and that we are not yet ourselves.'" I looked at them opening oranges and sipping drinks, staring at me. "'As long as I am weak I shall talk of Fate; whenever the God fills me with his fullness I shall see the disappearance of Fate.' Got that?"

The solidity of that small locker room was wavering.

"Look, I want to tell you about that Emerson fellow, known as Waldo to his friends. He lived in these parts—Concord, Mass., to be exact—and came from poverty. Started out as a schoolteacher and gave that up. Lost his wife to early death, and his past, and grew defeated, deeply so. Went to Europe for a year, recovered, and got rejuvenated. Returned to the States, got married again, and took up lecturing in a serious way. Began to travel around the country on wagon, stagecoach, sleigh, canal boat, steamboat, train. On tours that were frequently physical ordeals. For example, he had to walk across the Mississippi on ice, his stagecoach turned over several times, and he once had to escape from a burning hotel. But that was okay because he enjoyed the contact with the American people, never speaking down to them, always respecting them."

By now I could see them glancing at one another, munching and drinking slowly, wondering about the halftime diagnosis, the second half plans....

I glanced at my jumbled notes about boxing out and changing zones. "He believed in a form of mystical transcendence, in which man has in him Godliness, and doesn't need a Church

114

or Minister between him and God. The part of God in man is his *self*, every man relying on himself is trusting the God in him. Man has faculties in him that 'transcend' the senses, ideas and intuitions that 'transcend' his sensational experiences. Understood, gentlemen? And oh, yes, he thought these thoughts despite losing his little son Waldo in 1842, his beloved boy of six, which once again sent his life crashing into a deep black hole. But it didn't deter him, being down and out, it only made him more determined."

I paused to look at them, my beaten crew, and proceeded. "So God is immanent in man, is the omnipresent and benevolent Oversoul, a source of spiritual energy from which knowledge comes to man through intuition. He didn't call all this a systematic philosophy, you understand, but held forth on the 'infinitude of the private man.'"

Perspiring, I sipped water. "All right, gentlemen?"

They nodded dumbly, embarrassed.

"Okay, let's go get 'em."

On the way out Dennis came by and said, "That was quite a little... lecture, Mr. B. Uh, are you *feeling okay?*"

"Yeah. I'm fine."

He smiled his best curled-lip smile, charming in such a big fellow, and nodded—with sympathy, I thought—as he walked out.

Why not? I needed it.

Vargas and Eddie accompanied me. "What'd the boy die of?"

"What? Consumption. Common in those days."

Coming onto the floor Avram said, "Strange talk, Coach Berger. I never hear Coach talk that strange. But I like this Emerson, and will study him. Have you read Tolstoy's *Resurrection*? This 'Oversoul,' you spell it...?"

They played looser, stronger, smarter. They picked up on the little things—the offensive boards, the loose balls, the deflected passes. The boys in the middle—Eddie, Vargas, Dennis—used their bodies to control the boards. Twersky started getting the ball in his sure baseline spots and hitting the jumpers, on the break and off picks, plus a few trifectas. The Chief stole the ball from their flashy guard, sneaked by the immobile center and waylaid a fast break. Eddie the Red began to muscle his way in, moving steadily from right to left, and tossing in his little eight- or ten-footers. And Nurlan became Merlin, running the court with his deceptive speed, handling the dribble with fingertip beauty, overseeing the whole court. When he played that way, with ease and grace and perfect poise in the midst of hectic surroundings, he left behind East New York and crack dealers and streets of despair and made the court into his ballroom, where he was Astaire dancing up a storm. He turned two or three layups into three-point plays, waiting for his defender to come up close and then taking him on in for the basket and foul. And when a Cross bruiser tried to bang him hard, Dennis intercepted the fellow with a bodycheck hip and sent him flying. We had a rhythm, it was a show, it quieted the crowd and amazed me.

We lost by three, but had a victory: of the mind and spirit. Their coach, who had once coached at our place for a year, came over and shook my hand, saying, "I don't know what you fed them at halftime, but that was a different squad out there in the second half. We were lucky to come out with a win, very lucky. You should do pretty well if they can keep that up." He laughed. "And tape that halftime speech for me sometime, huh, buddy?"

In the locker room the boys were quietly elated. For the first time they kidded each other, and me too. Holy Cross was a power, a test. Now, having passed it, my Conway kids knew something, knew something true about themselves and their ability that was empirical, not just my rhetoric. *(Did I share that confidence?)*

"We showed some soul, huh Coach?" Jarrod.

Nurlan came up to me beaming and hugged me.

And outside the locker room a faintly familiar gentleman approached, hand extended. Speaking with a slight lisp, he said, "That was as good a college half against my alma mater in this gym as I've ever seen. Especially by an Ivy club. Heckuva job, Coach!"

"Why, thank you, Mr. Cousy. I feel honored."

"Where'd you find that playmaker? I came to see the Crusader kid and wound up dazzled by yours. That young man knows his way around the court. Arnold should see him. And what's *your* name again?"

On Thursday, back home on campus and in town, I felt a lilt in my step, and a sign from nature, too, in the first real snowfall of the season. At the Conway Co-op and Campion's on Main Street, I was greeted with newfound interest, as word had spread about our inspired half of basketball. The gloom and anxiety of the past few months opened a crack, allowing a sliver of light.

Now it was time to move from high (Emersonian) idealism to low contemporary reality, to problems beyond the court.

Jack Lightfoot was prompt about leaving his papers with me, and I read through the last two carefully. They were not bad at all; the prose uneven, the material of some interest. One essay, on sense of place, described his high school with apt detail; the second distinguished between the natural authority of nature versus man's artificial sort. The prof's comments scribbled all over in red seemed to be off base, the D grades ridiculously off. I called him up, introduced myself, said it was important that I saw him today. He tried to wave me aside. I persisted and he gave in.

In classy Sanborn, a 19th century brick building which housed—and coddled?—the English department, I sat outside the office of Professor Arlen Breitman and tried to sort out my strategy for dealing with the fellow. Through a mutual friend I gathered that he was a poet of sorts, a fashionable "radical in theory," but pompous and conservative in practice. The institutional disease, I figured, no more.

A demure coed emerged from the office, reduced to tears, and I changed strategies as I entered.

Glancing at his watch, he said, "Well, I can manage ten

minutes, Coach. Sit down."

The large room was cloaked with thick brocades adorning the round oak table and windows, creating a hovering sense of a monk's cell, via Xerox commercials, with a dark wooden globe set on a stand. The professor was a hulking fellow, maybe 55, with a long scraggly beard and wild white-flecked hair cascading over his ears, not quite covering a bald pate. His shirt and suit were equally rumpled—perhaps too equally?—and he wore suspenders. A would-be Whitman in Hart, Shaffner and Marx.

"I feel very awkward coming here like this, Professor Breitman, but the thing is, my player Jack Lightfoot has been having a difficult time, as you know. And I'm worried about him."

"Yes, yes," he intoned deeply. "I'm worried too. He just didn't have the proper high school training, I fear."

Gently, I said, "Professor, forgive me, but he's given me these essays here," I held up the folder, "and I've read through them, and," I shook my head, feigning a loss of words, "I think they're not bad at all. Certainly, according to my general estimation, not *failing*..."

The professor took out his pipe, tapped the bowl repeatedly, slowly inserted the tobacco using a silver tamp, and finally lit it, a ceremony of Kyoto proportions. I had trouble keeping a straight face during this self-parody.

"Do you teach, Coach?" He grinned. "Physical Education?"

"History."

He raised his eyebrows. "Hm. An adjunct?"

"Yes."

He nodded, not without sympathy. "The situation is difficult, I realize. Uh, what is your name?"

"Berger. Sydney Berger."

"Difficult, Sydney, as I was saying. They're not well trained when they come here, and then the only thing they're able to write about is personal experience. But you see, the acquisition of the art of writing entails conceptualizing, an ability to think abstractly, and that's where the minorities are simply behind the eight ball. Look, between you and me, this university does not fulfill its responsibility towards these youngsters because it doesn't give them the proper tutorial and remedial help that they need to stay afloat here, and not be forced into... into permanent closure."

The language was prompting me to try the pipe ceremony myself. Disputing his judgment here was not the right path, I saw.

"Is it possible," I tried, leaning forward, manufacturing a fresh reverence, "for Jack to hand in some revisions, or even a few new papers, before the term ends? Papers on subjects you mutually agree upon, and boundaries that are very clear for him?"

He glanced at me sideways, and the phone rang.

"Yes, yes, Stephen," he muttered, "I'm coming right along." To me he half-nodded and said mournfully, "Yes, he can try that, I suppose. He's not a bad young man, really. How's he doing on your team, Sydney? Can he play?" He guffawed, with great mirth.

"Oh yes, he's a starter in the backcourt."

He was already getting into his wool overcoat and reaching for his large grey fedora. "'Backcourt,' eh? I must employ that noun. Send him around to me for a 'powwow,'" he emitted a low laugh, "and we'll work out the guidelines."

With difficulty I forced out, "Thanks, you know."

Dealing with the social worker down in Cambridge was more human, but depressing in a different way. If the professor had tried to puff himself like a samurai with his pipe acts, the woman here was poignant with her piles of manila folder powerlessness.

Mrs. Julia O'Connor shook her head in her Cambridge office, chain-smoking, elbows leaning on two stacks of folders. "It's beyond my control," she explained, her dark hair streaked prematurely grey, "It's up to the courts, and the parole office, and they're both overloaded too, and frequently

119

make terrible mistakes. In this case, it's a mistake we see often enough, and can't do a thing about, because the victim in question accepts the abusive man back, and we don't really know whether it's out of fear alone or addictive emotions. In either case, it's not very healthy."

"Can anything be done about it?"

She exhaled, "I can stay on top of the case, along with this other dozen, say," she held up her folders, "and be there for Mrs. Vargas, if and when she should need us. Oh, we check in periodically with the parole fellows, but they think we're sort of squishy-soft in our attitudes."

"And you of them?"

She laughed with a youthful radiance. "No comment."

"If you need me, for any reason, please don't hesitate to call." I gave her my updated card. "And here's my home number, too."

She looked at it and stuck it in her purse. "By the way, how's the boy playing, what's his name, Roberto?"

I nodded. "Coming along."

"Do you play down here at all?"

"Well, yes. We have a date with B.U., at Walter Brown Arena."

"If you can get me a freebie, I'd be delighted. I'm a Celtic fan, but would love to see a good college game."

I jotted down a memo. "I'm not sure how *good* it'll be..."

The parole officer, one Gino Palozzo, agreed to meet me downtown for a coffee. At a greasy spoon near Government Center I expressed my concern and interest in the Vargas situation.

"Yeah, tough case, that one. But until he really injures her again, if he should..." He threw up his palms and half-grinned. "Between you and me, Coach, just another sleazeball, but not a hard-core type if you know what I mean. It'd be easier if he were that sort."

I accepted the bigotry, sipped my coffee, glanced over at this fellow sporting his huge Windsor knot and cynical grin.

"Of course, if he does anything to violate his parole rules...

or if this Mrs. Vargas were to report him for something, then we can slap his wrists a little harder, sure."

"Okay. But if you hear of anything I can help with, let me know, would you?"

"You bet, Coach. Now tell me, what's life like up there, in the higher altitudes of the Ivory Tower? You don't get crummy deals like this up there, I'll bet. Who knows, you may even save that kid, what's-his-name?"

Before returning to that high altitude and projected salvation, however, I had to play one more hand down there, in the lower inner-city depths.

Lily Vargas was cordial on the phone and agreed to meet me in the same East Cambridge restaurant where I had courted her son.

As she came toward the booth, I stood to greet her. Oh, she had been a knockout maybe five years before, and still was a looker—trim figure, jet black hair shoulder length, sensual lips. A young Gene Tierney? The skirt was too tight and the lipstick and makeup a tad too heavy, but the large silver crucifix around the neck would counter all that, right? "Hi. Glad you could come, Mrs. Vargas."

After ordering sandwiches I told her that Roberto was doing fine, really coming along now.

"He will graduate, won't he?"

"Well, I certainly hope so," I said. "I'll do whatever I can to help him get through in the next few years."

She shifted her compact, smiled. "I'd be most grateful for that."

I had to tread very easily here. "And I hope you'll do everything you can to help him, too."

Her face tensed up and her eyes shot me a look that signalled: Stop, Warning. "What do you mean?"

"Oh, I just mean that anything positive which you might contribute, please do." It wasn't the language, I knew, but the underlying message, the spirit of the thing. "You know, encouragement, support. The importance of college education."

This calmed her and she returned to her makeup.

"Yes. Of course."

"And keep things smooth for him," I slipped in, "lines of communication open. He's very fond of you, and also, I think,"—ah, the glory of the lie!—"very proud." When you wanted to get something, you had to give something. Like the politicians, the clergy... To recruit her for my side I was willing to peel off a layer of honesty. I had done worse.

She nodded. "We've always been very close, and I'm proud of him, too, Mr. Berger. I would never do anything to hurt him."

"Oh, I know that." Good; she lied just as easily as I did.

Finding her oversized crucifix, she acknowledged, "He does not get along with Luis, that's true. I try to keep them apart." She smiled coquettishly.

"Well, that's useful, Mrs. Vargas. And smart."

She accepted the compliment modestly. Then added, "If you ever think..."

She attended to the waiter moving about, the conversations and glasses tinkling, and to her own thoughts. "If you ever think that *I*... should *do* something, that would help *R*oberto"—she rolled the R roundly—"you will feel free to tell me?"

I nodded, feeling something like a shrewd priest working on a willful and perhaps dangerous parishioner. "Yes, Mrs. Vargas, thank you, I will remember that. Just remember, for Roberto's and your own sake, you've got to stay well and take care of yourself—but you also have friends out there, just in case."

She tensed up again, a cornered animal. "Just in case what?"

Just above Lily on the wall I noticed an ecstatic woman leaping in the air alongside her Toyota, saying "I love what you do for me!" Life was easier up there on the posters. To this needier woman I replied, "In case you should ever need help."

"Which friends do you mean?"

"Well, Roberto mentioned a Julia O'Connor. And myself, I hope."

She inhaled deeply and sighed. "Yes, I think we all need help at times. Thank you."

Driving back on Interstates 93 and 89, thoughts floated in and out with the looming night and mountain fog. Strategies for the team mingled with conceptions about my role, my identity. More and more I was feeling that my staff should include a shrink, a social worker, a chaplain, a detective. On the radio the female singer in Ten Thousand Maniacs was asking her man to "burden her" with his troubles. Well, I needed her as much as her lover did, I figured. What would old Ralph Waldo have thought, having to confront all this democratic chaos while trying to keep idealism alive, manhood intact, and victories coming? Did I need to have a long conversation with him, updating the times and confusions in men's souls?... Or maybe what I really needed was a brand new Saab, souped up with higher horsepower and a kind of spiritual turbo, so I could fly back and forth on these dark empty highways in swifter time, with clearer understanding? Something like leading the fast break by taking a few extra steps with such illusory speed that the refs (or law) could not quite detect the illegality? My beeping green radar set on the dash helped me some, but I needed more deceptive power, more cunning speed, than what I had going for me now. Otherwise, I feared, peering closely through the windshield, I was always going to be a little slow in saving souls, those of my players' or that elusive one of my own.

7 INSIDE THE GAME

Back up in IvyTowerLand all was right with the world again. The snow had blanked the sidestreets and hills, the citizens paraded in their teal warmup jackets and red ski parkas like birds of good cheer, the shops on Main Street were glistening with winter virtue. (Even the banks and real estate offices, metastasizing like cancer cells, had dolled themselves up.) Seedy problems, wife-beaters and parole officers were at bay somewhere out in the rural woodwork, far removed from the protective sanctity of town and college. Prescott was clean, Conway was pure, the whole Ivy tapestry was like a Platonic Essence, no matter how messy and dirty the world down below, in matter-of-fact America, remained.

And if that America were for sale—as it was nowadays to the highest bidder, the wealthy Japanese and Swiss and Germans who were buying up our farms, businesses, cities, airlines—at least good Conway was not. Not on your life. And as I wandered the tidy white campus during those early January days, that was a good feeling to have, I thought. Colleges like Conway seemed to be the last outposts of our nation's original independence and dignity, in the new discount department store called USA. Maybe there was something after all to the mystique of the college, the uniqueness of Conway Ivy. So, reluctantly, I found myself warming to the notion of "green pride"—there you go, Chip—of Sydney Berger belonging to a cozy, worthwhile, protected family.

And warmed too to my own team perhaps coming around the bend now—Coach too?—into the territory of the able and the respectable. If the good turning and good bounces continued.

Who understood the game? Who loved the game? Who *needed* the game?—you know, like stuff in your veins? Who knew what it was like to put in fifteen youthful years on the game, and then, in adulthood, another fifteen or twenty? The sort of spellbinding passion that gradually, inevitably, wore a groove into obsession. Like chess players, violinists, novelists who spent their mature years in chains, enslaved, running the same track, refining the skill. Player, fan, coach—especially coach—each had his way of participating in the process. But until you were on the inside of the game, like my father inside opera, trapped exquisitely by your own wellworn repetitions like a gerbil, or a confirmed bachelor, you didn't experience the game in its full, nuanced ripeness. As a thirty-year man I figured I was smack in the middle of my hopeless track, my boyish obsession.

Oh, I knew well too that full ripeness was as rare in the peachbasket game as anywhere else, whether on the high school, college or professional level. Think on it: to put five young men on the floor in swift motion, held together by the basketball, dribbling, passing, shooting, and wired by a *precise and sweet* timing, going against five dedicated opponents, this was no common matter. Teams won championships all the time, but that was ordinary stuff, not of great interest. To find a team that could escalate ordinary play and climb into a higher zone, however, even if only for a few minutes a game, that had been the vision I aspired to behold. That had been my passion.

I had seen it at work, on occasion. I had witnessed it with the CCNY club of 1953-54, coached by Nat Holman; in

1955-56 with the Cincinnati teams of Oscar Robertson and the Ohio State clubs of Havlicek and Lucas; with the University of San Francisco when Bill Russell blocked shots and K.C. Jones made defense a web of beauty; in high school with Brooklyn's Jefferson High, '55, and the Boys High clubs with SiHugo Green or Lenny Wilkins; with the John Wooden UCLA teams, when Hazzard and Goodrich fielded backcourt, or Lew Alcindor skyhooked and Walton defended and passed at center. Usually, though, the high zone was reached when there was no big man playing, upon whom the team became dependent. Such dependencies may have created victories, but they crippled fluidity and the rhythm of exquisite movement, or what I call High Flow, when, among many beautiful acts, passes were threaded like silvery intricacies and play resembled the woven gossamer designs in spiderwebs.

With Nurlan in full form I had hoped for such a possibility, and the 12-15 minutes in the second half at the Holy Cross gym opened into glimmerings of that vision. It was now up to me to work toward the higher team rhythm, shoot for its consistency, refine and polish it, try to push the envelope wider with each game. Of course that meant getting it down in practice, maneuvering or tricking the team into surpassing its own parts and running on the illusion of high. Practices would have to change somewhat, I decided, now that Nurlan was flashing himself again—might become a little boot camp where I would not be liked much.

So I became a kind of drill sergeant, disciplining and bullying the boys in an effort to weld them together, glue the parts, toughen them into consistency. I pushed Nurlan into releasing the ball more on fast breaks, and the Chief into getting back into passing lanes faster. Dennis I screamed at for his "dumb" positioning; and I had Eddie and Vargas run extra laps around the gym to improve their stamina. Avram and Jarrod were asked to stay an extra hour three times a week, dribbling up and down the floor, up and back; one lost dribble along the way and they had to add three trips. Spares like Tony and Antoine were forced to become defensive robots, forbidden to shoot back. The post-New-Year looks I received were not pleasant, I assure you.

How well the strategy worked was simple and immediate enough to see: we got blown out in Providence by Brown, and embarrassed the next night by 15 against a fair Harvard team. The bus ride back from Cambridge that Saturday night was quiet, deadly quiet.

Halfway up Nurlan came and sat beside me in the front, and spoke low: "Ya should just let us play more, Coach. We were gettin *smooth* ya know and suddenly..." In the darkness he checked to see I was understanding. "Hey, like the season's young, we'll get 'em. Jes be cool in practice. Let go, Coach, and you'll see us perk up. Jes cool yer jets, Mista B, and let us be." He patted my arm.

When ace pointguard talks, Coach listens. On Monday I called off my master sergeant boot camp and returned to old ways. Immediately practice turned upbeat again, relaxed, patterned, up-tempo. Nurlan led, the team followed. I felt the great fool. Somehow I had taught them to flow loose, then suddenly I had turned the spigot tight. By the end I was cheered.

Until the team manager (Pat Hinsdale, '91) brought me the local political rag, the controversial *Conway Review*. On the cover I read: HOOP COACH TURNS NATIVE SPORT INTO THIRD-WORLD POLITICAL EXPERIMENT! The colored illustration showed a caricature of me in the center of a maze, surrounded by a confused array: Indian with tomahawk, two blacks shooting up with syringes, a Puerto Rican carrying a Commonwealth First placard, a yarmulked Jew levitating with a basketball, a blue-eyed blond white kid crying over a lost scholarship, a big Polish boy trying to screw in a light bulb. My stomach dropped. On the third page, under the heading, "Coach Berger's Half-Year Report Card: Grade F," was the sad story, and I sagged to the bench under its weight. The lead paragraph ran this way:

There are a least four major casualties of Interim Coach Sydney Berger's radical experiment with the hoop team this year. First, the honor and dignity of the college itself. Second, the long-term credibility of the hoop program. Third, the interest of Big Green fans in basketball this year. Fourth, the probable Rhodes Scholarship of Dennis Healey, '90. It is hard to say which is the cruelest. And as for the minor injuries suffered, they are too legion to go into here. Suffice it to say, the risky gamble taken by Dick Porter, A.D., of hiring a questionable-at-best recruiter assistant to run a creditable hoop program has proved to be not merely a grand failure, but an utter humiliation to Conway. Already there can be heard whisperings up and down the corridors of the other Ivies: what's going on up there in Looney-Tunes Prescott?

My heart was pounding and I found it hard to breathe. Boys were coming around, but I couldn't look up. *Take it easy, Syddie,* Mama used to say, rocking me after a blow.

These whisperings began when Conway hired a coach with no experience in the first place, a man who had left Miami of Ohio under shadowy circumstances. Whisperings turned louder when rumors had it that the entire first squad of last year was being demoted, so that Coach Berger's lumpen-underlings could be promoted. And when that rumor became hard fact, the whisperings became loud and clear suspicions. And when yet a second rumor became fact, namely that the Coach in his new wisdom was going to bring in a zombie-druggie off the streets of Brooklyn to be readmitted to the college, against the advice of Admissions, suspicion became lament. Finally, when the third rumor proved itself true too, namely that a collection of social and academic misfits were going to constitute the Team this year, all led by that same druggie (now in Rehab thanks to Coachie's decision and WHOSE MONEY??), lament turned to anxiety and open mutiny.

Tears welled up. *"Knit one, purl two,"* recited Mrs. Gideon in Steiner School, for stress. I glanced through the next two paragraphs, bitchy interviews with the departed players from last year, and stopped in the next paragraph at:

> Is it true that the Coach put pressure on a renowned pro-
> fessor in the English Department, if not exactly to change
> a grade, then to look more 'kindly' upon one of his flunk-
> ing-out minority players? If this is the case, what comes
> next, when perhaps the star from the ghetto finds himself
> in deep doodoo with Trig or Soc Rel?...

I took three yoga-breaths from the center of my stomach
and released the air slowly.

> What shall we say now, when, at midseason, it is clear that
> the team is an abject failure, the season is lost, the players
> are disgruntled and confused, and its opening three games
> in Ivy play have been total humiliations? Is it too much to
> ask: who is responsible for this betrayal? Who is minding
> the store at Conway? And who will be the first to ask for
> the immediate resignation of this particular Berger, who
> would seem to be more fit for Burger King than Conway?...

By this time I had collected a small crowd around me, my
team. What could I say? Do?

I stood up wearily and handed the rag over to the boys.
Walked, slumped over in defeat, across the length of the floor,
like a man walking his last mile. Maybe I should have been, I
thought, hitting the exit at last.

For the first time I looked forward to my regular appoint-
ment at the periodontist, late that afternoon, at 5:00 p.m. I
had omitted gingivitis on my C.V. Would the *Review* be interested? Sitting in the chair and having Cheryl, the
heavy-handed hygienist, work me over for my periodic deep
scaling, I felt duly rewarded. Deep into my chronically in-
fected gums she used the ultrasonic tool like a jackhammer,
flailing the gums with particles of water but occasionally hitting an exposed nerve or irritated area.

I tried my best to focus elsewhere, of course. On upcoming games and trap and zone defenses, but what kept coming back to me was the ambush in the *Review*. Maybe after all I should give it up, call it quits, before they called me in to ask me to resign? I daydreamed of a quick lawsuit, like everyone else in America, but gave that up quickly. I knew that most people of good sense thought very little of that right-wing rag; still, maybe in sports matters, it had more credibility? The scurrility of several charges, the ranting personal smears, took my breath away and kept driving me back to the riveting on my gums.

Dr. Hutfin came in. In his dour, competent way he looked me over, measured the gum depth, mostly 3's and 4's, and said it was coming along fine—fine?—but I'd always be collecting plaque. Toasting my future!

Cheryl returned and spent the final fifteen minutes digging with the probe and mirror, poking about, and scraping away the tartar she had missed with the ultrasonic cavitron, which continued to pound at my gums. Because she had that heavy hand, was a dogged perfectionist and, at 45, wouldn't look at a modern book or movie ("too explicit") she was carving me up to her heart's delight, the repressed dear. Privately I rooted her on: "Go on, pal, give it to him good, pound the stupid son of a bitch!"

"How'd I do?" Cheryl wondered merrily, knowing how I had complained of her style in the past. "Was it too bad?"

"You did well this time," I told her. "Not only thorough-going, but exemplary."

She fluttered at my cryptic praise.

The calls started coming in the next morning, asking for my reaction to the piece. Friends, newspapers, local media. "Well, I'd prefer if Grantland Rice or Red Smith wrote the sports columns for them." I smiled for channel 31. "Or even Jimmy Cannon."

The A.D. poked his head in. "You're a celebrity. Once the Review marks you on the front page, watch out for *60*

Minutes."

Chip Bromley rang up, offering his sympathies. "What a rag! Yellow journalism just became canary-colored, the little snotnoses! You're not letting this affect you one bit, Syd, are you?"

Well, maybe one bit, Chip. "Nah, I've got my work cut out for me, up in Ithaca."

Oh, I had yet to make it up with the Admissions Office and Professor Breitman, but that could wait.

At a brief meeting with my coaches I asked their views. Roscoe said, "Cheap shot all the way. Everyone can see that. Don't give it two thoughts." Duddy Hamsun, my fiery German schnauzer, brandished his fist. "A punch in the nose would be the old way of handling those spoiled little rich bastards!" Percy Grimes made good sense: "Just make sure *our kids* took it okay."

In the gym for an early morning final practice before heading up north, I gathered the boys together and asked how they reacted to it? Did it really injure anyone's feelings?

No one answered, I waited, and finally turned to Avram to speak up. He said, "Like reading *Pravda* again. Only subjects changed."

"What's this Prav-da, man?"

"The Party paper."

"What party?" asked Vargas.

Avram shot him a look. "The Communist Party of the former Soviet Union. *Pravda* used to decide what are the facts to suit its principles. True fact no matter. Everyone reads it, laughs privately."

"And over there," I added, "until recently at least, Pravda was the only newspaper in town. Here, gentlemen, I assure you that no one reads the *Review* and gives it a second thought. Like reading the Sunday comics." A few grins. "Now onto foul shooting, fifty shots per man, and remember, bus leaves at 2:00 sharp today."

Walking off toward the basketballs the Chief caught me up.

"I think it hurt us," he confessed. "Our dignity."

I put my arm around his shoulders. "Never let someone else's dirt smear your dignity, Jack. Only your own actions can do that."

He nodded.

But was he paying attention? Were any of them?

Hiring Renee Flugman was the smartest thing I ever did, I figured quickly a few days later, as it immediately paid dividends. And like most good fortune, it came about by accident. My assistant Roscoe was hit by a sudden hernia condition and needed surgery. Just then Renee was up at the college, looking into possible employment. I desperately needed an assistant to replace Roscoe, who handled all the nitty-gritty PR things among his chores.

Enter Renee: short, dark frizzy hair, prominent chin, small darting eyes. When she focused on you, her look read: "I'm getting things done nicely or otherwise, whichever you prefer." The 36-year-old daughter of a German-Jewish professor of classics in New York, Renee had been an athlete at Barnard and then sustained her interest by coaching basketball, squash and tennis, first in high schools and then on the college level. Currently down the road at UNH, she had come up to inquire about the autumn vacancy-to-be in the women's hoop program.

I met her at lunch in the faculty dining room when the women's coach, Andrea Cox, invited me over to say hello. After a sandwich and an hour's lively talk, I impulsively asked Andrea if I were free to ask Renee if she might want to help me out for the remainder of the season? Would that interfere with her candidacy for Andrea's job? When Renee smiled, surprised, and said 'no,' I offered her the job, cautioning that I had to clear it with our A.D.

"Now that's a radical turn of events," Renee said, nibbling on a brownie and nodding. "It'd be a ball."

Later Dick Porter reacted with wry interest, saying, "Sure, why not? It might even help out our image. With Nell at least."

Right off Renee proved to be a tough, no-nonsense woman off the court and a sympathetic soul on it. Switching from wrap-around skirts to grey Bean's sweats easily was the way she handled the different roles of defensive aide and PR administrator. Importantly she understood have-not kids and their predicament at our college. (In a week she had earned the respect of the players. Dennis observed dryly, "So you realize at last that you've been missing a crucial element for The Temptation test. Good.") And at PR work she was cunningly able, I learned soon enough, as I observed her handle the *Review* crowd and reporters with composure and wit. She was always in control, neither flustered by insult nor irritated by stupid questions, and cheerily took sarcastic bait. Best of all, she was a master of the non-talk/double-talk cover, an increasing trouble spot for me.

No wonder even Old Boy Chip Bromley remarked to me, "Which angel delivered Renee to you? She is just what you needed—to free you up for coaching per se, pal. You might want to keep her on after the season ends, Sydney. And she's loyal to you too, I can tell."

He was right, I thought, on every count. For Renee became as much trusted bodyguard as right-hand helper. Whether it was handling media, publicity, or a dim trip for scouting, she was there. Her great virtue was not her straight basketball acumen, but rather her strong belief in competitive athletics for college kids. And it was axiomatic in our time and place that a woman who was smart would make a far more able politician, a more powerful ally around a campus, a truer all-around bodyguard, than any man.

So Renee came aboard just at the right time, when the ship was in some trouble, and was a most welcome mate. And she was shrewd enough to realize that the other three mates had been there longer and required the proper amount of stroking. So she stroked, deferred, labored, and swiftly became one of the boys, or crew—though she remained very much her own woman.

On the long bus ride up to Ithaca I sat next to every player for a brief chat, describing what I was looking for against Cornell. To Nurlan: "Work the break whenever you can, but also look to pull up for the little jumper. Remember, they have those two maulers in the middle." To Avram: "Get into that baseline spot as fast as you can, and get off that shot pronto." He made a face. "What is 'pronto'?" "Quick, and quicker." To Konepski: "Eddie boy, keep looking for the offense. Take it to the hole whenever you can, all right?" To Vargas: "This is the game we need you all over both boards. They're rough up there and will try to intimidate you, on the first few rebounds especially. Use your body, stay cool." I sat by Dennis. "Block the middle, right?" "Right." "Box out." "Got it." "Do not bait the refs, understand?" An embarrassed smile. "Would I do that?" I paused. "Worried about your Rhodes?" Pursed lips. "Would the Green Knight be worried about his scholarship if he were visiting the Court of Arthur?" I shook my head in despair. To Antoine I said, "Be ready, on guard. I may need you for their bullies." He stared at me, silent, and I hadn't the foggiest. With Jarrod I spoke softly: "You're gonna be playing about twenty minutes tonight. They'll know you're a freshman and come right after you, holding your shorts, calling you names. Ignore it, stay cool, under control. *Versteh*?" He nodded and half-smiled.

Were they listening? I wondered as we bumped along on the seven-hour trip. On their tape they played a rap group and "Wild Thing" by Tone Loc so often I had to have them shift to Walkmans. I filled in my own with Ruffo's greatest hits. Gazing out at the long farm landscape in winter I was reminded of Stilwell scouting around China via the Peking-Mukden Railway.

They might have been listening, but it didn't do much good in the first half. We played sloppily, foolishly, intensely; too intensely, I saw. Against a rugged but not skilled Big Red team we went off at halftime down by 14.

"Same old 'Green Eggs and Ham,' huh boys?" a fan encouraged as we walked off.

I felt stupid, bleak, useless. In the locker room the boys sat on the benches, heads down, munching desultorily on citrus. I stood by my blackboard, chalk and notes in hand, ready to go into a few new zones and stuff. The smells were pungent, dizzying. "Okay, listen up," I called out, and found myself writing on the board, "Vinegar Joe." I said: "Anyone ever hear of Stilwell, General Joe Stilwell?" And I was off and running.

"You see, this guy was an excellent *man* and excellent general, not some mini-dictator like Patton or MacArthur. Stilwell had common sense, and a sense of humor, which you don't often find in military men. Plus real integrity. And he respected great traditions and old societies, which made him perfect for China, where he lived for 13 years after the First World War. He had gone to West Point and spent four years in Fort Benning with George Marshall, a tough boss, and then, when he had a chance to return to his beloved China in the early forties, he grabbed it. He was there to see what the Japanese were doing in Manchuria, and to the Chinese; and there to see how Chiang Kai-shek was more interested in his own greed and power than the Chinese people. In other words, how and why Chiang was killing his own people first, because they were Communists, than in facing up to the Japanese challenge. I assure you, gentlemen, it didn't please Washington and Secretary of State Cordell Hull one bit when Stilwell told them how corrupt Chiang was; and it didn't please Chiang too much when General Stilwell was put in charge of all Chinese forces in 1944, the first time a foreigner ever held this post. So you had a great irony there—Stilwell saving Chiang's ass while hating him, and Chiang watching his forces saved, and the Japanese thrown back, by the American he distrusted and despised."

I took a drink of whatever, brushed my brow, loosened my tie. I saw them eyeing me, glancing at each other. My coaches slinked off quietly, furtively shaking their heads.

"Dennis, on defense, raise your hands in the middle but *don't* leave your feet. Nurlan, *bounce* that lane pass on the

break. Jack, float around and *cheat* more in the middle...
Where was I?

"Oh, yeah... Now you see the thing about this Joe was
that he was for real, a serious fellow, not a West Point card-
board cutout. He could have had a fat job back in the States,
but preferred the hot seat of China when it was in terrible,
terrible shape. You know, when the Allies, like we Americans and the British, were selling China down the drain so as
not to offend the Japanese and draw them into the war. And
when they drove Joe out of China he regrouped in India, using the old Chinese strategy of 'strategic retreat,' only to return
in a year or two, counterattack, and stun the Japanese. He
made it stick, too. The man was a man; in hard times, he was
there, sticking it out against a well-organized enemy with a
disorganized army, amidst Chiang's greed, the Washington
bureaucrats and cowards, the intolerable conditions and circumstances of a nation of deep poverty and backwardness
—because he loved the Chinese, and what they had stood for.
He was one gutsy, smart, courageous American, Vinegar Joe.
And by the way a great handball player, too, and a cross-
country runner, and a fellow who—"

"The second buzzer's rung, Mr. Berger," Pat called in
softly.

I nodded. "Yeah, yeah, I hear it." Of course I had heard
nothing. "All right, but just remember guys, there's more to
this story. Let's go."

On the way out, wry old Dennis said, "How come the 'Vinegar' nickname, you omitted that."

"Oh, that. His sense of humor: acerbic, unconventional.
One time during the First World War—"

Duddy pulled us along. "We gotta get out there, Syd. The
warmup period is just about over."

"Yeah. Sure. Sure." I was surprised, actually. Duddy was
pulling me. "I'm moving, Duddy, take it easy."

The crowd and the floor and the refs calling to us were a
bit of a shock, like the curtain going up and revealing a live
audience when you thought you were in a dress rehearsal.

136

Well, you know how it went, right? The catcalls and mocker-
ies from the Cornell crowd just stirred us up more. The players
stayed cool, worrying chiefly about me, it seemed. "You just
take it nice and slow, Coach," consoled Eddie. "We'll be fine
out there."

And, truth be told, fine they were. They played less
charged up, more relaxed and precise; and for those first few
crucial psychological minutes out of the chute, when you show
the opponent how halftime prepared you, they stayed all over
the backboards and hit three immediate baskets—a feathery
jumper by Avram, a drive by Nurlan, a tip-in by Vargas.
Cornell called a timeout and I said to the group: "Don't worry,
boys, I'm okay. And Stilwell's story is not done yet. I should
explain how he got his nickname..."

"Coach, excuse me," Jack inserted. "Do we stay in the 3-
2 zone?"

Lovely idea, as I met his smoky black eyes. "Nah, shift to
man to man, gentlemen, they're probably adjusting right now
for the zone."

Oh, we had some rhythm now, but Cornell helped us kick
into another gear when they sent Nurlan crashing to the floor
on a layup, and Dennis and Eddie got fired up. They banged
Roberto pretty good on a rebound, and while he was on the
foul line, called out to "Roberto dear" about his "garbage
collection." Time for an Antoine minute of bodyguard banging and fouling. And Vargas, you see, when he was pushed,
would wake up and push back, stretching his talent. As I had
hoped, he became a Silas-master on the offensive board, positioning himself under the basket just as the shot was released,
and keeping alive those balls which he couldn't actually tip
back in. A performance of subtlety. Avram became a baseline
scoring machine, taking the bounce passes from Nurlan on
the break, or working off picks from Dennis; he threw up
seven jumpers and hit six. Eddie was relentless, unstoppable,
driving always from his left to right and muscling his way in
like a mini-Dolph Schayes. Big Red began to diminish in size,
stature; getting no boards, getting eaten up on defense down

low, and losing the battle for the key at the top of the circle, which I, in my Nimzovitch mode, thought was essential. And when I threw in Jarrod the Minister as an all-purpose sub, the freshman played just the way a *senior* was supposed to, doing all the little things—loose ball recoveries, deflected passes, no turnovers—that secure victories. With three minutes to go Percy squeezed my arm, "We're doing it, Syd, we're doing it!" Shaking myself, I gripped his hand. For the first time in a decade we beat the stubborn Big Red in their own lair.

Though the bus ride down to the Big Apple was long and dark, for us it was like a trip back from the Valley of Death with our lives intact, spirits resurrected. I let them play as much Tone Loc and REO Speedwagon and whatever Ice-T rappers they wanted. I sat in the back, sealed off with headphones and soaring privately with Björling. Papa's gene weighing in; he always celebrated with a tenor.

Later on Nurlan leaned down and said, "Ya see, Coach. Nothin to worry bout once we set our minds ta it."

And Duddy Hamsun prophesied, "We got ourselves a club, buddyboy!"

Dennis slid into the seat alongside me, sporting a bandage over his eye where he'd taken an elbow. "Well, Coach, those are 'interesting' lectures you're springing on us these days. At first I thought you might turn out to be Bercilak, but now I'm not so sure. You may be Sir Gawain himself, if that isn't too simple. No, if I were a betting man I think I'd go with Morgan Le Fay."

"Who?"

He grinned slyly. "I see you know little of the Beheading Game or The Temptation to Adultery." He leaned closer and whispered, "One of the most mysterious sorceresses in Arthurian Legend, Coach. Supernatural powers. The secret planner of the plot in Sir Gawain. How else to account for those cunning lectures of yours, so obviously allegorical."

"*Obviously.* You did a good job in the second half, Denny, blocking out and setting picks. Keep that up and who knows, you might make first-team Oxford next year."

I liked that term, "the beheading game," and figured that I had avoided it for now with the nice sweet win in the upstate hinterlands. Evidently I should look into that Morgan Le Fay woman; learn a bit more about her bag of tricks.

I spent part of Saturday in my uptown Manhattan hotel room, lunching with the coaches and players. I made sure that when the kids traipsed out, they did so in groups of two and three, with Nurlan accompanied by Antoine, Dennis and Vargas, his roomie and regular companion. On my own I went to the Frick and stood by the Vermeer, mother's favorite dating from an art appreciation course. (She was always "improving" herself.) The small portrait of the woman pouring water from the pewter jug, in front of the window and thick brocade curtain, all bathed in that subtle light, worked wonders after a bit. That interior light of Vermeer calmed, instructed my soul, like my boyhood knitting. On my three visits to Europe I had managed to get over to the Hague and, at that elaborate private mansion called Muisthouse, I'd climbed up that wide mahogany staircase and sat in the room by the "View of Delft." Gradually the light in the sky had expanded in front of my eyes, expanded and lifted me.

Uplifted now, I mused: if we could do it tonight up at Columbia it would be a hell of a weekend. Though the Lions were a weaker club than Cornell, it was the second game on the trip, and it was easy to lose after a victory like last night's and the lengthy bus ride. I focused on the glistening pearls worn by the woman in the picture, the dimmer glow of the pewter, the richly-textured interior. Yes, that's what we needed tonight, I decided, a controlled game once we got a lead.

Back in the hotel room I dumped out the week's papers in my chaotic briefcase and came across an essay, passed on to me by a math prof, on shooting streaks in basketball. In a recent *Chance* magazine two psychologists, one with the nicely coincidental name of Tversky, argued that there was no such thing as "getting hot" in a game, that it was an illusion, no more. All a question of randomness appearing as

139

streaks, so that if you flipped a coin one hundred times, say, it could come up heads in consecutive order simply out of random chance, though it would still be fifty-fifty all told out of the hundred. Oh, it was amusing stuff, I can tell you, and I longed for the other Twersky, my Kiev gunner, to have a hot hand again tonight, for a fitting response. Imagine trying to put a logician up against a streak shooter, a Turing against a West or Sharman, a Russell against Vinnie Johnson, a Tversky against a Twersky?

I settled in with my biography of Crazy Horse and fell asleep for a solid hour, awakened by Duddy for a pre-game sandwich.

Later, up at Levine gym, we came through, and once again in the second half, and again despite the coach, you might say. I mean we were down with nine minutes to go when Nurlan took over and, in schoolyard dominion, controlled the ending. Roberto and Eddie began clearing out the boards and getting him the outlet pass swiftly, and he was off and running, with Jarrod and Chief on the wings for the fast break. Columbia urgently assigned two men to him, but he was too tricky a dribbler, too deft a passer, and the strategy backfired; easily he found the open man, Avram or Jack for the sideline jumpers, Jarrod or Eddie for the layups, Dennis and Vargas for the backdoor. Like the inimitable Cousy he never lost his dribble, using his thin body to shield the ball and his long fingers to control it perfectly. And using that peripheral vision of his to see the whole court and make a quick decision on whom to pass it to, and when. If you went for the dribble he was flying by you; and as soon as they doubled him, he fed it off and moved quickly toward the basket for the give-and-go. Once he got the ball back inside the foul line you couldn't stop him, but had to foul him, even though he was just under six feet. Too many moves, too much hang time, too much poise. And beaming, for courtlife was sweet, wasn't it?

I'm afraid, however, I lost my poise at the end, when a frustrated goon intentionally knocked Nurlan to the ground and the ref didn't call it.

"Hey, shmuck," I called to him, "they're trying to hurt the kid. Throw the thug out of the game so Columbia gets the message!" Plus the other teams, and the other refs, too, I thought.

The ref stuck one finger in my face and his other thumb in the air and whistled a technical. "You're the one gone, Coach! You're through for the evening. Blow off!"

Two assistants had to hold me as I yelled, "If my boy gets hurt in this game, you sonofabitches are going to pay!"

"If you guys don't clear your coach out immediately," the ox-eyed ref said, smiling gleefully, "it's a double T, and it's gonna cost you dough as well."

The squad huddled around me, seeking to calm and console me. I gave Percy and Duddy the reins and told the club, "Forget me and the refs. Play your game and keep feeding the ball to Nurlan. Oh yeah, remember Crazy Horse and White Bull, right?" And I stormed off, hit by a flying popcorn container.

In the locker room I was able to watch the last few minutes on closed-circuit TV, and the kids stayed cool as early cucumbers. I was beginning to see the obvious: the hotter and wilder I grew, the more stable they stayed, the more in control they played. As though they sensed something about me and sympathized with my condition... Which was what, I wondered myself?

Later, in fact, Dennis chirped, "Did you have a lecture in mind at halftime, Mr. B, that didn't quite emerge, sir?"

I stared at his wide blue eyes, and wondered if he was innocent or insolent? "Nah, the Crazy Horse narrative takes too long." To be sure, I think I had half-thought that I had delivered a little talk. But the young man had a point: I had gotten so wrought up at the actual game that I guess I was beginning to confuse the real with the imagined just a bit, or the classroom with the locker room. Something like that. I couldn't quite pin it down.

Coming home from that second win in two nights was

like sailing in on a lovely wind, basking in blue sky and tur-
quoise sea and bright sun you just watched the world move
on by.

On Sunday I was awakened by the doorbell and realized
it was Becka with Danny boy, for the day and his overnight.
Dark, slender, small-featured, pretty—she looked better than
ever, rid of me.

"Here's his backpack, his violin, his Legos. And snow
boots. Don't forget them." She leaned down and hugged the
boy. Then she said to me sternly, "Would you get him to his
violin lesson on time today? Clyde can get upset easily if
you're late."

Clyde or you, Becka? It only took two sentences or so,
but I knew how necessary it had been to leave finally. "Yes, I
will."

I said hello to Dan by punching the little guy's arm, and
he laughed and whacked me back.

"Well, you won again, I hear," she relented. "Congratulations."

I nodded. "Thanks."

She stood for an awkward minute, then turned and left.
She needed a steady fellow soon, for my sake as well as hers.

I settled his gear and he got out of his jacket. "Wanna see
my pictures from Friday in school?"

"Sure," I said, and asked if he wanted some late breakfast.

"Didja win last night, Papa?"

"Yeah, we did."

"Hmmm. That's good. Can I come to the next game?"

"Maybe. We'll see."

"Well," he said, "let's see where old Merlin is?..." and he
began searching for my cat, his pal.

Very soon I got a call from Dick Porter. "You deserve a
drink for your weekend. Five-thirty okay?"

I said sure, but that I'd probably have a little boy with me.
"Good, I'd like to see him again."

Later, at ten to noon, we were driving up Wheelock to Low Street and his teacher's house. "Did you practice this week?"

"Well, sort of," he explained. "Maybe... five minutes a day."

In Clyde Gallant's unfinished, woodsy living room, I sat on the couch in front of the grey enameled woodstove, and looked through my notes while the boy took his lesson.

Periodically I glanced over at him, wearing his blue crewneck over his shirt, and tucking his downsized violin under his neck, supported by a sponge. Before actually performing anything he chatted with her, elaborating on a distinction he was making on her original question about his practice songs.

I wanted to stop him, but held my words and read in Parkman.

Finally she got him to the work at hand. First she had him plucking the strings, which he did easily and well. "Okay," Clyde said, a curlyhaired, bespectacled woman in her thirties who had home-schooled her own two kids and wrote children's books. "Now let's see you practice your bowing. Go ahead, start with A."

So he began, tucking the violin under his chin and arching his back stiffly, scraping his bow along the strings, sometimes hitting the note serenely, more often screeching across. The coordination in his tiny hands, or attempt at it, fascinated me.

He scraped on A, slowly found C, lifted upward on D. Listening to him, observing his rapt concentration, I didn't want him ever to grow up and be his own man. He afforded me too much gorgeous pleasure as this small functioning creature, as my son.

While the boy played I was transported momentarily to my own childhood, when my father was vainly attempting to sing, practicing his arias in the evenings, trying to accompany his favorite tenors, Björling, Caruso, Schipa, Gigli... Those were his happiest and most ridiculous hours, away from high school duty and family drudgery (politics included?), and it pleased me to glance over at him, helpless as he was, with one hand on his chest, the other in the air, emoting, trying to catch the high C. He looked more like a walrus waving his shaving mug in his paw than an opera singer...

The scratching sounds of the boy returned me to the sun slanting across the pine floor, and I longed for the old man to see the boy playing here... Maybe the boy screeching away would make up for the son who was fiddling with a basketball team?

Midway between that ghost and this child I felt half-possessed, half-possessing. Boyfather myself at fifty-one.

"You know, Daniel," Clyde offered, "I think you're almost ready for 'Scotland is Burning.' Would you like to try?"

"Sure. Is it very hard?" And he glanced over at me, making sure I had heard the very high offer.

8   ZONE OF TRANQUILITY

On Monday morning, on my office desk, I found a paper-back copy of *Sir Gawain and the Green Knight*, with an intricate medieval castle on the cover, shaded in gloomy greens. Alongside it lay a green sash and a note saying, "For any moral lapses." Clever cookie, my precocious Irish medievalist. From Springfield, Vermont, to Balliol, Oxford; Dennis'd do all right over there. But what the hell did the sash mean? As for moral lapses, well, I had enough for the whole club. "Since the siege and the assault was ceased at Troy,/The walls breached and burnt down to brands and ashes,/The knight that had knotted the nets of deceit/Was impeached for his perfidy, proven most true." Hmm... was I that knight, awaiting impeachment? Could be.

But for now, the athletic office and gym building were astir with the weekend news. A Monday morning in grim February, after a weekend of depositing two victories in the Ivy bank away from home, was like a day in Dante's *Paradiso*, bathed in higher light. You see, only in the Ivy did you play back-to-back games without a night off; to win both was a sign of Providence or... perfect poise. Suddenly there were fresh smiles and cheery greetings from people all over campus and the streets, as though I had just surfaced from the underground after a few years in hiding. Wherever I strolled, to the bookstore or library, to the haberdashers (where I rewarded myself with a pair of Rooster's wool ties and Viyella *Argyle* socks!) or Peter Christian's for lunch, the feeling was there: the taste and aroma of victory. Coach had *class* perhaps after all, read the looks now. For me, that noun, victory, was summer sweet coming after the string of winter losses. That sweetness and light spread everywhere, whether I was cashing a check, eating a tuna sandwich, reading the Globe.

Or when I met Professor Breitman by chance in the bookstore.

"Well, look who's here," he bellowed, grinning broadly.

"Hello, Professor," I said, avoiding his hand. "Didn't know you had such a close connection with the *Review*."

He glanced at me sideways. "What do you mean?"

"That story they ran about me and the team. You were quoted as saying I tried to lean on you to change Jack Lightfoot's grade. Is that what you told their reporter?"

"Oh, that," he boomed, placing a hand on my shoulder. "I said I had a nice chat with you, as I recall. Nothing incriminating, *Sydney*, I assure you. Don't be so sensitive!" He guffawed at my innocence, my paranoia. "You know the *Review*, for godssakes. A tempest in a teapot."

The Poet was a fudger, a crook. "Aren't you being a bit disingenuous, *Arlen*, if not out-and-out deceptive? If they misrepresented you about so serious a charge, you should have called them on it immediately."

"Well, if that's your attitude, I see we have little to talk about, Coach. But I shall remember this chat."

Like Napoleon recalling a betrayal? "Remember this one *correctly*, at least," I said, and walked off.

Outside the store, in the brisk grey day, I stopped to browse at the long table filled with remainder books, just in case I came across a Clair Bee memoir or a good children's tale.

My arm was taken, and another Claire said, "Hello, stranger."

"Hey, hi. Gosh, my apologies. I... uh..."

"No, no. I just wondered how you were."

"Coaching." I smiled. "That's how."

"Does that mean not living?"

"Unfortunately, just about. During the season anyway."

She gave me that perky smile beneath her Chinese fur hat. "Well, when you want to live again, call me."

"You're on, I promise. This week, *maybe.*"

She stroked my cheek, which indeed urged me "to live again," and departed.

Strolling past the Hop, back toward the gym, still feeling the hand, I was hailed, "Syd, hey Sydney!"

Approaching me, wearing a camel-colored English mackintosh and a big smile was Chip Bromley. He shook my hand warmly. "You son of a gun, you won the two goddamned games on the road, champ!"

"Thanks, pal. Caught a little lightning in the bottle, I imagine."

"Whatever it is, it's a fact, doggone it, and we're gonna take advantage of it right off, I hope." He draped his bear's paw around my shoulders as we walked. "How 'bout talking to the Sports Alumni Club this week?"

"I'd like to, Chip, but you know, with Princeton and Penn coming up, well, can I get off for a week or two? Of course I may not be so lucky by then."

"Well, sure, I just thought you'd like to bask in the sun a little for a change."

"Oh, I would, Chip, I very much would. But I've got four days to prepare for the grizzlies. You know what it's like."

"Sure, sure." We passed the Alumni Gym. "Any chance of pulling an upset at one of those dens this weekend?"

"Well, there's always *a chance,* buddy."

"It'll be tough, huh?"

"With a capital T."

"Should I drive down with a few of the old boys and cheer you on?"

"That's up to you, and thanks for the thought. But don't come with great expectations."

"Tell me the truth: do you have a *fighting* chance, or a Chinaman's chance? Excuse the language."

"Well, truth is, I can't tell. These are young kids, just learning to play with each other, with my system." *(Really, Syd? Or learning without your system?)* "So you can't tell. One week up, the next could be down, way down." I raised my hands.

We stopped in front of the Perry Center and my office.

"Whether we come or not, good luck down there, okay?" He leaned closer. "Helluva job, honest!"

Later in the day UPS Overnight brought the Ivy League tapes of the most recent Tigers and Quakers games, and I set them up for viewing. First I'd have a private viewing, then show the assistants—and then later maybe the players. If you couldn't bear VCRs and video-watching, coaching was a bummer these days.

We had a light practice, where I worked with the trapping zone on defense, and, on the offense, continued refining the fast break and outlet pass, plus the shots coming off the picks. Though the practices went reasonably enough, I came away dissatisfied. I couldn't put my finger on why...

And that night while it snowed and most sane adults read books, watched TV and took it easy, I hibernated in my flickering cave. I watched Princeton and Penn tinker and toy with Harvard and Brown. Potent clubs, in different ways. Penn was an offensive powerhouse with inner-city leapers and helter-skelter shooters, Princeton a typical Pete Carril team, patient, disciplined, slow, torturous. Like going from a battle against panthers and cheetahs to one against a boa constrictor; choose your poison. What to do? Could we beat either?... *Sure you could, if you thought you could; sure you could, if you played the odds and had the right strategy.*

By the time I left at 10:30 p.m., redeyed and pessimistic, I had a great urge "to live," but figured it was a bit late for Claire at that hour. So I contented myself with walking about in the fresh snow, beneath the bluish luminescence of the campus streetlamps. Promenading at that time of night the place was a child's toy village, with the colonial buildings and Georgian-style frats and dorms topped in white, and the stockingcapped students strolling, snowballing, cross-country skiing. The college at night was framed, serene and textured, a Nurlan watercolor of placid beauty. I felt uneasy. Was it because I felt a connection now to these grounds, these buildings?... As I perambulated it suddenly hit me what was wrong, what had been wrong with the practice today.

Compelled, I walked to the library and, in the '02 room, located Dennis and Nurlan and, downstairs, in the computer room, Eddie and Avram. I told them to gather up the other boys and we'd meet in the gymnasium, in 15 minutes. They looked at me dumbfounded. "You know what time it is, Coach?" "Yeah, Denny, I know. Let's get it on, okay? Pronto."

While raccoons prowled and citizens slept we were in the gymnasium and I was lecturing the boys about what I had discovered in the video reruns, and what I needed from them. Against Princeton we'd have to guard against the backdoor play, used repeatedly for easy layups. "Offensive boards, get on them. And on defense, intercept their flow. Remember, they'll try to work that 45-second clock all the way down. Got it?" They yawned. "And when their forward number 21 or center gets the ball, especially in the corners, double-team 'em, right?" Helpless, they nodded. "Now, for Penn, defensive boxing out is a must. And I've designed an all-court zone trap, to be used for two minutes at a time, since their passing is suspect. You'll get your printouts by Wednesday afternoon, okay? Any questions?"

At first a silence, then an open sign or two, and finally Nurlan murmured, "Uh, can we go now, suh?"

I smiled and took two steps closer to them. "Now we hit the floor, Little Green. In your workout sweats, let's go!"

"Are you kidding, Coach?"

"We got classes tomorrow morning, Mista B."

"C'mon, let's hit it. You can sleep it off tomorrow afternoon."

"If we make it through till then," Konepski bemoaned.

"Try Fort Benning down in Georgia, sometime. Hustle it!"

They got up, bitched, and draggingly obeyed. So, at 11:20 at night we were running around, practicing the zone trap, jumping alertly to avoid or harass picks and screens, practicing weakside help against the backdoor, boxing out and throwing the outlet passes.

Not bad, I figured, blowing a stop after an hour or more. I opened two bags of bagels with cream cheese, and milk and fruit. Past midnight, by KXE Jazz, we needed some breakfast.

Antoine, who hadn't uttered a word to me all year, came over, looming and sweating, and said, "You are one bad dude, Coach. Bad and mad. You just might have some bro's blood in ya."

Fair enough. I stared up at him, nodded.

They sat on the benches, munching. No one was yawning or moving sleepily now; they ate alert, wide-eyed.

I repeated aloud Antoine's words, and added, "Unless we're a little 'mad' for this weekend, gents, we don't have a chance. Mad as in crazy, narrow, focused, determined, obsessed. All of us. It's our only chance. Eat, sleep, dream, plan: the slowdown game at Jadwin, the helter-skelter show at the Palestra. Believe me, that's why we're here at midnight."

"Coach," laughed Nurlan, "we're believin', rest 'sured."

"Yeah, you're comin' through," waved Roberto, "loud and clear."

Others grinned at the jackanapes: me.

"We miss only a midnight story, yes?" wondered Avram, animated, drawing an impatient look from some of the others.

Not Dennis. "Why not? Anything in your bag of reads?"

I smiled wryly at the wiseguys but, provoked, searched my tote bag and found a few books. "Well, gentlemen, since this weekend is a kind of voyage of self-discovery for you, here's a tale about an Old World voyager-discoverer. The date is December, 1681."

One leg up on a chair, I began reading. "'The season was far advanced. On the bare limbs of the forest hung a few withered remnants of its gay autumnal livery; and the smoke crept upward through the sullen November air from the squalid wigwams of La Salle's Abenaki and Mohegan allies. These, his new friends, were savages whose midnight yells had startled the border hamlets of New England; who had danced around Puritan scalps, and whom Puritan imagination painted as incarnate fiends.'"

"—Whoa, who wrote all this?" asked Jack.

"The writer is Francis Parkman, a peculiar Brahmin from Boston. Anyone hear of him? Two? Good. Francis was my favorite historian, in part because he was an insider-outsider— a man who fought against himself, and, in certain respects, against his class, despite what DeVoto says—and a writer with an eye for the tragic." I eyed the boys, working them. "This privileged and sickly Yankee was attracted to protagonists who, somewhat like himself, were destined to create their own destruction—little Ahabs, you could say. Maybe that's why Melville appreciated F.P. and wrote a laudatory review of *The Oregon Trail*. So listen up, lads, here's Parkman's account of La Salle, the great French explorer. And pay attention to the prose style because Francis writes literature, not mere history.

"'La Salle chose eighteen of them, whom he added to the twenty-three Frenchmen who remained with him, some of the rest having deserted and others lagged behind. The Indians insisted on taking their squaws with them. These were ten in number, besides three children; and thus the expedition included fifty-four persons, of whom some were useless, and others a burden.

"'On the 21st of December, Tonty and Membre set out from Fort Miami with some of the party in six canoes, and crossed to the little river Chicago. La Salle, with the rest of the men, joined them a few days later. It was the dead of winter, and the streams were frozen. They made sledges, placed on them canoes, the baggage, and a disabled Frenchman;

crossed from the Chicago to the northern branch of the Illinois, and filed in a long procession down its frozen course. They reached the site of the great Illinois village, found it tenantless, and continued their journey, still dragging their canoes, till at length they reached open water below Lake Peoria.

"'La Salle had abandoned for a time his original plan of building a vessel for the navigation of the Mississippi. Bitter experience had taught him the difficulty of the attempt, and he resolved to trust to his canoes alone. They embarked again, floating prosperously down between the leafless forests that flanked the tranquil river; till, on the sixth of February, they issued upon the majestic bosom of the Mississippi. Here, for the first time, their progress was stopped; for the river was full of floating ice. La Salle's Indians, too, had lagged behind; but within a week all had arrived, the navigation was once more free, and they resumed their course. Towards evening they saw on their right the mouth of a great river; and the clear current was invaded by the headlong torrent of the Missouri, opaque with mud. They built their camp-fires in the neighboring forest, and at daylight, embarking anew on the dark and mighty stream, drifted sweetly down towards unknown destinies. They passed a deserted town of the Tamaroas; saw, three days after, the mouth of the Ohio, and, gliding by the wastes of bordering swamp, landed on the 24th of February near the Third Chicksaw Bluffs.'"

I paused and looked up, wondering how much to read. They were all watching me, waiting. I skipped ahead.

"'Again they embarked; and with every stage of their adventurous progress the mystery of this vast New World was more and more unveiled. More and more they entered the realms of spring. The hazy sunlight, the warm and drowsy air, the tender foliage, the opening flowers, betokened the reviving life of Nature. For several days more they followed the writhings of the great river on its tortuous course through wastes of swamp and canebrake, till on the thirteenth of March they found themselves wrapped in a thick fog. Neither shore was visible; but they heard on the right the booming of an Indian drum and the shrill outcries of the war-dance. La Salle at once crossed to the opposite ridge, where, in less than an hour, his men threw up a rude fort of felled trees. Meanwhile the fog cleared; and from the farther bank the astonished Indians saw the strange visitors at their work. Some of the French advanced to the edge of the water, and beckoned them to come over. Several of them approached, in a wooden canoe, to within the distance of a gun shot. La Salle displayed the calumet and sent a Frenchman to meet them. He was well-received; and the friendly mood of the Indians being now apparent, the whole party crossed the river.

"'On landing, they found themselves at a town of the Kappa band of the Arkansas, a people dwelling near the mouth of the river which bears their name. "The whole village," writes Membré to his superior—'"

"Hey, who's talkin now, who's this Membré dude?"

I nodded. "He was a member of the actual expedition, and kept his own journal, one of the original sources for Parkman's history. Understood? Now, 'The whole village came down to the shore to meet us, except the women, who had run off. I cannot tell you the civility and kindness we received from these barbarians—'"

"Boo!"

"'...who brought us poles to make huts, supplied us with firewood during the three days we were among them, and took turns in feasting us. But, my Reverend Father, this gives no idea of the good qualities of these savages, who are gay, civil, and free-hearted. The young men, though the most alert and spirited we had seen, are nevertheless so modest that not one of them would take the liberty to enter our hut, but all stood quietly at the door. They are so well-formed that we were in admiration of their beauty. We did not lose the value of a pin while we were among them.'"

Did they take the point? The Chief and Jarrod were both grinning.

"'Various were the dances and ceremonies with which they

153

entertained the strangers who, on their part, responded with a solemnity which their hosts would have liked less if they had understood it better. La Salle and Tonty, at the head of their followers, marched to the open area in the midst of the village. Here, to the admiration of the gazing crowd of warriors, women and children, a cross was raised bearing the arms of France.'"

"When there's a cross raised," remarked Dennis, "can Hell be far behind?"

"'Membré, in canonicals, sang a hymn; the men shouted *Vive le roi!*; and La Salle, in the King's name, took formal possession of the country. The Friar, not, he flatters himself, without success, labored to expound by signs the mysteries of the Faith; while La Salle, by methods equally satisfactory, drew from the chief an acknowledgement of fealty to Louis XIV.'"

By now *I* was getting pretty tired, so I said I was skipping a bit and, though their faces showed disappointment, leaped over several paragraphs.

"'And now they neared their journey's end. On the sixth of April the river divided itself into three broad channels. La Salle followed that of the West, and Dautray that of the East; while Tonty took the middle passage. As he drifted down the turbid current, between the low and marshy shores, the brackish water changed to brine, and the breeze grew fresh with the salt breath of the sea. Then the broad bosom of the great Gulf opened on his sight—'"

"He like them bosoms, don't he?"

"'—tossing its restless billows, limitless, voiceless, lonely as when born of chaos, without a sail, without a sign of life.

"'La Salle, in a canoe, coasted the marshy borders of the sea; and then the reunited parties assembled on a spot of dry ground, a short distance above the mouth of the river. Here a column was made ready, bearing the arms of France, and inscribed with the words, "LOUIS LE GRAND, ROY DE FRANCE ET DE NAVARRE, REGNE; LE NEUVIEME AVRIL, 1682."

"'The Frenchmen were mustered under arms; and while the New England Indians and their squaws looked on in wondering silence, they chanted the Te Deum, the Exaudiat, and the Domine salvum fac Regem. Then, amid volleys of musketry and shouts of *Vive le roi!* La Salle planted the column in its place, and standing near it, proclaimed in a loud voice, "In the name of the most high, mighty, invincible, and victorious Prince, Louis the Great, by the grace of God, King of France and of Navarre, Fourteenth of that name, I, this ninth day of April, one thousand six-hundred and eighty-two, in virtue of the commission of his Majesty, which I hold in my hand, and which may be seen by all whom it may concern, have taken, and do now take, in the name of his Majesty, and of his successors to the crown, possession of this country of Louisiana, the seas, harbors, ports, bays, adjacent straights and all the nations, peoples, provinces, cities, towns, villages, mines, minerals, fisheries, streams and rivers, within the extent of the said Louisiana, from the mouth of the great river S. Louis, otherwise called the Ohio... as also along the river Colbert, or Mississippi, and the rivers which discharge themselves thereinto, from its source beyond the country of the Nadouessious... as far as its mouth at the sea, or Gulf of Mexico, and also to the mouth of the River of Palms—'"

"Hey, just how much is La Salle getting after all?"

I skipped a few more protocols. "'Shouts of *Vive le roi!* and volleys of musketry responded to his words. Then a cross was planted beside the column, and a leaden plate buried near it bearing the arms of France, with a Latin inscription, *Ludovicus Magnus regnat.*

"'The weatherbeaten voyagers joined their voices in the grand hymn of the *Vexilla Regis: "The banners of Heaven's King advance,/The mystery of the Cross shines forth,"* and renewed shouts of *Vive le roi!* closed the ceremony.

"'On that day, the realm of France received on parchment a stupendous accession. The fertile plains of Texas; the vast basin of the Mississippi, from its frozen norther springs to the sultry borders of the Gulf; from the woody ridges of the

Alleghenies to the bare peaks of the Rocky Mountains,—a region of savannas and forests, sun-cracked deserts, and grassy prairies, watered by a thousand rivers, ranged by a thousand warlike tribes, passed beneath the scepter of the Sultan of Versailles; and all by virtue of a feeble human voice, inaudible at half a mile.'"

"That motha La Salle got all a that for his King Louis?"

"Just by *declaring* it so?"

"That was all Louisiana?"

"And why the hell did they sell it all back to us later on, and so cheap, huh?"

"Hey Coach, how's this Parkman know all this stuff, like that someone talks in a loud voice?"

By this time I was exhausted, even if they were babbling, and I began gathering my things, telling the boys to call it a night, it was getting late.

"*Getting* late?" Vargas laughed.

As I left the gym Mr. Stallings was standing at the exit beaming, holding his bucket and broom. "You sure work those boys, suh, and yoself. Duty's nevah done when you be the skippa, huh?"

During the next few days I worked hard preparing the kids as a team and also individually. I hoped they played decently down south and won one at least. Meanwhile word had gotten out about the midnight practice and I heard remarks like,

"Who does he think he's coaching, UNLV, Kentucky?"

"These are Conway students, not his personal property."

"Coach seems to have something of an Ahab complex, and he's dragging his boys into it."

But I had little time to consider those errant pricks; my thoughts were elsewhere. Could we get decent execution, a few key breaks, a high level of play? Maybe even some underdog calls by the refs?

By Thursday night I found myself on a tightrope, nervous and high, and this time I decided "to live" and called Claire early and said I might drop by. And at 9 p.m., upon arriving, I felt I had done the right thing upon seeing her, at home and cozy, in her living room. Potted ferns adorned the place, Joan Armitrage serenaded it, herbal tea and jasmine exuded fragrance. And Claire, my Julie Andrews, looked pretty desirable in hugging tweed skirt and white blouse and cardigan; a plain-looker who emitted a sensual aroma.

I asked for a little scotch to mingle with—and concretize—my Celestial Seasonings (peppermint), and heard about her job with the roughed-up adolescents. The usual native stuff—rural incest on a high level, the teenage runaway prostitutes and druggies who became the state's wards (N.H. couldn't care less), child abuse. And as we moved into the realm of her own life, and her last painful divorce, I realized I had a delicate problem here. Claire Clarkson was looking for longterm caring, tenderness, closeness, a romance of the heart. While I, I knew, was gripped by a very different state of mind, and emotions.

I had been wrong with Dennis, I thought, sipping scotch and observing the sensuality of the bones and lips. Not moral lapses— emotional messes had been my bag. My history with women had been the usual bumpy series of emotional mishaps, you might say, where accidents of the flesh were as common as what was called real relationships. So maybe a green sash was not the right color or symbol for the likes of me?

Well, anyway, when the right moment approached for me to make a gesture, put on a move, I did so with some reluctance. After I had kissed her a few times, and felt her body grow insistent (along with mine), I decided to back up, and off. Temporarily at least. Apologizing, pleading fatigue and nerves about the next night's game, I stood up and made my way toward my jacket and the door, feeling like a heel. But maybe heel now was better than cruel bastard a little later. Who knew?

Ruefully she smiled, and managed, "Okay. Play it your way."

I admired her stiff upper lip. "Just for now, okay? See you."

Later, lying in bed and trying to concentrate on the strict Arthurian conventions and chivalric ways of *Green Knight*, I sensed I should have been happier as a medieval gent. Far preferable to have been bound by clearcut rules and definite manners than my own life of freelance freedom and dizzying choosing. You see, I had inherited my parents' spirit of anarchism all right, but had transmitted it into the erotic realm. Become an open taker of all kinds of loose and easy fun, from post-pubescent nymphets of sweet sixteen to well-rounded, seasoned ladies of forty-some. And truthfully, I had fallen for most of them, once I had slipped into their furry nests and tasted of their honeyed havens. After all, can you really tell the difference between the chains of sexual intoxication and that compulsive delusion called love in adult relations?

Alas, the parade of irresistible females had finally wearied me; I was paying more attention to their all-purpose powers than I was to the rest of life—reading, teaching, befriending. In midlife I needed a new wave of experience, I felt, to feel life anew, to receive it freshly. Hence, coaching, anarchism in American letters, and marriage, fathering. It had worked, too, giving me a voltage recharge in my forties. Before the marriage went sour...

Putting an end to my meditation I reached out to shut the light and found the small photo of my parents. Taken in their prime at a reunion of the Sacco-Vanzetti Club in the Poconos. She was a dark, intense, full-boned and sensual-lipped Slavic beauty; he was curly-haired, thickly mustached, Italian comic-vulnerable in looks; a committed pair, a serious couple. The passion and idealism might be read in their resolute look, though not their operatic emotional life. Oh Papa, Mama, does it disappoint you to look at what happened to all that passion, how it turned out now in your son, the coach? You'll both forgive me, won't you? (Son Number One is Serious enough for all of us, right?) You see I still read your dear Prince Kropotkin—whom you traveled to Wellesley to hear and meet—and still listen to your dear neglected giant, Ruffo, out of filial loyalty; but my heart lies elsewhere. In Dr. Naismith's game of peachbaskets, give-and-goes, fast breaks, hardwood floors. And with my own forms of breaking the rules. I know it's a kind of comedown, but, old beloveds, blame it on the New World.

Playing at the infamous Cage of Jadwin, against Carril's Princeton Tigers, was a little like playing veteran rats in a maze of their own construction. Pete Carril, the sly foxy coach, had drilled his middlin'-talented kids in the same repetitions for every year of his twenty plus years as coach, whether they were short or tall, swift or slow, star or gofer. There were maybe 7-8,000 fans in the gym that Bradley built, and no Roman ever enjoyed a gladiator event with more positive glee in the kill than a true Tiger fan. For that genteel soul knew well there was little chance to win in there, and took his sadistic delight in the slow crunch, the inexorable death-embrace. You know, see the opposition squeezed until it was out of patience, out of fight, out of breath, suffocated by the endless monotony of weaves, layups, picks, backdoors. Smothered by layups.

Of course I didn't tell my kids what I really thought, that we'd be lucky to be within 10 at the end. Instead I gave them the usual pap-pep, while R.E.M. and U.B. 40 played lightly for the 999th time on the portable player—whatever happened to the sweet melodies of Duke or Fats?—reminding them of the at-home beating that Princeton had administered, and the fact that we hadn't won a game in this joint in a decade. They looked up at me every now and then with their usual mugs: Nurlan beaming and bouncing his basketball, Dennis mirthful, Lightfoot stoical, Konepski devoted, Vargas anxious, Avram cocky, Jarrod curious. The subs looked on with polite boredom (except Antoine, sullen). As we ran onto the floor I felt like a betrayer of Sacco sending the innocent kids out with some hope into a real Tigers' den.

Carril came over and shook my hand. "Your kids broke out last weekend and looked like they're turning a corner.

Young kids with talent are the most dangerous. I'm worried."

The shrewd faker. "We'll try to make it competitive," I half-apologized on the sideline, "but I want you to know that, along with Smith and Wooden, you've been the best around."

The small roly-poly man took my hand in both of his and smiled. "Now don't go out and ruin all this flattery by beating me." Like a father-in-law who knows what's best.

It began the way they all began in that cage. Princeton hit seven of their first nine shots, half on layups, and two fouls, and caused three turnovers. We hit a jumper and a foul. At 16-3, the crowd rollicking at the fun-kill, I called a time out.

"They've hit seven shots from within the paint," I told the boys on the bench, "and you've taken *one* shot from inside it."

"But we soon start making ours, Mr. Berger," advised Avram.

"Don't worry, Mr. B, we've just got to settle down a bit," urged Eddie. "Get used to the floor and what they like to do."

"Sure, sure."

"Should we heat up the defense, Coach? All-court pressure?"

"Well, Jack, I wanted to save that for later on."

"May not be of much use *later*," he responded.

"Yeah, I see what you mean. Sure, go ahead. Two-one-two trapping zone. Go ahead."

Let them feel good, I figured, removing my tie.

On the first play we got burned for a layup, and on the second, we got lucky when a pass went askew. Avram then canned a 3-pointer and Vargas a tip-in.

Now the boys tightened up the trap, with the sly Chief cheating on the weakside, crouching low beneath the big center and signaling Dennis to risk fronting his man. Why yell at the poor suckers? Let them lose the way they wanted, I figured.

For a minute or two my mind drifted, a cloud of fluffy memory low in the sky of sure losses, with scenes from childhood running alongside the players... Father awkwardly trying to teach me to dribble a soccer ball, absurd in his large woolen overcoat... Mother teaching me geography, having me trace the boot of Italy with stencil paper... 16-year-old Robey whacking a stickball nearly three sewers with a broomstick while I looked on with little-brother pride...

"Hey, that trapping is givin 'em some trouble," Percy gripped my wrist. "You with us, Syd?"

Two minutes to go in the half and we were down by 10. Not bad, I thought, not bad. The boys were sitting there, toweling off. And I had a bright idea, seeing Nurlan breathing hard. "Okay, subs, you're in. Full-court press. Watch the fouling."

"You sure, Sydney?" Roscoe asked, his first game back.

"Yeah, sure. Let the subs run 'em, what the hell."

The scrubs grew redfaced and terrified, I saw. "Four passes before anyone shoots, right? Everyone handles the ball. No backcourt fouls."

Two minutes they had, these frisky underclassmen, and two seniors. Let them get their chance to fuck up. Why not?

Except they didn't. I mean, they didn't knock anyone over, but they did what they were told, they stalked the Princeton starters everywhere in a man-to-man press, and they even made a few shots on sheer freshness (Antoine tipped one in) and luck (Tony hit a jumper off the backboard). Amazing. At the half it was still reasonable, a nine-point deficit, to my surprise.

I walked off, toweling my neck and face, and sensing how nervous I had been, perspiring wildly.

In the locker room I settled for a Hopje sucking candy instead of a scotch, and walked up and back, figuring things out.

I began diagramming on the board, and gave some specific instructions. "Inside guys, you should be climbing all over those milquetoasts. Eat 'em up! come on, get angry. Avram, where the hell are you? For only one shot were you in the right position! And fast break, where hath thou gone?

161

Eddie, Dennis, get that *outlet pass* going right off. Nurlan, what the hell are you grinning that way for?"

"We be fired up right you give us a fairy-tale lesson..."

"Now?"

"We still got time..."

They were nodding their heads, even brazen Dennis. What the hell was going on?

I began feeling odd, sweet, as if I'd been injected with morphine for minor surgery. Were they putting me on? Did they know something I didn't? They gave no signal, only munched, drank, waited.

"All right: how many of you have ever heard of this pair of immigrant radicals from the twenties?"

I proceeded to scribble on the blackboard, across the foul lane, the names of Sacco and Vanzetti. Only Dennis, Eddie and Jarrod had raised their hands.

"Well, they were poor Italians, like my father, see, who came to America for a new life maybe in 1918, and in 1921 or thereabouts were convicted of murdering a paymaster in Dedham, Mass., during a robbery, and some seven years later, executed for the crime. But the evidence at the trial was quite dubious, and the handling of the case and courtroom by the judge extremely irregular and suspect. So, were they convicted because they were the criminals, or because they were radicals, anarchists to be precise, in an age when Americans were hysterical about foreigners and radicalism of every sort? A hysteria that seems to afflict us every few decades or so. And were they also executed because they were little guys in a judicial system that honored, or at least worked best, for the big guys, the rich and wealthy? Those are still key questions for us today. Still, in 1961 there was some evidence found that might suggest that Sacco did own the pistol which killed the guard, and that he *might* have been guilty, while Vanzetti was innocent. But even if that were the case, the trial was an embarrassing example of American justice, and came just after the period of the Palmer Raids, more Red-baiting."

I saw Nurlan and Vargas shaking their heads, bewildered.

"Anti-communism. You understand that, right? The commies are our enemy, that's been the line since the Second World War, when they were our allies...Anyway, the other thing I wanted to tell you about those Italian immigrants was that, while in jail, Vanzetti wrote some of the most moving and powerful letters to his wife and son. That's what I'd like you to read some time, to get the feel of their situation and his surprising literary powers. You see—"

"Coach, halftime's over," Pat Hinsdale called out, signalling.

"So soon? Well... All right guys, stick with it, tough on defense, keep your poise, and... and... 'keep the aspidistra flying!'"

They cheered my non sequitur and ran out of the locker room.

Percy Grimes mused, "You know, Coach, that seems to fire 'em up for some reason."

But as we walked out to the corridor Roscoe Grumman whispered, "You don't really think they were innocent, do you?"

"Who knows," I acceded, "but they were my mother's heroes, you know."

"Your *mother?*"

"An anarchist, Roscoe, true-blue, black and red. Old man too."

When I took my place on the wooden bench my head was still spinning. The caged arena, the crowd's catcalls, the sudden flood of light, the orangey floor and squeaking of sneaks, the smells of popcorn and resin, why it all affected me like returning to land after being out on the wide sea, free and easy and transforming. My senses newly inundated, my sense too was returning. Good, good.

"Okay, boys," I told the team circling me, "stick with it now, tough man-to-man defense, wide bodies on the boards, and play smart. Get Water the ball on the break. Spread the lanes. Make the extra pass. Stay poised, cool. Forget the refs, the crowd. Make the game come to you. Yeah?"

The second half started well enough, a trading of baskets, giving me time to catch my breath, perceive my folly. Christ. I had a moment's recall of marching with Mom in front of Gracie Mansion in the early fifties, carrying a placard on the anniversary of Sacco's execution. At eleven or so I was embarrassed to be marching in that small motley parade of shabby protesters, missing school, and mocked by passersby. "Fifth columnists!" we were called, and I nearly cried, until Mom leaned down and said, "We're the real patriots, Syddie."

"They're picking it up." Percy grabbed my arm. "They're picking it up!"

True enough, they were. Smiling at the white guard jiving him, Nurlan headfaked and dribbled right by him and through two others, gliding above the big forward for a layup and a foul. Jack, anticipating perfectly, stole a weave handoff and Avram drilled a jumper. The Tiger's vulnerable number 21 forward was double-teamed on the sideline and, holding it a second too long, had it knocked free, resulting in a basket by Dennis. Next a Princeton miss was rebounded by Eddie the Red, who outletted the ball and raced down the court to get it back and dream in a reverse layup. Now, from behind, Roberto blocked an easy bank shot and fired the ball downcourt to Chief, who took it on in. The crowd, amazed, grew hushed, and Carril called a time out.

The boys took their seats in front of me. I asked who was winded, and replaced Eddie with Jarrod, and Vargas with Antoine.

"You guys keep it up," I said. "Same trapping pressure, same fast breaking. Any questions?"

"I bet both of them was innocent," said Nurlan. "How you gonna believe some jive about the gun so long after they tried the guy..."

An odd thing happened out on that Jadwin court in the next crucial five or six minutes. I fully expected Princeton to mount a comeback and put it to us, which they tried, slowing it down, making a few layups. But I, and everyone else in the gym, didn't expect the boys in green to keep their poise, stay in their rhythm, play loosey-goosey as though they were out there practicing nice and easy and getting it right, just right. In fact you might say that they were hitting a stretch of High Flow, except that, against a team like the Tigers, this was not fully possible, because they slowed the game to a walking contest on offense. But we owned the boards now—our Daggoo, Tashtego, Queequeg trio of Dennis, Vargas, Konepski—so Princeton got only one shot and out, while we frequently had two and three; and we had Water, who was fluid, swift, elusive, controlling the ball and the game, dribbling and laughing, not out of mockery but out of fun, sheer pleasure, like a man sailing or skiing. Playmaking was *his element*, far from airless streets and familyless rooms, and as he was driving our whole green machine, you felt your adrenaline rush, and knew that coaching was irrelevant. The machine was purring, hitting on all cylinders, tuned up like a V-8, and the driver was one happy soul, oh yes.

We won by nine, 64-55, an upset of shocking proportions in the Cage. But maybe that was not as *interesting* as that run of five minutes?

Did Carril sense this when he shook my hand and said, "Hard to believe those boys are not ringers, Syd. When they got it going in the second half they looked like they could take on the big boys. Congratulations, you beat me with players *and* with coaching, and I don't usually have to confess that."

Not the right moment to tell him he was wrong about the coaching, all wrong.

At Penn the next night the play continued. Our play, the visionary play. Except that here the Quakers were totally willing to run and gun, not really believing we'd dare to stay with them. The large crowd at the Palestra was, like the Tiger fans, geared for easy prey. Their band banged the drums and blew the horns and noisemakers whenever we had a foul shot, and the coach did his best to work up the refs, so the whole atmosphere bordered on the out-of-control. Of course the

Quaker club itself was, as I knew, mostly a rough-and-tumble gang, a gaggle of gyroscopic leapers from the Philadelphia projects, more geared to the schoolyard game of one-on-one than a team game. This was a significant advantage for us, now. That, plus the fact that they had already beaten us easily, and were as cocky as could be.

My boys were ready. It just took some time to speed up from the slowdown game of the night before at Jadwin. We hit the boards well, cutting down their fast break; our defense was alert, weakside help everywhere, causing disruptions in their flow; our tempers stayed cool, despite some heavy traffic in flying elbows and jive talking. And Avram was hot, hitting six jumpers in a row, three for three-pointers. You know what hot means: the basket looks spacious, the front rim vanishes, the release of the ball is directed by a line of concentration as perfectly focused as a laser beam from hand to hoop. The opposition is mind only, not another player; mental ease and zen deliberation are all.

At halftime we were three points ahead and we hadn't hit our full flow yet by any means. We would, I wagered privately.

Over Gatorade and oranges I made a few simple adjustments: an alternating 2-1-2 and 1-3-1 zone, an additional double-pick play for Avram on the half-court offense.

In my briefcase I found the psychologists' articles on streak shooting, and sat between Avram and Nurlan.

"So the boy's hot, huh?" I remarked.

Avram shrugged, blushed.

"Six jumpers in a row was it?" Nurlan smiled. "Yeah, I'd say the mother's hot."

"Well," I said, "it's probably an illusion. Here, see, 'The Hot Hand in Basketball: On the Misperception of Random Sequences,' and this, 'The "Hot Hand": Statistical Reality or Cognitive Illusion?'"

Avram took the offprints in his hand and began reading. "By another Tversky yet? Some kind of joke?"

"No joke," I replied, "but you know what? It may indeed

be a cognitive illusion, or 'random sequences misunderstood,' but Nurlan, feed him the ball every chance you get, right?"

Nurlan took Avram around. "My man's got it. Jes yah keep shootin, Kiev. Who knows, yah might get thirty or forty points all by yerself, and wouldn't that be a party?"

Avram, uncomfortable in the limelight, shifted awkwardly and said, "Coach, we get our halftime storylesson, yes?"

That "our" caught my attention.

To my surprise, his request was being chorused by the others.

In my totebag I searched amid my paperbacks and notebooks.

"All right, while you're relaxing here, I'll read to you a letter from Bartolomeo Vanzetti to a woman who had written to him sympathetically in May 1927, after seven years of imprisonment. The letter is written in the English that Venzetti learned while in prison, first in evening classes in the Charlestown prison, and then by way of a correspondence course. In three months' time, on August 22, he and Sacco were executed.

"'Dear Friend,' meaning Mrs. Sarah Root Adams,

"'Nick and I are now at Dedham Jail where we will be kept until ten days before execution when we will be taken to the death house of the State Prison in Charlestown. So I have received your letter of May 1 and also read the one which you sent to Nick. Since your letters breathe sincerity, love and earnest good will...' He goes on to say words aren't enough to thank them."

I read ahead, sipping my drink. Then began aloud:

"'I have understood from the beginning that Judge Thayer wanted to kill us because we were hated and feared by the ragged and the golden rabbles so that he will be recompensed by them by being appointed judge of the Massachusetts Supreme Court—this vanity has been the obsession of his live. Yet, for a while, I hoped that I would have won by showing my innocence. But since I had been found guilty at the Plymouth trial'—that was an earlier trial—'I understood that I was lost except if my friends would become physically stronger than my enemies. Were not the first Christians believed to be blood-drinkers? Yes, they were believed so and insulted, tortured—'"

I saw a hand go up, a face in painful doubt, but I shook my head.

"'...insulted, tortured, martyrized by the ragged and golden mobs of their time. Even the so sage Marcus Aurelius feared, hated, insulted, and killed them. Of course the first Christians were outlaws because they were against the laws who legalize slavery; against the powerful Roman Empire oppressing mankind and master of the Courts and laws; they were gods-destroyers but destroyers of false gods. In this was their right, greatness, sanctity; for this they were put to death. What chance of fair deal and acquittal those not only innocent first Christians could have had in being tried by pagans to whom the fact of one being Christian was all the crimes and all the guilts at once and in one. From those times, I could come down through the centuries showing you that the same dealings has been imposed by the golden and the ragged mobs to all those who have discovered, wished, and labored for a little more of truth, justice, freedom, triumph and sublimization of the men, women and of the life—down, down to this very date...'"

"Who are these golden and ragged mobs," asked Eddie, "the people who conform?"

I half-smiled and read on. "'Radicalism is a very general term, applicable to several parties and doctrine each of which differs from the other ones. Both Nick and I are anarchists— the radical of the radical—the black cats, the terrors of many, of all the bigots, exploitators, charlatans, fakers and oppressors. Consequently, we are also the more slandered, misrepresented, misunderstood and persecuted of all. After all we are socialists as the social-democrats, the socialists, the communists, and the I.W.W. are all Socialists. The difference—the fundamental one—between us and all the other is that they are authoritarian while we're libertarian; they believe in a State or Government of their own; we believe in no State or Government.'"

I glanced up to see if I still had them. All eyes and ears.

"'I have been born of a Catholic family and believed in Roman Church until my 18 year. But actually, as far as religion goes, I believe in no religion, though I try to learn and practice all that to me seems to be of truth and good in each and all of them. Just for this reason I am for the utmost liberty of conscience, and I made no difference and therefore I neither fear nor hate any sincere believer, be he a Christian, a Jew, a Maomettan, a Buddhist, or what not. My bases, measures and relation from man to man, is as man to man—and nothing else.

"'Now, few words on the statement which you suggested to us to send out because it would help our freedom. We cannot make it because it is a thing against our understanding and conscience... We too have a faith, a dignity, a sincerity. Our faith is cursed, as all the old ones were at their beginning. But we stick to it as long as we honestly believe we are right. Both I and Nick would have followed our old beliefs, practiced the old moral and life sanctioned by laws and churches—we could have grown rich on the poor, have women, horses, wealth, honors, children, all rests, boundnesses and pleasures and joys of life. We have renounced voluntarily to almost all of even the most honest joys of life when we were at our twenties. Lately we have sacrificed all to our faith. And now we are old, sick, crushed, near death; should we now after having endured these three deaths and lost all, should we now quack, recant, renegate, be vile for the love of our pitiable carcasses? Never, never, never, dear friend Adams. We are ready to suffer as much as we have suffered, to die, but be men to the last. On the contrary, if I am shown to be wrong—then I would change. This is the only thing which would change me.

"'Well, this is almost all for now.'"

"Nope," intruded Duddy, "this is all. Second half time, Syd, we better go." Delicately he slipped the book from my hand and in the same manner guided me out from the locker room and onto the floor. As though the adjustment from the world of text to the reality of gym was akin to the shifting of a patient from his hospital bed to the visitor's room.

The boys came out for the second half fresh and focused, and picked up from where they had left off—the defense smart, the boards swept, and Avram still scoring (thanks to Nurlan). And sure enough, by the seven minute mark they hit their stride, that river of flow. Only this evening, unlike the Princeton game, they were given the opportunity to move it steadily to a higher level. Penn was playing its standard wideopen game, and before they knew what had hit them, they were down fourteen. At their Palestra. Effortlessly, and almost imperceptibly, like an optical illusion, the gang of Green played the higher game. The passes arrived at points where players would be, not were; the player motion was constant and purposeful without the ball; the shots were relaxed and just, the percentages high; the players were parts of a whole, not isolated. At the center of all this swift motion was Nurlan spinning, whirling, beaming, a dribbling centripetal force for illusion and wonder.

Water drove and passed, Roberto tipped, Avram shot, Dennis screened, Jarrod skied, Jack intercepted, Eddie rebounded; the ball seemed suspended on a rubber band among the five players. Blind passes were on a magnet, the defense was on glancing alert, disrupting and deflecting, the Penn squad could barely get a shot off before it was turning the ball over, and the green jerseys were headed the other way; and for about six or seven minutes the machine was running with refined calibration, the normal level of basketball eclipsed by this newfound ascendance. Something like an Oldsmobile 88 transforming itself into a Boeing 727, as in a 60-second beer commercial fantasy, and taking off. You sensed it was higher stuff, beyond game-gravity, a zone of tranquility set smack in the midst of speeding latitudes. The partisan fans quieted suddenly, hushed to watch, and, when a second timeout was called, they did something most unusual: they stood and began to applaud the visitor's special performance. The applause gathered steadily, too. The score hardly mattered, the competition was nearly forgotten, the level of the Conway game was the thing. A level the fan didn't see, or the players reach, often.

And as the boys came toward me I thought: this is High Flow in the great college tradition. For six or seven long basketball minutes we were up there with 1950s USF and CCNY, 1960s UCLA, 1970s Ohio State and North Carolina. I sat the boys down, told them to take it easy and sent the subs in, my heart still aflutter with transcendent beauty. The ordinary details of the gym spun about me, the smells of sweat and squeaking of sneakers, the PA announcement and the crowd buzzing. And for once I was grateful for the little whirring camera eyes shooting around the court, and for the video recorder memory box awaiting me, knowing the game replayed next week would be like viewing a scene from Fellini or Kurosawa for the second or third time. Six minutes' worth of the pure thing imprinted on the celluloid, a kind of immortal witness to the beauties of the game, the essential truths of play.

Feeling blessed I walked along my bench and touched each one of the boys.

9 WINNING GAMES, LOSING GROUND

Winning, like losing, becomes a habit, a way of life, a state of mind. In life, in the game. Illusion or not, an outcome generates a momentum of its own. From having been on the losing side for a long time, I knew that lesson well. After a few repeats with winning, the Mind gets the point, and the Will enters into the equation (and game), infiltrates external circumstances and makes its own separate rendezvous with victory.

We kept winning. The kids believed they could, and they did; in some sense it was as improbable as that. In another sense, of course, that was only half the struggle. The remaining half was refining physical skill, practice effort, team talent (and team comfort), shots falling. Without the ball swishing through the nets at crucial moments, especially in the endgame, you got nowhere. Plus some progressive education; improve the parts with each game—like improving the speed with which you could do puzzle-solving—and intensify the clarity of the focus without distraction. A focus on the innermost part of the game, its passing soul.

We won from early February on, including the balancing pair at home on the March 2-3 weekend against Yale and Brown. Nurlan was king of the court, magical, wise and just, delighting in passing off for baskets and setting up teammates; and judging shrewdly when it was appropriate to drive all the way in or stop and pop (the little jumper). Nothing could erase the child's grin on his face when he got the ball for the break, like getting his ice-cream cone by our foul circle, and heading upcourt, two on one, one on one, or one on two. Dribbling with those long pianist's fingers and gliding forward in concert with his streaking pals, he resembled the leader of a flock of Canadian geese, flying in perfect and exquisite formation. He was schoolyard star and *team* playmaker rolled into one, saintly and selfish, a pointguard prince. Interesting—with all the millions of kids playing the hoop game, his combination was rare, produced only once every few years among the sort who can make it over the high school hurdle and into college. ("He's *bad*," was how street kids had praised him, playing subversively with white language and values.)

Indeed in college Water was doing as I thought he might: squeezing by in the regular subjects and in art showing serious talent. My "tinkering" with his admissions application was proving to be what I had expected: an immoral means toward an excellent end. I had helped him get into that advanced studio course and the professor there, Sam Begosian, was truly surprised. "The kid can draw, he can *really* draw, Syd, and he has great color imagination too. I'm impressed. And he picks up things fast. If he wants to take an independent with me next term I'll gladly sign him on." Nice to hear; my hands were getting cleaner and cleaner, I felt. I'd make sure to get "Bugsy" and his son, a fan, a pair of tickets to a big game sometime.

Alongside the flowering of my black prince, the rotating of forwards in the center's position was also raising levels. The absence of a true center and its replacement by my 6' 5"/ 6' 6" mobile units had become a surprise weapon. The other clubs, coming in with their tall pivot player, simply figured the paint was theirs, the boards too. No, no. It wasn't height that gave you the inside; it was instinct, timing, touch, the right body. Roberto by himself was a handful, and tougher in tandem with Eddie; but three bodies meant triple trouble. You just couldn't block three gents like Vargas, Dennis, Eddie, off of their spots at once. Once they got to know how each moved, and what each preferred—Roberto the offensive rebound fake and putback, Eddie the defensive board and outlet, Dennis the body blockout—they became like the three heads of Cerberus at the Gates of Hell, a hard ring to crash. It was like having Rudy LaRusso out there again—the tough star of the last great Conway squad, in the 60s—banging away; only now two LaRussos, plus a Dennis. You see these guys loved the board game, the black and blue banging challenge, the art of the glass. Especially in the baby Ivies, three tough hombres were not merely a handful, they were a security force not to be messed with. (Think of Arkansas in '78, with their 6' 4" leapers, Moncrief and Brewer.)

The game had its parts. If you owned the boards at both ends you controlled the ball off the misses; and if you owned the court length with your playmaker, and through him, the passing lanes, you were going to get a large share of easy buckets: layups, short bank shots, foul line jumpers, tip-ins. All you really needed then was a pure shooter.

Enter the Ukrainian Gunner: Avram the improbable. He had become a scoring machine, his percentage about 55 (nobody on the Celtics shot that), shots taken around 15-20 per game. He learned to move to his positions on the floor like a toy soldier attracted by a magnet. No sooner was he planted than he received the ball, and in a second, it was released. All that he added, in the last month, was a three-point shot. Oh, he'd get trash-talked, get his back elbowed and thigh kneed. No sweat. "Kibbutz league dirtier, much," he explained, lifting himself up. This young man was not in a one-game hot spell, but a month-long streak. I sent a note to the other Tversky, out at Stanford, inviting him to come see his Double and doublecheck his dubious theory. Down the stretch in February my Twersky gave us 24 points a game, while trying to solve a "Positive Rates" problem in probability theory.

Toss into the pot my defensive wizard, Jack Lightfoot,

who would cheat down inside and out, disrupt set patterns, bother the opposition star shooters. Free to roam in my all-court pressure traps and zones, the Chief was a one-man vigilante gang, breaking rules, dodging laws, causing turn-overs. Doing naturally what he had done at Olde Towne High: playing the night guerrilla out on ambush patrol. There was not much about that game—fast hands, sly vision, gambler's instinct—that you could teach him. A vigilante was a vigilante, an ambush an ambush, on any turf.

Then there was Coach, faithful to his boys and theories, rigorous about his drills and repetitions, on the lookout for High Flow but ready for sudden fire alarm, sure of disaster and surprised by victory, calm on the outside but neurotic-overheated internally, especially during tight games. To relax himself, though he blamed the lads, he continued with his half-time lectures on Americans of note. Thus whomever he might be reading, or reading about, in his wayward eclectic way, entered the locker room: Gompers and Paul Robeson, Horace Mann and Jefferson, Crazy Horse, Hofstadter, DuBois and Dreiser. Oh, they were as mixed a bag as the players themselves. And whether read to or lectured or coached the boys responded with goodhumored smiles, questions of interest, second halves of distinction.

So we sailed on through Penn and Princeton, Cornell and Columbia, Yale and Brown, during those last weeks of the Ivy season. In a way, as I've signalled, *I* had little to do with our success, though I was starting to gain some attention. Dick Porter came in one morning and Redford-smiled. "Unless you've got these kids on steroids, Syd, you may very well be Coach of the Year. You're doing a helluva job, pal." A note arrived through campus mail from the sports-minded Provost saying, "Bravo, Mr. Berger, bravo! I saw the Princeton game and it was a performance to remember. Congratulations, and hope to go with you to the NCAA's." The benedictions of an institution. Even old adversary Wim Haarhus caught up with me at the mailboxes in History, where I checked in every few weeks. "Well, Mowgli, my boy, you're making a bit of a hit down in the jungles, I notice." Lightly he slapped my face, just lightly enough to keep me from swinging. "You devil, you may turn out to be a Head Coach after all—and then you can stop playing the history teacher." He wore the thinnest smile on his pallid face, like some subhuman creature from comic-book childhood. "You see, we all surprise each other in the long run, don't we? *If* we're worth anything." Whatever he was babbling about, I didn't bother to ask.

I was coerced into a few interviews for the college newspaper and the Conway alumni magazine, and tried my best to say as little as possible, drawing down the curtain of platitudes—crediting the players and their progress as a team, the maturing of young talent and the settling into the season—on the real truth. Which was: *I didn't really know how or why Conway was winning.* It was a mystery, more Poe than Hammett, one beyond my strategy or understanding, but of course I couldn't say that. Current platitudes were better, were indeed in demand, for the news.

As we won and my head bobbed up into the balmy air of congratulation, I also began to develop a curious emotion: a surge of native-feeling. As we won, the team and I began to be the news of the college, *the* news from the north country during the long New England winter. With phone calls and letters suddenly offering me invitations to talk, and the *Boston Globe* and *Herald* taking notice, the monthly culture wheel was turning in my direction, and even working its visible charms upon me, inducing surprising pulls of chauvinism, patriotism. Our dear beloved country (and college) adored a winner, for somehow it reflected upon itself, making itself more beloved, I saw, in the eyes of the one on top. Was the whole world like that, putting a higher premium on success than on self-worth, integrity, serious achievement?

The canvas-covered, awning-striped wagons of the U.S.A., success, power and adulation, were beginning to circle around Sydney Berger, and the noise and rattling were making him nervous.

Meanwhile, Dennis Healey heard the big news in January: the ironic Medievalist was a Rhodes Scholar. A month later we had our little celebration, during our winning streak. I offered the team its choice of three restaurants, and they chose the Chinese Dragon Royale over in West Lebanon, where they put four tables together in their banquet room. Each kid picked a different dish, after the opening soups and fried dumplings. Dennis ordered Peking Duck, Antoine the Hunan lamb with hoisin sauce, Nurlan the General Tso's chicken ("Did they really cook that back in the 'Ching Dynasty,' man? How dya know that?"). Eddie opted for the spicy crispy fish, Jack the Prawn Amazing (large whole shrimp, stir-fried with a variety of Chinese vegetables), and Roberto, Neptune's Blessing from Shanghai ("Yah gotta go with the names, huh?"). Over Chinese beers and Cokes the boys toasted and roasted the scholarship boy.

"To the man in the center, may you acquire an English accent," advised Jarrod, "and Savile Row tailor!"

"Don't get caught coppin' any ol' manuscripts from that Bodleian, baby," warned Roberto. "Look bad for the boys."

Playing the orator, Nurlan read solemnly from a slip of paper: " *'Quae nocent docent,'* man." Cicero via Brownsville.

The merry band of homeworkers clapped and whistled; Dennis reddened.

"Know what it means? Betta look it up in her OED, Menace, or you'll look kinda grey up here." Water tapped his temple.

"If you should spend three days with your host's wife," Jack proclaimed, "make sure you bring along protection!"

"Yeah, and wear your Conway sweats in the gym," added Eddie, "it'll remind you of scrimmaging back at Alumni and make you homesick for my elbows and knees!"

"To Sir Dennis!" the coach saluted him, "may he return to the Round Table of the Big Green in one native piece."

So it went round and round in spicy festivity, a grand comradely Sunday matinee high.

I was still high the next day, walking back with Duddy to my office in preparation for late afternoon practice, when I noticed a white Celica passing me by slowly, with Kansas license plates. A déjà vu sensation passed over me and I realized that I had seen that car earlier in the week. What the hell was up? I watched it drift down Wheelock, up ahead, and I wondered if I were drifting toward paranoia?... But later on, after a ninety-minute workout I saw the short shark parked right across from the gym and knew that Toyota meant trouble. Dope trouble? As I went to collect my things from the office, a stranger was waiting there.

Tall, slender, fiftyish, he flashed his wallet toward me, and asked if he might see me for a few minutes.

I invited him inside and asked who he was.

"Oh, you didn't read the card? Sorry. Gaines, Kenneth Gaines, Jr. I'm from the NCAA, Coach, and we're doing a little investigating of your program here." His inflection was Midwestern flat.

I didn't invite him to sit. "What do you mean, 'a little?'"

He smiled pleasurelessly. He had a long head topped by a crewcut and wore a plaid sports jacket. "A preliminary inquiry to see if a full-scale one is in order. We've heard of some... irregularities, and simply want to check them out or dismiss them."

I nodded and glanced at my watch. "Well, go to it, Kenneth. Should I have the college counsel in on this by the way?"

"Oh, I don't think there's any need for that just yet. This is merely informal right now."

I nodded again. Call my own lawyer immediately? If I brought in the college counsel, whose side would he be on, the company's or mine?

"Do you mind if I ask a few questions, actually?"

"Not at all. But just now, I have a dinner date."

"Oh." He looked disappointed. "When?"

"How about Thursday morning at 10:00?"

"But that's nearly 72 hours away."

"Is it? Well, that's not too long. Now, Mr. Gaines, if you'll excuse me, I must run. Where in Kansas you from?"

"Mission. Just outside Kansas City. Do you know it?"

"I know downtown KC at 5:00 p.m. when the prettiest women in the country get out from work. Or at 9:30 when I can hear the best jazz."

He stared at me, not knowing how to take these remarks.

"I better run."

"Look, I'll leave you my card. I'm staying at the Inn in case you could get free earlier than Thursday. I'd appreciate that."

At home I doubled up on tasks of cleaning, organizing. Cleared up the mess of sweaters and trousers that had accumulated on the bedside chair, folding them or making a pile for the cleaners. Pulled about the orange Mighty Mac, vacuuming the little bobs of dust at the edges and corners of the two bedrooms, where the cleaning person never ventured. Shined up the silver faucets and basins with Comet and moved into 15 minutes of trimming my beard with an ancient pair of Dubl-Duck scissors. Acts of tiny pride which calmed me when I was burdened with a problem and tried to think it through, whether it was Parkman's view of the French or NCAA insidiousness. When I was a high-strung 13-year-old mother had placed me in the Steiner School, where they took away my violin and put me on knitting. A partial success. I still wound up shaking my feet when sitting, or fussing with my lips or hair. Tidying up, beard trimming, inheritances from father, always worked better.

"'Irregularities,' that wonderful catchall term. Oh, I'd have loved to hear Aquinas or Maimonides argue with those Minds from Mission. Assuredly they'd have little chance against the NCAA Judges and Hypocrites. Sure, there had been irregularities, I lived and breathed that way. Who didn't who had to live by official rules these days, and wished to remain interesting? If it came to sports irregularities, just take half of the top ten teams in the country, in any competitive sport, and you'd find hazardous waste dumps that were cleaner. Could they sue me for being an irregular American, like the old Hoover bullyboys? Well, if not sue me, break me? Sure.

The thing about living alone in middle age is that you're not really alone. You're in the company of your barnacle habits and eccentricities. At 51 is there better company? More trusted or pleasing company? You've earned these ways. At some high cost to your personality you've paid for your odd paths of living—what mug for coffee; what chair, what hour to read the newspaper; what radio disc-jockey fantasies; the particular item, such as shoes, for which you have an unusual affinity. Were you going to go and spoil that perfect cocoon of the self, that diaphanous bubble of harmless narcissism, by bringing an outsider-intruder onto the scene?

I sat at the kitchen table and, overlooking the frozen Connecticut, made a short list of professional indiscretions. Helping Nurlan with the rehab, and having him and Vargas rewrite an essay or two; buying a few pair of dungarees and winter parkas as Christmas presents for the poorest lads; well, and outfitting them for college with my own dough; putting some pressure on the Admissions officers; making some recruiting promises (about playing time) that perhaps were best left out; paying for a few visits by parents to see their sons play; and so on. No cardinal sins, just venial ones, at best. But enough to hang me with, probably. So, fight the executioners or set my head in the noose and plead for mercy? Are you kidding? Mercy from that lynch mob of self-interested sheriffs, the latest version of Salem witch-hunters? As for mercy from Conway...

Seeing the time I dressed quickly, throwing on a sweater under my jacket, and rushed off to my dinner, at Claire's place. For some reason Parkman's description of La Salle's assassination floated by and I jotted a note about finding it.

"Where've you been all these weeks?" she asked finally, over fresh flounder and lemon. "I thought we got along rather well, and you were going to call me."

"We did. And I was." I shook my head feebly. "But the truth is, when I'm coaching, I don't have time for living."

"What do you mean?" She wore that Julie A. smile on her

pretty, small-featured face.

"Really, just what I said. Coaching seems to take up all my time, real time. I don't do much else, except see the boy."

"How is he? He was quite charming, the one time I met him."

"Oh, he's doing fine. Growing up, enlarging his powers for mischief."

She smiled and sipped her wine. "You're lucky to have him. I wish I had another."

I nodded, no touching that.

"Seeing other women?" She blushed slightly at her boldness.

"No, not really."

"Just being alone, all this time?"

My turn to smile. "It's not been years, you know. And I've not been in solitary confinement."

"Sounds like you have, actually."

I nibbled lettuce, and wondered, was she right?

"This salad's first-class," I offered. "For some reason I never buy this seaweed. But it tastes pretty good."

"Hmm. By the way, is coaching all that interesting?"

I dabbed at my mouth and considered that. "Probably not, to anyone on the outside. Inside, however, it's a different story. Like most lines of work, I imagine."

"Oh?"

"Well, I mean it is interesting. And it isn't. But it's... what I do. What I know. My passion."

"*Really*. What do you mean by that?"

"You're right, I should have said 'illness.' It's more like a chronic illness. Something that hits you, that knocks you out regularly, on schedule, something you're stuck with. History for example is a passion, but I don't *need* to teach it." I shook my head. "Coaching is in my blood. As to whether it's 'interesting' to an outsider—is multiple sclerosis of any interest to anyone who doesn't have it, or isn't studying it? Doubtful. But there it is."

She shook her head and smiled. "I see now that you weren't

kidding when you said you had little time for living. That *is* too bad."

"Yes, it is. But the season stops at a certain point. And soon, too—then I can come up for air and live again."

"Like spring, hey? Aren't you lucky? What are your friends supposed to do while you're hibernating for six months—sleep too?"

I laughed. "No. Not at all. They're on their own, doing what they regularly do—which is, I suppose, sleepwalking most of the time, and calling it entertainment."

"My, you're cynical, aren't you?"

"Yeah, but don't take it too seriously." I ran my hand along her smooth cheek. "I'm just cynical for half the year."

After dinner I gave up thoughts of returning to the office for video-viewing and stayed on for Claire-viewing. Her French designer jeans, with thin white stripes down the legs, gave superior definition to her well-shaped figure.

"If you like holding me so much," she asked, pausing during a long serious kiss, "how come you don't do it more often?"

"You have a point," I replied, "but who told you I liked holding you that much?" and slipped back to the kissing ardor.

Presently, post diaphragm-placement, we were hard at erotic work on the living room couch, and I learned soon enough how out of synch for such play my body had become from temporary disuse. Meaning, I had lost my powers of firm control, and came much too soon.

"Sorry," I offered, "out of practice."

She urged me to continue with my hand, and I did until she reached her pleasure, too.

"That was sweet," she said, making me feel better.

In her arms my mind drifted through hazy obligations and obdurate faces, from the game on Saturday night to the NCAA spy waiting at the Inn. I felt suddenly edgy, restless. I needed a Schipa aria or a John McCormack lullaby from Papa.

"What's wrong?"

"I better get going."

"You're always going," she noted, and I couldn't read her tone.

I continued dressing and soon was saying goodnight at the door.

"See you in two months?" she mused. Quizzically? A wan daisy in white nightwrap.

I went with the banter, avoiding a serious turn.

"Spring—as soon as I stretch and yawn."

And it would be spring, though I didn't know it then.

Kenneth Gaines was brighteyed and bushytailed on Thursday morning when we met for coffee at the Ivy Grill. The pitch clearly was to be cordial, as he shook my hand and smiled his best choirboy smile. Besides cordiality, however, there lay on the table a long trim journalist's notebook and a Cross gold pencil.

Did he know that a tape recorder would have kept me from taking without a lawyer? Sure.

"You're certainly lucky to be coaching here, Mr. Berger." Flat, nasal, Indiana speech. "I mean, this is a delightful and classy campus. The surrounding hills, the lovely river, the wonderful sense of tradition."

"I have an hour, Kenneth. What is it you'd like to ask?"

"Huh? Well, Coach, there are certain irregularities, as I mentioned the other day, and perhaps they can be gotten rid of easily. Or... perhaps not." He half-smiled... half-embarrassed?

I stirred my coffee and waited, searching for his furtive grey eyes.

"Well, perhaps I should get right into specifics, Coach. Did you give any of your boys cash of any sort at any time?"

Did bus-ticket loans count, I wondered? An extra few twenties for a sports bag, good sneaks? "No."

"Did you ever promise financial compensation, or know about any, over and beyond the Conway scholarship-need package, as part of a college recruitment pitch?"

Easy. "No."

He made a check with his gold pencil, a flick of questionable power. "Gifts of any sort? Accepted by you or given by you?"

The waiter approached with more coffee and I nodded, grateful for the hot refill and the few extra seconds. Was a planned gift the same as a spontaneous one, in dictionary English? My summer-camp outfit was a loan of sorts. "No."

"Did you exert pressure of any sort on professors to alter grades or change class marks for your student-athletes?

"No." *Professor Breitman, your view please?*

"During high school recruitment, did you contact sophomores and juniors, especially once you became the official Head Coach?"

I shook my head.

"Have you violated, knowingly or perhaps unknowingly, any code or regulation of the NCAA College Rules for Basketball as set forth in the Rules Book for 1989-90?"

I was happy now that I had never read through all those restrictive clauses. "Well, Ken, if it's been done unknowingly, it's unknowing."

"Something you *may* know about *now?*"

I smiled, thinking how rich and varied were the rivers of sin and wrongdoing, and the many tributaries of guilt. "No."

He looked up at me like a priest magnanimously giving his parishioner one last chance at confession. "Anything, Coach, you'd like to add? Off the record or on?"

At last I located his small eyes, enlarging with pleasure in the little inquisition. "Your organization is not by any chance trying to deflect attention from embarrassing sharks like UNLV by coming after little fish like Conway and me?"

"That doesn't merit an answer, Coach."

I glanced at my wristwatch.

"You realize," he said, shifting over into the prosecutor, "that if any of these statements made by you are contradicted by the actual evidence, we will initiate a full-scale investigation."

"That sounds like some sort of harassment threat, Mr. Gaines. Do you enjoy threatening people?"

His look lightened and he shook his flattop head. "No, not particularly. But I think you should know the possible consequences."

"As well as my rights, yes?"

"Huh? I don't get you."

"Rights. Citizens' rights. Bill of Rights rights. Coach's rights." I stood up. "Have to get to work now, Ken. Be seeing you."

He stood up, slightly taken aback, and put out his hand. "Thanks for your time, Coach. If we need you we'll—"

I waved and turned at the same moment, and marched out of the darkened room. My heart felt congested, my head swirled, and I needed natural light and fresh air badly.

On Wheelock Street the cold air slapped at me and I walked on, passing the Hop, not really knowing if I had lied or simply not told the whole or fine truth. Wasn't a fact part of a context, a sentence a piece of a paragraph, an incident part of a whole story? Was the aid I gave to Nurlan a terrible wrong, for example, when placed within the entire moral context and ultimate benevolent consequence? Who was capable of judging that, the NCAA neanderthals or a Holmes, a Spinoza?

"Coach Berger. Hey, Coach!"

Gaines had run up behind me and stood there out of breath, grinning. He handed over my blue canvas briefcase. "I'm not so bad after all, am I?" Like a cuckoo clock asking not to be blamed for popping out foolishly every hour.

"By the way, Ken, how long does it take for you to... clear this up, give us a clean bill of health?"

"Yes," he acknowledged, "we do tend to move slowly, don't we? Well, we're trying our best, but we are very short-handed, you know."

Good, I thought, breathing easier. Good. "Thanks for the case."

A week later, two days before our playoff game against

Princeton for the Ivy championship, another unsettling event occurred.

I got a call from Cambridge, from that straight-shooting social worker I had met several months before, Julia O'Connor.

"You told me to let you know, Coach, if there's been a troubling development in the Vargas domestic situation. Well, it's happened, as we feared. He got on the sauce and beat her up pretty badly this time, including a three-inch gash with a bread knife. Lily Vargas is in Cambridge City Hospital, in serious condition. Do *you* want to tell the boy?"

I took a deep breath. "Yeah, I guess so. Is she conscious?"

"In and out of a coma. Want me to keep you posted?"

"Would you? And where's the he-man sonofabitch?"

"Back in the clink. Maybe this time it'll be for a few years."

"Julia, you're a gem. I'll hear from you soon, then."

At my desk I looked at the calendar, the clock, the game plan for Monday night's big game. What timing, eh Sydney? The Ivy on the line, and Roberto's stepdad decides to go macho berserk again. Don't be a fool, Syd, tell the boy right off and let him make the decision whether to go down or not... On the other hand, what's the difference of 48 hours if she's in a coma or just out of it, and he can't even communicate with her? Let him play, let him shine maybe, and then inform him. Why not? You won't beat Princeton without that kid, and who knows, you may be doing him a favor in the long run. Get him to the NCAA's and some pro scout just might notice him, and then, why he could buy his mother an escape hatch maybe, a three-bedroom ranch in Medford somewhere...

Deliberating with such casuistry I let the minutes tick away, sliding slowly into the game plan for Princeton. Vargas was a central part of that plan, needless to say.

So Lucky Ruiz stuck a shiv into Lily Vargas's belly, should I help to ensure that he cut into Roberto's life as well, and into my team? Did dentists, doctors, lawyers, associate professors have to live down in the lower depths with the patients and students the way I did? Take upon their backs the daily burden of the Robertos and Nurlans?

Ah, Saint Berger, dost thou deserve a medallion? Or a certificate of official wrongdoing for not informing the boy? Yet....

Princeton fell handily and Vargas was a major factor. We won the Ivy and a celebration was held at the fancy French restaurant on Route 10. All through the meal I glanced over at Roberto, laughing dreamily, and spruced up in his flowery white shirt with the huge collar turned halfway up in back, and I felt like a heel. The kids looked like a bunch of Babar animals out for a day with the Old Lady; rich classy patrons of D'Artagnan's stared and smiled politely, enjoying the spectacle.

The next morning I did my duty and gave Vargas the news. To assuage my guilt I offered to drive him down myself to Cambridge. Big heart, huh? In the car he was quiet and brooding, twisting his neck this way and that in visible pain; I said all the right, consoling things. And kept my vision straight ahead, and on the curving meridian line—and also on the week ahead, and our schedule for the NCAA's. No way was I going to lose my young pal here, my forward, to extended grief in Cambridge town, no way. Though he didn't know it yet, Vargas had about 48 hours to stand vigil over his mother, 48 to console and mourn her, and 48 to get himself together again. Saint Berger would see to that. And who knows, maybe the whole event would be a blessing in disguise, with Roberto taking out his fury on our first-round opponent in New Mexico next week...

During the first 48 hours I stayed with Vargas the whole time, ministering to him at the same time that he ministered to his mother. I didn't trust him out of my sight, figuring he'd either go bananas and seek revenge, or get depressed and give up Conway. In the hospital it wasn't easy, to put it mildly, seeing that olive-colored, smooth-skinned woman turned into a black and blue pulp, a limp frozen cabbage, wired by tubes. While Vargas sat in the room with his comatose mother I sat twenty yards away, in the floor lounge, filling up a graph book with diagrams for half-court traps and matchup zones. It was convenient, actually, to be away from the college just then, alone, at my own unreachable command post. Too much unnecessary attention up there now. For lunches we'd use the hospital cafeteria, but for dinner, I'd coerce him, literally drag him out with me. We'd walk up Cambridge Street to Inman Square and an old favorite, Casa Portugal, or one of the new ethnic restaurants.

"I knew I shouldn't have left her alone with that alcoholic sleazeball," he'd start in, working the same groove over and over. "I shouldn't have come to college and left her by herself with a hot-tempered thug."

"She *wanted* him back, Roberto," I reminded him. "Nothing you could have done..."

He curled, creaked his neck. "Yeah, I know, I know. Still... I coulda helped had I been around. Ever hear of Bravura? The courage to take action, no matter how scared you are. He wouldn't have beaten her this way if I was still around."

But he'd have gone after you, pal. "Eat your steak, it's getting cold. C'mon. And think of number 21, and how he would have handled it." And I made him look at the determined mouth of his namesake hero, Clemente.

Her sister, Roberto's aunt, showed up, a heavyset woman of 45, wearing a nun's habit. Fondling her large crucifix, she shook her head disapprovingly.

"Lily wouldn't listen to me, ever, about anything. This man was scum and she... she didn't care. She wasn't much better herself. She shouldn't have raised the boy with *her* attitudes and habits. It's a shame. Poor Lily. When she left the Church and God, she left morals. I hate to say it, sir, but she made her bed and now she's lying in it." The green-grey eyes in the round dark face were stone hard.

Getting Vargas away from that punishing rack took some doing. He kept saying, "No way I can go back now to campus or to the tournament, Coach. I'm real sorry to do this to the team and you right now, but..." Fortunately I had gotten the good Julia MSW to come over and meet with us, and swear that on the first sign of his mother's emergency from the coma, she'd let us know immediately. That, and his "team responsibility" edged him back north with me. Even when I had him in the car, having overloaded the poor sucker with sandbags of guilt, he still was mumbling his protest: "No way I can be leaving her now, Coach, no way..."

Alas, irony caught up with me. Seeing Roberto back on campus, walking amidst the neat snowfilled greens and rows of fraternities and L.L.Bean- and Turbo-model-outfitted students, and knowing what frenzy was whirling inside, I too felt pangs of guilt. Imagine. And I realized that the Berlin Wall was no more emphatic a boundary line or closed border than that between the ordered lives of the white middle-class students here, and the chaotic lives of my lumpenproletariat crew.

On Friday I had my own boy with me, and after reading to him about Koala bears and Peregrine falcons in Ranger Rick, I left him to his own devices—the battles of space Legos—and played a few of my father's old records. Arias by Björling, *"Salut, demeure chaste et pure..."* and *"Nessun dorma..."* and by Gigli, *"Dalla sua pace..."* from Don Giovanni. I'd never loved the stuff as he had, but it was like being home in Brooklyn and upstate again, seeing the old man lathering up with his shaving cream mug and waiting for his cue to break into a duet with the big tenors. Now Ruffo, as Rigoletto, *"Pari siamo..."* Raising the roof.

"This was one of Grandpa's favorite songs, right?"

"Yeah, that's right. How'd you remember?"

The boy shrugged. He scampered to one corner of the living room with his vehicle, calling out in deep mock bass to the adversary, "This is your last chance, Eucalyptian, give up now or you'll *languish* in jail once you're captured!"

Björling sang. Daniel attacked. I reflected. Winning the games had been at least as much work as fun, maybe more. (Was it now going to be hard work not to lose outside the court as well? A year-away problem, thank god.) Concentrate on New Mexico State, I chastised myself, and strategies to use against a taller, stronger opponent. Patience and defense would be all-important, and I outlined a changing defense of camouflage zones, halfcourt traps, man-to-man stuff. Despite all the strategy, however, it would still be up to the boys to improvise when things weren't going well, to keep their poise and will, to pump up the balloon of confidence against bigger athletes, to play with the power of an illusion. Then they had a chance. (Me too?)

"C'mon, Papa, you promised to play the Patagonians in one war at least!"

We had one last practice before departing in quest of the Holy Grail, the NCAA Final Four.

The team seemed flat and uninspired, so I cut it short, gathered them together and said, "All right, relax. I'm going to tell you about a fellow who was a real long shot to make it as a great historian, and turned out to be the greatest America ever produced. I've read you his work before."

Several voices supplied the name Parkman.

"That's right, Francis Parkman. I can't remember exactly what I told you about him, but he very much wanted to escape his privileged life as a refined Boston gentleman and enter into the real life of the nation, but not being too well— he had very weak eyesight, and he suffered several nervous breakdowns—he did this by learning about America's history, and then bringing it back to life in his books. He loved flowers, he loved wilderness, and he loved America, and whenever he got the chance he escaped to mountains and wilderness, at first in the West, where he went to see the Indians and the great emigration of 1846, and produced his first book, called *The Oregon Trail*, and then frequently journeyed to the north country—"

"You mean around here?" asked Eddie.

"No, way up north, up in Canada. When it was still completely wild and empty. And there, too, he began to reflect upon what would have happened if the French, and not the English, had won out in the battle for the New World. He began writing a series of books in which he recreated the early history of the French and English in our hemisphere, and their battles with each other and with the Indians, for domination of this land. And he writes this history, as you've heard, with a vivid eye for what he imagined it was really like—the scenery, the battles, the soldiers and generals, the philosophies. Some of the principal characters he wrote about in addition to La Salle were Champlain, Frontenac, Pontiac, Montcalm and Wolfe. By now some of those names should be familiar to you..."

The boys identified Champlain as the man for whom the lake was named. One thought there might be a Frontenac somewhere, and another made a crack about Pontiac cars.

I slipped on my specs and opened my paperback. "Now listen, I told you before that the man could write, and that besides telling a dramatic story, he possessed a real prose style. Now I want you to hear his description of La Salle's assassination."

"Wait a min—by who, Coach? How?" Jarrod asked.

"By a few of his comrades who were afraid he was leading them to their destruction."

"Betrayed, huh?" noted Jack mournfully. "The low way to go."

"'It was the eighteenth of March, Moranget and his companions had been expected to return the night before, but the whole day passed, and they did not appear. La Salle became very anxious. He resolved to go and look for them; but not well knowing the way, he told the Indians who were about the camp that he would give them a hatchet if they would guide him. One of them accepted the offer, and La Salle prepared to set out in the morning, at the same time directing Joutel to be ready to go with him. Joutel says—in his Journal, that is—"That evening, while we were talking about what could have happened to the absent men, he seemed to have a presentiment of what was to take place. He asked me if I had heard of any machinations against them, or if I had noticed any bad design on the part of Duhaut and the rest. I answered that I had heard nothing, except that they sometimes complained of being found fault with so often; and that this was all I knew; besides which, as they were persuaded that I was in his interest, they would not have told me of any bad design they might have. We were very uneasy all the rest of the evening.

"'In the morning La Salle set out with his Indian guide. He had changed his mind with regard to Joutel, whom he now directed to remain in charge of the camp and to keep a careful watch. He told the friar Anastase Douay to come with him instead of Joutel, whose gun, which was the best in the party, he borrowed for the occasion, as well as his pistol. The three proceeded on their way—La Salle, the friar, and the Indian. "All the way," writes the friar, "he spoke to me of nothing but matters of piety, grace and predestination; enlarging on the debt he owed to God, who had saved him from so many perils during more than twenty years of travel in America. suddenly I saw him overwhelmed with a profound sadness, for which he himself could not account. He was so much moved that I scarcely knew him.' That was the friar speaking. Now Parkman again. 'He soon recovered his usual calmness; and they walked on till they approached the camp of Duhaut, which was on the farther side of a small river. Looking about him with the eye of a woodsman, La Salle saw two eagles circling in the air nearly over him as if attracted by carcasses of beasts or men.'"

Avram inquired about the detail of the eagles circling. Too much imagination, perhaps?

"'He fired his gun and his pistol, as a summons to any of his followers who might be within hearing. The shots reached the ears of the conspirators. Rightly conjecturing by whom they were fired, several of them, led by Duhaut, crossed the river at a little distance above where trees or other intervening objects hid them from sight. Duhaut and the surgeon crouched like Indians in the long, dry, reed-like grass of the last summer's growth, while L'Archevêque stood in sight near the bank. La Salle, continuing to advance, soon saw him, and, calling to him, demanded where was Moranget. The man, without lifting his hat, or any show of respect, replied in an agitated and broken voice, but with a tone of studied insolence, that Moranget was strolling about somewhere. La Salle rebuked and menaced him. He rejoined with increasing insolence, drawing back, as he spoke, towards the ambuscade, while the incensed commander advanced to chastise him. At that moment a shot was fired from the grass, instantly followed by another; and, pierced through the brain, La Salle dropped dead.'"

There were murmurs, moans. I wanted to skip ahead, but dared not, they were so caught up.

"'The friar at his side stood terror-stricken, unable to advance or fly; when Duhaut, rising from the ambuscade, called out to him to take courage, for he had nothing to fear. The murderers now came forward, and with wild looks gathered about their victim. "There thou liest, great Bashaw! There thou liest!" (from Joutel...) exclaimed the surgeon Liotot, in base exultation over the unconscious corpse. With mockery and insult, they stripped it naked, dragged it into the bushes, and left it there, a prey to the buzzards and wolves.'"

"Cowards!" Vargas's voice was low.

"Now, gentleman, attention to the writing, yes? 'Thus in the vigor of his manhood, at the age of forty-three, died Robert Cavelier de la Salle, "one of the greatest men," writes Tonty, "of this age"; without question one of the most remarkable explorers whose names live in history. His faithful officer Joutel thus sketches his portrait: "His firmness, his courage, his great knowledge of the arts and sciences, which makes him equal to every undertaking, and his untiring energy, which enabled him to surmount every obstacle, would have won at last a glorious success for his grand enterprise, had not all his fine qualities been counterbalanced by a haughtiness of manner which often made him insupportable, and by a harshness toward those under his command which drew upon him an implacable hatred, and was at last the cause of his death.'"

"Now, pure Parkman. 'The enthusiasm of the disinterested and chivalrous Champlain was not the enthusiasm of La Salle; nor had he any part in the self-devoted zeal of the early Jesuit explorers. He belonged not to the age of the knight-errant and the saint, but to the modern world of practical study and practical action. He was the hero not of a principle nor of a faith, but simply of a fixed idea and a determined purpose. As often happens with concentrated and energetic natures, his purpose was to him a passion and an inspiration; and he clung to it with a certain fanaticism of devotion. It was the offspring of an ambition vast and comprehensive, yet acting in the interest both of France and civilization.'"

"'His purpose was to him a passion,'" repeated Vargas, rapt.

"'Serious in all things, incapable of the lighter pleasures, incapable of repose, finding no joy but in the pursuit of great designs, too shy for society and too reserved for popularity, schooled to universal distrust, stern to his followers and pitiless to himself, bearing the brunt of every hardship and every danger, demanding of others an equal constancy joined to an implicit deference, heeding no counsel but his own, attempting the impossible and grasping at what was too vast to hold—he contained in his own complex and painful nature the chief springs of his triumphs, his failures, and his death.'"

"Who was the more romantic," Dennis wondered, "La Salle or Parkman? Or Coach Berger?"

I paused. The boys waited. "'It is easy to reckon up his defects, but it is not easy to hide from sight the Roman virtues that redeemed them. Beset by a throng of enemies, he stands, like the King of Israel, head and shoulders above them all. He was a tower of adamant, against whose impregnable front hardship and danger, the rage of man and of the elements, the southern sun, the northern blast, fatigue, famine, disease, delay, disappointment and deferred hope emptied their quivers in vain. That very pride which, Coriolanus-like, declared itself most sternly in the thickest press of foes, has in it something to challenge admiration.

"'Never under the impenetrable mail of paladin or crusader beat a heart of more intrepid mettle than within the stoic panoply that armed the breast of La Salle. To estimate aright the marvels of his patient fortitude, one must follow on his track through the vast scene of weary miles of forest, marsh, and river, where, again and again, in the bitterness of baffled striving, the untiring pilgrim pushed onward toward the goal which he was never to attain—'"

"Man, the man is driven," muttered Nurlan.

He was and I could feel him driving me.

"'America owes him an enduring memory; for in this masculine figure—'"

"Sexist!"

"'...she sees the pioneer who guided her to the possession of her richest heritage.'"

I lowered my book and drained my water glass.

"A-men." Almost together.

All's well that ends well, right Sydney? When you're riding Lady Luck, dig your spurs in and ride, boy, ride! Forget the tricky curves of moral responsibility, and giddyap down the straight ground of pragmatism. Meaning this: good ol' Lily V. pulled out of her coma, her bruises and wounds healed up, and she came back to the living again. When Vargas went down to visit her before going west, he saw a familiar body, a functioning mother.

"She's sure Jesus did it for her," Roberto told me, smiling. "Gave her a second chance."

I nodded and patted his broad shoulder. "Who knows, maybe she's right? Now maybe He can take care of Luis Whatever, too, if and when he's returned to the streets and comes around."

My boy's face tightened. "If He won't, someone will have to."

"*Someone,* yes." I held his arm. *"Not you."*

And I made a note to speak with Julia O'Connor, and maybe even hire a private detective down the line to be that *someone.*

10 THE JOURNEY WEST, THE BIG TIME

We traveled out to Salt Lake City on the evening of March 13th in order to get in a practice on the next day for the game on the 15th. For winning the Ivy we were rewarded with a ranking of 64th in a field of 64, and a place in the West Regionals, against UCLA, ranked 2nd out there. That was fine with me, however, and with the boys. Why not go up against the tough ones early on? Yet who wasn't tough in that gloried, rarefied atmosphere of the Final Sixty-four? Out there on the new floor of the Special Conventions Center we went through some basic drills, getting used to the bounce of the ball off the overly-waxed hardwood, the springy glass backboards and soft rims, the glare spots in the lighting. (No way of seeing the 45-second shot clock from one side of the court.) The 16,000 seats were empty just now, and the TV cameras were not yet set up at 7:30 a.m., and it was like being in a museum of one's own, with no visitors tramping through. A true up-to-date Dr. Naismith museum.

This was the first "big time" for the kids, and for me, and it was going to be interesting to see how it might affect all of us. When we had entered our hotel downtown, for example, the clerks were mildly curious about Conway, surprised to hear that it was in the Ivy League and believing it was "in

Vermont or Connecticut somewhere." The welcome was quite different for UCLA, Missouri, and top-seeded Indiana, when those hotshot teams came strutting in. Indeed even I was a bit awestruck by the actual sight of the renowned coach of the Hoosiers, who looked middle-aged Rabbit-grey and battle-weary in a wool overcoat and cardigan. I didn't dare try to introduce myself, but turned away with my newspaper.

On the floor my boys looked loose and easy, running and passing in threes, the guards dribbling in pairs, shooting hoops around the horn to the voices of Ray Charles and Stevie Wonder. As they squeaked in their sneakers I checked the springiness of the rims and walked around with my private squeegee, noting the soft spots, hand-mopping resin into slippery areas of the floor. No need to lose a player before the games began. Kneeling and rubbing, I wondered if we would lose by twenty or thirty? Be humiliated in the first ten minutes and lose our cool? Get flustered by the cowed refs, who undoubtedly would give every close call to the bigtime teams? I had seen all that happen before in the NCAA's. Little guys stayed little guys, unless someone up there, on CBS say, took a shine to you.

Well, I had to give them a pep talk at some point; was this the moment? When I had gathered the team around me I decided rather to let them scrimmage and save the bad news for later on. Like how not to get down on themselves because the opponent was bigger and faster? After all, they were playing against full-fledged athletic scholarship kids—what could they or I expect? Moreover, we had already had our great year and championship celebration. This was simply icing on the Ivy cake, I told myself, blowing the whistle when I spotted Vargas failing to box out, or noticed Chief and Eddie failing to get back fast enough on the defense transition.

Later, that evening at the hotel, the NCAA held a press conference for the eight coaches and I was taken aback at the number of reporters. There must have been fifty to a hundred, at least, besides college personnel and onlookers. The stars of course were the coaches from the Hoosiers and the

Bruins and the local favorite from BYU. All sorts of questions were put to them, with especial deference to the unholy terror, the volatile Hoosier, Bobby Knight. And yours truly? I was used as comic relief, a kind of Ivy foil to big-time hoop seriousness.

"What do you think of the 500 to 1 line against your squad?'

"Long shots are always worth a bet."

"No offense, Coach Berger, but do you really think you should be here in the first place, when teams like Ohio State and UTEP and a half-dozen others were left out?"

"Why not? We won our League, and the Ivy's been around for a lot longer than most conferences. In fact, if you want to look it up, Conway even played in a NCAA championship final, losing to Stanford in '43, I think. And to me, this tournament is as much about carrying on a tradition as the Rose or Orange Bowls. Otherwise it's just Hicksville, USA. Or a tournament in Tokyo."

Voices buzzed at my huffiness.

"So you definitely think it's a mistake to do away with your automatic bid some time in the next few years?"

"Definitely."

"Has your conference taken this up with the NCAA committee?"

"Oh, I'm not sure."

"Excuse me, Coach, but is it true that yours is the only non-scholarship school admitted into the playoffs right now?"

I nodded. "I think that is true."

"Well," retorted the Utah reporter, "I guess we'll see tomorrow night if that sort of policy is fit for Division I play. Maybe you should try to get your school to change its policies and views?"

"You may be right, considering today's world. On the other hand, maybe Conway and our League has it right, and the NCAA and you guys wrong. Maybe academics should come ahead of sports, for the real colleges and universities. Our total budget for running some 31 sports is a million and a half. Now for those schools that form the farm system for the NBA clubs, let sports dominate there, and academics take second or third place—you know, at graduation time give those kids B.A.s from the Knicks or diplomas in Latin from the Lakers."

Laughter, jeers, applause. "Good sermon, Coach!"

"Could you be specific, and name some of those 'farm system' colleges?"

The moderator cleared his throat diplomatically. "Gentlemen, I think we should return to the Western Regionals tournament at hand here in Salt Lake in the next few days. Any further questions pertinent to this topic?"

Afterwards I was surrounded by the sports reporters, questioned, and looked upon—rather politely—as though I were some freak from the circus. Already I was sorry I had spoken out that way in such a forum, on the eve of the tournament. No need. So here, with the group of a dozen news-hungries from places like Laramie, Boise, Provo, Tulsa, Reno, I was nice and tame. And tried to give them a sense of Conway, and how it was a bit different from a UTEP, Arkansas or Tennessee State, in history, ambitions, scope.

At the hotel's front desk there were several telegrams. One was from the athletic office at Jadwin gym, Princeton: "Forget the hoopla, focus on the opponent/Get a good game plan/ Keep your players level-headed./Good Luck from Ivy colleagues and players!"

Signed, Pete Carril. A missive of cheer which I would save and frame. The next, from the Conway Alumni Club: "Go Big Green!/With you all the way/150 fans arrive SLC Friday night." Signed, Chip Bromley. Good fellow. The third was from the college President: "The eyes of Conway are upon you. Win, lose, or draw, you've been a great success! Remember Matthew 3-3: *Vox clamantis in deserto.*" Not bad, I thought. Sew the motto on our uniforms?

After an early dinner I took the boys out for an evening stroll. A lovely spring evening, cool and crisp, the sun blood-red in the sky and the mountains snow-capped in the near distance. I asked the way to the Mormon Tabernacle, and discovering it was a ten-minute walk from our Doubletree Inn, we ambled over there. Inside the hallowed walls of the private grounds we meandered about the various churches of Zion. The virtuous visitors and lily-white Mormons eyed our curious crew as though we were Foreign Legionnaires, in for some AIDS convention, perhaps.

I found the original tabernacle building and we entered and quietly walked about. The large wooden structure with the semi-domed ceiling was most elegant, and the magnificent thick timbers of the original 19th-century were intact. A smallish group was just getting ready to watch a video history of the place, and we joined them in the back pews. Nothing like a little Americana, I thought, to extend their horizons and take their minds off the game. As we sat, I counted my players like campers to make sure we hadn't lost any stragglers. Easy to spot them in their "Western Regionals" white caps.

The forty-minute video described the journey west of Joseph Smith and his ardent followers, the revelation of the Book of Mormon, the original stops in western Missouri and Nauvoo, Illinois, where Smith and his brother were eventually arrested and murdered. Next the baton of leadership was passed to Brigham Young and the site changed to the valley by the Great Salt Lake. What was striking in all this, to me, was the isolation of the Mormons, their persecution (by the "Gentiles"), their devotion to their community and its Biblical principles against all outside odds. Well, I began to form my own spiel now, remaining outwardly quiet.

Outside presently I gathered the troops around a bench in the park-like atmosphere, and spoke softly. "Sons, we need a purity and devotion like the kind you just saw. If one of you makes a mistake, you have to make up for it by personally creating two. And let nothing block your path tomorrow. Not the referees, not the crowd, not the spectacle, not the other team. We have to play the game in our minds first, according to *our own* aspirations and ideals, *our own* rules for excellence." *(High Flow was my private vision.)* "If we do that, perform on that level, we will achieve something. Something approaching victory in its deeper meaning. Reflect on this tonight, focus in on the game and your roles, and we'll fulfill ourselves and our mission tomorrow. Are you with me?"

A small crowd had gathered around us and applauded. One asked kindly, "Which mission do you head, sir?"

Strolling back, Dennis murmured quietly, "How come they, or you, didn't mention the polygamy thing, Coach? Out of bounds?"

I shook my head. "You'll always be a Jesuit at heart, my boy. Distinctions, always distinctions."

He pursed his lips and smirked.

Later, in the hotel room with the players and assistants, I went over the game plan and the UCLA team. Start off with a variety of zones and see how they worked. Doubleteam their vulnerable pointguard if it was a fastbreak situation. Trap the sidelines in the last few minutes of the half. Slow down the tempo and work the clock; UCLA was impatient. Look for backdoor layups in the halfcourt game. "Our only chance is to play steady, make few turnovers, take the high-percentage shots and hit fifty percent. Grab the defensive boards and make our foul shots. And be nice to the refs, no matter what. Okay? Here's the sheets again, gents." I handed out an updated instruction list for each player. Ridiculous list.

Later, about ten, I got a drink in the bar. Glancing around and spotting the pack of reporter wolves I decided to take it upstairs. In my room I turned on the television, lay on my vast bed, sipped my straight Daniels. My remote control flicked from station to station, giving me a CNN news clip about a serial killer terrorizing Phoenix—a grotesque iron-pumping contest among muscle-bulging women—a teenage gang drug war in Los Angeles—a hockey game from Edmonton—a Japanese industrialist shaking hands with an Idaho farmer over a huge land purchase. Escaping this America I found a movie starring the young Ida Lupino, and stayed.

The drink warmed my stomach and rippled in my mind. The old movie drifted me into calm. With the country going to hell I was sitting in the catbird seat, as ol' Red used to say. Waiting for my team to take the court. But where were we, where was I? Should I have told Vargas about his new family problem? Sure. Had I done wrong with Nurlan, helping him out early on and straight through? Legalistically yes, ethically no. (On whose behalf was I hustling, my own or that of a just cause?) Should I have given in to the NCAA mudslingers, that legal mafia, cut a deal and taken my misdemeanor punishment? Fuck 'em. Why were we selling out the country, just for money? Christ. Half Washington should have been strung up as traitors for starting the mess, or even countenancing it. Concentrate on the game, buddy boy, the game. By tomorrow night you'll be out of here, out of the hotseat, that is, and be free and clear. To look for another job, another profession?...Another self?

I sipped and reflected, watching Ida—in terror of this psychotic (Robert Ryan) she's mistakenly taken in to clean her house and help out—try to escape her bad judgment.

The game. It was everything, young, energetic, hungry in our tired, bloated USA-land. *The game.* The rest sucked canal water, to use the student phrase. Politics, religion, television, business, higher education. Down the tubes, like the rest of the country, from the farms and the real estate to the banks and the schools. Sucked. *The game.* Pick a game and get to know it, feel it; it's all there is. (Look, there's Ida, beautiful in terror, trying to duke out the psychopath; such a simple, spare tale, so well done.) Didn't matter if it was football or basketball—or even baseball, though that's down for good, the outfielders can no longer catch fly balls, the pitchers are not allowed to pitch out of jams, the good hitter hits .280. *The game.* Get inside one and stay inside, don't come up for air, the air was lousy and polluted, and it wasn't going to get cleaner. Not for a long time. Sydney boy, do you think Jefferson or Emerson would have hung around here for long?

So stay right where you are, focusing on Conway versus UCLA, on the subtle angles and small ways of pulling off the upset. Stay right with it, on the probability of percentages and the nuances of decisionmaking that the fan doesn't see, and see if you can out-coach that six-figured recruiter snob and steal one tomorrow. Oh, the boys'll have to do their part, but you'll have to hold up your end, smart-alec; outcoach the PR fucker. Pick up the slightest wind and sail with it. Pull her into High Flow and don't look back.

Sydney, you're drunk on one double-Daniels.

And the next day I was in my usual game trance; parallel lines of nerves and calm. By the time it had started I had blocked out the ESPN boys, the UCLA girls (disco cheerleaders), the Conway boosters, the sparse crowd (I accepted the insult of very few Bruin fans even showing up for this early shoo-in against baby-Ivy Green). I focused on pieces of defense... Did the three-two zone or box-and-one bother UCLA the most? Were Vargas, Eddie and Dennis using their bodies as well as elbows to keep the jumping jacks off the boards? Could the Chief handle their schoolyard pointguard off the dribble all by himself? On offense: were we making our mandatory 5-6 passes before taking a shot, and was Nurlan penetrating only to pass off at the last moment? Had UCLA prepared smartly for Avram, meaning were they leaving the Kiev Rifle's baseline spots empty and was he getting there quickly enough, for the pass? Was knightly Dennis being *mean* enough on the picks he was setting? What about the Coach's gamble of restraining Water from opening the throttle full until second half? High-risk folly or shrewd strategy?

Coolly, in the first ten minutes of play, Coach made his dozen or so decisions and slight adjustments, reckonings; otherwise, he knew, the score at halftime would be too lopsided. The kids played decently, not great. UCLA was a bunch of talented individuals but not an awesome, disciplined Wooden team; we walked off at halftime down by six. So far, not bad. It didn't hurt that the UCLA kids taunted Nurlan and Vargas in the runway about playing in the Ivies. I took Nurlan aside.

"Okay, you're a free agent in the second half." He beamed. "Bout time, Mr. B."

In the locker room, adorned with Water's serene wiry landscapes, I was in a whirl and couldn't wait to get started, all pumped up with notions and notations. At the chalkboard I wrote in block letters SECONDARY CUTTERS and INTERIOR PASSING, and scribbled away, chattering on about their number 31 down low and working our reverse screens on him, since he was so slow in coming off the pick. "Now, on the trapping zone, Jarrod and Jack..."

The boys were smiling oddly, shaking heads, telling me they were cool, they would do just fine. The odor of sweat, resin, wet uniforms was exotic to me, I was elsewhere. I put down the chalk, stared at my smudged hand.

"You must take easy, Mr. Berger," Avram declared. "We not play that well. The shots not go down. But law of percentages, they will next half. Besides this, Water will let loose more, as planned, yes?"

They were gathering around Avram, grinning at me, munching oranges, draining Gatorades, big wet eyes fixed on me. Did I seem so wired, so overwrought? Were they trying to cool me down, or themselves?... I sat down, crossed my legs, put away my spiral pad of notes, and took out my current reading. From the corner of my eye I saw the assistants giving each other the fish-eye, signalling, "Uh-oh, here he goes..." They were right,too, I half-knew, but what could I do? Helplessly I was high as a kite, my heart was pounding with the Event, and my head was swimming with ideas. Did they sense this?

"Gentlemen, how many of you have heard of Captains Lewis and Clark? And know about their Westward Expedition from 1803 to 1805?" A chewing, coughing silence. "Well, let me begin with the Louisiana Purchase, the greatest bargain in our history, which doubled the land mass of America and opened the West." I spent two minutes detailing the circumstances surrounding that event, focusing on the negotiating powers of Jefferson, who recognized that the land had to be kept away from Napoleon, and joined to the States for powerful economic and political reasons. Erasing the halfcourt diagram on the blackboard, I drew a quick sketch of the Purchase, emphasizing the Rockies and the snaking Missouri River. I now came to that heroic pair, Meriwether Lewis and William Clark. "Their job in effect was to find out what was actually out there, in the West; did the Missouri somehow connect up with the Pacific? How long would it take to make a trip like that? What were the mountains like, and were there other major rivers we didn't know about? How about the various Indian tribes? Could they be persuaded to be friendly despite their allegiance to the British because of cheap goods, etc.? Might our China trade be increased ten-fold with the shorter overland route to the Pacific? And so on. In Lewis and Clark, Jefferson had picked the most intelligent pair of explorers imaginable. (Along with Sacajawea, the remarkable Indian woman who was their guide.) Here, a few paragraphs of their unique diary."

"Sydney," implored Roscoe, perturbed, "don't you want to go over some of the important plays? This is the NCAA's for godssakes!"

Yes, of course. "You're absolutely right, Roscoe. Thanks."

"No, no, Coach," interceded Eddie to my astonishment. "Please read."

"Yes, Lewis and Clark, this must be," agreed Avram. "We get ball to Water, we pass more, shots fall, percentage on our side. All to be fine."

The squad clapped, whistled. What could I do but read?

"'Friday, August 16th, 1805,'" I began, in a tizzy, "'I sent Drewyer and Shields before this morning in order to kill some meat as neither the Indians nor ourselves had anything to eat...'" I skipped ahead, worried that the scene would take too long to set up. "'After the hunters had been gone about an hour we set out. We had just passed through the narrows when we saw one of the spies coming up the level plain under the whip, the chief paused a little and seemed somewhat concerned. I felt a good deal so myself and began to suspect that by some unfortunate accident that perhaps some of their enemies had straggled hither at this unlucky moment; but we were all agreeably disappointed on the arrival of the young man to learn that he had come to inform us that one of the white men had killed a deer.'"

I looked up at their munching faces and they were glued to me, raptly attentive, so I nodded and went on.

"'In an instant they all gave their horses the whip and I was taken nearly a mile before I could learn what were the tidings; as I was without stirrups and an Indian behind me the jostling was disagreeable, I therefore reined up my horse and forbid the Indian to whip him who had given him the lash at every jump for a mile fearing he should lose a part of the feast. The fellow was so uneasy that he left me the horse, dismounted and ran on foot at full speed, I am confident, a mile. When they arrived where the deer was which was in view of me they dismounted and ran in tumbling over each other like a parcel of famished dogs, each seizing and tearing away a part of the intestines.'"

Not one of their faces showed repulsion at this gruesome scene. Nor did mine, I supposed.

"'...some were eating the kidneys, the melt (spleen) and liver and the blood running from the corners of their mouths, others were in a situation with the paunch and guts but the exuding substance in this case from their lips was of a different description. One of the last who attracted my attention particularly had been fortunate in his allotment or rather active in the division; he had provided himself with about nine feet of the small guts, one end of which he was chewing on.'"

"Hey, Sydney, give us a break, please!" Percy urged, and Renee concurred. They both moved away.

Entranced, I went on, "'...while with his hands he was squeezing the contents out at the other. I really did not until now think that human nature ever presented itself in a shape so nearly allied to the brute creation.

"'I viewed these poor starved devils with pity and compassion. I directed McNeal to skin the deer and reserved a quarter; the balance I gave the Chief to be divided among his people; they devoured the whole of it nearly without cooking.

"'I now bore obliquely to the left in order to intercept the creek where there was some brush to make a fire, and arrived at this stream where Drewyer had killed a second deer; here nearly—'"

The warning buzzer screeched, and Duddy took my arm and book. "C'mon Chief, we better get out there." As the kids trotted by some patted my arm and some winked. I felt exhausted, in a different world.

We were able to get in three minutes of shooting warmup before the intermission was over. Our boys entered the second half with firmness and poise, not rushing things, and cut up the vaunted UCLA team with smart defense and precise passing which produced high percentage shots. And Nurlan now went full steam ahead. Smooth as silk and fluidly in control, he easily took the play away from the wild Bruin guard whose one-on-one game became more and more erratic. (He tried to upset Nurlan with trash talk, "C'mon boy, why you wanna play like a honkie?", but Nurlan just smiled.) And when, some ten minutes into the half, the Bruins began to sense that there was an operation being performed, they doubleteamed the surgeon; but that didn't help. Nurlan penetrated the first line of defense easily with his dribble and immediately whipped the ball to Avram for a jumper or to Eddie or Vargas for a crashing layup. And if the second line laid back, he'd cruise on in by himself. As the upset began to unfold, the outcome inching toward the inevitable, I was reminded of Daniel's favorite creature in the local science museum, Stanley the boa, sometimes mistaken for a harmless snake, taking its prey in its grip and tightening the hold. Just as it began to sense its error, UCLA was already gasping for air.

Our hold didn't lessen or mitigate. The year of solid repetitions, of the right mix of capacities and roles, of an emphasis on defense, rebounding, the passing game and pointguard play, had become a recording in its groove. Even the refs, who had started out giving UCLA every single close call, switched to calling it even, seeing the sustained finesse, skill and poise of the Green jerseys. The crowd had grown in size, coming in for the second game (a doozy, New Mexico versus BYU), and they were gradually perceiving what was happening. With six minutes to go we were up by twelve, UCLA began fouling, and I wandered up and down in a tizzy. Our kids responded: the guards didn't get rattled, the four corners spread their wings and we passed smartly (getting several easy layups), and we hit 80 percent of our foul shots. Won going away.

At the end it was mild mayhem, the coaches grabbing me, the 150 Conway fans pouring down to congratulate, the large crowd, amazed, surprised us with an ovation. Our players hugged each other but eschewed any wild shenanigans, celebrating quietly. Embracing me, Nurlan confided, "We got a further destination fore we really dance."

In the dressing room there were relatively quiet cheers and controlled festivity, with brief speeches coming from the A.D. and a Graduate Dean who had flown out to join us.

"You did it, you son of a gun." Dick Porter took my hand. "You did it! Who would have believed it, huh? *Who!*"

"Well, thanks, Dick. And thanks for the chance, and year."

"There'll be more, Syd! This is the biggest basketball victory for Conway not only in my time, but in four decades at least, and maybe more, considering how college ball has changed."

"Well, you may be right, Dick."

Dennis, sporting a mischievous grin, said, "This is definitely more of a rush than getting my letter from the Rhodes. I didn't quite realize what you were up to all these months."

"Oh?"

He half-smirked. "Those... odd lectures."

I nodded, not at all understanding what he meant.

Roberto whispered, *"We're movin' on, Coach B, we're movin' on."*

Seeing his big shining eyes and Brando grin, I nodded, still in debt.

But what I understood clearly was, I had one day and a half to get them ready for Saturday afternoon's game against the winner of the nightcap. Did we have any chance there?

After 20 minutes of showering, cleaning up, accepting kudos, I raced upstairs for a peek at the opposition. One club was slick, the other tough. Put them together and they'd be unbeatable. But apart, as separate teams, they had shortcomings. Was there enough time, however, for me and the kids to see how to take advantage of them?

Doubtful. The next 36 hours was an orgy of plans, nerves, strategies, avoidances (publicity). At a small celebration given by the Friends of Conway I was asked to speak and bumbled a few words out before sitting back down. Dennis, Jarrod and Avram on the other hand stood up and helped out. Jarrod was even elegant in giving a thank you to the Boosters for their support through the year. In double-breasted Glen Plaid suit he added, "It's too early to say whether we have the best team, but what other club can boast of a Rhodes Scholar in its starting lineup, a Van Gogh for a pointguard, an 'off the wall' history buff for its coach?" The crowd of 150 roared.

No, we really didn't have the time to drill our kids in BYU's deficiencies. (We practiced foul shooting, passing.) At this point in the NCAA's you were playing on your season-long habits, your stamina, your level of confidence and will. The other team was to be overcome, yes; but you had to do it, if you were like Conway and not superathletic, by running that same groove of repetition, by adhering to the long curve of one's aspiration. The acquired gene of team rhythm. In a word, the competing was against your own game. My pitch. Well, yes and no was how they responded to it; and how the game went.

BYU had its usual squad of tall, gangling Mormon kids— with a token black thrown in—who could shoot and run, and rebound some. Truth was, however, they couldn't crash the boards against Dennis, Eddie, Vargas; and they couldn't con-

trol the center of the floor, offense or defense, against Chief
and Water. (See Papa, Nimzovich again.) If you don't rebound
on the defensive board, you don't fast break; and if you're
suddenly double-team pressured and don't have the passing
game, you're going to be thrown off-balance. For much of
the game BYU played off-balance, its rhythm askew, its splendid shooting out of kilter. Add to this the focused energy of
Water on offense, his gliding brown superiority to the slower,
less subtle white counterpart, and we had clear advantages.
While the home crowd found it hard to comprehend how the
little kids from the Ivy League could be sticking it to their
higher, semi-divine team, I found it easy. We were a much
sounder club, a far superior clockwork. Of course you
wouldn't tell it from my behavior: I was as nervous on the
bench as a pregnant cat, prowling up and down, querulous
and ready to pounce (on the refs), bearing cups of water up
and back from the cooler as though it were the Great Salt
Lake desert inside.

At halftime of an apparently close game Nurlan put his
arm around me going down the runway and cooed, "Sheet,
Doctah B, reelax. Betsy Head is much tougha ground. How
bout anotha one a those Captain Clark and Lewis chapters?
They were *real* fine-sounding the otha night, ya know."

"You fellows truly enjoy those things? Why, Nurlan?"

His dark matte face lit up mischievously. "Caint truly put
it into words, Coach. It's jess our halftime stories. And
somethin like a *higha* education."

What could I do but give in to my—or was it now
'their'?—strange addiction? Once they were settled in,
sprawled on benches, gulping citrus and looking at me, I said,
"Okay, gentlemen, Captain Lewis again, from that August
16, 1805, entry of the other night."

"'...a fire being kindled we cooked and ate and gave the
balance of the two deer to the Indians who ate the whole of
them even to the soft parts of the hooves. Drewyer joined us
at breakfast with a third deer. Of this I reserved a quarter and
gave the balance to the Indians. They all appeared now to

have filled themselves and were in a good humor...' I'm skipping, men. '...being now informed of the place at which I expected to meet Captain C. and the party they insisted on making halt, which was complied with. We now dismounted and the Chief with much ceremony put tippets about our necks such as they themselves wore. I readily perceived that this was to disguise us and owed its origin to the same cause already mentioned. To give them further confidence I put my cocked hat with feather on the chief and my over-shirt being of the Indian form my hair disheveled and skin well-browned with the sun I wanted no further addition to make me a complete Indian in appearance, the men followed my example and we were soon completely metamorphosed.'"

Someone whistled loud and I skimmed down a bit.

"'We now set out and rode briskly within sight of the forks, making one of the Indians carry the flag that our own party should know who they were. When we arrived in sight at the distance of about 2 miles I discovered to my mortification that the party had not arrived, and the Indians slackened their pace. I now scarcely knew what to do and feared every moment when they would halt altogether. I now determined to restore their confidence, cost what it might, and therefore gave the Chief my gun and told him that if his enemies were in those bushes before him that he could defend himself with that gun, that for my own part I was not afraid to die, and if I deceived him he might make what use of the gun he thought proper, or in other words that he might shoot me. The men also gave their guns to other Indians, which seemed to inspire them with more confidence; they sent their spies before them at some distance, and when I drew near the place I thought of the notes which I had left and directed Drewyer to go with an Indian man and bring them to me, which he did. The Indian seeing him take the notes from the stake on which they had been placed.

"'I now had recourse to a stratagem in which I thought myself justified by the occasion, but which I must confess set a little awkward. It had its desired effect. After reading the notes, which were the same I had left, I told the Chief that when I had left my brother Chief with the party below where the river entered the mountain that we both agreed not to bring the canoes higher up than the next forks of the river above us wherever this might happen, that there he was to wait my return, should he arrive first, and that in the event of his not being able to travel as fast as usual from the difficulty of the water, that he was to send up to the first forks above him and leave a note informing me where he was, that this note was left here today and he informed me that he was just below the mountains and was coming slowly up, and added that I should wait here for him, but if they did not believe me that I should send a man at any rate to the Chief and they might also send one of their young men with him, that myself and two others would remain with them at this place. This plan was readily adopted and one of the young men offered his services; I promised him a knife and some beads as a reward for his confidence in us. Most of them seemed satisfied, but there were several that complained of the Chief's exposing them to danger unnecessarily and said that we told different stories; in short, a few were much dissatisfied. I wrote a note to Captain Clark by the light of some willow brush and directed Drewyer to set out early being confident that there was not a moment to spare. The chief and five or six others slept about my fire and the others hid themselves in various parts of the willow brush to avoid the enemy whom they were fearful would attack them in the course of the night. I now entertained various conjectures myself with respect to the cause of Captain Clark's detention—'"

The first warning buzzer sounded. But I held up my hand. "I'm skipping a little. '...my mind was in reality quite as gloomy all this evening as the most affrighted Indian but I affected cheerfulness to keep the Indians so who were about me. We finally laid down and the Chief placed himself by the side of my mosquito bier. I slept but little as might be well expected, my mind dwelling on the state of the expedition which I have ever held in equal estimation with my own existence'"—I looked up, "Nice thought, huh, gentlemen?—'and the fate of which appeared at this moment to depend in a great measure upon the caprice of a few savages who are ever as fickle as the wind. I had mentioned to the Chief several times that we had with us a woman of his nation who had been taken prisoner by the Minetares, and that by means of her I hoped to explain myself more fully than I could do by signs; some of the party had also told the Indians that we had a man with us who was black and had short curling hair, and this had excited their curiosity very much, and they seemed quite as anxious to see this monster as they were the merchandise which we had to barter for their horses.'"

I sipped water, the second warning buzzer went off, and I was persuaded or coerced to stop by Percy, Duddy, Roscoe.

As we walked out, Jack said to me, "He doesn't really trust those Indians after all, does he?"

"He does, in his way. Certain ones like Sacajawea in the next section, who—"

"How could he trust 'savages'?" He stared icily.

Jarrod wondered, "Did he really mean monsters, sir?"

I tried to explain, reached for a distinction, but there was no time, everyone pressed urgently forward.

Poised, purposeful, highly efficient, the greenshirts cruised in the next half, passing beautifully, and lifting into five minutes of High Flow that made my heart palpitate. To my surprise the largely Mormon crowd tossed names at us and a good many ethnic slurs. But I took that as the heat of battle, the keen disappointment of losing on their own turf, no more. Afterwards the BYU coach felt amiss and apologized to me during congratulations. "Your kids are something, Coach— especially that Hebe kid... Man, I'd sneak a jewboy in too if I could get him to jumpshoot like that. Bet on it."

11 LAND OF ENCHANTMENT, OR
ENTER SYDNEY: HALLUCINATING

When you look up and it's late March and you're still playing college basketball, you're spinning in a different galaxy.

While others were stuck deep in mud season, cabin fever, tax forms, I was running inside this kaleidoscope of colors and shapes called the NCAA Regionals, barely keeping my balance. Truthfully, it wasn't that easy, especially for a potential Cinderella of that native religious festival, followed devotedly on TV for three and a half weeks by farmers in the Texas panhandle, professors in Berkeley and Ann Arbor, ranchers in Montana, suburbanites and city folk in New York and Chicago, rural fans in Idaho, Maine, Oregon. Yes, they were sending notes of good luck and talismans from all over, a bracelet from Sleepy Eye (Minnesota), an Indian arrowhead (Aberdeen, South Dakota), a collage of orange blossoms (Chattahoochee, Florida). And everybody wanted a piece of us, from the locals to the Lettermans and Gumbels—a nation always on the hunt for freakish success stories like Conway's. Horatio Alger with a basketball.

I had a week, no, about five days, to get things in order. To see the videos on the team ahead next Friday, to prepare a game plan, to keep my own squad in shape, mentally sharp.

215

And to prepare myself: ego alert, id in order, body light. The frequencies—team fundamentals, individual tasks—must be checked out, fine-tuned. The tropical zone of March playoff reality has to be dealt with, absorbed, a continent away from the actual arena. In spring the dominion of coaching expands way beyond the gym.

The heroism of our deeds had become, via newspapers and other media, well-known. *USA Today* ran a special red and blue border section on Conway the Giantkiller. Happily, they foresaw the bursting of the bubble that next weekend, against the big boys. Good. (ESPN ran a Special focusing on past Cinderellas and us, with Dick Vitale going wild about the coach.) I assigned Renee to handle the deluge, freeing me to focus on strategy, matchups, practices, the game.

For playoff nutrition I ordered a cutdown on greasy foods and excessive protein. "Breads, pastas, fish, extra carotene, a good beer now and then, wholewheat crust pizza, and, oh yes, apples and bananas—grab one whenever you're hungry. Duddy, let's have bunches of bananas on hand daily. And listen, if you're reaching for chocolate, we'll have a punchbowl of these Tiger's Milk nutrition bars," and I held up the dark brown wrapper of a bar from the Co-op.

The boys fussed with their caps, grinned and shook their heads. Roberto observed, "That's carob-covered, not chocolate."

"So what? It tastes just as good."

Checking later with Dennis, I knew my folly: they'd stick with pizzas, cheeseburgers, french fries, Doritos chips, yodels. Tough.

The excitement of the week was hot and palpable, like being in a boxing ring or combat zone, I imagined; a native bubble at 90 degrees Fahrenheit. Everyone in our sedate little town seemed touched by the event, their bland lives microwaved. CBS had already declared that our game was the main early attraction that Friday evening. Outside life, with meals and sleep and classes and dinner dates, all that seemed incidental, duller than ever. Even the larger world events, like the USSR falling apart and Germany coming together, paled into insignificance. (Yeltsin vs. Manning? Germany vs. Lobos or Wolverines? No contest.) The big time, the center ring, was occupied by the college basketball championships. And Conway was in it.

The college president, a genial fellow and hoop fan, invited me to lunch with Dick Porter, and I couldn't resist. (Well, I had practical and political reasons too, right? What if the NCAA boys pursued my case next year; how hard would President Grayson back me up?)

A Rudy Vallee lookalike with hair parted down the middle and rimless spectacles, he was eager to hear all about our chances against the mighty Hoosiers.

I put him off with as much flimflam chat as I could. "They're throwing us to the lions right off. Midnight comes early for Ivy Cinderellas in the NCAA's, especially in the Pitt. And there's no way that Bobby Knight is not going to get into the regional finals."

"You're not saying it's fixed?" He smiled.

I lit my pipe. "Not fixed in the ordinary sense. Just say our chances are very slim, in the referees' minds, *before* we start."

"Well," the President went on jovially, "we'll be there rooting you on, Syd. Lee and I wouldn't miss this for anything!" He paused and twinkled. "Tell me, what's it like to be out there on the floor for a big game, at a timeout, say?"

While I went through the motions to answer him, even using the salt and pepper shakers as props, I deliberated privately on the real goods—the several Indiana weaknesses: their inside game, slow transition on defense, weak ballhandling. Oh, they could shoot from the perimeter all right, and play man-to-man fine. But the Big Ten was a run-and-shoot league, not a "finesse-and-intelligence" conference. So no matter how Knight had schooled his boys, they were used to playing against hotshot gunners on the lookout for NBA agents. If my young green ingenues stayed cool, played their fundamentals, pressured the guards and the touted slowfooted

217

jumpshooter, while making the extra pass and slipping in some easy baskets on turnovers and fast breaks, we had a fair chance. And if we were to hit High Flow for six or seven minutes, fair would be fat.

"So if you can stay within ten you'd be happy?"

"Oh, yes. Happy indeed." I smiled, puffed. "Would coming close convince you to fight for some real athletic scholarships for us?"

He took that quite gravely and protested. "Oh, we'd have to take that up with the whole Ivy League, I'm afraid."

I nodded, smiled, wondered: whose side would he take in a crunch?

"I do want you to know, however, that what you're doing for our League is simply terrific. Its image in the athletic community has shot up significantly. We appreciate that very much, Sydney."

"Not to mention what you've done for Conway," added Dick, "for its alumni, boosters and students. Even the faculty is buzzing. It gives a lift to the entire Athletic program, across the board. It's been amazing."

The President's eyes behind the specs lit up playfully. "And I imagine Dick here will be rewarding you shortly for your phenomenal success!"

Dick laughed. "I imagine so."

Oh, that sounded sweet, as in "three-year contract" sweet.

So what if, beneath sound, my heart was being hit by intermittent depth charges of anxiety, urgency.

Pressured more as the week progressed, I couldn't help retreating one late afternoon for a therapeutic session. Was there a better therapy than deep massage? (Another win in the big tournament?)

The half-hour drive from town, up rural Route 10 through Lyme till the outskirts of Orford, was therapy in itself. A landscape of sloping river farms on one side, and rolling snow-covered mountains on the other. With white clapboard or red brick houses dotting the countryside, and the two tidy general-store towns pulling me into an old postcard, the real world and the NCAA's seemed far, far away, a mirage. (I had turned off Indigo Girls and Heart on the radio.) Just what my equilibrium required.

Grete Schuman was late forties, slender, dark, forlorn, past prime (thank goodness), fatigued in life but possessing strong hands and "Shiatsu wisdom." She knew the pressure points in my neck, back, feet, shoulders, thighs. I clasped her hands to say hello, undressed, and lay down on the thick workout mat in her living room, covered by a sheet. While she arranged the Mozart on the stereo I eyed the small photo of her father on the table: his stern face and stiffly-parted hair suggested, I thought, his Spanish gene. Of his Jewish gene, however... perhaps the nose? But of his role as a top Nazi engineer during the war, no observable evidence; that came from his still loving Grete. Indeed, right up to his recent end at 87, he used with pride his wartime designation of Field Marshal Schuman.

Grete began at my temples and eyes, pressing, massaging, smoothing my skin. Gradually my soul was massaged too. And I drifted off into distant half-dreams and flashing prints... Mother holding my hand *very tight* while Dr. Winard, without anaesthetic, sews up the hole in the crown of my head made by Gaby's wild swing with a rusty pipe... Robey pitching to me with a tennis ball in the schoolyard, now and then breaking off a torturous curve and smiling... Papa marching, holding my hand in a Lincoln Brigade memorial parade, while singing an aria... Scented Claire *(Grete?)* leaning down, whispering, her breasts touching me... The Good Humor man hawking his ice cream at Coney Island and, as I wait my turn, a teenager swipes my dime and runs!... Someone coming up behind me to poke me in the shoulderblades!

"Are you all right, Sydney? Do I hurt you?"

I shake my head, half-open my heavy-lidded eyes, and return to my semi-amniotic state. Only now, as those fingers move up and down my chest, finding points, stopping to dig in, I design the metaphor. The game, like the anatomy, has its pressure points, its decisive moments for determining the outcome; control those, especially in the second half, and you can win the game before the finish. The right players in the right position for the percentages to be favorable. A quick deflection, pass and (made) shot creating the demoralizing turn, and you had your advantage, way beyond actual play. Pricking the opponent's poise.

Wim suddenly appears, eyes narrow and yellow. "In life, too, Mowgli-Boy, the same holds true. Consider yours, where you've been in the wrong spot mostly, and, when in the right spot, chosen the wrong path. Your fate, Sydney?"

I try to focus on Daniel, but Robey the graduate student is grinning. "Always trying to be different, eh, Syddie? But leaving high school to ship out to sea? *Come on.* You know what it'll do to Mom."

I turn and twist, and am facing the Midwestern flattop. "There's the little matter of... extra gifts, Coach. The sneakers, gym bag treatments... oh, that entrance essay and... shall I go on Coach or—"

"You feel awfully stiff today, Sydney. Something is wrong?"

I shake my head. "Nothing really, Grete. Just..."

"Shall I stop?"

"Oh no, not at all."

"So: you turn over please."

I do as she says. With her almondy lotion I sense her lathering me up, and then traversing from the neck down my back in long hard strokes. I do my best to let go of the disturbing faces and charges, and concentrate on the kneading, the thumbing, the rubbing. Presently I'm confined within the semi-circles of pressure, the slow dissections of force, a piece of dough in a baker's hands, a gingerbread coach rolled and readied for the oven....

Before leaving for Albuquerque on Thursday I gathered up my schedules, notebooks, reading, and growing batch of telegrams and mail. I started going through the latter, but gave it up as too arduous, and asked responsible Renee to sort it through for anything important. A surprising crowd of maybe a thousand fans turned up at the tiny Lebanon airport to cheer us off! And the gigantic bonfire rally Wednesday night on the Green had been attended, it seemed, by the entire campus body, faculty too, and townspeople.

"This is how it used to be around here in the good old days," burbled Chip Bromley, taking my arm, "when Julian or Blackman or Ozzie were the helmsmen, and we had players like Gus or Audley and later, Rudy. You've brought back the old glory, Sydney." He held me close in the wildly windy air. "I knew you were the Coach for us, *you shaman*, I just knew it!" He lifted me up in a bear hug. "And no matter what happens from here on in, you're the man of the year. Good luck, you son of a gun. Good luck!"

Just as though I were his son, going off to the wars.

On the little prop airplane carrying us down to Logan in Boston, I observed the lovely terrain of snowcovered hills and frozen lakes and the snaking rivers. Was I really up there with those gloried coaches of yesteryear in Big Green mythology? A legend already? Well, if so, I hoped it would last awhile, at least another season or two, say.

To my surprise, the Dornier flew down smoothly, without its usual turbulence. A high sign, Syd?

On the jumbo 747, however, turbulence developed. Not from Boeing however, but from Mission, Kansas.

"I think you ought to read this one on top first, Sydney," advised Renee, handing me the batch of telegrams. "The rest are pure fun."

Addressed to me at the college, it read:

WE REGRET TO INFORM YOU THAT THERE IS SUF-FICIENT EVIDENCE OF RULES INFRACTIONS AT CONWAY COLLEGE IN OUR PRELIMINARY INQUIRY TO WARRANT A FULL-SCALE OFFICIAL INVESTIGA-TION OF THE BASKETBALL PROGRAM. THIS

INVESTIGATION WILL COMMENCE IMMEDIATELY.
WE LOOK FORWARD TO YOUR FULL COOPERATION
IN THE MATTER.
    R. SCHULTZ, CHAIRMAN
    COPIES TO: PRESIDENT M. GRAYSON, CONWAY
COLLEGE/ATHLETIC DIRECTOR: RICHARD PORTER/
DEAN OF FACULTY: JAMES SIMPSON

I had approximately six hours to fly and I realized that, if I didn't watch myself, I would use it all up on brooding, moral, legal and psychological. Instead of devoting my time to Pete Newell and John Wooden on aspects of the game, and Nimzovitch and Capablanca on tangential strategy. So I settled in with de Tocqueville, Chapter X, "On the Taste for Physical Well-Being in America."

The Pit in Albuquerque, home of the New Mexico State Lobos, was the place where you shined or withered. Great teams had come in there and fallen by the wayside because, in part, the crowd noise could be so deafening. Fortunately, there was no home team to play against now; rather, just a few of the big boys of college ball. But to wither in front of twenty-million plus, via the cruel eye of CBS, would be remembered. On the one hand I had no pressure at all; we were the overwhelming underdogs, by 16 points. On the other, we were right there on the threshold of deliverance, of a whole new era for Conway; not to cross over now would hurt. Expectations had been raised, exaltation was near...

In the shootaround on Friday, Billy Packer, the knowledgeable CBS announcer, came by. "I wanted to meet you, Mr. Berger, and tell you what a heck of a job you've done. To me, you're the Coach of the Year in Division I ball, no matter what you do here." He put out his hand.

I took it and thanked him.

"Off the record, Sydney, do you have a chance tonight?"

"Off the record, yes, we've got a pretty fair one."

"Really?" He looked astonished.

"Really, Billy."

"Well, since you're being frank, what about the rumors of an NCAA investigation of the program at Conway?"

I had to gauge my "timing" quickly. What did the Committee mean by "commencing immediately?" What would that have to do with results a year or more away?

I took a chance and said, "Off the record, I've heard those rumors myself, Billy, and would very much like to know who's started them. For example, who told you?"

"Well, coach," he shook his head anxiously, "I'm afraid I can't reveal my sources on this one. As a journalist, I mean."

I nodded. "I just hope whoever started them is not trying to unnerve me right before a big game. An intentional nasty leak. That would be dirty pool, don't you think?"

Billy reflected. "Sounds that way, doesn't it? The timing is off-putting and a little coincidental."

He had taken my fishing rod now, handed over to him conveniently enough, and maybe would go fishing himself. Who knows, maybe even mention it on the telecast, putting more pressure on the stoolie. And if it were an NCAA stoolie, why that would be very interesting, maybe even very illegal. Damage control could include, on my part, an ambush attack here and there. The plotting and intriguing could go two ways.

While the boys shot around, under the supervision of Percy, Roscoe, Duddy—who would make sure that the starters got in their fifty foul shots and fifteen-footers apiece—I went over the floor carefully. I took my customary 31 yard-long strides (plus a foot) up and back the length, and my 17 across the width; found a janitor with a ladder and measured the 10-foot basket height; got on my knees at random points and wiped the wooden court surface with my handkerchief, searching for undue wax or resin.

"Afraid we're not gonna get it right out here in the sticks, Coach?" said a half-smiling, sallow fellow in a light windbreaker. A tall Wim.

"Just an old habit of mine," I remarked casually. Then I looked up to ask, "By the way, who are you?"

223

But he had already walked on by, apparently out of hearing.

I continued my pursuit of irregularities, checking backboards, baskets, twine, lighting, and, when none turned up, I returned to the boys on the floor. Made sure that they were practicing what they would be doing later on: Water dribbling from foul line to foul line, Avram jumpshooting from both baselines, Eddie and Robert rebounding misses to get the feel of the springy rims and backboard, and so on. I took the Chief aside to caution him again about their one trifecta shooter, and his need to take one little dribble before going up. "You've told me three times, Coach. Take it easy." Truth was, I was nervous as hell already, here, in late morning.

When the whistle blew signalling time for us to leave the court and the next squad to have its turn, I waited around just a bit to make sure everyone had cleared out, and also to see which team was coming on. Sure enough, it was the Hoosiers, and I found myself half-mesmerized by their aura, their slick red and white warmups, their legendary coach.

The great man himself walked on presently, wearing one of his patented old sweaters; spotting me, he pointed, freezing me.

I stammered, "I was just—"

He gripped my arm just above the elbow, held it tight, and fixed me with stern blue eyes. "Your club is just the kind I didn't want to face, Berger. Smart. Feisty. Poised. Rough off the boards. With a real quarterback." He leaned closer, a breath away. *"But you're going to have to beat me, Coach.* Remember that."

The fierce stare, and line, stunned me.

I reached for his hand, and only after another ten seconds did he relent, and release me.

"Well, I'll try, Mr. Knight," I mumbled, and wandered off slowly, trying to disguise my daze.

It took about an hour, and some reading, to wash him away.

The same number that he had performed on me, he did on

the refs in the first half of the game. He worked them brilliantly in the early minutes, prodding them about Water's first step and dribble; calling Dennis twice for three-seconds violations; citing Vargas's inside offensive positioning as "swim-stroke" arm movement fouling. Each ref he worked differently, one with cajoling, another with angry bellowing, a third with reasoned talk. It didn't help that the third, and head ref—whom he treated most respectfully—was the same sallow fellow who had chided me for looking for floor irregularities. Careless, stupid me! I had lost an even footing right off.

Indiana led throughout the half by scores of 14-10, 22-17, 29-23. Every time we had a small run going, Bobby the Intimidator would call out a critical word, a stern caution, and we'd get stalled by a foul, a questionable call. In the huddle I told the boys to stay calm, play their game. Water shook his head, "That cat is trippin' me every chance he gets, Mr. B. An the ref turns his head away." Perplexed, Roberto protested, "I never push number 24 'round, no need to. He's a jelly bean, no strength, man." I heard them out and said, "Play the basics, don't bait the refs. We'll get our share of the calls. Now, let's vary the defense..."

Near the end of the half we're down by four and the Chief steals the ball and flings it ahead to Water, who glides upcourt. Slyly, he waits an instant for two Hoosiers nearly to catch up, and gluing them to his hip, takes the ball on in for the layup, getting banged to the floor. Whistle blows. I'm cheering like a kid for the 3-points and the momentum, when suddenly I see the head ref, who's been out yonder at halfcourt, overrule the call against defense and call it a charge on Nurlan! Hurting, my boy looks up in disbelief.

I scream out, "What? That's not your call! How can you?"

The lanky ref approaches, wags his finger at me, and warns, "Any more outbursts, you got a T."

"Why would you overrule? On what basis? What'd my boy do?"

Nodding to me, he adds, "And that's a shooting foul for

defense."

Restraining myself, I repeat slowly, "What'd my boy do?"

He approached me closer, "Used his elbow on the way up." Grinning, he adds, "That'll cost you a T, Coach."

He blows his whistle and yells out, "Technical, Green coach!"

I am beyond fury at this point, and the assistants grab me, trying to pull me away. I stand in his path, in his face, and say, "If the baseline ref didn't see that, how could you? You were way out of position. You're biased, ref. Or is it bullied by Knight?"

"One more word, Coach, just one," he proclaims loudly for my assistants and the scorer's table, "and you're gone from the game." Then he leans down and, as crafty as Iago teasing Othello, whispers, "Never knew a kike who wasn't a hothead sore loser."

As I cock my fist I'm grabbed from behind by Percy and jerked away, heart pumping crazily.

The crowd is surprised. My players are shocked. Like a lunatic who's just had a psychotic episode, I'm escorted out and down the runway by two assistants, who get me to the locker room. Firmly but calmly, I'm undressed and set in the shower. Just like that. Strangely, I submit.

Soon, when the boys come in, I gather that Indiana has made the technical, and made both ends of the one and one. Instead of leaving the court at halftime one point down, we're now down by seven, a turnaround of six points in a close, tough contest.

I take some yoga breaths while the boys settle in, collect their Gatorade and oranges, change shirts, towel off. Clearly they are despondent, taken aback, confused about the turn of events.

My head spinning, chest thumping, I find myself in a rage and throw cold water on my face. Looking in the mirror I see a rumpled, oversensitive jerk, and nod at him. I return to the boys and tell them they did splendidly, I fucked up.

"Just play our game, pick up the defense a notch and move

without the ball." Then I pick up my paperback. "All right, boys, you've all heard of Thoreau, right? Now hear this, and take it to heart. This is the real stuff. From chapter 2 of Walden: 'To be awake is to be alive. I have never yet met a man who was quite awake. How could I have looked him in the face?

"'We must learn to reawaken and keep ourselves awake, not by mechanical aids, but by an infinite expectation of the dawn—'"

I looked round at them doubtfully. This was more abstract than I'd remembered, but they were all with me and Konepski asked if Thoreau had looked ahead to CDs and movies.

I went on, "'I know of no more encouraging fact than the unquestioning ability of man to elevate his life by a conscious endeavor. It is something to be able to paint a particular picture, or carve a statue, and so to make a few objects beautiful, but it is far more glorious to carve and paint the very atmosphere and medium through which we look, which morally we can do. To affect the quality of the day, that is the highest of the arts. Every man is tasked to make his life, even in its details, worthy of the contemplation of his most elevated and critical hour...

"'I went to the woods because I wished to live deliberately, to front only the essential facts of life, and see if I could not learn what it had to teach, and not, when I came to die, discover that I had not lived. I did not wish to live that which was not life, living is so dear—'"

Nurlan shook his head, orange peels in hand, beret on, relaxed now. "Live that which wasn't life?"

"The essentials, he means, Water. The important things he didn't want to miss in life."

They were really listening. "Here, more. 'I wanted to live deep and suck out the marrow of life, to live so sturdily and Spartan-like as to put to rout all that was not life... to drive life into a corner and reduce it to its lowest terms, and, if it proved to be mean, why then to get the whole and genuine meanness of it, and publish its meanness to the world; or if it were sublime, to know it by experience, and be able to give a true account of it in my next excursion. If life is brutal and nasty, then so be it... I'll take that then.'"

I searched down and read on. "'Still, we live meanly, like ants; though the fable tells us that we were long ago changed into men; like pygmies we fight with cranes; it is error upon error, and clout upon clout, and our best virtue has for its occasion a superfluous and evitable wretchedness. Our life is frittered away by detail. An honest man has hardly need to count more than his ten fingers, or in extreme cases he may add his ten toes, and lump the rest.'" I paused for the ripple of laughter. "'Simplicity, simplicity, simplicity! I say, let your affairs be as two or three, and not by a hundred or thousand; instead of a million, count half a dozen, and keep your accounts on your thumb nail. In the midst of this chopping sea of civilized life, such are the clouds and storms and quicksands and thousand-and-one items to be allowed for, that a man has to live, if he would not founder and go to the bottom, and not make his port at all, by dead reckoning, and he must be a great calculator indeed who succeeds. Simplify, simplify.'"

Dennis was beaming; what was that about? Anyway, "'Why should we live with such hurry and waste of life? We are determined to be starved before we are hungry. Men say that a stitch in time saves nine, and so they take a thousand stitches today to save nine tomorrow. As for *work*, we haven't any of any consequence. We have the Saint Vitus dance, and cannot possibly keep our heads still.'"

Now Roberto was nodding in agreement. I went on. "'Shams and delusions are esteemed for soundest truths, while reality is fabulous. If men would steadily observe realities only, and not allow themselves to be deluded, life, to compare it with such things as we know, would be like a fairy tale and the Arabian Nights' entertainments. If we respected only what is inevitable and has a right to be, music and poetry would resound along the streets...'"

Nurlan repeated, "Reality *is* fabulous, ain't it?"

I held the book toward them and searched down the page

with my other hand. "'...I perceive that we inhabitants of New England live this mean life that we do because our vision does not penetrate the surface of things. We think that that *is* which *appears* to be. If a man should walk through this town and see only the reality, where—'" the first buzzer rang— "'where, think you, would the "Milldam" go to? If he should give us an account of the realities he beheld there, we should not recognize the place in his description. Look at a meeting-house, or a courthouse, or a jail, or a shop, or a dwelling-house, and say what that thing really is before a true gaze, and they would all go to pieces in your account of them.'"

Eddie interrupted. "Coach, are you referring here to the *reffing* in all this?"

I stared at hopeless Eddie, then went on. "'Men esteem truth remote, in the outskirts of the system, behind the farthest star, before Adam and after the last man. In eternity there is indeed something true and sublime. But all these times and places and occasions are here.'"

The second buzzer sounded and the assistants began getting the balls and the boys ready, though they still waited. "'God himself culminates in the present moment, and will never be more divine in the lapse of all the ages. And we are unable to apprehend at all what is sublime and noble only'— by that Thoreau means *except*—'only by the perpetual instilling and drenching of the reality that surrounds us.'" I looked up at the boys, bless their souls, who were right there with me still.

"Have you ever heard a more perfect definition of transcendentalism, fellows?" I asked. They looked at each other, checking it out, smiled and shook their heads.

"You mean better than Mister Emerson's?" Jack asked.

"We've *got* to take them out, Sydney," begged Duddy. *"Please!"*

"Just this: 'The universe constantly and obediently answers to our conceptions; whether we travel fast or slow, the track is laid for us. Let us spend our lives in conceiving then. The poet or artist never yet had so fair and noble a design but some of his posterity at least could accomplish it.

"'Let us spend one day as deliberately as Nature and not be thrown off the track by every nutshell and mosquito's wing—'"

"That's it, Syd, sorry. Let's go boys!"

A flurry of activity. I'm not sure how it happened, but I found myself out on the floor with the team, the half about to begin. To Chief I said: "No dribble for 16." To Eddie: "Aggressive to the hoop." To Nurlan: "Extra pass off the break." To Avram: "Release faster." To Dennis: "Baseline picks." To Roberto: "Use the body." To Jarrod: "Weakside help." To the team: "Remember, boys. *Simplicity—*"

"Simplify, simplify!" Nurlan shouted with glee.

"And dance the St. Vitus's dance, huh, Coach?" added Vargas.

"And also," added Dennis, "let's not be thrown off by 'every nutshell and mosquito wing.'"

I nodded to my ally in irony. "Yes. Quite."

Well, they went out there and I'd like to report that all went well and better, but it didn't. The same sorts of niggardly calls impeded our progress. A walking violation. A three-second lane infraction. A hold on Vargas instead of an offensive tip-in.

There was only one thing to do, so I did it. At the next bad call, with five-forty gone in the half, I called over the same head honcho, and spoke very calmly, "You know, Dwayne, I don't think you understand clearly the Principle of Verticality. May I read to you here from the Rulebook?"

"I'm warning you, Berger, don't get into it with me now."

"Dwayne, you can't call a block on my boy there, just listen. 'If the defensive player's arms are held vertically and are maintained in this position, no offensive player may cause contact *even if the defensive player jumps vertically to a higher position.*' Dwayne, your call is missing the last clause..."

"Berger, one more word and—"

"But these are special guidelines for officials, Dwayne, see?" I held up my evidence, the little orange NCAA Rules booklet. "Would you like to borrow it for the rest of the game, really?"

His face colored as he digested the words, and he let go: "You're gone, Berger! A second T against Green coach! He's outta here, for good!"

The boys encircled me immediately, fearing an explosion. But I was calm, almost serene. Mission, and motivation maybe, accomplished. In parting I declared to the squad, "'Be it life or death, we crave only reality. If we are really dying, let us hear the rattle in our throats and feel cold in the extremities; if we are alive, let us go about our business.'"

The boys nodded solemnly, seeming to get the full point.

And yet, to confess the entire truth, I believe there were genuine tears in my eyes as Renee and Percy led me away.

In the dressing room I didn't bother showering or changing, but took a soda, sneaked in flask-scotch, and watched the team perform on the closed-TV. I expected them to go about their business, hoping that my sacrificial exit would have worked. Meaning, the two other referees would be influenced accordingly, and give the boys of green an even shot at the calls. If they didn't, it was over. But with a level of fairness introduced, the kids might find a surface for their rhythm, a lift for their belief. In the next minute Avram went up for a quick jumper, the defender was called for a foul, the replay showed a questionable call at best. Now it was the Great Hoosier's turn to protest, and he did. A tad too much, I sensed. Good signs. I might not beat him out there coaching, *but back here, ejected, maybe.*

I sat back and watched, something of a detached observer now. For it has always been my theory that, if you teach your students well, they should be able to perform on their own, when necessary, without your constant cues or expert presence. When the curtain went up, there were just the actors on stage, with the director just another spectator. Why not so with a finely-tuned, well-trained hoop team? The stage was theirs now, the repertoire was familiar, they could play Ibsen, Shakespeare, Aeschylus, Wooden, Iba, Berger. (My assistants knew enough not to interfere.)

They played the game, our game of fundamentals and lovely passing, and Indiana couldn't shake them; Conway stayed 3-4 points behind. I put my feet up. At about the twelfth minute, something clicked. Avram floated a jumper off a perfect (Dennis) pick. On the inbound, the Chief stole it and fed a soft bounce pass to Vargas, who hit the layin and a foul shot. On the next inbound Nurlan slapped away the dribble from their playmaker and without breaking stride took it all the way home. Indiana timeout, and Knight tried the whip. Cursing, yelling. No diff. When play resumed my boys were still focused, still elevating toward High Flow. A swiping Jarrod deflection of a pass into the pivot and Nurlan was fastbreaking, laying it off to Eddie for the layup. Again, with Indiana on the dribble their offguard was doubleteamed just over centercourt, Chief stripped him clean, and we were off and flying, with Dennis banking the easy one. Indiana grew frantic, rushed down and threw up a wild jumper, which Roberto rebounded and in one motion outletted to Water, who took three long easy dribbles and, at the foul line, passed to Avram on the baseline for another corkscrew jumper; the defender, a second late, fouled. Swish, three points. The huge loud Hoosier crowd grew very quiet—a Greek audience suspended in disbelief as Clytemnestra emerged bloodsoaked from her husband's bath. Indiana tried yet again to bring it up and score a single point; double-teamed on the sideline, the slowfooted shooter threw an errant pass. Quickly, Nurlan brought it back down, feinting one way to Avram, feinting the other way to Eddie—and grinning while faking out the Hoosiers—did a relaxed 360-degree whirl, laying it up and in with a fingertip roll. He was hit, too (a foul again called by another ref). Beaming still, he made it. Knight called another time, this one for plea and supplication, but it was too late, too late, our run was 17 points in a row in the space of nearly four minutes. The hoop audience of 18,332 fans stood and applauded, having witnessed the complex and true art of the game, wherein the eye was more accurate than the mind in perceiving the essence; so swift and immaculate was the appearance. As the TV camera panned the vast auditorium and crowd in full appreciation of Conway, I must confess, my heart leaped high.

The game was over, everyone knew, though the remaining minutes had to be played out. We had been sublime, we had been exhilarating, we had been transcendental. Reality *was* fabulous. Yes, Waldo? Henry?

And something else happened for me: when the television replay did a slow-mo of the last 30 seconds of play, with Billy P analyzing the conventional items, I discovered something new about High Flow, something deeper. Watching Vargas rebound and Nurlan dribble and Chief deflect and Avram float one in, I understood that in the midst of apparent speed, there was relaxation; in the eye of the hurricane, there was an unrushed quality, a point of equipoise held at the center. Maybe something like light held and caught in prismatic refraction. For when the boys returned to the floor and kept it up for another two minutes, I was able to see the speed of the game in terms of an inner time; beneath swift motion I perceived its serenity; no wonder Nurlan could spin and beam, pleasure was leisure in the middle of motion, and the boy knew this secret. I searched for other terms, starting with the notion that the game's true beauty was that its hidden quality was its effortless center; in High Flow, time was altered, clock time was transformed into inner timelessness, the eye (and mind) were tricked by the external movement of players and ball. So that at the innermost heart of the game, when play lifted up into its higher zone, was paradox and illusion, but it took mind in repose, in reflection, to perceive and name it. And I felt a nice bit of self-irony, too, in recalling how, during the season, I had cautioned Nurlan and the boys not to rush things, to take their time, to feel relaxed even on the fast break, for I had been saying more than I knew, uttering an unconscious revelation behind a line of conventional wisdom...

Thus after years of watching, Sydney was now discovering; sitting there ejected, Coach learned a bit more about the game.

Later, in celebration—or in dream?——I took the bus of kids up to the mountains outside Santa Fe, where we would have our burgers and malts and watch the full sky show. They protested, but I didn't care. One art deserved another, I reasoned.

"Is this not the 'Land of Enchantment,' fellows?"

"It's freezing up heah, man," answered Vargas.

"Can't we put on some Hammer, Coach?"

"Coach B, give us a break, huh? The Big Macs just ain't the same up here, honest."

"Look up, gentlemen, at Orion and tell me you've ever seen it before? Over there, Nurlan, Eddie, see? And look, the moon's so bright up here you can practically read by it, right, Roberto? Yes, Dennis? And what was it Thoreau said, 'that perpetual instilling and drenching of the reality that surrounds us...'"

"Coach, like we got no boots on, and the ground's snowy— caint we do this some other night maybe?"

I was only slightly dismayed. After all, so what if they were ordinary out here, in life? Hadn't they been extraordinary onstage, down there on the court, where it counted?

I smiled at Nurlan and stroked his lovely brown cheek; took the Chief around the waist, and called the other boys closer in, too, until we formed a kind of circle, holding hands; and if we didn't offer up a formal prayer, at least we were together, and the gods could see that. Huddled together, beneath the white peaks of the Sangre de Cristos, we could see each other's breath in the fine cold clear night, and it was bracing. A higher music. (I stopped hearing their noises.) For just a minute or two, we probably looked like some ancient people in strange ritual, communing with the immortal gods in a remote Stonehenge, out here in the enchanted New World.

12 SHADOWS OF VICTORY

Victory High. Is there any drug sweeter or stronger than the morning after victory, when one can savor the taste in one's palate, and let it slide down and around slowly, revving up your entire body and mind in one long grateful high? A suffusion of potency. In that Western Motel the next morning I devoured the accounts of our upset in the *Albuquerque Journal* and *USA Today*. I took to heart remarks like "the cool unflappable poise of the Ivy League boys, obviously instilled in them by the shrewd though hot-tempered coach, who resisted adversity and kept their focus on the ultimate prize." And: "Was it Coach Berger's plan all along to get tossed out for purposes of inspiration, à la Auerbach in the old Celtic days?" Or: "The remarkable upset is testimony to what is possible in college ball when a team plays as a whole, and forgoes catering to star recruits who demand the ball, among many special compensations." And my favorite: "If there's been a better-coached club, or a better ten-minute run of pure basketball, than Conway College displayed last night in the Pit in Albuquerque, this reporter has not seen it since the days of the great UCLA teams of John Wooden." Alone at 7:15 a.m. in the coffeeshop and reading those winning marks, I felt saluted and honored, a stage director reading the opening night raves or a Navy skipper just having come ashore from an uphill sea-battle. The SS Conway fighting in Midway.

To boot I already found telegrams in my box. One was from the impeccable Carril at Princeton: "IVY CONGRATU-LATIONS ON SPLENDID VICTORY! BEAUTIFUL TO WATCH!" A second was from Dave Gavitt of the Big East: "HOW DOES THE GLASS SLIPPER FEEL, CINDERELLA? THE FIT SEEMS PERFECT." A third, from a U.S. Senator named Bradley: "YOUR VICTORY BIGGEST BOOST TO IVY SPORTS SINCE PRINCETON IN '68 OR CONWAY IN ROSE BOWL, 1942!" I couldn't resist pouring whole milk upon my corn flakes and sliced banana; a richness forgotten.

Presently my four assistants wandered in and sat down, grinning like party children.

"No bagels, Syd?"

"Oh, I had my rewards last night," I told Duddy.

"You better be prepared for some bigtime offers," said Renee, taking coffee and juice and referring to the newspapers.

"Ain't that a fact?" added Percy. "You've just become *one hot property.* Take me along if it's the Sunny Coast!"

"Well, you guys were terrific last night when I was asked to 'step aside,'" I said, "you kept them focused."

"They kept themselves focused, Syd," put in Roscoe, shaking his head. "I've seen kids determined before, but never that collected and poised. Completely poised."

Percy added, "And relaxed, Sydney, relaxed. That was the key."

"As though you were right there," laughed Duddy, "*reading aloud* to them."

"Yeah, something like that," concurred Percy. "Can you keep them that way for the big bad nasties?"

"UNLV is something, isn't it?" I said. "Boy I bet they could do as well in the NBA as any new expansion team. It'll be something just to be on the floor against them. 'Conway versus Las Vegas in the Western Regional Final,' has a nice ring to it, hey?"

"The winner getting a ticket to the Big Ball," murmured Duddy. "Do we have a chance, Syd—realistically? Honestly?"

The waitress came and set down three more breakfasts.

I accepted a muffin and buttered it. "Sure, you always have a chance, no matter how long the odds are. Sure. But we've got to cut down on the odds, on the court at least. Nudge them a bit off stride." I nudged a crumb. "Just enough to frustrate them. Then hit the shots we shouldn't miss. And hold onto the ball."

"But do we have time to prepare, in one day?"

I shook my head. "We've had all season to prepare, Roscoe. Now's the time to do what we did last night: stay poised, relaxed, efficient. Make few mistakes. And hit a high stride for crucial minutes down the stretch." High Flow I'd keep private, like a religious preference.

"Against that defense? Those jumping jacks? Those shooters?"

"Two practices today, gents. At noon and at six p.m. Nothing heavy, I assure you."

They nodded, jotted, ate.

"Just one question, Syd." Roscoe. "Did you purposely get tossed last night? I hadn't considered that till later on."

Superstitious like the next fellow about my innermost secrets, I held up my muffin: "I'll bet anyone a sawbuck—this isn't a Thomas's!"

After they left I sat around daydreaming. ("Coach Berger, this is Stanford calling...") Planning the practice sessions. The dour waitress filled my cup two more times at least, while I doodled on a few napkins. Then suddenly a hand reached across me in the booth and placed a rumpled paper bag at my place. Cocaine plant?

"Lox," whispered a familiar voice, "with cream cheese and bagels. It took me an hour and a half to find the real thing." Hugging me tightly and kissing my cheek, Chip Bromley sat down opposite me. "You son of a gun, you deserve it."

I read the scribbled logo of "Goldy's Deli," and believed

he was right. "I'm going to save it for lunch, okay?"

"You can save it for the Final Four, if you wish," he winked. "Make that dance and I'll personally fly some in from Barney Greengrass's."

"Don't kid yourself," I smiled. "UNLV's talent is overwhelming."

"So are you. *Don't kid yourself.* You've taken a crew of nobodies and made them into the smoothest unit in college basketball. One that the whole country is buzzing about. It's nothing short of phenomenal. Sydney, what can I tell you?"

"Thanks, Chip. You've been a help and support all the way."

The waitress brought his coffee and he slipped a bagel out of the bag. "Jan would kill me, but what the hell? Mind? You still have half a dozen."

"Half a dozen? Who are you feeding, Berger and Sons?"

He chomped, sipped coffee, and spoke, low, "I hear some rumors floating about an investigation. Hell, whatever it is, I'm there to help you out, remember? And I have friends, too, with clout."

"Thanks, pal."

"Look, buddy, I trust you more than I trust any damned investigators. And I know you well enough to know that you haven't done anything to tarnish the college." He shrugged. "Even if you might have helped out a lad here or there."

I decided upon half a bagel.

"Two rights don't make a wrong in my book," Chip continued. His long oval face was puffy from past drinking; the furrows in his forehead were jagged and pronounced, a sign of his hard reckoning.

He *believed* in me, all right. But did I have the same conviction? I wasn't sure.

"Well, we don't have to bother about this stuff now, here, with the immediate task at hand. The big focus is tomorrow, huh?"

Indicating the lox, I noted: "This is not bad, considering it's not Nova Scotia."

"You know," he said, missing my distinction, "with you at the helm, I have the same feelings that I used to have when I watched Doggie Julian or Bob Blackmon coaching. Conway *always* had a chance, no matter what the odds or the other guy's talent. I used to figure the other team had to make up maybe a full touchdown, because of our coaching superiority. With you I figure the other club starts maybe... ten points behind. Roughly."

"Should we advise the scorekeeper of that, or just pretend?"

At the noon practice I talked to the boys about the Vegas fastbreak and their offensive board climbers. "Dennis, Roberto, Eddie, if you don't put your bodies on theirs and protect our defensive board, we go nowhere. Understood? Next, defensive rotation, weakside help on the man down low is *everything*. Every pass into the pivotman, especially if it's Johnson, has to be harassed, the ball slapped at. Got that? He's so strong-bodied that our job is to make him give up the ball *as soon as he gets it*, since his judgment is questionable. Chief, Jarrod, Eddie, you're the Harassment Squad—go ahead and smirk, but that's your task. And Antoine, it may be your day of reckoning; fight LJ down low, for positioning. On offense, Water, you can expect to be double-teamed, maybe even in backcourt; be prepared. Get rid of the ball, upcourt, and keep it in the center, not sidelines. One of you three forwards needs to come up quickly, take that first pass, and immediately look downcourt for the next pass, to Avram for the open jumper on the baseline, or down low to one of the other two. Denny, start out on top and we can alternate. In other words we play the double-team aggressively, make them pay for it. If we miss the jumper or the chippie, too bad. In the halfcourt game, we work the clock down for 30-35 seconds, make them lazy, bored, impatient, and sneak in the layup. Got it?"

They nodded and I sent them out to work.

For two hours we ran through the 30-second countdown and setup drill; not bad. On the trap I exchanged Dennis for Roberto as my first passer. On defense I ran a switching man-to-man defense which slid deceptively over into disguised sagging zones. For twenty laborious minutes the "H. Squad" went to work, bemoaning the routine but getting the point. Finished up with passing drills, and the mandatory fifty foul shots apiece. Did it matter against monster UNLV? Wishful fantasy. I took them off the court before they worked up a full pace. The race wasn't until tomorrow at 4 p.m., and I still had a 6 p.m. workout planned, to repeat routines and work on set plays.

In the locker room Dennis remarked idly, "Do you think a reading is in order, sir?"

"Oh, I don't think—"

"Yeah, Coach Berger, that'd be a blast!"

"Now? Really?"

"Yeah, sir, why not?" Eddie said. "Timing's sort of perfect."

Huh? Alas, while the boys opened up their motel box lunches—ordered by me, to keep them away from reporters and fans, groupies and druggies—I searched for de Tocqueville, but found only my portable Thoreau. Pressed I turned to an old standard.

"Here, gentlemen, a classic lecture. 'On the Duty of Civil Disobedience.' How many know it? ...Some education. Let me skip around to give you the full flavor. Here, for example.

"'It is not a man's duty, as a matter of course, to devote himself to the eradication of any, even the most enormous, wrong; he may still properly have other concerns to engage him; but it is his duty, at least to wash his hands of it, and, if he gives it no thought longer, not to give it practically his support... See what gross inconsistency is tolerated. I have heard some of my townsmen say, "I should like to have them order me out to help put down an insurrection of the slaves, or to march to Mexico—see if I would go"; and yet those very men have each, directly by their allegiance, and so, indirectly at least, by their money, furnished a substitute. The soldier is applauded who refuses to serve in an unjust war by those who do not refuse to sustain the unjust government which makes the war; is applauded by those whose own act and authority he disregards and sets at naught; as if the state were penitent—'"

I stopped and checked their interest; their eyes were upon me. "'—penitent to that degree that it hired one to scourge it while it sinned, but not to that degree that it left off sinning for a moment. Thus, under the name of Order and Civil Government, we are all made at last to pay homage to and support our own meanness. How can a man be satisfied to entertain an opinion merely, and enjoy *it?* Is there any enjoyment in it, if his opinion is that he is aggrieved?'"

"Sounds like he's pretty ripped himself, though."

Jarrod, critically.

"Yes, but on the other hand...'Action from principle, the perception and performance of right, changes things and relations; it is essentially revolutionary, and—'"

"'Scuse me, Coach B, could you rehearse that line again?"

I nodded and, just as I was about to repeat the line, I noticed Dick Porter standing by the door, arms folded, listening. I flinched. My god, now I was in for it all right.

"Yes, it is a good line, Jarrod. Here it is again. 'Action from principle, the perception and performance of right, changes things and relations; it is essentially revolutionary, and does not consist wholly with anything which was. It not only divides States and Churches, it divides families; ay, it divides the *individual*, separating the diabolical in him from the divine.

"'Unjust laws exist; shall we be content to obey them or shall we endeavor to amend them, and obey them until we have succeeded, or shall we transgress them at once?'"

"All right, man, now go for it!" Nurlan, exultant.

I glanced at the A.D., and he was standing there, leaning against the door, listening. *Thinking what?*

"'If the injustice is part of the necessary friction of the machine of government, let it go, let it go:—' skipping—'but if it is of such a nature that it requires you to be the agent of injustice to another, then, I say, break the law. Let your life be a counter-friction to stop the machine. What I have to do is to see, at any rate, that I do not lend myself to the wrong which I condemn.'"

Eddie asked about that line, if it meant not just going along and cited the "action from principle" theory.

"Right, Eddie." I turned to Dick, and asked if he wanted a word with me...?

"Yes, I would, Syd. But why not finish first."

The sport. "All right. One more paragraph, gents. Here: 'Under a government which imprisons any unjustly, the true place for a just man is also a prison. The proper place today, the only true place which Massachusetts has provided for her freer and less desponding spirits, is in her prisons, to be put out and locked out of the State by her own act, as they have already put themselves out by their principles. It is there that the fugitive slave, and the Mexican prisoner on parole, and the Indian come to plead the wrong of his race should find them; on that separate, but more free and honorable, ground, where the State places those who are not *with* her, but *against* her—the only house in a slave State in which a free man can abide with honor. If any think that their influence would be lost there, and their voices no longer afflict the ear of the State, that they would not be as an enemy within its walls, they do not know by how much truth is stronger than error, nor how much more eloquently and effectively he can combat injustice who has experienced a little in his own person. Cast your whole vote, not a strip of paper merely, but your whole influence. A minority is powerless while it conforms to the majority; it is not even a minority then; but it is irresistible when it clogs by its own weight.'"

Roberto intruded here, eating a banana, repeating to himself: "'clogs by its own weight.'"

"Clogging the middle, man." Nurlan was fingertipping the ball. "Ya know what that means. So, a minority can do that too, to the system, if it wants ta."

Roberto nodded slowly.

I read: "'If the alternative is to keep all just men in prison, or give up war and slavery, the State will not hesitate which to choose. If a thousand men were not to pay their tax-bills this year, that would not be a violent and bloody measure, as it would be to pay them, and enable the State to commit violence, and shed innocent blood. This is, in fact, the definition of a peaceable revolution, if any such is possible. If the tax-gatherer, or any other public officer, asks me, as one has done, "But what shall I do?" my answer is, "If you really wish to do something, resign your office." When the subject has refused allegiance, and the officer has resigned his office, then the revolution is accomplished. But even suppose blood should flow. Is there not a sort of blood shed when the conscience is wounded? Through this wound a man's real manhood and immortality flow out, and he bleeds to an everlasting death. I see this blood flowing now.'"

"Whoa, hold on," interrupted Jarrod. "That's pretty cool stuff." The others concurred, except for Dennis, who commented: "Rather sophisticated reasoning for revolution. Perhaps sophisticated to the point of casuistry?"

"To the point of *who?*" The Chief stared at him haughtily.

"False reasoning performed very well," I said.

"Well, I don't find the reasoning *that* false, you know," Roberto explained, craning his neck. "If your conscience is wounded, your mind is messed with, and then your manhood is on the line, hey?"

"And do not forget Mr. Thoreau's answer to the public officer," observed Avram, "'if you really wish to do anything, resign your office.' That too takes courage, much courage. That message is everywhere in Tolstoy, Chekhov, you remember. For example, Ivan Ilytch, who should resign and doesn't. And—"

I called a halt to the literary lesson. "We better get on with it. The A.D. here has been patient enough." Grinning, everyone turned to him. "Six o'clock sharp, boys. Get some rest."

I put Thoreau to rest and went over to Dick, who took us

along the runway and back out to the empty court. We strolled around the floor.

"My oh my, I've never seen a session like that, Syd. I had heard a little about your 'pep-talk readings' but I had never realized that it was that sort of material...sort of like a seminar."

I shrugged, embarrassed.

"I'm thoroughly impressed." He faced me with his lake-blue eyes. "Which makes what I have to do all the more difficult. In fact I can't quite believe it myself. Here." And he handed me a telegram from the college; specifically, from the office of the President.

NCAA RULES COMMITTEE INVESTIGATION HAS CHARGED SERIOUS ALLEGATIONS OF IRREGULARITY AND ILLEGALITY IN YOUR METHODS AND PRACTICES AS COACH OF BASKETBALL TEAM. STOP.

REGRET TO INFORM YOU THAT YOU ARE HEREWITH AND IMMEDIATELY SUSPENDED FROM YOUR POSITION UNTIL ALLEGATIONS ARE PROVEN ACCURATE OR INACCURATE. STOP.

OUR LEGAL COUNSEL AT COLLEGE RECOMMENDS THIS ACTION.

VERY SORRY.

DR. MARTIN GRAYSON, PRESIDENT

I looked up and shook my head.

"I know what you must be feeling."

"I don't think I'm feeling anything," I said. "I don't even understand what this means... for me, now."

"I'm afraid it means the worst: you're officially suspended, effective immediately."

"And tomorrow's game?"

He shook his head. "Someone else will have to coach it."

A death of a friend, a wife's betrayal—the stuff that defied the conventions of language to approximate emotions. "Really?"

"Really."

"I see," I said. Or was it the network of emotions that was shortcircuited, tricked haywire?

"It's hard, Syd. For you, for me, for the boys most of all."

I breathed deeply, gazed at the sacred court, let my head spin.

"Want me to tell them?" he offered, putting a hand on my arm.

"Sure," I said, not caring. "Why not? Say that... Whatever."

He nodded. "I don't know what to say. The legal boys are surely overreacting... but if there's anything I can do, I will."

I turned slowly and walked off.

Before I had taken ten steps however, I turned back. "No, Dick, I'll do it. I'll tell them. Maybe I'll catch them now."

I jogged quickly back down the runway to the locker room. But when I got there, they had already scattered. What should I do? Collect them by the pool? Their rooms?

I ran upstairs and searched for the A.D., but he too had left.

Where to go, what to do? I found myself returning to the golden floor, like a homing pigeon. Slowly I strolled around it, focusing on the polished tongue and groove hardwood. My dream was embedded right there, tomorrow. The game of meaning. But it would be played without me. I found it hard to comprehend.

Hurting and suddenly deeply fatigued, I wandered away.

In my rented Toyota van in the parking lot, I drove off. Took the main highway out of town and drove, listening to the radio, oldies, pop stuff. The Eagles sang of the depressed doings at a hotel in California, Gloria Estefan offered musings about the heart in a deep, sonorous voice. I followed the vanishing meridian line as though it were a guide for the perplexed, a direction of purpose. My head told me to get back to the hotel and take care of business, like giving the kids the news. But they'd learn it on their own, I figured. And I'd see them at the six o'clock practice.

At one point I pulled over and took a walk on the hardstubble, amidst the low brush. It was chilly, grey, an altogether forbidding place. I walked among large boulders and still couldn't quite fathom it all. How I had shot up so high and then fallen so quickly... Why now? Had I deserved it?

Sure you deserved it, Sydney boy. You broke the rules, remember, for the sake of your boys; for your own principles. The anarchist streak in your blood, right? At least Mom and Dad would be proud. (Really?) Now swallow your medicine like a big boy and get on with it. Move on, to the next rung down. How'd Odessa Junior College in Texas sound for starters? And let big brother Robey have one final smirk.

Back in the van I wrote out a formal letter for the media, and for the college. Nothing much, just denying the allegations, blah, blah. In Albuquerque I found a copy shop and made a few copies of the telegram, and my own statement. Strangely I found myself comforted in that hurly-burly shop, watching the copier machines spitting out their sheets. I had to pull myself away from the hypnotic repetition.

In the motel I sneaked into my room, took the phone off the receiver and grabbed a shower. And tried to sleep.

No luck.

Yet maybe good luck, it turned out. For I was clearheaded about my strategies for UNLV. I sat and jotted down two or three notes. Then, to soothe my soul, I read several sections on how students were taught in anarchist schools, one from Josiah Warren, one from Paul Goodman (a novel), and the third from Tolstoy's school at Yasnaya Polyana. These forty-odd pages of moral and aesthetic education by serious educators—not the sort of careerists who generally ruled today's college departments—revitalized my spirit. I felt on firmer ground with my own actions, my own moral, if unorthodox choices. That real education seemed so very remote, so intensely apart, from the packaged wisdom being dispensed in ninety-nine percent of our schools these days, Conway included. Under the umbrella of such truths—or were they thin rationalizations?—I felt somewhat consoled.

In the next hour and a half I made contact with my lawyer back in Prescott and heard what I expected: there'd be little hope of getting an injunction to stay the college order. There were also several knocks on my door, but I didn't bother to answer. I had to keep my head clear, for hoop strategies, personal strategy. I read some William Godwin, some Clair Bee, and, on the tube, saw some Marx Brothers. The trio was just right for someone in my condition.

At 6:00 p.m. sharp I was on the gym floor pacing up and back as the boys came on, the coaches too.

"Why didn't you tell us immediately?" asked Percy.

"Where the hell you been?" Duddy exclaimed. "Everyone in the world has been trying to get to see you, for chrissakes!"

"Honest, Sydney, we're your friends," chastised Renee, "not merely your *professional* associates. Why haven't you let us help out today?"

Even icy Roscoe seemed affected. "You got a raw deal, Syd. To do this to you now, on the eve of the biggest game." He shook his head. "You deserved better, much better. We're with you in this, down the line."

I tapped his shoulder. "Thanks, all of you. Okay, guys," I turned to the squad. "Gather round. I've got some news for you."

The boys gathered, sitting on the benches, dribbling, standing. They wore their old grey practice shorts and ragged Conway shirts and green baseball caps. Except Nurlan, with his beret, twirling the ball on his fingers, in front. Seeing them and knowing where we were, my feelings almost welled up and over before I could say anything. "There's been some news, fellas. I don't know how to tell you, so I'll—"

"Excuse me, Coach," interceded Dennis, "but the team already knows the news. *Your* news."

I blinked hard, my head spinning. "Huh? How? When?"

"It's all over town, Coach," said Roberto. "We been accosted all day by news reporters, TV media people and stuff."

"Yeah, we went over to the A.D.'s room," explained Eddie, "and told him 'bout the rumors flyin 'n all. He told us you'd tell us, but we informed him we had to know right then if it was gossip or what. So he gave us the whole scoop."

I nodded. "Oh, I see. Then you gentlemen do know. Good. Good."

Dumbfounded, I stood there scratching my scalp. "So there's nothing for me to say on that score. Instead I'll simply say this," I declared, heading into a reverse Gipper pitch: "No matter who's coaching you tomorrow, and we'll get into this in a minute or two, I want you fellows to go out and give it your all. Don't let up, not for a minute. Forget me, and what's happening around me, for now. Focus on the game. And when you're out there tomorrow afternoon—"

"Uh, Coach," interrupted Jack Lightfoot. "We have some news for you too. For you I mean."

"What do you mean?"

"Well, like, we had our own meeting, see," explained the Chief, "and we've come to our decision, sir. We've decided we're not gonna go out tomorrow afternoon and play."

I stared at Jack, his dark intense eyes following me resolutely. Slowly I shifted to that whole odd bunch now facing me with solemnity. I didn't fully get it, and broke into a befuddled grin. "Well, gentlemen, thanks a lot. That's just fine. But," I declared emphatically, "you will play and you'll play well, too. See, we're talking about an issue that concerns *me*, not you fellows. Your responsibilities lie elsewhere, on the floor tomorrow. And—"

"Excuse me, Coach," interrupted Avram. "But we have resolved on this. Discussed, resolved, and it's unanimous. We will not go out on the floor when the buzzer rings and the game begins. We decided we won't play without you, Doctor Berger. This fact is solid."

Doctor, suddenly? I glanced over at my assistants, who shrugged and shook their heads.

"Ya see, suh," advanced Nurlan, beaming and twirling, "we figgah we all be in this togetha, and if one a us is prohib-i-ted from takin part, well, then all a us will follow suit. Stick togetha like stickum."

"Yeah, that's the story," added Roberto. "We won't play."

"Look, guys," I said, searching for words, feeling nervous and weirdly prideful. "I appreciate the support. Very much. In fact I'm, I'm... moved by it, but you see it may turn out that..."

"I don't think you understand, really, Coach," Jarrod put in firmly. "This is an issue of principles that does involve us. Have you forgotten what you read to us from Thoreau about that? 'Action from principle,' sir, and 'the perception and performance of right,' well, that sort of 'changes things and relations. It is essentially revolutionary.'"

"Yeah, yeah."

"Amen, brother." Vargas. "Revolutionary."

Stunned. Foolish. Disconcerted. I tugged my short beard, took off my glasses and breathed into the lenses. I looked around trying to get a handle on it all. What the hell were they up to?

"Did someone put you up to all this? Come on, come clean."

"Yeah, kind of," Chief answered, grinning darkly. "You, Coach."

I didn't like what I was hearing one bit. "Me? How?"

"Come, sir. Your half-time lessons, yes?" advised Avram. "It is only inevitable this. Our firm decision and action now."

"Don't you see, Coach?" Dennis asked, lips puckered. "Don't you?"

Did I see? All I saw was a crew of bedraggled boys, facing me with a curious kind of collective stare, a mixture of wonder, devotion, and wry bemusement. Or so I read it. And beyond that, three or four adults, arms akimbo, turned sideways almost, in... benevolent embarrassment? All this in a huge empty auditorium, 20,000 vacant seats in the dim background, with a floor lit by a bright cone of yellow light—maybe the fitting setting for such a peculiar revolt? Go tell Captain Daniel Shays, I figured.

Did I see? From my good-humored scattered readings, this, now? A lost chance for the boys, a lost Rhodes for Dennis, a lost—

"See what, gentlemen? Folly, imprudence, caprice? Yeah, I see all that. But for Conway's sake, you're going to be out there tomorrow, for Conway's and your own." I sensed my words were making little headway, like a conventional tide pushing against a reinforced beachfront.

Indeed as I continued on through the motions of pleading with them, actually working up a good little angry diatribe and sweat, I already was trying to figure out the repercussions of their odd resolve, a resolve that bewildered me, unnerved me. Something like taking the ball out and being caught suddenly in a backcourt zone press and, trapped on the baseline by Chief and Nurlan, having no one to throw the ball to.

"So I think you're beginning to see that I'll do the thinking for you on this matter, right?..."

13   REVOLT IN THE DESERT

In the next three to four hours the shit hit the fan and blew upon me from everywhere. My hotel room became like Pearl Harbor, a Center for the Bombing of Berger. The media interpretation was simple: Coach Berger, trying to save his tarnished skin, talked his squad into staging the odd little rebellion on his behalf. Conway too bought into this version of reality.

"I recommend strongly that you talk sense into those boys and get them out on the floor tomorrow, Coach, or you'll have hell to pay. And you'll likely pay it from jail, for incitement." Ralph Jestud, college Provost.

"Is the rumor true, Coach Berger, that you blackmailed three or four crucial players on the team by threatening to reveal how they had managed—or cheated?—to stay in college with passing grades this year, unless they agreed to join this radical boycott?" CBS Analyst.

"College sports has reached a new low-point today, beneath the contempt of sleazy agents and venal programs, by the behavior of Coach Syd Berger of—who would have thought it?—Conway College. It wasn't enough that he was suspended from his job by his own Ivy college for allegations of NCAA rules infractions, but he has attempted to drag down the boys on his own team on the eve of their most important game in decades." CNN sports commentator.

"If Conway College should fail to field a team for tomorrow afternoon's game against University of Nevada at Las Vegas, Conway will face *longterm banishment* from NCAA competition on all levels of intercollegiate sports." NCAA rules committee telegram.

"Sydney, please, for the sake of your friends at the college—and you have many, none better than myself—don't allow this situation to deteriorate any farther. You've had a sensational season, and I believe you'll weather the current allegations, but *absolutely not* if there's a *forfeit* tomorrow. Persuade the boys to play, however you can." Chip Bromley, phone.

For me, the most beguiling comments came in next morning's New York Times, via George Vecsey's column: "Shays' Rebellion in the NCAA Finals? Ivy college players say No to playing without beloved but abruptly suspended coach. Who's right in this odd moral debate?"

"Odd moral debate?" But who was debating whom? I saw no debating opponent, only a mass reaction of vituperative pressure and vilification. Saturday night and Sunday morning, for twelve hours, intense calumnies were fired at me. I was being banged up and smashed down at dizzying speeds, a human particle in a linear accelerator. A bad divorce or custody battle, a misconstrued military or business venture, a good book hatcheted in the press; these must have brought on kindred feelings of shame and undeserved dishonor.

The good, gentlemanly A.D. appealed to me strongly, persistently, in a quiet room away from reporters, hired by the college, at the hotel. "Look, Sydney, for whatever reasons and however misguided the investigation by the NCAA, and the subsequent decision by the lawyers at the college, which resulted in your suspension—a suspension I personally find premature at least, and unfair in its timing—you have to overlook all of it, for everyone's sake. Yours, the kids', Conway's, mine too. First of all, we will automatically lose the money involved, money which will go straight into the coffers of the Athletic Department. And even though we share it with all the Ivies, the total figure of one million, one hundred forty-six thousand bucks is no small matter. The other Ivies will never forgive us, either, don't forget. Let alone all future and past Conway alumni. *You just don't forfeit games in the big-time, period—no ifs, ands or buts.* There's too much riding on it nowadays."

I sweated, drank tea, smoked my pipe and Cuban cigarillos. I explained. "Dick, it's their decision, not mine. I wanted them to play, I encouraged them to, and I will again, tomorrow morning. You can be there with me, if you wish, and talk to them yourself."

"It's you, Syd, who guides them." He shook his head. "You've become their guru, not merely their coach. I saw it myself the other day, today I mean—you see, I'm losing all track of time, this thing has me going round so much. You're the only one they'll listen to at all."

After a few hours he had removed his tie and shoes, popped a pill of some sort, and had a second scotch. "It's my job too that's on the line, and my future, Sydney. Look, I hate to bring this up, but, don't forget, it was I who gave you the break in the first place. And if you don't get us out of this mess now, I'm down the drain with you, pal. No more credibility to this A.D. in college sports. Nearly thirty-odd years down the tubes. You understand?"

"I do, Dick, I do." But I was running out of interior room to encompass it all.

"Look, if I could field a representative team of any sort, I would. But it's too short a notice, and too long a distance. I'm trapped. So it's up to you to get us off the hook. And I'll promise you this, buddy." He leaned down to my chair, clear blue eyes in wide, "*get them to play* and I'll back you to the hilt against the NCAA posse. Hide you, outfox them, countersue, whatever it takes to free you from their kangaroo court. And that's a promise, Syd. Have I ever broken one to you?"

I shook my head. No. Still, I didn't think that he, or any-one, understood that team's resolve, their crazy resolve.

"I'll give it my best shot, Dick. Honest."

He nodded. "One other person wants to speak to you on this, if you'll just wait a moment." He dialed, and in just a few seconds, like a USSR-USA hotline, he handed me the telephone.

"Hi, Sydney, how are you? I bet it's been rough. Very rough."

Thank you, I almost blurted. "Yes, sir, I think so too."

"Well, I want you to know that Conway is behind you in all this. I mean we will provide whatever legal assistance is called for in the NCAA inquiry. That's one point. The more important point, however, Syd, is that your great accomplish-ment, and the team's great accomplishment, will be wiped away and tarred by this most unfortunate situation, if it is allowed to continue. And what will be remembered instead is the dark day of the forfeit, something like the 1920s Black Sox scandal in baseball. I don't think you, or the boys, or Conway, want that. Do you?"

"I agree, Mr. President." Pressured himself, I saw now. "I think."

"You 'think,' Sydney? How do you mean that, if I may ask."

"I mean, I agree, Mr. President." Too many ambiguities, confusions, were circling my brain for me to untangle them now, here.

"Good, Sydney. I sincerely hope things will work out to-morrow afternoon... and later on. And who knows, Syd, that squad of yours is so well-coached that it may just go on and win tomorrow, with you there in spirit only." A little laugh. "And if they should win, why I'd imagine we'd work hard with our legal office to have you reinstated for the Final Four next weekend, Syd."

I paused over that legalistic "I'd imagine." "Thanks, sir, for the thoughts." I handed the phone back to the A.D., who said a last word.

"Just as the college is recovering from its own image problem..." He half-smiled.

"I'll do my best, Dick. Look, I'll get the boys up at 6:30 a.m. and—"

"Why not tonight, later, meet with them? In case it takes you two meetings, not one, to convince them?"

"Sure, yeah, I'll try that," I said, recruited now to the side of Conway, and The System.

I had an idea. Got hold of Duddy, my backpacking specialist, and told him to round up, in town somewhere, enough gear for an overnight. (He gave me the fisheye, but said he'd get the stuff.) And so, at ten-thirty p.m., bagging my doubts and stuffing my secret pride (in the boys and their revolt), I collected my bewildered team into the two vans and began driving. The music blared, talk ricocheted, the lights and noises of town receded. In a half hour we were out into the cool, vacant desert, lit by a full moon.

"What's up, Coach. Where you takin' us?"

"Hey, Mista B, you makin' hostages outta us?'"

"An odd time of night, sir, don't you think, to make the return trip to the Green Knight's castle?"

I drove, quiet, letting them come forth with their jokes and jabs, letting them feel whatever oddness they were feeling. To nurture their comfort they played their Walkmans—UB 40, George Michael, Prince—an addiction to cease soon, I knew.

I drove on in the silent soft night.

"What's goin' down, Coach, huh?"

"And all this camping gear, sir?"

"It ain't gonna work, whatever ya have in mind, Mr. B."

Away from civilization and CBS/ESPN/USA Today Surround Sound, I turned off the road with my 4-wheel-drive Toyota and nosed toward the shadows of the looming mountains. In just a few miles I pulled up within the crepuscular shadows of the high, jagged Sierras.

Immediately, outside, I was accosted by Roscoe, Percy. "What the hell are we supposed to be—"

"Shhh, take it easy. Listen to the desert, will you? And if you're uneasy, any of you, go back, honest."

"Where's Renee, and why are—"

"I left her at the hotel to take care of late-callers. Now just hold on, please." And to the boys: "Okay, guys, get out the tents and sleeping bags, we're gonna be settin' up camp out here. A little bivouac action."

I heard whisperings, mutterings... "What the fuck!"... "The man's gone loco...Absolutely bananas!" "Who's he think he is, a master sergeant at Fort Benning? Shit, we're not marines!"

"C'mon, fellas, stop grousing and move it! The sooner we get set up, the sooner we can get to the business at hand. Shake it."

If they began to resent me, so much the better, I figured.

Luckily that earlier training back at Mt. Moosilauke in old "Live Free or Die" was coming in handy, a rehearsal for the real thing. A half-dozen odd-sized tents were pitched, sleeping bags were issued, bitching and moaning shifted into high gear. With Sydney Berger catching the main flak.

In the cool night air Duddy, after obtaining a few boys' help in collecting kindling, built a splendid fire, and they huddled around it. Over warm cocoa and sodas and coffee-tea (for the grownups), I addressed them.

"I want you fellas to listen up. We're not talking here about tomorrow's game—we, I, am talking about your whole lives, present and future. And you're not going to throw them away because the NCAA is putting some pressure on your coach. Make no mistake about it," I declared, pacing back and forth in front of them, "don't get on the floor tomorrow afternoon and your basketball lives, and personal lives, will be worth zip. You'll be remembered always, and treated always, like traitors, outlaws, criminals, bums, goodfornothings. As for something like your Rhodes scholarship, Dennis my boy, forget it. They'll find a way of taking it away from you. And Nurlan, as for a pro tryout, no chance. No one will touch you. And Eddie, your name will be mud in the Polish community of Brattleboro. Just another dumb Polack, and you'll be lucky to get a dishwasher's job in a greasy dive. And Jack, all the glory you're supposed to bring home to Olde Towne and the Penobscots, it'll be transformed to shame. Think on that. And Roberto, forget any chance of playing for Puerto Rico in the Olympics; they don't take on *quitters*... Yeah, I see you guys are beginning to get the picture. Good. Avram, boy, is that why your dad left Kiev or a kibbutz, so you can quit on him here? As for someone like you, Jarrod, just starting out," I shook my head slowly, "forget Conway or the Ivies. You better start looking into some Texas JC."

I sipped my coffee and let the message sink in, staring at them. Feeling like the traitor myself. "Any questions thus far?"

"Yeah, Coach, I don't get it," wondered Jarrod gently. "Why are you doing this to us, to yourself?"

"You shmuck! I want you guys to understand the consequences for your planned martyrdom. It's not going to be pleasant back there, not one bit." I waited. "And one other item to consider this night. The real screw-turner."

I spoke more slowly. *"You can beat those guys tomorrow. You can really handle them. Oh, they're powerful as hell, they can shoot and jump, but they can be had. You guys have what it takes to defeat them, and get a ticket into the Big Dance.* There's the saddest irony of your choosing not to play. No one believes this in the basketball world, no one, but you and I know it, don't we?" A dramatic pause; and, on cue, a long high call from the desert.

"Are there wolves or coyotes out here, Coach?"

"They wouldn't nohow come round here though, right?"

"Hey, what bout them lizards or scorpions, can they sneak unda tents like?"

"You get what I'm saying?" I declared impatiently. "One more win and you'll be the Cinderella who's made it. Not many have, and no one like you in recent years—the last one was Bill Bradley's Princeton team in 1965, that's *25 years ago, and you guys have faced stiffer competition by far. Consider, you'll be in all the record books, almanacs,* along with that club. *And you can do it,* if only you will. And if you don't fuck up your chance, I'll show you how, once you give me the Go Ahead sign, tomorrow morning, that you'll play. So think on that tonight, think on it."

More dramatic pacing, eyeball to eyeball confronting. "And one last point: we've worked our tails off, coaches, players, fans too, to get us here. And I know what you've tried to express, and have expressed in saying *no.* Believe me, gents, I appreciate the gesture, totally. So I'm asking you now for another, larger gesture: forget your *immediate* reaction, bypass your momentary anger, think of my wishes and your interests in the longer term. And, tomorrow, *play the game:* for my sake, for your sakes. And for the sake of basketball too: the fans and coaches need to see little Conway play big against a big-time school."

I paused, gazing around at the mirage of mountains and darkening sky. "Just tell me, friends, is this not *right* our here, just right? Look around and feel it. Have I ever steered you wrong before?"

I liked that extra spontaneous bit at the end there; quite soothing that. I felt heady like a serious con man, the native sort that cons himself first and the client only second. Yes, I believed all the malarkey I had dished out; or made myself think I believed it. Actually, I thought something else, something more complicated and ironic than my stated pitch. But I wasn't there for complexity and irony, I was there to get them on line, back in the system, on the court. And I sensed I had them, too.

"So you guys sleep on all that, okay? And nice and early we'll hit the decks and see what you think."

A silence ensued.

Good, I thought. Moved by me into reflection—at last.

"Jes one question, Coach: can you read somethin' to us now? One a them stories?"

That was quite... touching. "Sure, why not, Nurlan? I'll get something from the van." After all, I figured, if we wanted a change of heart here, we needed some of the old ways repeated, like a nighttime lullaby. What should I go for, de Tocqueville, DeVoto, Turner, Bourne?

I returned after a minute. "All right, I'm going to read from the journals of a man who was an illegitimate child, son of a French sea captain and his Creole mistress. A fellow who was inept in school and bored in business in Kentucky, a man who became the greatest ornithologist and illustrator of birds in North America. But he loved more than birds—the entire outdoors, the wilderness. His name is John James Audubon, and he died in 1851."

Mutters from the boys about bird-watchers and Nurlan, skeptical: "Hey, was he really *illegitimate?*"

I proceeded. "Here's what he wrote from an 1820 Journal, for example: 'Ever since a boy I have had an astonishing desire to see much of the world and particularly to acquire a true knowledge of the birds of North America, consequently, I hunted whenever I had an opportunity, and drew every new specimen as I could, or dared *steal time* from my business.'

"And again, he wrote of his aspiration: 'I saw here (at the confluence of the Ohio and the Mississippi) two Indians in a canoe, they spoke some French, had bear traps, uncommonly clean kept, a few venison hams, a gun, and looked so independent, free and unconcerned with the world that I gazed on them, admired their spirits, and wished for their condition.'

"I'm going to skip now, and read from a later work, *Delineations of American Scenery and Character.*

"'When I think of these times'—his early years in Kentucky—'and call back to my mind the grandeur and beauty of those almost uninhabited shores; when I picture to myself the dense and lofty summits of the forest, that everywhere spread along the hills, and overhung the margins of the stream, unmolested by the axe of the settler; when I know how dearly purchased the safe navigation of that river has been by the blood of many worthy Virginians; when I see that no longer any Aborigines are to be found there,' and by the way, Jack, that's a good clean word, aborigine. Means native to a particular place. Indigenous. Descriptive, not pejorative. Now,

Audubon again: 'When I see that no longer any Aborigines are to be found there, and that the vast herds of elk, deer, and buffaloes which once pastured on these hills and in these valleys, making for themselves great roads to the several salt-springs, have ceased to exist; when I reflect that all this grand portion of our Union, instead of being in a state of nature, is now more or less covered with villages, farms and towns, where the din of hammers and machinery is constantly heard; that the woods are fast disappearing under the axe by day, and the fire by night; that hundreds of steam-boats are gliding to and fro, over the whole length of the majestic river, forcing commerce to take root and to prosper at every spot; when I see the surplus population of Europe coming to assist in the destruction of the forest, and transplanting civilization into its darkest recesses; —when I remember that these extraordinary changes have all taken place in the short period of twenty years, I pause, wonder, and, although I know all to be fact can scarcely believe its reality.'"

Jack looked thoughtful, I observed. Convinced...?

"'Whether these changes are for the better or for the worse, I shall not pretend to say; but in whatever way my conclusions may incline, I feel with regret that there are on record no satisfactory accounts of the state of that portion of the country, from the time when our people first settled in it.'"

"He should see the old virgin land now, huh?" remarked Dennis.

"I'm going to skip... 'However, it is not too late yet... I hope to read ere I close my earthly career, accounts from those delightful writers...' He's referring to Irving and Cooper... 'of the progress of civilization in our western country. They will speak of the Clarks, the Croghans, the Boones, and many other men of great and daring enterprise. They will analyze, as it were, into each component part, the country as it once existed, and will render the picture, as it ought to be, immortal.'" I closed the paperback and looked up. "As he did, in his life, and some of his writings, of course."

"Of course, if you peeked round these parts," said Nurlan,

turning about, "it's still vanilla empty, ya know. Scope it out, I don't see nothin but miles an miles a desert and mountains. No population 'splosion here, huh?"

"Is that why you brought us out here, Mr. B? I mean, to take note of all this...?"

"And what's playing or not playing got to do with it, huh?"

"Just listen to the quiet music of the place tonight, boys, and replay my words. *Why you have to play, should play, will play.*"

"Where are them drawings a his, Coach? Can we get to see 'em?"

"Absolutely, Nurlan. There are several fine editions. Now get some sleep, you'll need it for four o'clock tomorrow."

I watched them saunter toward their Sierra tents, lean, zip, enter. Presently I heard Roberto entertaining with his guitar. I privately played Ruffo and Caruso in my headset, Iago and Othello singing their great duet *(Si pel ciel marmoreo giuro!)*, one the voice of passionate fury and the other of dark deceit. Never before had I *felt* so clearly their disturbing resonances.

The morning was bright, the desert glorious, and I was up early, despite the fact that I had slept very little. Nerves, thoughts, new sounds, hard ground had interfered. The ground of this desert was rib-cracked and rockhard flat, and I saw a darting lizard stop suddenly to observe the curious intruders. The camp was quiet, the sounds were calls from birds, and I was just getting the coffee ready on Duddy's tidy gas burner, when Duddy showed up.

"The way to live, huh?" he said, in his red fleece Patagonia windbreaker and shorts.

"Christ, aren't you freezing?"

"Hey, Sydney, this is spring! Can't you feel it? Think of them poor suckers a few miles down the road, hitting their garages or sidewalks instead of *all this*." He waved his arms.

I gestured toward the boys. "You think they slept?"

"Sure. Doubling and tripling them up in the tent was the

trick. Like peas in a pod, safe and secure. Should we wake 'em?"

"Nah," I said. "Let them have their beauty rest. Put them in a better frame of mind for their decision, and better condition for the game."

"Think they'll go ahead with it?"

I nodded. "Unless I can't read people, or they're complete fools. Anyway, they had better. Or I'll have them wandering in the wilderness for the next 40 years. Come on, let's see the Colombian you can brew here."

The air was cool and the desert fresh, like new air that had just been brewed, never breathed before. No trees, no houses, no roads, no cars, just the vast blue-grey sky slowly lightening, kissing the distant earth. Birds chirping. A bliss of wilderness. A rush of rightness. Reluctantly I felt myself getting converted.

"Duddy, you can lend me that Aldo Leopold or Wendell Berry you've been preaching to me, I'm going soft."

Big smile. "You mean greening, huh?"

That color again. "Have it your way."

Later, when the boys got up and straggled in, between 8:30 and 9:00 a.m., we fed them breakfast of rolls and jam, snack boxes of cornflakes and milk, coffee and tea (Nurlan and Dennis). We chatted, the kids whining amiably about animals and rodents in the night. ("Man, I tell ya the way that creature was scratching and pawing at the tent I couldn't move if you had paid me!" and "Do they have rattlers out here, Duddy? I coulda swore I heard one for a good hour or two trying to spook us out.") Indeed I detected a kind of pride in the boys at having done this wild thing: camping out. As though they'd accompanied Powell on the Green River.

"Ya know what, Coach? This was a neat idea after all, I'm beginning to think," said Eddie, wiping strands of red hair from his eyes.

"Yeah, it not only kept us away from the reporter types, but it cleared our heads, sort of," Roberto said with part of a muffin in his mouth. "Made things clearer, simpler."

"Really," assented the Chief. "It was the right way to go. We all sorta came to that."

"Different from Conway lawns and dorms, that's for sure."

"An' different from Betsy Head and Brownsville, too."

"Big spaces remind me of area in Siberia, near Lake Baikal."

"You know, Coach," observed Jarrod, scooping scrambled eggs, *"you are one different dude,* for sure. One different dude."

"Well, son, show me how that difference is rewarded— on the court at 4:00 p.m. today."

He winked. "You're right, Coach. We can take 'em."

It wasn't at four but at 10:30 a.m. that they showed me something. Through the A.D., the team called a press conference. But the conference room at the Doubletree Inn was way too small for the crowd of media people that had assembled there to cover it. A mutiny on the hardwood floor, especially an Ivy college one, was not a daily occurrence. In the smoke-filled Grand Ballroom at least five hundred were on hand, notebooks and cameras ready, to cover the unique happening. From newspapers like Ann Arbor News, Providence Journal, Newport Daily News, Kalamazoo Gazette, St. Paul Pioneer Press and Dispatch, Tulsa World, Lexington Herald-Leader, Toledo Blade, St. Petersburg Times, Christian Science Monitor, Seattle Times, not to mention the biggies or the cable stations. And not all sports reporters, either. (I saw tags from *Paris-Match, La Repubblica, Politiken, Manchester Guardian.)* As for me, I stood way in back, an interested spectator, wearing a straw hat, loud tie and shirt, sunglasses—sporting a scrambled nametag and holding a notepad. Coach as Journalist Spy, ready to hear the formal announcement of "Play Ball."

The team had chosen Dennis, Jack and Jarrod to be their representatives. On a raised platform, with the whole squad (including Assistants) behind them, the three were introduced by Dick Porter. Dressed in their green and white Conway windbreakers and baseball caps, they stepped forward to speak before a lectern.

"First, we would like to read our statement, and afterwards," announced Dennis cordially, "if there are any questions, we'd be pleased to answer them." He turned to the others, smiling, and added, "I think."

The crowd appreciated the touch of wit.

A *Miami Herald* reporter alongside me, in red suspenders and porkpie hat, muttered, "Next thing you know, they'll be reading from teleprompters."

Jarrod stepped forward and, cracking a book, spoke low into a mike. "I'll begin by reading a passage from W. E. B. DuBois's *The Souls of Black Folk.*" He put on reading glasses while the crowd buzzed, puzzled.

The reporter huffed, "Ho-o-o-o-o-ly Je-e-e-sus, is this Sunday morning Mass at the Methodist Church? Are we really here to hear *sermons?*"

"'Scuse me fella," a man in a fedora called out, "but where's the Statement? Are you guys playin' ball or not?"

"The name is Jarrod, sir, Jarrod Stalleybrass. I think if you'll be patient, and hear us out fully, you'll understand our reasoning better. Ladies and gentlemen, this is the DuBois text: 'A prominent Southern journal voiced this in a recent editorial, in 1900:

"The experiment that has been made to give the colored students classical training has not been satisfactory. Even though many were able to pursue the course, most of them did so in a parrot-like way, learning what was taught, but not seeming to appropriate the truth and import of their instruction, and graduating without sensible aim or valuable occupation for their future. The whole scheme has proved a waste of time, efforts, and the money of the state.'"

"Now Dubois comments. 'While most fair-minded men would recognize this as extreme and overdrawn, still without doubt many are asking, "Are there a sufficient number of Negroes ready for college training to warrant the undertaking? Are not too many students prematurely forced into this work?

Does it not have the effect of dissatisfying the young Negro with his environment? And do these graduates succeed in real life? Such natural questions cannot be evaded, nor on the other hand must a Nation naturally skeptical as to Negro ability assume an unfavorable answer without careful inquiry and patient openness to conviction. We must not forget that most Americans answer all queries regarding the Negro *a priori*, and that the least that human courtesy can do is to listen to evidence.'"

He paused to drink water.

"Friggin' radicals!" my colleague noted, and the crowd stirred.

"'The advocates of the higher education of the Negro,'" Jarrod went on, "'would be the last to deny the incompleteness and glaring defects of the present system: too many institutions have attempted to do college work, the work in some cases has not been thoroughly done, and quantity rather than quality has sometimes been sought. But all this can be said of higher education throughout the land; it is the almost inevitable incident of educational growth, and leaves the deeper question of the legitimate demand for the higher training of the Negro untouched. And—'"

"'Scuse me, uh, Jack," interrupted a reporter, "but can't we get to the point? I mean, we're here for some news, hard news. Are you guys going to play or—"

"I am coming to that, sir," answered Jarrod. "But you can appreciate what Mr. DuBois was saying then, and by analogy maybe, what we are saying now, about the faults of higher education for poor folk, minority folk." He smiled rather serenely, and looked like a gleaming black Buddha.

"I don't get at all what you are saying. And we, I—"

"As I, or Mr. DuBois was saying," Jarrod went on pleasantly, his high, fine voice imitating a style I recognized only too well, "'If we leave out of view all institutions which have not actually graduated students from a course not higher...'"

Leaning against me, my pal winced. "Have you ever in your fun-filled life seen anything quite like this fuckin' minstrel roadshow?"

"'...Through the shining trees that whisper before me as I write, I catch glimpses of New England granite, covering a grave, which graduates of Atlanta University have placed there, with this inscription:

"In grateful memory of their former teacher and friend and of the unselfish life he lived. And the noble work he wrought that they, their children, and their children's children might be blessed."

"'This was the gift of New England to the freed Negro; not alms, but a friend; not cash, but character.'" Jarrod paused at that, looked up, and drank water slowly.

The man in the fedora stood up and called out, "Please, Jerry, we believe you. Honest, fella, we do. But could you come to an end for godssakes and tell us if you're going to be playing today?"

Jarrod nodded. "I repeat that last line, if I may. 'This was the gift of New England to the freed Negro; not alms, but a friend; not cash, but character. It was not and is not money these seething millions want, but love and sympathy, the pulse of hearts beating with red blood;—a gift which today only their own kindred and race can bring to the masses, but which once saintly souls brought to their favored children in the crusade of the sixties, that finest thing in American history—'"

"I tolja lefties, didn't I?" Red suspenders pounced fiercely. "Still selling the sixties, can you imagine?"

"'...and one of the few things untainted by sordid greed and cheap vainglory. The teachers in these institutions came not to keep the Negroes in their place, but to raise them out of the defilement of the places where slavery had wallowed them. The colleges they founded were social settlements; homes where the best of the sons of the freedmen came in close and sympathetic touch with the best traditions of New England. They lived and ate together, studied and worked, hoped and harkened in the dawning light. In actual formal content their curriculum was doubtless old-fashioned, but in educational power it was supreme, for it was the contact of living souls.'"

Jarrod looked up, half-smiled and stepped back.

This speech had taken up nearly a half-hour, since he had read the words very deliberately. And now that he was done, the packed house didn't know what to make of it, how to react. A few clapped out of courtesy, others buzzed to each other. Many remained silent, waiting.

"Is it the question period now, John?"

"Jarrod, as in the Bible, sir," corrected Dennis. "Hmm... Jack, do you have something to say?"

Jack stepped forward. "Coach taught us character, on and off the floor. Character first, never cash. Made college into home."

Eddie awkwardly took a step out, coughed. "It's true, he ate and worked and studied with us. We were sorta like that 'social settlement' that Mr. DuBois mentions." He retreated.

Nurlan came forward, in beret. "Yeah, Coach B gave us a lot a that love and sympathy. But you folks have ta remember something else, an I quote: 'Unjust laws exist; shall we be content to obey them or shall we endevah ta amend them, and obey them 'til we have succeeded, or shall we trans-gress them, *at once?*'" He beamed.

Dennis walked up. "I'd say he was a kind of Scholar-Coach, offering me along the way some subtle readings of the Green Knight."

"Uh, son, are you referring to the Purple Knights by any chance? I'm afraid I never heard of the Green Knights."

"Well," Dennis answered, "I'd go along with what Parkman said about La Salle," and he read: "'He belonged not to the age of the knight-errant and the saint, but to the modern world of practical action and practical study. He was the hero not of a principle nor of a faith, but simply of a fixed idea and a determined purpose.'"

My chest was beginning to pound, and tears welled up, I was so oddly moved. I hadn't realized that... that...

"What's La Salle got to do with this? Or Rutgers?"

"Where is your coach, by the way, son? Why isn't he here now?"

"*That* sonofabitch," muttered my partner, elbowing me. "Probably put this comical crew up to staging this friggin' farce all along."

Another reporter stood up. "Look, sports, are you characters playing today or not? That's what we're here for, and you gathered us here for that, remember? Is this preparation for a yes or no?"

"Where's your A.D.? Why doesn't he speak here?" Others joined him in the same plea!

Dick Porter strode wearily to the lecturn and said, "Gentlemen, I'm afraid I'm as much in the dark about the boys' decision as you are." He held out his hands. "So, let's hear them out and see what's on their minds. What do you say?"

"Hey, Dick, where you been for the past hour and a half, holed up back in New England? We've been listening to what's on their minds, and listening, and listening."

Helpless, he said, "I know, Jud, but let's not lose our patience now."

During the pause Dennis took the microphone. "I think a few of the other boys might want to say something. Hmm. Antoine?"

The tall gangling silent black swaggered forward. Would my ebony Bartleby really talk? He fidgeted a bit, fussed with his cap. "Well, ya know, Coach had an interest in that 'contact of living souls.'" He stayed put for three or four long minutes, looked about as though searching the universe, saying nothing. He turned and walked back.

You could feel the patience sliding, the anger growing.

Roberto came forward. "I never talked 'fore this size crowd before and," he laughed and stretched his neck, "it's kinda scary. Anyway, what I wanta say is this. Coach is a man, and makes ya feel like a man. And that means... everything."

Avram marched forward and recited rapidly: "Emerson says: 'Whoso would be a man, would be a nonconformist.

Nothing is at last sacred but the integrity of your own mind. Absolve you to yourself, and you shall have the suffrage of the world.'" He marched back.

"So ya ain't gonna play then, is that what you guys are saying?" cried out the man in the fedora. "Then go ahead and say it, goddammit! Say it!"

"You see," Jack said calmly, "the thing is, we can think for ourselves on this issue, and others."

Nurlan took the mike. "An we ain't slaves no more. On the court neither."

Dennis added, smirking slightly, "Or even indentured servants."

Then Nurlan took over. "Thass true, really true. We ain't like otha clubs ya know that are treated more or less like 'human chattel.' Do this, do that, boy, or you lose your scholarship, and be washed up at college. No sir. Now," he paused, opening another book, "let's check out Chapter 10, from the life of Frederick Douglass. Chief?"

Jack came forward and the audience groaned aloud.

"The balls, the balls of these characters!" My companion was steaming. "Tell me this is not happening, it's all a dream, a bad dream, come on, it's gotta be!"

Jack was reading: "'"Learning would spoil the best nigger in the world," Master Hugh would say, "if you teach that nigger"—speaking of myself—"how to read the Bible, there will be no keeping him; it would forever unfit him for the duties of a slave; and as to himself, learning would do him no good, but probably, a great deal of harm—making him disconsolate and unhappy. If you learn him how to read, he'll want to know how to write; and, this accomplished, he'll be running away with himself." Such was the tenor of Master Hugh's oracular exposition of the true philosophy of training a human chattel; and it must be confessed that he very clearly comprehended the nature and the requirements of the relation of master and slave...'"

As he continued, however, the audience slowly began to file out. At last they had had enough.

Oh, I understood them all right, and sympathized, and also understood the boys, and felt emotional—slightly over-whelmed. I had taught them well, perhaps too well. (Or badly?) They had grown impertinent, stubborn, stiff-yoked, relent-less, longwinded. Maybe educated?

"Don't tell me you're staying around?" demanded red sus-penders. "Come on buddy, I'll buy us a few Coors and we'll file this crazy fucking unbelievable yarn." He took my arm.

I released it. "Nah, I think I'll stick around till the end."

"The bitter end, you mean? When they stick it to us and announce they'll play after all?"

"Whatever... whatever."

"Well, good luck fella. Looks like there are a few dozen suckers like you sticking around." He shook his head. "Who'd you say you worked for again?"

I thought fast. "Didn't. Just one of the cables."

He squinted at me. "Figures. You bleeding hearts don't know these types off the floor do yah? Come down to Miami sometime and I'll take you on a tour." He shook his head and departed.

He was right, there were a few dozen of us who stayed put, most taking chairs, realizing we were here for a long haul.

For some reason I stayed standing, back against the wall, listening to Jack drone on with the Douglass narration, think-ing how this was the kind of speech that Fidel used to deliver, in the old glory days, with his Cuban audience glued for four to six hours, true believers of the revolution. *(Or even Sydney Berger?)*

Me, I was as skeptical of this revolt as the next fellow, even though it was made on my behalf, in my name. But skep-ticism didn't prevent my heart from fluttering, my brain from whirling. Oh, the revolt was getting monotonous all right, but it did have its bracing, poignant side, for me anyway.

"Look at you, in that shit-eating disguise," said Bobby Knight, my old adversary. "We should string you up alive, and let you swing on the Pit floor for two whole days and nights. And let everyone get a good look at the sucker who caused this whole cockamamie mess. Or better yet, send you so far from the big leagues of coaching you'll think the fuckin' desert is home. Yeah, from here on in, you're going to be toiling in some Gulag, and watching the big boys on the tube like the rest of the poor peasants. For beginning today, your coaching career is at an official end, a dead-end, in case you didn't know it."

Then, as if in slow motion, he took out a penknife, opened a pair of small scissors, and proceeded to clip my tie off just below the Windsor knot.

But that was all right, the act was minor, I figured, next to the Frederick Douglass story that was droning on and on, and the boys standing up there straight and firm, like a fatigued but driven group of Lincoln Brigaders saying No to perceived injustice—and Yes to loyalty?—in this unique and oddly articulate way. Too bad Mom and Dad weren't around to see the sight, and maybe Kropotkin too, here at the Marriott Hotel Ballroom. Revolution on native ground; anarchy native-style.

14   HEARTS AND MINDS

Oh, I was moved and impressed by their noble speeches and emotions, for sure. And charmed by their monkey-like mimicry and newfound erudition. To think that through all those halftime intermissions, while I flailed away, they had imbibed more than the Gatorade. What I had taken to be... idle eruptions and harmless charades of self-melodrama, the boys had taken to be fundamentals of Scripture. Moral imperatives. *Real* school lessons. Well, now they had taught me a thing or two.

A poetic statement and an exemplary act, wasn't it? Like some exquisite Kierkegaardian monologue, read by school-children.

And yet, yet, as I sat in my comfortable hotel room and stared out at the endless desert—with the telephone ringing—I couldn't help wondering: was it suddenly all over, the whole season? On the tube the Albuquerque news anchors were filling in everyone on the big news of the Conway "No." Was this really the way it was going to end then? The remarkable magic season sent up in a bonfire of high-minded altruism and team loyalties? All on behalf of "truth" and Sydney Berger, that anointed moral and strategic captain of the ship? With our goal, our white whale, say, just there in sight: the

NCAA Final Four. The end, really?

Other thoughts were swirling in my head, however. One more game, this afternoon, and, if we got some breaks and played well and happened to win, why then Little Jack Conway would get to climb the Beanstalk and go up against the real giants and ogres next week. Proceed onto the sacred ground of semi-final Saturday and who knows, Holy Grail Monday as well?... Why, even if we lost today, as the 10-1 odds indicated we should, just to play against powerful UNLV in the Western Regional Final was a victory in itself, a major accomplishment. Coach Berger would have made his point, his mark. My chest began to quaver and I got up and prowled the L-shaped room, flipping the station to a Home Shopping Channel and twangy voice selling rhinestone necklaces for $19.95. Was that my destiny down the road in NCAA history, to be called The Rhinestone Coach? Was that my due reward, too? Bullshit. I could outcoach 99% of the simpleminded duds who called themselves coaches. And all because of some silly spouting by me, and some imprudent infractions of dumb rules. Was the whole beautiful season, a feat of great delicate engineering, to go down the tubes in this... ungainly forfeit? The thought ate at me. It was becoming clear that *Coach Berger* had been running up against a subtle and devious opponent—*Citizen Berger.*

Picking up the Sunday N.Y. Times, with the Conway story making the front page, I knew I deserved better. My team, too. Despite themselves, despite me. So, for both of our sakes, I decided that I had to do something. Something swift, something rhinestonish, for the sake of the exalted end.

An act against me and my ideals, against coaches Wooden or Smith, against heroes Emerson, Whitman, Thoreau?!

Oh, that would hurt! Well, good. Good. "What I must do is all that concerns me, not what people think." "Right on, Ralph Waldo," I would add, "and not what your conscience thinks." In fact only when you went *against* your declared ideals and aspirations, on behalf of your deeper wants and needs, could you be true to yourself, right? With basketball in my blood, the season in my bones, all paths of virtue led to the Final Four. How could I resist?

Heated up by my court casuistry, I picked up the phone and told a perplexed Duddy to round up the boys, pronto, and find a good hiding place for a powwow. I thought fast, jotted a few notes on a hotel envelope, and made a pit stop at the Radisson business office for a bit of business.

By noon, at a dingy Hacienda Motel on the outskirts of town, we got a "suite," and privacy, anonymity. The Chicano proprietor was delighted at the sudden Sunday clientele.

The boys were still glowing with pride over their performance, and I told them how well they had done, how splendid their play had been. "Arthur Miller couldn't have scripted it better, boys. With Jean-Luc Godard directing, in his heyday."

"It was your victory as much as ours, Coach," Jack remarked.

"True, Mister B," added Jarrod, "we're your *pupils* as much as your players."

"I hate to admit it," allowed Dennis, "but you've really been our... Thomas Aquinas."

"Yeah," seconded Roberto, "and without ever preaching on us."

Everyone cheered in agreement and nibbled at the blue corn cheese nachos and Cokes we had brought in.

I nodded thanks and gathered them in front of me on the Mediterranean couch and shag carpet. "A great performance on the stage, boys. A wonderful scene. But now it's a great performance on that Pit floor that we need, and a different scene." I spoke slowly here. *"One that you're going to give."*

"Hey, Coach, c'mon, we already been through this earlier—"

Waving Eddie quiet I sipped my coffee and saw their looks ask: What's going down here? "A performance that you're going to have to give, on the court. What I mean, boys, is that *something new* has developed, and it would be amiss of me if I didn't inform you of the matter and give you my best counsel on it." *Lay it on thick, Aquinas.*

Their faces furrowed and bodies shifted uncomfortably. "I'm referring to some very nasty mail—or blackmail—that's suddenly come down the chute via the black fax." I held up and waved slowly a sheet of thermal fax paper, as though it were a criminal indictment. "Almost directly upon receiving word of your decision not to play, our pals at the *Review,* the infamous *Conway Review,* faxed us at the hotel to declare that, in the event you don't get out there and play, you'll be paying for that refusal for the rest of your lives—no decent schools, no decent jobs, no clean track record. Character assassination will pursue each young traitor everywhere. Furthermore, and this is the really dirty part, friends," I paused for full effect, "they intend to make sure that the parents are hit too. They will do a profile not only of the *quitters*, as they call you, but an investigative report on 'the *quitter's parents,* '" I had begun to read and tried to sound restrained, "'and make them pay as well. Since they, along with Coach Berger, are responsible for their training in sportsmanship and manners, for their lack of understanding of Conway values, they as much as the boys will suffer the consequences. Research is already under way to hit them where it hurts most, in their home towns and jobs.'"

A stunned silence, then bursts of obscenities.

"Are they nuts? This is still America!" shouted Eddie.

"Oh, c'mon, sir, that's just scare tactics of the cheapest sort," Roberto asserted confidentially. "Who do they think they are, the CIA?"

I leaned forward and spoke quietly. "Here's the really scary part: the specifics, and I have no idea how they got this info— such as Mr. Konepski on the Vermont State Highway Department, Reverend Stalleybrass in his St. Alban's Church affairs, Principal Edward Healy at the Hartford High School, Mrs. Lily Vargas down there in East Cambridge, Johnny Lightfoot in Olde Towne, Maine, and so on." I nodded solemnly and felt the lies sink in, like worms, nice and deep. I even felt badly for the good boys, having the mud spoil their Virtue Party so soon. But, sacrifice was in order for the higher good. And *my* good, too, I acknowledged. Anyway, weren't lies sometimes necessary for... memories of virtue? Penitence could always come later, after victory.

"Coach, are you sure of all this?" asked a confused Jack.

"Could they really get away with this kind of messing around, sir?" Jarrod pondered.

"Dirty tricks, like Nixon, huh?" said a mournful Antoine.

For evidence I held up the nefarious piece of paper and wagged it in their faces. "That's what they are there for, to manufacture the offal and then spread it on real thick." Oh, how useful the *Review* had suddenly become!

"May I see the fax, sir?" asked Dennis.

I stared at his blue eyes of mirth and firm brow, and reluctantly handed it over to him. Thank god I had taken that little precaution, just in case, at the Radisson's efficient office.

The piece of paper with the fabricated message fascinated and compelled the boys as though it were a shrunken head lifted out from the formaldehyde. They looked at the thin paper and dark message, and handled it with disbelief, curses, and growing fear.

"The dirty bastards!"

"Why would they do this, just for Conway?"

I told them to sit back down and hold on, stay cool. "Right now these are just threats, not acts. So the question is, do you want to gamble that they'll remain just threats and stay virtuous —or play and take revenge later on? Legal revenge?" They stared bewildered at me, and shook their heads, torn.

"I'm afraid I agree with you," I resumed. "We'll play and then fight 'em. Play first," I said, liking the sound of the piety, "fight second. And we'll make them pay, later on, don't worry." I shook my head, knowing there was no later on. "But first we'll play, so our parents and families are protected." My blood was pumping now.

"Won't we look like... cowards?"

"And be humiliated?"

I shook my head. "Once the whistle blows, and the game

begins, the only thing that counts or that will be remembered, is how you play and what the final score is."

"Could they really get away with those threats, sir?" Eddie persisted, obsessed.

"I don't really know, to tell you the truth. But it's too high a gamble, I'd say, and therefore—"

"Nope, we won't do it," Jarrod said, "parents be damned."

"Yeah, let them threaten us, blackmail us," seconded Jack. "What good is a principle if it doesn't cost you something, sir?"

The wavering boys now joined Jack and Jarrod, nodding, agreeing verbally.

The stubborn bastards! I stared at them, walked about, felt the season slip down the drain and my head begin to spin, perspire. I had one last shot, and took it slowly. "Boys, what about me, how could you do this to me? Think of me, Sydney Berger, your man on the floor, your man on the street. Me, your recruiter, your counselor. Sydney Berger, Conway outcast and NCAA loser. *Well, I need you guys now.* Go out there and trade in your philosophical principles for your Berger fastbreaks. *Just now I need a victory out on the floor more than you need a moral victory.*" I urged my eyes to well up. Then, like Olivier on the war fields, I crouched down in front of my soldiers. "I really do need you out there, boys, for my honor... my salvation." The highfalutin nouns and artful appeal were true, though, weren't they?

Uncomfortably now they shifted, glanced at each other, and reluctantly gave up, caved in, saying things like, "Okay, Coach, you got us," and "Didn't realize that it mean *all that* to you, I guess." "Berger over Thoreau, sir?"

I winced privately, patted this shoulder and that butt, and said, in a surprisingly cool tone, "Okay boys, now let's get on to today's opponent, UNLV. Tough team, but they can be had."

First I stepped outside into the adjoining room and told Roscoe and Percy to call the NCAA Regional Committee immediately, announcing the change of heart of my team.

"Christ," proclaimed Percy, animated, "what the hell did you promise them, Syd, a trip to Australia?"

"I hope not cash, whatever it was," added Roscoe, only half-joking.

"You're a magician, Sydney, and you deserve Coach of the Year award." Duddy was bursting. "A fuckin' Merlin!"

Back in the room with the boys, I took out the portable blackboard and went to work designing the game. "Now here's the thing about the Rebels, gang, they like to run and they like to lead, that's what makes them most comfortable. So w hatw e'lldo ism ake them *uncomfortable*, especially at first, yes?"

Henry David T. had his ways and Sydney Carton B. had his, was the way I looked at it. Plus, circumstances had changed. "So at first we slow it down, play the halfcourt game, and give them no second shots on the offensive board, right? Stay nose to nose with them..."

What can you say about my excitement, my anxiety, my blood running before a game like that? The opportunity of a whole lifetime was at hand, to go against a top four team and design a plan to topple them? This was it, friends, this was the chase hot and real, coming to a fateful end. Oh Jesus, to think that I almost blew it, for the sake of... virtue, honor, reward. And self-esteem. Had I forgotten that America was the god here, and its motto was "Victory Is The Only Morality."

"So, the first thing we do is run the clock down on the set offense, and on defense, you three mates on the boards, Tashtego, Daggoo, and Queequeg—"

I grinned with them, trying to settle myself down.

"By the way, Coach, will you be out on the court with us?"

I shook my head. "Not allowed. But don't worry, you'll hear from me, and know exactly what I'm thinking. So, where was I?..."

The game was a honey, and watching it on closed video,

in the locker room, was in many ways better than on the bench, especially with the slow-mo repeats, where you could make a quick study. Also, I was less wired, being remote that way and sending out my advice and counsel via a platoon of messengers. What was so special about the game was the contrast between the apparent rhythm of the score versus the real rhythm of the underlying pattern. Of course that didn't kick in till the second half, when the odds of probability began to take hold. But the basic questions, for me, were answered in the first half. Were we able to rebound defensively? Interrupt their fast break and force them into a halfcourt game? Intrude upon their powerhouse center, making him give up the ball? On offense, were we in synch, spread out, making the extra pass? Were they making the strategic mistake of not doubleteaming Water? The fact that Avram was not hitting on all cylinders yet because of tight defense—that I could correct; the fact that we had not yet hit a stretch of High Flow—that I could hope for. So, at halftime, with us down by four, I felt pretty good.

"As you know, lads, I'm not here to coach, let's make that clear. Because that's what Roscoe and Duddy and Percy are here for. I'm here to give you fellas a peaceful reading of a text, that's all. If you should like it, fine. If not, fine too, understand?"

They smiled, munched their fruit, drank, sprawled out, towelled off. My sentries stood in the door, just in case. (In case the A.D. came along? Fortunately I had been given no crude specifics of my banishment, merely the guideline of a Conway gentleman's agreement. Well, after all, was reading aloud criminal to the NCAA or Conway?)

Forsaking a Moby Dick chapter (no need for anger just now), I instead turned to an interesting fellow I hadn't read since my Miami of Ohio teaching days, when the middle-class kids had put him down as a "crybaby." Working with my ancient yellow teaching marks I began: *"Santayana on America*, gentlemen. A Spanish philosopher who spent half his life in America, as student and teacher at Harvard, he was both critic and fan of this country. Pay heed, 'cause I'm going to skip about."

The boys hunkered down, wide-eyed and intent.

"Here, concerning William James, Santayana wrote that 'he enjoyed a stimulating if slightly irregular education: he never acquired that reposeful mastery of particular authors and those safe ways of feeling and judging which are fostered in great schools and universities. In consequence he showed an almost physical horror of club sentiment and of the stifling atmosphere of all officialdom... His excursions into philosophy were accordingly in the nature of raids...'" I looked up, saw Jack smiling, and heard him wonder if James was a kind of "anarchist or guerrilla, making him so attractive for Coach?"

Mock cheers!

Smart Jack. I proceeded: "'He saw that experience, as we endure it, is not a mosaic of distinct sensations, nor the expression of separate hostile faculties, such as reason and the passions, or sense and the categories; it is rather a flow of mental discourse, like a dream, in which all divisions and units are vague and shifting, and the whole is continually merging together and drifting apart.'"

They nodded their understanding, Nurlan saying, "Flow, sir. Flow." And Jarrod added: "And motion, motion."

"Further down: 'The implication was that experience or mental discourse not only constituted a set of substantive facts, but the only substantive facts; all else, even that material world which his psychology had postulated, could be nothing but a verbal or fantastic symbol for sensations in their experienced order so that while nominally the door was kept open to any hypothesis regarding the conditions of the psychological flux, in truth the question was prejudged... That flux itself, therefore, which he could picture so vividly, was the fundamental existence. The sense of bounding over the waves, the sense of being on an adventurous voyage, was the living fact; the rest was dead reckoning. Where one's gift is, there will one's faith be also; and to this poet,' James, he means, 'appearance was the only reality.'"

I looked up and they seemed to be with me. One cited "faith," another "flux," and a third said, "Dead reckoning, like Thoreau, huh?" Good work, Jack, good.

Skipping down I found an underlined sentence. "'The tragedy and comedy of life lie precisely in the contrast between the illusions and passions of the characters and their true condition and fate, hidden from them at first, but evident to the author and the public.'" Oh, they preened at that, as though they were the characters in question!

"And from another essay, this odd paragraph: 'The heartiness of American ways, the feminine gush and the masculine go, the girlishness and high jinks and perpetual joking and obligatory jollity may prove fatiguing sometimes; but children often overdo their sports'"—I looked up to see thumbs up and arms pumping—"'which does not prove that they are not spontaneous fundamentally. Social intercourse is essentially play,'"—a cheer arose!—"'a kind of perpetual amiable comedy; the relish of it comes of liking our part and feeling we are doing it nicely, and that the others are playing up as they should.'" Eddie was nodding and mumbling something about teamwork. Good. "'The atmosphere of sport, fashion and wealth is agreeable and intoxicating; certainly it is frivolous, unless some passion is at work beneath, and even then it is all vanity; but in that sense, so is life itself... The point is that it should be spontaneous, innocent and happily worked out, like a piece of music well-played. Isn't American life distinctly successful in expressing its own spirit?'"

They seemed to be with me. Jarrod wondered if, in the vanity bit, I was referring to excessive solo drives? Nurlan, turning his beret, said yeah, we hadn't played with "passion or pleasure," and probably did look "frivolous." Oh? Well, let them be.

I forged on. "'Freedom—and young America furnishes a proof of this—does not make for enlightenment; it makes for play.'" Again they started to cheer, but I restrained them. "'A free society would create sports, feasts, religion, poetry, music; its enlightenment would be confined to a few scattered sages, as in antiquity. What brings enlightenment is experience, in the sad sense of this word—the pressure of hard facts and unintelligible troubles... Enlightenment is cold water. Education is quite another matter. "The purpose of this college," I heard the Master of Balliol say in 1887, "is to rear servants to the Queen."'" Laughter, jeers. "'Education is the transmission of a moral and intellectual tradition, with its religion, manners, sentiments and loyalties. It is not the instruction given in American schools and colleges that matters much or that constitutes an American education;'"—first bell rang!—"'what matters is the tradition of alacrity, inquisitiveness, self-trust, spontaneous cooperation and club-spirit; all of which can ripen, in the better minds, into openness to light and fidelity to duty.'"

Dennis noted that tests were indeed folly and Antoine intoned "club-spirit."

"'If American education does not transmit such a perfect human discipline as that of a Greek city or of the British upper classes, that is not its fault; it works on a vaster canvas with thinner pigments. But its defect lies in not being thoroughly and deeply enough the very thing which Mr. Lovett condemns it for being—a transmitted life.'"

A voice called out now, "That's enough for now, Sydney. You shouldn't be here, didn't you understand?"

I nodded at the firm A.D. as he approached and said, "Just reading, Dick, no coaching." And went on. "'The prevalence of insanity, of "breaking down," and of "nervous depression" is one of the most significant things in America. It goes with overwork, with not having a religion or "getting religion" (which is incident to not having one)—'"

"Now come on, Syd, please. Don't make it harder on yourself, or on me."

"'...with absence of pleasures, forced optimism, routine, essential solitude. An intense family life would prevent all these miseries, but it would take away personal liberty. The modern family is only the eggshell from which you are hatched; there you have your bed, clothes, meals, and relations; your life is what occupies you when you are out.'"

The second buzzer rang now and Dick gently took my arm.

"'But as you foregather only with chicks of your own age, who are as destitute as yourself, you remain without the moral necessaries.'"

Firmly I was grasped by two assistants and the A.D. and as I was transported out, I finished the passage. "'The test of a good school or college is its capacity to supply them. It is the only remaining spiritual home.'"

In the tunnel, Dick asked, "You all right?"

I stared at his concerned blue eyes. "Oh yes. Yes."

As the boys marched by they stopped to comment. Jack tapped my arm knowingly, "'In the nature of raids.'" Jarrod said: "'Where one's gift is, there will one's faith also be.'" Nurlan came up, whispered, "The flow, huh, the flow; like the man says, just like a dream. I getcha." And Dennis offered—with irony— "Which is more evident to our public, sir, the comedy or the tragedy?"

Dick and Duddy escorted me to my seat in the loge, cautioning, "You stay put now, remember? No matter what. Dick paused and reflected aloud, "You know, those boys seem to take in what you read to them, though in peculiar ways, don't you think?"

Well, it was fine, some 25 rows above floor level; you could observe the overall design and spacing better than on the bench. And as I watched the boys go about their business, on their own, more or less, I felt it was a truer test of my coaching. Without me to pester them constantly, to be their hoop superego, say. My crew was out there, an extension of myself and my intentions, maybe more *intentional* even, since they and I knew that they were only out there because of me, against their will and fulfilling mine.

So there I sat, feeling perverse. My quarterdeck below. One of the crowd of fifteen thousand souls, I felt alone in a spiraling moment of guilt, pleasure and intensity.

We were up against a taller, more powerful, higher-leaping opponent, against athletes who had been primed since the eighth grade for the NBA. There were coached by a man who had been charged with about 150 rules infractions in the past decade, but who was still out there. Well, actually, he didn't really coach during a game, he was a cheerleader; game strategy was left to his assistants. UNLV had a widebody center, a wonderful defensive forward, a sharpshooting guard, a ferocious/cocky attitude. How did you beat such a monster team, posing as a college club? Or have a chance?

I watched, searching for the small items at first, to see if the boys had heeded my between-the-lines messages. Two quick baskets by Las Vegas, one on a terrible shot; but it was countered by a jumper by Avram behind a Dennis pick. And the next time down Vegas put the ball down low to Johnson, their ferocious center; immediately Roberto went for the ball, forcing Johnson to turn to the blind side to keep it, whereupon Jack was waiting, took it away, and tossed it upcourt to Water, who had one man to beat, their cocky guard, and he took him in on his hip, fingertipping it under and in and drawing the foul. We were down by three. Next, their defensive forward was allowed the side jumper, he banked it too hard, Eddie rebounded it and outletted it to Water, who took two dribbles and bouncepassed it to a cutting Vargas for the basket. Down by one. The western crowd was surprised and confused. Vegas came down, their guard talking trash, and he tried to take it one on one on Nurlan; Jack cut him off, knocked his dribble away, Eddie grabbed it and flung it down to Nurlan who took it down and gave it over to Avram. Avram missed the short one but Vargas was there to tip it back in. Conway up by one. Vegas called time out; their cheerleaders danced, their coaches yelled. Roscoe looked up in my direction, where I kept nodding.

Vegas was now facing a box-and-one zone when they came down, a surprise. Offbalance, their guard nevertheless tried Johnson down low. A mistake. As he turned and took a dribble it was one dribble too much. Two fellows knocked it away,

Dennis grabbed it and got it to Jack, who flung it upcourt to Avram for an open fifteen-footer. Up by three. Vegas came down more slowly now, passed it around sloppily—they were not a passing club—and their offguard tried a 3-pointer, which rolled off the rim. Vargas got the rebound and we went the other way, the Vegas assistant screaming at the poor choice of shot. We worked the ball around, weaved and picked, Eddie came off a screen on the left side and dribbled right, into the lane à la Schayes or Havlicek, and using his body for protection, banked in a short hook and was fouled. He swished it for a 6-point lead.

The crowd stood, or was lifted by our play, and clapped. Their faces were clean and well-scrubbed, their love of God and family showed in alumni sweaters and polyester caps and jackets, their lives of ordinary routine and emotion were momentarily suspended.

I said to myself, to the team: stay focused, stay poised.

Vegas came back, scored a few baskets, but the boys were right there, poised, focused, relentless. The UNLV leaping, the trash-talking, the pounding inside didn't distract them. We played our game, the same game we had been refining all season, and it was a beautiful game. We rebounded hard and well; we defended with skill and strategy; we played fastbreak and we slowed down; we let Water dribble and direct, Dennis and Vargas pick, Avram jumpshoot and Jack troubleshoot, and we passed the extra pass. This *team* basketball worked its clockwork rhythm, each piece (or player) doing its thing, no more no less, the mechanism ticking routinely in expert gear. It proved the axiom that the clockwork team was far better than its parts and better too than the parts of their superior opposition. Like the art of the sonnet, the art of the game required a summation of repetitions (team), and strategies of genius (coach). Ah, Repetition, all honor to thee! (I had jumped up and was asked to sit back down.)

We kept the lead steady between six and ten points, a more impressive feat than a melodramatic last-second victory. The boys were my fleshly extension, my body, I knew, and I tingled with excitement and tension. You could feel their focus like a spiritual force, sense the awed and loud crowd blocked out, see that a mistake was quickly followed by a resumption of regularity; the zone of play had reached the higher level. All that down in The Pit, in The Land of Enchantment, while the banished coach watched devoutly from the stands, his invisible presence driving like a shoot through every one of the boys. The Conway five was straight on course like some purposeful ship on automatic pilot and no storm or opposition was going to deter it from the chase. And I, their driven Captain, felt a certain ease, a surge of relief, like a man who has had a heart attack but who has now been given his wonderdrug, his streptokinase.

In the hullabaloo that followed I found myself on the floor grabbed by this fan or that player. UNLV's Johnson took hold of my arm, grinned, and said, "Man, come on up to the pros, I'll play for you anytime!" Did he know, or think, I had coached? Or what? Chaos, screaming, hugging, kissing, bedlam! Amidst the frenetic rush the A.D. was upon me, saying, "Syd, Syd, that's one heck of a performance. You did it, they did it, thanks for getting them back on the floor. I'm going to do everything I can to get you reinstated for next week. Glad you stayed away from the bench, and," he winked, "the locker room, right?" I nodded, dumb. The boys were lifted and congratulated by alumni, by students, by fans, so I didn't bother to intrude upon them. Besides, I felt two or three ways about this victory, and I was already powerless from exhaustion.

Suddenly I was strongarmed by a fellow who said he worked for CBS and insisted that I come along to appear with the team for a postgame interview.

Thus I was forcefully pulled along to the sideline, where I was introduced again to Billy Packer, the sportscaster, and the whole team, my lost and newly found boys, were assembled all around us. The cameraman and sound guy adjusted our position, Billy chatted with me and Nurlan and Percy, and the crowd was still cheering. Then the red light was flashing, indicating ON AIR.

"Coach, and to me you're still the coach of this team, did you ever dream you could come this far?"

Someone shoved a Final Four cap onto my head, and the boys roared. "In America, I suppose, anything is possible, Billy."

He laughed. "No, seriously. What did it? What brought this unbelievable victory? To me it was the discipline, the incredible discipline of this team performing to their level without you on the bench."

"Yes, the boys played well, and stayed on course, true course."

"Ah, you're too darn modest." Turning to Water he said: "Now here's the great playmaker himself, Nurlan Waterford Reeves. What a great game, comparable to the old games where the playmakers like Cousy or Andy Phillips dominated. Waterford, how were you able to keep control of the game the way you did, even when they began doubleteaming you at the end?"

Water beamed, removed his white NCAA Final Four cap, and said, "Coach always said, 'You're the man, do your thing.'"

The little liar, I never spoke that way.

"And you three come on in here—the great inside game, not a one of them above 6' 6" in this era of giants. That's the best team rebounding job that I've seen since that great Arkansas squad with Moncrief and Brewer. But three rebounders? How do you keep from getting in each other's way?"

Dennis offered, "I'm the decoy."

Billy hit his arm. "No really, how do you do it?"

Roberto laughed, "Man, we're already black and blue from practices!"

"Coach, any word on your status for next week? Will you be allowed back onto the bench? Do you know yet?"

I shook my head. "I have no idea, Billy."

"Well, I personally think it'll be a great shame if you're not invited back, based on allegations alone. For if there's anyone who deserves to be in Seattle next week, it's you,

Syd. What a masterful coaching strategy! Good luck next week, all of you!"

"May I say hello to my father in Brattleboro, sir?"

The red light blinked off. Billy said privately, "It'll be more than a shame, Syd, it'll be a scandal. Got a good lawyer?"

Our celebration was a mixed affair, and short, since we had to catch a plane out of there. The boys were high and jubilant from the immense physical victory, yet every moment or two a thrust of regret or sliver of melancholy slipped through.

"We coulda been heroes of a different sort, ya know," said Jarrod, packing gear. "One a little more unique."

"Or cowards, a little unique," I retorted, sipping seltzer.

"Well, we'll just have to see how history records us, huh?"

"Yeah, Eddie. History."

"Coach," wondered Jack, "did you really think in your heart and mind that we could beat the Running Rebels?"

"All the way," I said, thinking of their hearts and minds.

"You are gonna take care of that *Review* though, right?"

"Right!"

Just as we were leaving an elderly gentleman came up to me. Offering his hand, he declared, "Coach, that's the best bit of coaching I've seen since the Wooden days, and maybe better, considering the difference in talent. The discipline, the strategy, the conceptualizing of three forwards, the emphasis on passing," he shook his head and smiled, "it was here, like the old days. I'm Pete Newell, if that name means anything to you."

"It does, Mr. Newell, a whole lot. Your Cal teams were special. And I've read your books. I appreciate your words."

"You can write your own ticket now on where you want to go, from what I see and hear. Just clean up that little mess at Conway and then pick your college. Good luck next week, and congratulations. You've brought *basketball* back to the game."

When he moved off Percy hit my arm and winked. "Tolja!"

The bus ride was dark and sober, given the victory. The moon slid in and out of the clouds. The boys were shrewd or sensitive enough to understand the exchange that had been made by our Faustian contract. Credit them again. After the assistants got through complimenting me—and I them—I settled in with myself, my own counsel. A win was a win was a win, I began. And, as Coach Newell suggested, my future might very well be a yellow-brick road paved by that prodigious upset. Conway defeats UNLV, Ivy League Conway as the Western Champion, those were strange, powerful words. And they could carry a career a long way, *if the little mess* could be cleared up. But my spirit, my nervous system, that was another matter. Much as I wanted, I couldn't really feel the full glory, or climb inside the victory and stretch, stretch! Instead I felt a certain undertow tugging me, an undertow of betrayal, self and other. By pushing the boys back up through the chute of their brave, smart revolt—the intelligence of their "No" resonated—I ensured my own fate as a cad, a coward, a crook. So be it then. Coach didn't have to be an upright citizen, he needed to be a Coach first and foremost. To win against the odds, that signified coaching. To drive the boys beyond their individual talent, that was coaching. To go up against your own highest interests for the sake of the team, to slip the shiv into your own ribs for the sake of victory—that was a coach's courage. The rest was piety, PR puffing, cheerleading. So be it, I repeated, lighting my pipe.

For an idle minute I pictured my reward—a place in the sun like UCLA, a place in the tradition like Kentucky, a place among the real athletes and athletic scholarships like Michigan?

Then the remote moon slipped back into the clouds and the little mess reappeared, dissolving my picture. Victory in the game, I thought, confusion and despair in the soul. Well, that too went with the territory, perhaps, the territory of Syd Berger, Coach or ex-Coach.

My reward came sooner than I had thought, however, when I received a late night call from the man himself. "Coach Berger, this is Sonny Vaccaro from Nike. That was a great upset victory you pulled off, and your whole run in the tournament has been spectacular. I'd like very much to sit down with you and talk about an exclusive Nike endorsement contract. We're talking six figures, Coach, and you'd be in some very exclusive company, with the coaches from Duke and Georgetown and Seton Hall. Hey, you'd be the first coach in the Ivy League to be invited to join our team. Quite an honor, eh, Coach? And of course your boys will be donning the best Nike sneakers for years to come, gratis, of course. What do you say to all that?"

But before I could stumble out an answer, the voice added, "You know, win this whole thing and I think maybe we could run a prime time commercial around you and your club. You know, stressing the underdog thing, something every American kid out there in the schoolyards and playgrounds can relate to, right? Yeah, that sounds pretty good to me. Congratulations, Coach, and you'll be hearing from our team real soon."

The legendary king of high school boys' hoop dreams had spoken, and waved his six-figure wand, and I, his newest emissary, was struck dumb by the possibility of enchantment.

But I'd keep the news to myself and try to focus on the real for a while yet.

15 THE CHASE

Back in the cozy streets the hometown was abuzz with the game, the victory, the national glamour. And Sydney Berger, far from returning home as a cad or criminal, had become a sort of Robin Hood, the outlaw coach who had taken his scrawny band of peasants to the magical forest of the Final Four. The last time little Conway had been this far was back in the 1940s, before basketball had a Final Four. The news of our peculiar ordeal and surprise journey was picked up everywhere, from the *New York Times* to the *Today* show and *Le Monde*. No way that allegations and charges by an athletic outfit like the NCAA were going to hold that much credibility, in light of our athletic achievement and the glow of national attention. America was beckoning. Thus it was the university administration, as well as me, that was on the hot seat; it found itself up against public sentiment, and even up against a good portion of its own people—faculty, students, alumni. The university lawyers had made a rather hasty decision in suspending me in the first place, and the higher-ups in the administration, Provost and/or President, had gone along with it. (Or was it the other way around? Would we ever know?) A mistake, it seemed now, after the great victory. (If you thought it difficult to fire a MacArthur or Patton after a military victory, imagine a great coach nowadays.)

The ensuing week provided three levels of entertainment; the legal arena, the national media, the play in the gym.

A city friend put me in touch with a New York civil rights lawyer, a heavy hitter who turned out to be a lovely intellectual and basketball fan. A curly-haired Copperfield story from the Bronx, Marty Frommer flew up to Prescott and, in 24 hours, found out what he needed to know. For Wednesday he arranged a meeting with the Conway lawyers. At breakfast that morning I told him I was a bit nervous. He smiled. "You're nervous? What about them? It's their call, and it's a tough one. If they stick by their highly irregular, if not illegal decision of a week ago, we sue Conway; if they back off, they have to come up with a good excuse. And, they've already violated your contract, which they may or may not be aware of yet. Don't worry, you're gonna come out smelling like a rose. Do you want some dough out of this by the way?"

I couldn't believe his words. Weren't those corporate waspy lawyers of Conway tougher than this Stuyvesant High boy imagined? "No money. I just want to be on the sidelines with my team in the Superdome. But won't they try to put the pressure on you, and me?"

His smile blossomed slowly. "Oh, maybe they will try, at first. I don't think they'll get very far. I checked with the NCAA's lawyers in Kansas, and as far as they're concerned, until any of the allegations are proven and the inquiry is completed, you're just another coach. And an innocent man. Furthermore, I read the Conway regulations booklet. Your case was handled sloppily."

I nodded, feeling hot over the ambiguity of that innocence. "Look, Marty, what are you looking for in all of this, if I take no money? I don't make—"

"Relax, don't worry," he said, taking my arm. "I'm a hoop junkie. I want to be out there behind the bench for Saturday's game. I take other cases for the money. Besides, there's principle involved, your rights versus university power. Let's see how this plays itself out, though I don't think it'll be too bad."

I considered his bespectacled face, his soft unlined skin, and his tough background. "Will any of the real bigwigs be present today?"

Marty wiped his mouth with a napkin. "Oh, I doubt it. They try to keep their hands as clean as possible. You know, they could use a West Side bagel shop up here. By the way I looked through your stack of media invitations, and I'm impressed. I may make mention of one or two during this hour, okay? You should go on one, actually. Let's go."

No, the meeting wasn't too bad. For me, in fact, it was an education in the ways of the world. Three Conway lawyers sat like grey-suited, button-down sharks waiting for my blood; the innocuous Provost and the President's assistant seemed to be witnesses to make the kill fair and square. The long wooden conference table had a tray of coffees and coffeecake, and a view of the green. Marty and I sat together while they ringed us on the other side and corners. Yet only the first twenty minutes or so were what you would call rough.

The Conway lawyers began by questioning me about my job description and normal activities. Then, for five or ten minutes, they peppered me with queries about extra-curricular activities, but when they proceeded to asking me directly about my "improper" activities, Marty interceded, saying: "Excuse me, are you thinking to conduct an official legal inquiry here of Coach Berger? If so, under what legal auspices? And let me say to you gentlemen, right off the bat, so's you know why *we're here*"—and Marty reached down to his briefcase and took out a thick folder of legal documents, from which he removed a contract—"that so far as I can see you have breached my client's contract, first of all; secondly, you have violated his First Amendment rights as a citizen; and third, you are in probable violation," and he rummaged through the pages again, "of statute 102a of the Conway rules and Regulations, regarding due process, which, I may add, in the case of Morrison vs. UNH in a 1988 New Hampshire Supreme Court ruling, turned out positive for the plaintiff. Furthermore," he paused, "after speaking to the NCAA legal staff in Kansas yesterday, I'm being conservative when I say 'probable violation.'"

Oh, that language on my behalf was every bit as lovely as "Shall I compare thee to a summer's day..."

The lawyers began to counterattack, but I couldn't follow it all. Besides being ignorant, I was too overwrought. (I had a curious impulse to pull out my Parkman and read!) The first fellow, a youngish blond wearing natty red suspenders, attacked rather sarcastically Marty's interpretation of the Conway statute and the Supreme Court ruling; the second, "Scotty something Junior," attacked me personally in a condescending manner, making a thing of "the shame" I was bringing upon the college; I stood to retaliate but Marty restrained me. Then they both went after him as a New York City "hit man" and an "ACLU type, coming up here to besmirch an Ivy school." To this and other cracks Marty listened quietly, doodling on a pad.

After giving them the stage for about ten minutes of vituperative anger, Marty sat up alertly and said, "Gentlemen, the thing is, you have a problem there, and I suggest you attend to it now and here, while we're around. Later, it will be too late."

Suspenders grew furious and said what the hell did he mean. Marty replied that his firm was ready to file an immediate brief for an injunction on their ruling keeping me off the court, and the ensuing publicity, which would be national, wouldn't do Conway any good at all. "You realize of course that Mr. Berger has been invited to appear on the *Today* show and *Nightline*, just to show you the scope of this affair."

Scotty Jr. cried out, "You ambulance-chasing shyster!" and Suspenders cursed aloud, but this time he was held back by the third, older colleague, who up to that time had sat imperturbably, looking on. Now he signalled a time out and stood to huddle with his colleagues, along with the Provost and the President's assistant; while they whispered at the far end Marty took a coffee and piece of Danish, and offered me a piece. Taking a bite he said, "Someone is going to make a bundle one day with a real deli up here, you wait and see."

After several minutes they broke from their huddle and came back to the table. Now John Ferguson, the more "mature" gentleman, spoke up: "Mr. Frommer, we're here to find an amicable solution to this rather difficult situation. Do you have any suggestions?"

"Mr. Ferguson," Marty responded, amicably, "we have a common interest here. Litigation or nasty publicity is not on our agenda, I can assure you. Mr. Berger is a superb coach, the team misses him and the game misses him, and we simply want him back out there on the court for this next crucial weekend."

Thick-jowled Mr. Ferguson nodded, paused, asked, "What else does your client want?"

Marty leaned forward just slightly, his fine chin edging forward maybe a millimeter toward John Ferguson. "You know, there's a lot more we could ask for, I believe, but all my client wishes, and I honor those wishes, is for him to be reinstated, swiftly, as the Conway basketball coach."

He glanced at his younger colleagues and back at Marty, and finally toward me.

"And the publicity, Mr. Frommer?"

Marty shook his head. "There will be no public statements on the matter that will go beyond what the school will announce. And I know the school can come up with a statement that will be fair and beneficial for all concerned."

Ferguson waved his colleagues around him, they conferred for a minute, and he turned back to us. "Well, I think that's a very fair and decent proposal, Mr. Frommer, and Mr. Berger, and while we'll have to consult of course with the proper officials of the university, I'd say that for our part we will recommend a rescinding of the suspension. Are you staying at the Inn, Mr. Frommer? Can we let you know by the end of the afternoon perhaps?"

"The middle of the afternoon would suit my client better, so that he can practice with his team later today. Practice time is growing short."

John Ferguson smiled slowly, a wan smile, I thought. "I know what you mean. Once upon a time I played hockey for this school, Mr. Frommer, and how you practiced went a long way to determining how you played the actual game. My old coach never tired of reminding us of that, and he was right!"

There was a surprisingly cordial breakup of the meeting with their team shaking hands with us and smiling, and presently we were outside in the crisp late March air, walking past the Green, blanketed still with a few inches of snow.

My heart was beating fast. "Was that it? All that stress for this hour and a half? Pretty damned friendly there at the end."

"Well, they got off so easy," Marty observed. "I can't believe that Ferguson went along with that telegram of suspension. Jumping the gun that way. Shmucks. *We could have really nailed them*, and the school, if you had wanted to. God, it's really the life up here, isn't it? Look at those kids, playing frisbee without a care, their jackets on the ground. An oasis, huh? Mind if I come to the practice? I've never really seen one."

The decision was delivered to the Inn at 3:00 p.m. in a sealed envelope. We read it in the lounge. "Delighted to inform you that the University has rescinded its one-week paid suspension of Coach Berger, due to our misunderstanding of NCAA rules, and wishes him and the team all the best of luck in the Tournament next weekend." The President had signed it.

"Paid suspension?" I repeated.

Marty smiled. "I saw something in that Conway Co-op for my daughter. See you later in the gym. What time again?"

The practice began at 5:00 p.m. and the boys and assistants arranged a surprise ice-cream cake from Ben and Jerry's, inscribed with "NCAA Final 4," welcoming me back. Charming. I ran through sets of passing drills, off the break and half-court offense; high post pick 'n rolls, and backdoor plays; a series of picks, screens and double blockouts for the cutter and Avram's jumper; on defense I designed a midcourt trap against the key Duke playmaker, and a series of flexing zones,

3-2, 2-3, 2-1-2, to be used where down low Vargas, Dennis, Eddie were constantly in rotation, guarding no one man but shifting to replace each other.

It was 7:30 p.m. when Percy and Duddy begged for a break to feed. Sure, I said, adding, "Back at, let's say, 8:45, okay?"

Marty came over. "A regular Fort Benning you run, Sydney."

"I'm a drill sergeant at heart, I suppose," I said, toweling off. "I love the discipline of repetitions. Do you know Kierkegaard's slim volume on the subject? Besides, this may be my encore week with them."

"Kierkegaard? I had heard about your... wide reading and unique lectures. I see..."

While the boys grabbed pizzas at Eba's, supervised by Duddy, I had Chinese food brought in for Marty and me, and I watched videos of Duke with Roscoe, who handled the phone as well. At one point he called me over. "This one you should field for yourself." It was the great Koppel himself, who said he had sent a telegram and then had his producer try to get through without luck. (I had not looked at the pile of phone messages and telegrams that had poured in; too nervous, no time.) Could I come on his show tomorrow night? "The entire country is following your Cinderella squad, and you, and I'd very much like to talk about it."

I replied that I was very short on time; no way could I fly down to New York. "Fine, that's understandable. We'll take a crew up there, to you. How would that be?" Let me think on it, I said.

When I informed Marty, he smiled. "Why not? It could be interesting. Regarding your reinstatement, I would simply say that things have been worked out amicably. Use their word, 'misunderstanding,' and move on from there. Now, what's on for tonight?"

I smiled. At 8:45 p.m. we were back on the floor. First my oral quiz on game situation: what traps are run in the last few minutes, and on whom? Name Duke's weakest ballhandlers, foulshooters? What are the out-of-bounds and timeout rules for the last two minutes? What are our rotations against zones? They scored 85 percent. Not bad. A half-hour later we scrimmaged, trying out the complicated defenses and zone traps; I blew the stop-whistle often. I had less than three days to turn strategy into routine, and routine into instinct; fat chance. If I had a month, maybe. I pointed to the few Duke weaknesses—uncertainty if the pointguard is harassed, inconsistent rebounding—and emphasized putting pressure on those points, especially at crucial moments. Hoop acupuncture. Then, drill and more drill; and freeing Nurlan to run the break and defy the press. If he had a fine game, we had a shot. By 11:00 p.m. the boys had had it.

"Sir," Eddie asked, "have you told Mr. Frommer about the *Review*'s nasty ways? What's he suggest we do, file charges?"

I winked at Marty. "We decided to deal with that after the weekend. Now, any questions?"

"Sure, Coach," said Roberto, grinning. "For old time's sake, how bout a little story or narration, sir."

"*Now?* Aren't you fellas pretty exhausted?"

"Never too exhausted for a rivetin' tale, Mister B," teased Jack.

What could I do? I looked through my explosive tote bag, saw a few enticing titles, Josiah Royce's *Basic Writings, The Radical Will* by Randolph Bourne, *Portable Whitman, Montcalm and Wolfe,* but suddenly grew self-conscious in Marty's presence. "Well, *I'm exhausted.* Hit the sack, get your rest, be back here for foul shooting before your eight o'clocks. In just two days we're on the road again. Come on now, don't look at me like disappointed pups, get showered and get your shuteye. See you in the gym bright and early; 7:15, say?"

Mild boos and jeers while they wearily ambled off to the locker rooms. Marty said, "Too bad. I was kind of looking forward to one of those... sessions or seminars or whatever."

"Next time."

"Do I have my pair of tickets for the Kingdome?"

"Done deal."

"Thanks. Good luck tomorrow night. I'll watch you from New York."

I nodded, shook his hand, and waited till all my boys had left, saying a word or two to each as they passed. Then I took my usual promenade up and down the one hundred and twenty feet of wooden floor, and walked it again, nervous, alert, ready... for what? For the ultimate sighting, the NCAA finals? I was already there, in a way. Saturday's semi-finals was about as good as Monday's finals. The gym, this gym, this huge cave of play and youthful passion, filled me with excitement and longing. Did it matter how far I'd come or wanted to go? In a way, yes; but in another, no. This was where I wanted to be, was; running my drills, seeing the weaves, watching the passing game. The only thing that would really sting, really wound, would be banishment from this cave. Exile from the boys and scrimmages. All the rest really was gravy, pure gravy.

I took one last walk across the burnished floor, scribbled a note about the matchup zone, flipped the switch for the lights. Good night, sweet gym, see you anon, and slipped on my parka.

When I got home, however, the cat didn't race to greet me with a neglect-squeal, so I knew something was up.

"Hi. I was worried. Are you okay?"

Claire looked lovely. She dropped Merlin and hugged me hello. "You said spring, right? I checked the date." She showed me her wristwatch, smiling mischievously.

I got us drinks in the kitchen—white wine for Claire, mandarin orange-flavored seltzer for me—and we sat on the couch. As she began to chat her green-grey eyes sparkled an appeal, but I knew that her agenda of warmth and comfort, let alone companionship and respectability, was not mine, for now or the foreseeable future. Too many other things were on my plate. What could I say, though, without sounding callous, cruel?

"Are those your parents in that picture on your desk?"

I nodded and asked if she minded a little music, a late night habit when I could manage it.

"Sure," she said, squeezing my hand.

I put on a CD of Ruffo. As the great baritone voice began to sweeten the room my mind drifted back to father, and his stories of first seeing his idol in Pisa when he was a boy. I wondered if Claire knew of him.

"I've never heard of him, I must admit," she said.

"Not surprising, he's remained rather obscure. Too bad, because my father thought he was the best baritone of this century, and maybe the best singer. Of course Papa also loved him because he was an outspoken opponent of the Blackshirts, and refused to sing in Italy while Mussolini ruled." I shushed myself with a finger to my lips. "He's singing the Prologue from *Pagliacci*, originally made in 1912. Listen to his range..." While the powerful deep voice of the clown Tonio poured upon us, Claire got up and went to the desk. She brought back the small photo in its oval frame and set it down on the coffee table before us. Father with his thick curly black hair and handlebar mustache, and dark suit, the real-life clown in pain, and mother, brunette, Slavic, strong-boned, strong-willed, who kept the family afloat with her great common sense; oh, I missed them, more and more as the time passed.

"Where was he from? What did he do here?"

I put my finger to my mouth again to hear the rest of the *Si può?* aria. Then said, "Città di Costello, in Umbria. Not too far from Florence. A high-school math teacher, when he had a job. Otherwise, during his many seasons of unemployment, stamp-collecting and bathroom tenoring, while Mom worked."

She took my arm and edged closer. "Take me to Umbria sometime, will you? And that City-something."

"Well, if I ever go again, I'll let you know. First I have to go to Seattle and play a game or two."

"Basketball and baritones. The high and the low life, right? You're a man of parts!"

I tapped her playfully on the arm. "You're getting to know

me, huh? The two selves of Berger: paleface and redskin," I said, referring to an elegant essay by the critic Rahv.

"What's that mean?" She looked up at me, wanting to move, I thought, to another stage. "And which is your truer self?"

"The tired self," I sighed, kissing her softly but without passion. "I'm going to call it a night—even though it's spring."

She stared at me, injured, but I couldn't answer her wanting. I offered her the guest room to stay in, but she declined and left, leaving the front-door key behind.

Coaching had come to replace relationships, I understood, and it wasn't a bad exchange, not bad at all.

Koppel's crew set up the interview in my office, setting up the klieg lights, pancaking me, pinning me with a microphone, and fussing with all the other tedious paraphernalia in preparation for putting my kisser in some thirty million homes.

The helpful producer, Edie, smoothed my hair and told me to speak clearly and relax. "Pretend Ted's right here, in your office, chatting away."

Sure. Anyway, just before air time, Mr. Koppel's assistant called to check the connection and tell me that our segment was scheduled for a full half hour, so I could take my time, and then he'd switch for fifteen minutes of commentary by two outside observers, a well-known coach and university official. If I wished I could respond to that pair, too.

After the full day of practicing, watching videos, accepting congratulations, I was rather beat, and wondered what the hell was I doing there, and why? Of course the boys were proud, like crazy; TV fame was what counted in their big wide world. (Koppel had asked permission to have them too on the tube, but I had a curfew on, and made sure they were tucked in securely.)

I must say that Koppel's opening was flattering. "If Germany had its moment of national reckoning with the Berlin Wall coming down some six months ago, it's fair to say that America has its moment of reckoning with regard to sports.

And no story this year beats the story of little Conway College making it to the Final Four of the NCAA tournament, defeating giants along the way like UNLV and Indiana. And no man is more controversial than the coach of this Cinderella team, Doctor Sydney Berger, our guest tonight. Until yesterday suspended by his own college, Dr. Berger was officially reinstated and will be on the bench for Saturday's game against favorite Duke. Welcome, Dr. Berger."

The little red eye lit "on" and I gave a weak, "Hello, Mr. Koppel."

"Let me begin by referring to two quotes by formidable coaches around the country. The first is from Dean Smith of North Carolina: 'The job done by Coach Berger in this tournament is the best coaching I've seen in two decades.' And the second, from the honorary Dean of college coaches, Pete Newell: 'All around, his team has performed according to the highest level of classic basketball, which just shows you that there still is room, in the day and age of the slamdunk and monster center, for the success of classic team play.' Would you like to comment on these remarks at all?"

Slightly embarrassed, I said, "Thank you, I'm flattered, is the most that I can say, really." Why get into the fact that it wasn't really classic basketball that I was conducting out there, with three forwards in place of a center, sliding zones, and other wrinkles.

"Well, that's gracious of you, I'm sure. I read those quotes not to embarrass you, sir, but rather to establish the fact of your great techniques and skills as a coach. Because at the same time, of course, there's been much controversy about other aspects of your...uh...behavior, let's say. I'm thinking first of the NCAA investigation of your offcourt habits and the program you've established at Conway. So what I'd like to ask you first is, how do you feel about that investigation? More specifically, do you feel a coach should be allowed to coach in the Final Four while he's under such a cloud? A cloud that compelled your own college to suspend you just last week?"

Take your time. Don't blink too often. "Well, the fact that the college has now rescinded the suspension due to a 'misunderstanding' of the NCAA rules should answer one part of that. As for coaching under a cloud, Mr. Koppel, I don't feel that way at all. The only cloud for me is Duke, our opponent on Saturday. Don't laugh, Mr. Koppel, it's true. Universities, and various departments, get investigated all the time, by all sorts of agencies, such as the Federal Government or the NIH. It's part of the regulatory bureaucracy, Mr. Koppel. Some prove helpful, others not." I paused, tried to look relaxed, checked the red light and Koppel in my ear and on the adjoining screen.

"All right, Mr. Berger, that's fair. Let me inject a more personal question then: have you done anything to warrant this investigation? Speaking bluntly, has your program been run illegally, or have your procedures been highly irregular, perhaps?"

Relax in the shoulders, white lie with a smile. "Oh, I have my own ways of doing things, no doubt. And perhaps some of them are 'irregular,' as you say. I'm sure there are accounting procedures, for example, that could be done one of several ways, especially with the changing laws." I adjusted my tie.

"Are there NCAA rules which you find particularly unjust or unfair: or even *quite worthy of breaking,* Mr. Berger?"

Tread easily here. "Oh, probably, Mr. Koppel. I'm sure you feel the same about some of the FCC rules, for example."

"Well, could you be specific here?"

"Mr. Koppel, I think it's very important to understand *who* these new student athletes are: poor kids who come from weak school backgrounds, whose one chance upward in this society, *and* in higher education, comes via sports. Now, I understand the NCAA's trying to keep out the corruption of loose money from agents or gamblers or shoe sponsors or what-have-you, that follows these kids; that's a worthy concern. But you can't lose track of the fact that these young men, coming from poverty, are thrown into a culture of privilege and plenty. Would you deny a kid like that a new sports bag for 39.95, or even a bus ticket home for 79 dollars? Would you call those infractions 'evidence' of serious corruption? Would you suspend a school's program, or a coach, for *those sorts* of infractions?"

Ted smiled sympathetically. "I understand what you're getting at here, Coach. Do you have a remedy for correcting those mistaken rules or misguided boundaries? Was Proposition 48 helpful, for example? Do you agree with John Thompson that academic standards should be loosened for student athletes? And in a few sentences, since we have to take a break here."

I forced a grin. "My answers need equal time, Mr. Koppel. Anyway, I think the NCAA rules need some real updating, a revision to be implemented by the likes of a few Madisons and Jeffersons so that they reflect the very complicated nature of America today, and sports in college society today. The revision should not be left up to ordinary bureaucrats, sir, but put into the hands of our best legal and philosophical minds. Along with a respected sports figure or two."

"A New American Constitution for Sports, is that it? On that note, let's take a short break for our sponsors."

Red light off, Edie raises two thumbs up. And Ted says to me privately, "Well done, Sydney. My scouts were right, you are most articulate. The next segment will change course a bit, and get into your own rather unorthodox coaching habits, all right?"

"I'm at your service, Ted."

Edie handed me a glass of water and I worried about that crack about the bureaucrats. Oh well. Edie signalled, Koppel was back on, my little red light flickered anew.

"Now, Mr. Berger, let me shift gears here and ask you about your unorthodox methods as a coach. I'm thinking specifically here about the well-known lengthy summations, the vaunted lectures or readings, well, whatever they might be called, that you seem to deliver at halftime intermissions, which have little to do with basketball. Is this correct, sir?"

I was rather taken aback. "Well, I suppose so."

"Come now, could you tell us a bit about those unorthodox pep talks? How you see their purpose? Obviously they've
worked, both in the games and outside, to judge by your team's
extraordinary second-half play, and their revolt. Go ahead,
please."

I took out my pipe and took some time lighting it, almost
burning myself.

Edie rolled her hands frantically.

"Come now, Mr. Berger, please don't go shy on us here
about this most interesting matter. Well, let me start with the
most obvious facts. Is it true that you really don't design basketball plays at halftime, but rather offer the boys seminars
or lectures in American history and philosophy? For example,
I understand that you've used," he glanced at his notes,
"among others, Emerson, Thoreau, Parkman..."

As Koppel reeled off the names I was stunned, as if he
had just exposed me to the nation as a child molester or a
child victim myself! Why?... I puffed, and nodded, and
watched Edie signal frantically.

"Mr. Berger, can you hear me? Has something gone wrong
with the connection? Sydney?" He looked about for technical help.

Choked up inside, I exhaled smoke softly. "Oh yes, those,"
I said. "Yes, yes."

He stared blankly for a moment. "So what we wonder is,
what was the meaning of those readings, sir? Was there a
shrewd psychological point, or...?"

Slowly I regained my voice, enough to say, "Well, Mr.
Koppel, I believe I did say some things during those intermissions which were, ah, somewhat irrelevant to the game at
hand, yes. But those little talks were nothing more than... The
truth is, I don't really remember them all that well. You see,
a coach tries anything..." I had at last located a platitude mode.
"...everything that he can to motivate, to lift the team, to inspire. You know, the way Rockne did, or Lombardi, say." I
waited and sat back in my chair, sweating solidly now.

Koppel wore a bemused smirk. "I must say, Coach Berger,

I think you're either being very modest or very disingenuous, I can't tell which or why. You've taken a club from the depths of Ivy League competition to the heights of the national championship with a most unorthodox method, and we simply want to talk about it here, sir. And to give you credit for your marvelous originality." He smiled, goodnaturedly perplexed.

So was I, my heart pounding and the perspiration pouring. "Why thank you, Mr. Koppel."

"Well, Coach, I must say, for a man so very articulate to go so quiet and still suddenly is most surprising. What can be wrong? Have I offended you in some way in putting the matter, Coach? Was I in some way referring to scandalous material? Not from what my notes tell me. On the contrary."

I blew my nose and wiped my brow. I tried to recover my composure, my position... "Flourishes, Mr. Koppel. Bits of drama. Overheated locker rooms... Propositions that seemed of permanent interest."

"Allegorical, then, Mr. Berger?"

I appreciated his attempt to help out. "Yes, perhaps that!"

He nodded and looked at me with the wonderful lucid gaze of a kindly doctor trying his best to diagnose a patient's mysterious symptoms. "Basketball allegory, right? How interesting, to tie up native thinkers with a native game. Could you give us a little of your vision there?"

You can imagine how quickly downhill it went from there. I muttered some stuff, pure mumbo-jumbo, about anarchism and the all-court press, transcendentalism and High Flow, and it was a disaster, a humiliation. The other guests were eyeing each other, bewildered. I was near tears by the time Ted graciously cut me off.

Edie patted my arm during the break and offered me an aspirin and another glass of water. I sat quietly during the next segment while the well-known coach, college president and NCAA official pursued the discussion reasonably with Mr. Koppel. Only once did he turn to me for my opinion, during a severe chastisement, but I had none. Silently, I rather welcomed the attack.

Duke, at 5 p.m. on Saturday afternoon at the Kingdome in Seattle, was an easier opponent than I myself had been as my own worst enemy on TV. Meaning it was clear what they were up to, unlike the confusing Koppel and company, and how effective a well-coached team with twelve full athletic scholarships could be. They had everything, too: speed, height, rebounding, playmaking, shooters, plus a dose of arrogance and cocksureness. And my club was not rehearsed enough in our traps, zones, press, to disturb their particular rhythm. Against Duke I needed a full week at least, preferably several weeks, like the break before New Year's Day bowls, to put in place a serious scheme of disruption and annoyance. (Offense would take care of itself.) Also, the boys and I had peaked emotionally the week before, not merely with the exaltation of victory, but with the revolt and its aftermath. Then there was the potent glare of the intense publicity, poured down on us all week, but especially Friday and Saturday. Only on the inside, during a sports championship, did you really see the emergence of Amerika, a new reality imposed upon the daily one. Lobbies filled with hustlers, hookers, agents, coaches, shoe sponsors, sports junkies, reporters, recruiters, dopers, owners, actors, superstars, bodyguards. You name 'em, we had 'em. And all of them hot in pursuit of yours truly, who, by then, was considered truly looney-tunes, though somehow, still, a coaching genius. Neither image helped.

No, it didn't surprise me that at the end of the first half we were down by twelve, and lucky at that. We had not played badly, just commonly; and they had played merely efficiently. A ragtag collection of Ivy bushleaguers, up against a glamorous ACC champ. The big crowd was disappointed, quiet. We were headed for great disaster, I saw, full humiliation ahead. The NBC announcer grabbed me as I headed for the locker room. "What do you have to tell the kids at halftime, Coach? What adjustments do you have to make?" Ha. "Rematch, new night?" I said. "No, really." I excused myself.

The locker room was appointed with thick carpets, Eurostyle toilets and three-way showers, built-in hairdryers and scented liquid soaps, superior video (and audio) replay equipment and padded, plush seating. A designer's showroom more than an athlete's locker room. The comfort was discomforting. We locked the doors securely and I posted my sentries.

The boys huddled up front, a sodden defeated bunch, and I walked up and back in front of them.

"Coach, why'd you go blank like that in front of Koppel?" Eddie surprised me.

I stared at him and his question. "Huh?"

"Yeah, why couldn't you talk straight out about that stuff?" said Jack. "It sort of bothered us, you know."

I looked at them, shook my head, and picked up the pace.

"You are ashamed of these lectures, Coach Berger?" Avram asked. "Please advise us, yes? We are proud."

"Very," seconded Vargas.

"Really," added Jarrod.

I shook my head. "It wasn't shame, don't you see. It was... privacy. A pact between us, a... contract between you and me. Also, these talks are not entirely *explainable* to an outsider. Not so..." I smiled feebly, "rational, you might say."

I paused, then started to move in the mobile chalkboard.

"You see, Coach," explained Jarrod, "we were very honored to have you up there on *Nightline*, celebrated in front of the whole country and representing us. And then you went sort of... flat, absent, not there."

I looked at these kids, once again taken aback by their bold emotions and surprising expectations. An air purifier was purring, otherwise it was marvelously quiet inside there, the superior soundproofing creating a cave of hibernation.

Befuddled I took the blackboard and began designing a new defensive pattern.

"Coach, maybe you can give us one last reading here?" Dennis was grinning puckishly, legs crossed.

"Yeah, we know what to do out there, ya know," smiled Water, beret sitting rakishly. "Even though we ain't quite done it yet."

What a relentless band. I had shot them up with this dopey

stuff and now they couldn't stay off it. Addicted.

In the magic worn-out tote I searched and found a book that felt right. "*Democratic Vistas*, Walt Whitman, 1871."

"Poetry, sir?"

"Sort of. In prose. Here goes. 'It may be claim'd (and I admit the weight of the claim) that common and general worldly prosperity, and a populace well-to-do, and with all life's material comforts, is the main thing, and is enough. It may be argued that our republic is, in performance, really enacting today the grandest arts, poems, etc., by beating up the wilderness into fertile farms, and in her railroads, ships, machinery, etc. And it may be ask'd, Are these not better, indeed, for America, than any utterances even of greatest rhapsode, artist, or literatus? I too hail those achievements with pride and joy; then answer that the soul of man will not with such only—nay not with such at all—be finally satisfied; but needs what (standing on these and all things, as the feet stand on the ground), is addressed to the loftiest, to itself alone.

"'Out of such considerations, such truths, arises for treatment in these Vistas the important question of character, of an American stock-personality, with literatures and arts for outlets and return expressions, and, of course, to correspond, within outlines common to all. To these, the main affair, the thinkers of the United States, in general so acute, have either given feeble attention, or have remain'd, and remain, in a state of somnolence.'"

Were they with me, I wondered, glancing around. Nurlan was sketching in his lap, a little like me as a boy, knitting and listening intently.

"'For my part, I would alarm and caution even the political and business reader, and to the utmost extent, against the prevailing delusion that the establishment of free political institutions, and plentiful intellectual smartness, with general good order, physical plenty, industry, etc. (desirable and precious advantages as they all are), do of themselves determine and yield to our experiment of democracy the fruitage of success.'"

Here Avram interjected a comment on today's technology. No, I mustn't underestimate them.

"'With such advantages at present fully, or almost fully, possess'd'—with unprecedented materialistic advancement— 'society in these States, is cankered, crude, superstitious, and rotten.'"

Now all their heads were up, astonished at the heavy artillery.

I nodded at them and continued. 'In any vigor, the element of the moral conscience, the most important, the vertebrer to State of man, seems to me either entirely lacking, or seriously enfeebled or ungrown...'" I skipped ahead again without telling them. "'Genuine belief seems to have left us. The underlying principles of the States are not honestly believ'd in (for all this hectic glow, and these melodramatic screamings), nor is humanity itself believed in. What penetrating eye does not everywhere see through the mask? The spectacle is appalling. We live in an atmosphere of hypocrisy throughout.'"

"You mean, just like now, eh, Coach?" Roberto.

Roscoe signalled to me, "Five minutes, Syd."

I looked up at the clock and leaned towards the blackboard, when Antoine, of all souls, demanded, "We're waiting, Coach."

All right, the little addicts! "'The men believe not in the women, nor the women in the men. A scornful superciliousness rules in literature. The aim of all *litterateurs* is to find something to make fun of. A lot of churches, sects, etc., the most dismal phantasms I know, usurp the name of religion. Conversation is a mass of badinage. From deceit in the spirit, the mother of all false deeds, the offspring is already incalculable.'"

I heard the murmured echo of "deceit in the spirit."

"'The official services of America, national, state and municipal, in all their branches and departments, except the judiciary, are saturated in corruption, bribery, falsehood, maladministration; and the judiciary is tainted. The great cities reek with respectable as much as non-respectable robbery and scoundrelism.'"

"Dad should hear this oratory," Jarrod said, smiling.

"The Reagan years, one hundred years ago!" Roberto cried. "Not much has changed, huh?"

"'In fashionable life, flippancy, tepid amours, weak infidelism, small aims or no aims at all, only to kill time. In business (this all-devouring modern word, business) the one sole object is, by any means, pecuniary gain. The magician's serpent in the fable ate up all the other serpents, remaining today the sole master of the field. The best class we show, is but a mob of fashionably dressed speculators and vulgarians.'"

"Almost time, Syd!"

I nodded, still grooved. "'True, indeed, behind this fantastic farce, enacted on the visible stage of society, solid things and stupendous labors are to be discover'd, existing crudely and going on in the background, to advance and tell themselves in time. Yet the truths are nonetheless terrible.'"

"Amen, amen!" Jack.

Serious or mocking? "'I say that our New World democracy, however great a success in uplifting the masses out of their slough, in materialistic development, products, and in a certain highly deceptive superficial popular intellectuality, is, so far, an almost complete failure in its social aspects, and in really grand religious, moral, literary, and aesthetic results.'"

First buzzer ran loud and long.

I held up a finger for another minute. "'In vain do we march with unprecedented strides to empire so colossal, outvying the antique, beyond Alexander's, beyond the proudest sway of Rome. In vain have we annex'd Texas, California, Alaska, and reach north for Canada and south for Cuba. It is as if we were somehow being endow'd with a vast and—'"

Second buzzer rang! The assistants started corralling the boys.

"'—more and more thoroughly appointed body, and then left with little or no soul.'"

"All that land *in vain*," said Jack. "With no soul. That man knew some things."

We were herded from the room into the Muzak corridor.

"Hey, I didn't know we had our sights on Canada and Cuba!"

I looked at Nurlan's small brown eyes and matte-face and said, "Their guard's beating you off the dribble, pal."

In a moment Roberto came up. "Some things don't change, huh, Coach? 1871's just about like 1990, right?"

I faced him squarely. "How can you allow that skinny Laettner to push you off the boards that way?"

And emerging from the tunnel Avram was alongside. "He speaks with very Russian accent of moralistic judgment. Like Tolstoy, Solzhenitsyn. You think so?"

"Yes, and I think you're not playing your hardest. You're *soft* coming off the pick, and *soft* on going up for the shot. Don't clutch on us now, Rooskie."

He stared back, hurt. What else could I say to these naifs?

They circled me before the half started and I told them this was Alumni Gym, and this was a practice scrimmage, no more. They held hands and let out a fainthearted roar. Whistle blew, play began, Duke got a jumper from the corner, we missed a jumper, they came down and hit an inside shot, and we were down by sixteen. I called a timeout.

And as they came around to sit down I kept them standing, ringing me; I too had been soft, too soft. Especially here, at the end of the chase. Would a jockey turn into a scholar in the backstretch, you prick? "Listen, you green rubes, you're soft all around, in every aspect of the game. You've forgotten how to pass, you've forgotten how to bang the boards, you're scared of fighting with these guys. And why? Because I've spoiled you with all this fucking learning! And with my becoming a fucking little God for you guys. Well, I got news for you: the *Review* never tricked you pigeons, I did! They never were going to blackmail you, but I was, and did! I needed your asses back out there on the court, for my own interests, got it? Think on that when you go back out there."

The look on their faces, I must admit, was quite stunning: mouths dropped, eyes widened, even tears. Their faces were filling with pain, revelation, and vulnerability, and, in that metamorphosis, they looked like butterflies becoming moths. I thought of Piero della Francesca, come in to paint five young warriors.

"So you have no soul, either, Coach?" Vargas mumbled. I grinned hard.

"'Deceit of the spirit,' hah, Mr. B," charged Dennis quietly.

"You got it, son," and I gazed at his blue, mirthless eyes.

Now they were sent back out, like soldiers of patriotism informed that they were mere mercenaries. What else could I do but try my last card? Down by 16, what else was there to try but whipping and scalding them? (Myself too, of course.) Either they would fold in self-pity or fight like furious streetfighters.

The Duke guard took a runner in the lane, missed the roll, and Robert ripped the ball away from their forward. We came down, Nurlan faked and, instead of passing off as he had been doing, he took it on in for a scoop layin. Duke came down, their guard was trapped hard just beyond the center line, his errant pass was stolen by Eddie, who led the field and laid it in. Once again Duke brought it back, passed it around and down into their cocky center, who went up with a short jumper, but got nudged a bit (not called; when you play tough D, you get the calls) and missed; rebound to Roberto, who outletted to Water, who, after three dribbles tossed over to Avram for a corner jumper, and swish! Lead down to 10 and Duke called time. The crowd of forty thousand felt the excitement, stood. The boys came around me, angry still. Good.

First Jack. "You, not the *Review*, really?"
"Really."
"Why?"
"Get you playing."
He shakes his head.

"I didn't think you'd ever deceive us that way, sir." Now Eddie is shaking his head sadly.

"Had to, Eddie. Had to."

They get up to go back to work, the crowd encouraging them strongly, but I know their heads are elsewhere.

Duke takes it out and brings it into the halfcourt offense, passing it around to slow things down, regain the momentum, take the right shot. The ball goes from side to side, and then their little pointguard, eager to be The Man, takes it on in; Jack, in ambush, just like at Olde Towne High, slides off his man on the weakside and deftly deflects the dribble. Jarrod picks it up and goes the other way, finding Water, who dribbles through two Duke players and lays a neat bounce pass to the cutter, Vargas, for the deuce and foul. He makes it, the lead is 7, the crowd is roaring. The moment of truth has arrived: will Duke stay poised? On their offense their shrewd Coach K calls out a set play. There's a pick for the lithe leaping forward from the West Indies who take the ball and, getting a step on Jack, dribbles the lane for a leaner, and makes it. We come back, I'm signalling frantically, but Water calmly calls out a two blue for a double screen and Avram jumpshot and we're back to 7. It's a game. My Ivy does are for real. Duke again tries the same forward, he's doubleteamed immediately and tied up, but the arrow points their way and they keep the ball; oh, for the old jump ball! This time their hotshot Laettner takes the ball at the top of the key, turns as though to pass, tosses in a soft jumper. Backbreaker? Water dribbles down, smiling, signals a weave, our big guys rotate down low, but instead of an extra rotation, Dennis takes a quick, forced shot, a mistake; Duke rebounds. Hurley the guard dribbles it up, talks trash to Nurlan, then whirls about needlessly, and Nurlan taps the ball away with his left hand à la Frazier and heads downcourt, loping, so that the humiliated white boy can catch up and foul him for the three-point play. It happens, and we're down by 6. It's a show. Everyone's a believer now. Especially their Coach K, who, genuinely frightened by what he sees, screams openly at his guard to cut out the dribbling and distribute the ball! He understands now that his guard is no match for mine, and will make do without him. "Christian! Christian!" he directs, and the ball goes again to their 6' 10" star in the corner, who, using his elbow to hold off Vargas, turns and drives. Cunningly Coach K calls at the ref to watch it!

A moment of worldly truth. Little nobodies playing tourney darlings, and great CBS star/top NBA pick taking the ball in on a crucial drive, while my sly ace Jack cheats off his main to doubleteam star as he goes up... and he and Roberto actually block the shot and squeeze the ball! But the ref won't buy it, kids that small from the lowly Ivy, no way they can block the tall darling's shot without fouling him, and so instead of us getting the ball, he gets two foul shots and makes both. Fair Dennis protests vehemently, gets hit with a technical, and Laettner makes that, too, running back and slipping Dennis the furtive finger. A 5-point turnaround, Duke's up by 9 instead of a possible 4. Momentum lost. Furious, I say, nice and tart, to the passing ref, "Too much skill for Christian and you, hey?" Mistake. He hits me with a T, too, and we're ten down and gone. I try to rush him, but am pulled away by Percy and Duddy. If you don't hold a decent lead down the stretch against a honcho club like Duke, forget it. The refs will slice you up and deliver you, dead on delivery, to the opposing coach.

I'm on steady boil. We make another run, they hold us off and win by seven. It's been an effort, and should have been a win or overtime. In the raucous tumult out on the floor, I search for my lost boys. Finding Water, I hug him, saying, "You're The Point Guard in the country today," but his smile is wan, worn, disconsolate. I find Robert sitting in tears and say, "You were the Chairman of the Boards in the second half, no question." Jack comes over, shakes his head: "We blocked the sonofabitch clean and they gave it to him anyway. Four-point difference." Linking arms with him I tell him, "Five." To Eddie, cut on the bridge of the nose, I say: "They're gonna name a street for you in Brattleboro, maybe Warsaw." Choked up, he laments, "We had 'em, we had 'em." Scanning for the others I'm corralled by the Duke coach, who pumps my hand vigorously and says, "Quite a game your boys put up, Coach. Sorry someone had to lose." "Yeah," I reply, "You worked those refs over pretty good. Do they get their lumps of sugar, now?" His face tightens. "You friggin' sore loser!" I wink and move off.

In the locker room I clear out family and alumni, everyone but our own crew, and try to express to them how wonderfully they played, against all odds. But the boys are in a state of utter dejection, heads sunken, bodies paralyzed. My words fall feebly short of the complex feelings, the depleted emotions. So I decide on a different tack. Right there, smack in the middle of the brutal defeat. I take out our portable CD player and slip in my opera disk. The first aria is *"La donna è mobile,"* with Schipa singing; next we get Caruso doing *"Vesti la giubba,"* and then Jussi Björling singing *"Celeste Aida."* The voices of the tenors soar across the room, filling it with sweet Italian melody and dissolving the whole dingy affair, and no one protests. Indeed as the singing expands it seals us off into a submarine of sweetened sound, lifting the boys' heads and propping their exhausted bodies.

Only by the fourth or fifth aria does Jarrod pipe up to plead, "How 'bout a little Mingus now, eh, Coach?"

"Sure, good idea," and as I prepare to exchange my disk for his, I know they're coming back up from the shrapnel and ether, and getting ready for the peace again. The very tough peace of what's ahead.

16 THIS SPORTING LIFE

At the narrow Island on the Gulf Coast the sky was bright azure, the gulf water was turquoise-blue, the evenings were bands of pastel pink and subtle mauve. And the Florida air, after New Hampshire's cold, enveloped us in softness. The boy and I walked the pristine white beach three or four times daily, collecting seashells, watching shorebirds, taking swims and snorkeling. Also we'd take a short drive and visit a nearby nature preserve, where the elegant white egrets and pouchy pelicans flew and sparkled, and the great blue heron gazed about in secure dignity. Rapt, we watched the impressive streamers of the flights of the white ibis, as groups drifted over the marsh. Ducks appeared, too, iridescent blue- and green-winged teals flying in controlled formation, like boys on the fast break. A long day brimming over with exotic birds, watercolors, and ocean smells, filling the soul with a kind of pastel ease, a Lethe of forgetfulness. For dinner we'd walk over to one of the restaurants on the island and watch the tarpon fishing boats come in.

"Was Mr. Gas-pa-rilla really a pirate?"

"Sure."

"From where?"

"Spain, I think."

"What'd he actually do, Papa? Being a *real* pirate."

"Hang out there by the cove, on the lookout for a splendid-looking ship to go by, then chase it down, seize it, and grab the booty. Hey, eat your dinner."

He chewed slowly, hazel eyes big with wonder. "Kill the crew?"

"Probably."

A spreading shy smile. "Did they catch him?"

"Yes. The last official pirate caught by the government."

"Whoa!" His favorite sign of awe. "You think that he buried any of his treasures 'round here?"

"Could be."

Where once upon a time pirates ruled, now condo dwellers reigned. Nights in our rented condo were filled with reading, Lego constructions or checkers, or an occasional video. I had with me DeVoto's *The Year of Decision* and Hawthorne's *The Scarlet Letter*, newly interested in that writer's fascination with guilt and wrongdoing. (Once again I discovered that old reading took on a new freshness when one's life resembled the content in some fashion.) For little Dan I narrated his regular bedtime serials and, for reading aloud, Stevenson's *Kidnapped*, in the original, enchanted him. Privately, I adored the physical proximity with him, watching his rapt face concentrate totally on the robust adventure, or his small dexterous hands as they built elaborate Lego towers and space stations. We slept in a Queen-size bed, and he'd roll into me, his sleep smell and boy's skin delicious. A paternal Eden. Reluctantly I'd turn him back over to his side, looking forward to the morning and his one greyblue eye slowly opening.

When he finally got to sleep I would sit on the veranda and look out at the dark bay, seeing an occasional yacht glittering by, or a commercial jet streaking for Tampa. The air was feathery, the Gulf wind a sirocco, the sleepy island a good place to forget.

Except that I didn't, couldn't. Oh, I sure as heck didn't want to go back to that pressure-cooker up north. But I missed the boys, the team, and felt crummy about leaving them up there, alone, to fend for themselves. (Though I'd chosen a good time to take off and vacation. Despite feelings of confusion, and their estrangement from me, when I left they had been heroes on campus and in the town.)

The dark bay rippled with a fishing boat and lights dappled the moonlit darkness. All was rippling smooth and easy in Boca Grande, but not so in Syd Berger.

That was another matter. I had to make a choice, several hard choices in fact, yet my options were... in flux? Changing rapidly, maybe daily. Who knew whether I was being indicted by the NCAA by now; asked to leave by diplomatic Conway; or, simultaneously, invited by another Big Ten or Pac Eight university to shore up their basketball program for a hundred or two hundred grand in base salary? Was I headed for the lower depths, a junior college basement and exile, or for a UCLA of big money, big athletes, big exposure?

On the veranda I sat in my webbed chaise longue, in soft limbo, not knowing the future or how to think about things. Hawthorne was in my hand, the boy in bed, my other boys on my mind. Seeing Nurlan dribbling and beaming, Jack defending, Dennis roughhousing, Roberto sweeping the boards and grinning, Jarrod dressed to the nines, Antoine stonefaced, Eddie driving hard—well, I faced the simple truth. I had come to love those boys. En masse, as the team, the family. Simple, huh? Well, I had betrayed them of course, just as I had betrayed myself. Their brave No!, declared in sporting thunder, had been erased by me, their moral guide. Good work, Sydney boy, two cheers for you and for others of your ilk, such as... Why name the scoundrels? Does it suffice to say that each of them had his or her own peculiar history of treason buried beneath high ideals and loyal intentions?

I spent another 48 hours at Gasparilla, wounded by my sense of bereavement and remorse, and finally cut short the vacation by two days. I told Daniel I'd make it up to him. Lotusland had become slow, sure torture.

Back up north things went surprisingly well at first. Cam-

319

pus rallies for the team were still in full swing, and a sense of powerful excitement, like some electronic circuitry, still wired the place, thanks to the intense focus supplied by the national and international media. *(La Repubblica, Le Monde, Politiken* and *Manchester Guardian* were all doing special features on "The Little Team That Could Think.") One week later, in mid-April, the Coaches and Sportswriters voted, almost unanimously, for Dr. Sydney Berger as coach of the Year. Bingo! On the front cover of *Sports Illustrated* and Sporting News sat yours truly, dark curly hair and handsome pipe and Harris tweed, looking reticent and scholarly; a violinist or physicist sooner than a sports coach. (SI lead: "Victory for the Egg-heads!") For the first time in fifty years an Ivy coach, let alone a Conway man, had won that prestigious honor. Feeling roguish I was rewarded and fêted.

Even locally I was earning plaudits from unexpected sources, as when dear tart Wim sighted me in Lou's and quipped, "You know, Mowgli boy, there's more skill and stamina in you than I had imagined. If you go down, you're going to bounce back up, I bet, you cunning wolf!"

And if I received a few feelers before, once the coaching honor was posted on the national board, the calls, 'grams and faxes poured in from everywhere, asking about my future plans. Schools like UCLA inquired—Texas, Stanford, St. John's, Arizona, Tennessee, Washington, Michigan, Oregon, Iowa, BYU, UNLV. Not to mention Europe's pro clubs, like Real Madrid and the Tel Aviv Maccabees, and the NBA's Timberwolves and L. A. Clippers. So while the boys were toasted and banqueted, I too was being stroked and courted. The honeymoon was on. Why, even President Grayson, dear friend, hosted a full-fledged dinner in my honor, inviting the faculty.

The only moments of social discomfort during those sweet three or four weeks were when I had to see the boys alone, and they tried to figure out what had really happened, what I had really done. They asked the right questions, and I didn't see the point of lying any more, so that when Jack figured it out one afternoon, and said that the *Review* had never really threatened them, did they? I acknowledged that that was true. Their immediate reaction was surprise and disillusionment, even amazement, and they stared in silence, betrayed in their house of religion, the gym.

After a while Eddie asked, "Did you do it for us or for you?"

Well, why split hairs now, after the fact? "Let's say for both of us, but yes, for me first."

He shook his head, trying hard not to believe it.

There they sat, quietly, trying to take it in or not to.

"I'd say, *for us,*" Roberto finally spoke up, "no matter *what* you say now."

"Yeah, Coach," Jarrod seconded, "no matter what you say."

"Motion passed, unless I hear any nays?" said Dennis, looking about. "No monkey on your back, I'm afraid, sir. Sorry."

"You gentlemen can think what you want," I retorted. "But I wanted that prize badly, and you boys were ready and willing to give it up, turn it back in, for Principles. There's the fact, and there's the nobility. Yours, all yours."

They moved about, fidgeted, dribbled, and at last Nurlan judged, "What's the diff, ya know? We were there, at the end, in the Final Four, and that's what we'll have left in our scrapbooks." He giggled. "Show 'n tell the grandchildren about."

Everyone laughed, several calling out "Yeah" and "Right on."

"Something else, too," reminded Jack. "Just like you said, we 'showcased' our talents, and that counts for a lot. Water, Robert, Eddie maybe are on the big map now, and got a shot at the big bucks down the line. Or immediately."

"And Dad's real proud of me, us, this way," said Eddie, "while like had you encouraged or allowed us to take the other route, well, he'd have been ashamed, pissed. That *nobility* would have passed him right by, sir."

Oh, they were clever, weren't they? So there it was, the

perfect way out supplied by my boys, giving me complete absolution. The little fools! If they needed more training it was to be by Aquinas or Maimonides, not Berger. To my astonishment, however, they were asking for a story, and not just for "old times."

Such innocence, huh? Such looney loyalty. By rote I rummaged in my magic tote and pulled out a lovely Josiah Royce, my specialist in the philosophy of loyalty. But as I started to find a place to begin I had second thoughts... So, against their will, and against mine, too, I told them No, not just now. Waved my hand and left.

The shit began percolating down about mid-May, conveniently enough for the College since everyone was leaving or left; that's the way things were done around Conway, and perhaps other institutions. I was called into the A.D.'s office and given the news on the same day that UCLA called to invite me to take a trip to Westwood to look things over. "Sorry, Syd," said Dick Porter, "the higherups have decided not to renew. You're a free man."

I nodded, not surprised. "And the boys?"

"Well, that's a bit complicated, I think." Despite the kids' popularity on campus, the negative pressure from the alumni was overwhelming (and at Conway the alumni minded the business of the college very closely). As he proceeded to describe the situation I knew that "complicated" meant they were going to be eased out, benevolently. Asked to go elsewhere; in gentlemanly fashion shown the way to distant towns like Edmond, Oklahoma; El Paso, Texas; Wichita, Kansas; Bellingham, Washington; Long Beach, California. "Of course they'll get letters of recommendation from Conway, and from my department. Who knows, they might wind up with much sweeter scholarships!" He stared at me with those sincere baby blues. "I'm genuinely sorry, and believe Administration is making a big mistake. Unless they know something I don't." He walked over to me from his desk and put out his hand. "That was a great season, the greatest, thanks to you. A real stint of coaching. Between you and me, you deserve a bigger and better program than what we can offer. And you'll get it, from what I hear."

I stood and took his firm handshake.

"Conway will miss you, and I'll miss you."

"Why, that's very nice of you, Dick. Just do me one favor, if you will."

"Sure, what's that?"

"If one of my boys does get to hang around by accident, look after him for me. In fact, help to make him a gentleman."

He half-laughed, a little unsure how to take me. "You mean a Conway gentleman?"

"Maybe just a gentleman, Dickens-style." I patted his arm.

As I turned to leave, he said, "Is that what you were after in all those halftime talks and discussions?"

I considered that. "Nah. I was just sort of... shooting my mouth off. Or maybe even... hallucinating?"

He smiled warmly, a thawing Redford. "Well, you're a hell of a hallucinator then!"

After the news I took a few days off to travel out to Los Angeles and meet with the UCLA sports braintrust, and look things over. (On the way back I had a maybe stop in Provo, for BYU.) In the blazing May sun I was escorted around the lovely campus, with its glittering buildings and lawns; tanned, lithe students; rich impressive museums. And then I was taken into the grandest museum of all, the Pauley Pavilion, or the House of Wooden. It was a little like walking out to the monuments in deepest center field in (old) Yankee Stadium or onto the parquet floor in Boston Garden, houses of native worship where our chosen gods, heroes and saints reigned. The unfurled blue banners of twelve NCAA national championships hung from the rafters, signalling the best in modern college basketball. Oh, I was sixteen again!

And then the *pièce de résistance* was brought out: the grand old wizard himself, John Wooden. Slender and white-haired, he shook my hand and spoke in a hoarse voice. "How are you Mr. Berger? I hope you're enjoying your visit out West."

I told him I was, my voice cracking just slightly.

The legendary coach took my arm and, leaving his three bodyguard assistants, walked alone with me. "Let's be honest. We've had a terrible time in the past decade. And the only thing that can turn this around is a fellow who can handle the coaching as well as the recruiting. A fellow who can motivate and discipline. A coach who knows that basketball has changed, and hasn't changed. *And* a fellow who can handle an idea or two beyond the court. What with AIDS, Gays and Drugs, you need to think about these things as they affect our kids. Someone with a brain instead of a doughnut. From what I see, and hear, you fit the bill."

"I'm flattered, sir."

We had walked halfway around the court, the lights having been turned on just for this promenade. Once, during intermission at the Bolshoi Ballet in Moscow, I had circled the glittering ballroom built just for such promenading, and the current trek was similar. A journey through American history.

He stopped me by the bench and looked at me directly, like a prosecutor demanding a deep truth from a witness. "I want you to come, son, and restore the true glory of this place. You understand me?"

"Yes, sir." But the man's pale intensity, and the physical arena and aura, made his command unintelligible to me.

"You're the Chosen," he smiled for the first time, "in more ways than one. Pete Newell and I agree on that, at least. I will promise you that I'll help you in whatever way you wish. I want to leave this place, my only real home, in good hands. Can I have your promise now, here, that you'll come?"

My chest was surging from the pressure, from his closeup intensity! Is that how he had gotten Abdul-Jabbar and Walton and all the other stars to come, subdue their huge egos and perform as a team, *his* team, at incredible levels?

I stood there silent, surging.

Removing his familiar glasses, he leaned even closer. "Look well at me. You know what you see, son? An old man, and a lonely man, who's watched his... his empire fall apart. The entire house that I built... has been crumbling for years. First this impostor, then that one... a shambles. You know what it feels like, for me? For the fans? It's been a cross to bear. Promise me you'll come and take it off."

Finally I found some words to mumble. "Sir, I don't know if I... I can *fulfill* all that."

His face relaxed, and he took me firmly by both shoulders. "I waited a long time before sticking my two cents in, Sydney. I *wanted to make sure.* I needed the coaching, but I also need the *character.* When I heard what the halftimes were like, and coupled that with how that team performed in second halves, I knew we had that special character. I know you can put my house together again. Make the tradition live again. *Promise me.*"

The arena swam before me. What else was there but to promise?

Back in Conway's high-schoolish gym I said goodbye to the squad. "Time to fly the coop, boys," I began, determined to sever the knot once and for all. "We did this great thing, made our own Long March—"

"Where was that, Mr. B?"

"—and now it's time, gents, to move on out in separate directions. Split up, take your own paths, and if I can be of help..." No promises to them that I couldn't keep.

"Sir, where are you heading?" Eddie asked. "Is the Herald report true about UCLA? Or just a rumor?"

I paused. "Until I'm signed, sealed and delivered, it's a rumor." Laughter. "I'm heading for the countryside for the summer. Rural retreat. Reading, writing and contemplating."

"Coach, 'fore you head off," Nurlan said, shifting his Kingdome cap, "maybe we can heah anothah piece of readin'?"

I stared at him, them—the eager, youthful faces I might

325

not ever see again. "Why?"

Water beamed. "Your voice, Mr. B. It's sort of... soothing."

"Yeah, and kind of nutritional," Jack said, smiling. "Like a bowl of cream for the cat." Teammates yowled support for the image.

"And the other voices," Roberto paused. He too was grinning broadly. "Different. Ed-u-ca-tion-al."

I scratched my ever-thinning hair, shuffled in the tote, brought up *Radical Will* by Bourne. "All right, lads, here's a taste of a rather obscure and original American thinker, Randolph Bourne, one of my Mom's favorite socialists. If he had lived long enough she would have invited him to Ratner's to talk to her anarchist group. He grew up in New Jersey at the turn of the century, and settled in Greenwich Village, where he became a bohemian and radical, opposing our entrance into World War One and writing a series of essays trying to define a new kind of American nationalism. Bourne was afflicted with a twisted face and hunched back—he wrote a forthright essay about being handicapped—yet his spirit remained wonderfully open to fresh ideas and idealistic feeling. One of his chief ideals was a more fluid, more expansive definition of American identity and culture, one that avoided the European model of a strong majority imposing its dominant will upon its minorities. Here, from an essay called 'Transnational America,' Bourne is pressing for a deeper investigation of Americanism: 'It is to ask ourselves whether our ideal has been broad or narrow—whether perhaps the time has not come to assert a higher ideal than the "melting-pot."' Familiar term, right?"

To my surprise Antoine spoke up. "My Soc 101 was called 'Beyond the Melting Pot,' Coach, but there was no Mista Bourne in it."

My sullen Buddha had come a long way. I nodded and continued. "'Surely we cannot be certain of our spiritual democracy when, claiming to melt the nations within us to a comprehension of our free and democratic institutions, we fly into panic at the first sign of their own will and tendency. We act as if we wanted Americanization to take place *only on our own terms*—my italics—and not by the consent of the governed. All our elaborate machinery of settlement and school and union, of social and political naturalization, however, will move with friction just in so far as it neglects to take into account this strong and virile insistence that America shall be what the immigrant will have a hand in making it, and not what a ruling class, descendant of those British stocks which were the first immigrants, decide that America shall be made. This is a condition that confronts us, and which demands a clear and general readjustment of our attitude and our ideal.'"

I looked up to see if there were any questions, and Jack wondered if by "immigrant will" Bourne also meant the wills of native Americans and slaves' grandsons, and I said, yes, emphatically yes.

"'It is just this English-American conservatism that has been our chief obstacle to social advance,'" I began, and skipped down. "'Let us cease to think of ideals like democracy as magical qualities inherent in certain peoples. Let us speak, not of inferior races, but of inferior civilizations. We are all to educate and to be educated. These peoples in America are in a common enterprise. It is not what we are now that concerns us, but what this plastic next generation may become in the light of a new cosmopolitan ideal.'"

The gym in late May was not the place to be, I thought, beginning to perspire. The boys were right there with me, sweating too, waiting.

"Further down, 'The truth is that no more tenacious cultural allegiance to the mother country has been shown by an alien nation than by the ruling class of Anglo-Saxon descendants in these American states. English snobberies, English religion, English literary styles, English literary reverences and canons, English ethics, English superiorities, have been the cultural food that we have drunk from our mothers' breasts. The distinctively American spirit—pioneer, as distinguished from the reminiscently English—that appears in Whitman and Emerson and James—'"

A collective cheer sprang up!

"'—that spirit has had to exist on sufferance alongside of this other cult, unconsciously belittled by our cultural makers of opinion.' I'm skipping down a paragraph. 'It is only because it has been the ruling class in this country that bestowed the epithets that we have not heard copiously and scornfully of "hyphenated English-Americans."'"

I looked up and Jack offered, "Like some might say Native-Americans or African-Americans or Jewish-Americans, huh?"

Oh, Bourne would have liked this. I nodded and said, "Now after putting down the ideal of assimilation as a fruitful Americanism, Bourne says, 'there is no distinctively American culture. It is apparently our lot to be a federation of cultures. This we have been for half a century, and the war has made it ever more evident that this is what we are destined to remain. This will not mean, however, that there are not expressions of indigenous genius that could not have sprung from any other soil.'"

I looked at them in the slanting light, and nodded to Nurlan, who waved his cap slightly. "Like basketball, Coach?"

I smiled. "Invented by a Canadian, remember."

"How bout jazz, baseball, Melville, Marx Brothers, sir?"

I nodded to Avram and went on. "'The failure of the melting-pot, far from closing the great American democratic experiment, means that it has only just begun.' Bourne goes on to describe how the Anglo-Saxon who comes to a university will find his true friends among many diverse types. 'Meeting now with this common American background, all of them yet retain that distinctiveness of their native cultures and their national spiritual slants. They are more valuable and interesting to each other for being different, yet that difference could not be creative were it not for this new cosmopolitan outlook which America has given them and which they all equally possess.'"

I paused and drank water.

Eddie murmured, "I get it. Being different can be positive, sir."

I went on. "'America is coming to be, not a nationality, but a trans-nationality, a weaving back and forth, with the other lands, of many threads of all sizes and colors. Any movement which attempts to thwart this weaving, or to dye the fabric any one color, or disentangle the threads of the strands, is false to this cosmopolitan vision.' And these last lines, boys: 'Let us look at our reluctance'—meaning on the part of the ruling class to accept that weaving and dyeing of the fabric—'rather as the first crude beginnings of assertion on the part of certain strands in our nationality that they have a right to a voice in the construction of the American ideal. Let us face realistically the America we have around us. Let us work with the forces that are at work. Let us make something of this trans-national spirit instead of outlawing it.'" I looked up, hot and tired. "Not so bad for seventy years ago. Time's up, gents."

"One question, Doctor Berger," said Avram. *"May we look realistically* at our situation around us? This team's?"

"Yeah, sir," Jack seconded, "what about our spirit now?"

I stared at the crew, inscribing their looks of pressing inquiry in my mind, and realized how enlightened they had become in the art of reading. They paid attention. And I was learning to pay attention to them.

I closed my text and packed up, deliberately, while the boys sat confused. Then, nodding slowly at them, but not knowing how to end, I waved limply and moved off.

Realizing what was happening they called out to me, called for me to return. "Coach!" "Mr. Berger! Please!" but I just kept walking through the strips of shadow. Oh, I'd forget all of this crazy stuff, this unnatural attachment, this strange addiction, out there in straightforward UCLA. Turn my attention pure and narrow to repetitions, strategy, recruitment. And write off all of this intense brooding and reluctant affection to New England and the lingering effects of transcendentalism, circuited crazily to the peachbasket game. Something like that.

Skip ahead three months to the heat of late August. I had rented an old house out in the countryside, in a small town down the river maybe ten miles. A ramshackle farmhouse, where I mowed the lawn, fixed a thing or two, tried to forget myself. Had the boy on weekends, a very occasional female friend for an evening, and my monograph on anarchist literature for daily work. Plus the mail, which had accumulated into a Mt. Washington of correspondence and articles. While trying to face—or avoid—that mountain, I listened to Björling, Gigli, Schipa, Caruso, McCormack—and Ruffo, whose voice seemed to summon in me, now especially, the same haunting favor that it had from my father. Papa had been right; one could forget one's life, one's frustrations, listening to those voices of the past. Bereaved and unraveled, occasionally feverish with delusion, I felt my body under the influence of a low-grade flu that wouldn't disappear. It helped me to enter a realm of forgetfulness.

The NCAA had chipped in with its judgment: no Sydney Berger coaching for one year, and one year of probation for the Conway hoop program. Suspensions for numerous violations of NCAA rules. (You name the minor rule, I broke it.) The college acted ashamed and angry—no Ivy team had been punished that way in years—while others like Wim and Dick thought I had gotten a raw deal. On my behalf Marty Frommer was suing the NCAA for infringement of my First Amendment rights and character defamation. Suing for damages equal to my UCLA salary and benefits, a sum near seven figures. UCLA reacted in gentlemanly fashion, publicly declaring that I was still their coach for 1992-93. The war of threats, counterthreats and looming litigation consumed the local FedEx and USPS and heated up my telephone during the early summer, until I simply shut down my communication wires and remained unplugged and unwired for several weeks.

As I said, I distracted myself with my anarchist literary monograph, with Dan on weekends, with my attempt at a garden; life grew boring and obscure. I turned back visits from brother Robey, ex-wife Becky and even Claire, who'd called once to talk about "the futility of us," hoping, perhaps, that I no longer saw us quite that way. However, I had no tolerance for family or intimacy. In idle moments, when driving to town four miles away or further, to Rich's Shopping Plaza on 12A, I'd allow a fuller meditation on the fortunes of myself and try to figure out: What happened? What next?

In late July the boys started showing up. How'd they find me? ("Man, that's easy, Coach," said Jarrod. "Just a little detective work, first at the college and then at your son's house in Canaan.") Jarrod and Dennis arrived together, the former to announce that he had been accepted to Georgia Tech, and Dennis to say goodbye before heading off to Oxford. Destinations. They spent an afternoon, small chat stuff, Jarrod giving me new CD editions of Mingus and Billie Holiday, and it was okay. Nothing big or heavy discussed. Their company was tender, like being around a favorite old plant or pet.

In a week, however, Vargas had come up; things had turned out "really bad" down in East Cambridge. Lily Vargas got mixed up with "the creep" again; he'd beaten her and gotten himself killed in a Dorchester robbery; Lily blamed son Roberto. Crazy, but there he was, alone and vulnerable, and disconsolate. Damn! What could I do? So I gave him a room (temporary), and he got a job at a video store at a mall. (Next year he was scheduled for Michigan and a red-shirt year.) He played guitar upstairs evenings, and actually it wasn't too bad; lots of Segovia and Rodriguez stuff. (He reminded me of his studies with Rodrigo Riera, assistant to Segovia; and he wanted now to study with a protégé who lived somewhere in the area. Let him babble, I thought.)

Then Jack called, saying he was unhappy up in Olde Towne, needed some time away from family and tribe, could he come down for a short stay? I said no, that wouldn't do, really. Two days later he arrived in a beatup Ford pickup, eyes narrow (with guilt, for defying me?), and I simply turned away, in apparent indifference. It turned out that Jack not only had fast hands, he had a green thumb. In a week he had put my shabby overgrown garden into green shape; everything had been weeded, separated (radishes, carrots, tomatoes), freshly hoed, and was newly shooting up. Plus he planted three rows of potatoes (mixed with nasturtiums), brussels sprouts, kale. Oh well.

Avram showed up unannounced in the last week of August, apologized, and wore a new MIT sweatshirt ($E=MC^2$ formula), having transferred back there. He proceeded to take a huge carton from the back of his old station wagon. I turned back inside to my work. Well, two hours later, when I walked out from my study, the three of them were playing HORSE; they had rigged up a K-Mart backboard and basket on a tree by the barn where there was flat ground. I couldn't quite believe it, and when they asked me to shoot around a bit, I was dumbfounded; we even played a two on two for 7 baskets. Oh, I was out of shape and had forgotten what it was like to go up against real players, in condition.

For the weekend Avram had brought up meat piroshkis from Brookline's Russian bakery, and homemade borscht from his mother; though we ate together, I stayed quiet, purposefully glum, and retreated from the table as soon as possible. They didn't try to draw me into their circle of talk, and I was grateful for that.

I didn't understand the gathering. Didn't want to inquire, actually. I had had enough "community," I felt, for a lifetime. Or was it their community?

Anyway, Avram departed on Sunday, leaving Jack (employed now at a local garage) and Roberto. Then a phone call from Jarrod... He had heard that Nurlan was in trouble over in Albany. Maybe we should go and get him? He had gone there to play CBA ball for the Albany Patroons, and had gotten mixed up with the wrong crowd, was in danger of coking out again. My god, one minute out of my sight and care and he was in trouble! I mumbled that I didn't care and went back to the higher life, Emerson and self-reliance, Melville and allegory, Whitman and the self. Was I running a babysitting service for these kids? Sure enough, the next day Jarrod and Avram drove up with Nurlan in hand. Only three months later and he looked three years older, his smile pale and his thin torso thinner; a coat on a stick. He wore his Conway windbreaker, though it was still summery, and he sported a new goatee. "How ya doin', Coach?" He put out his feeble hand and I complimented him for his new navy beret. He laughed and gave it a little twirl, saying, "Ya always did 'preciate my caps, ya know." Getting choked, I turned away, recalling the time just a year ago when I had visited him in the jungles of Brownsville and saw a Conradian papier-mâché figure rocking and groaning in Betsy Head gym. How innocent had I been, thinking he was all cleaned up, once and for all!... Later, inside, he leaned into my study and said, "Albany's no Prescott, Coach. And CBA ball is one big mess of gunners and shootouts. Makin' the pretty pass or defendin', well, they don't rate too high." He smiled, and said, "Man, ya sure got a bunch of rooms round here. Sorta like a hotel."

Yeah, the Hotel Despair, run by Warden Berger. All right, let him have a room for a bit, stay around and put some meat on his bones, before I send him packing. Them. Indeed, the next week, as though on cue, Antoine showed, satchel in hand, brown paper bag of apples for the teacher, and staring at me; all right, come on in.

There it was, a comic utopia or sporting halfway house, with me as the reluctant director. Many thanks. For the time being I let it slide, out of inertia. You see, I myself was in limbo, waiting for a firm direction, a destination; where was I headed? And where was my spirit heading, for the depths or for recovery?... While I waited, why couldn't they wait with me, perhaps? (Chip in to pay the rent, those who could?) Weren't they four players in search of a coach? So ran my fuzzy reasoning during those Indian-summer weeks of September.

When the boys weren't working they helped out with the

chores, stacking wood, harvesting vegetables, tinkering inside, cleaning up the barn, and, surprisingly, cooking. Turned
out that Jack and Robert liked to cook and were not at all
bad—once you got used to their dishes. ("Cooking's like playing ball. It relaxes you, Coach," proclaimed Vargas.) I found
myself eating beef stews with plantains and potatoes, cold
plates of marinated codfish, thick corn soups (made with
hambone, white hominy, red kidney beans, and eaten with
bread), a legendary beef stew called *wastunkala* ("made in
the old days with dog meat"), and *wojapi*, a fruit pudding,
along with a spicy lobster stew "popular on the island." While
not exactly northern Italian, it was good, filling stuff once
you got over the taste hump.

At night, after dinner, the boys hung around the living
room, the radio playing jazz, Nurlan sketching or napping
(he slept a lot, as though he were home from combat), Robert
playing guitar or checkers, Jack working on my spare (Kaypro)
computer. To their credit they left me alone, sensing my mood.
(Only once did Jack tentatively ask if I felt like reading something aloud, but quickly saw my lack of enthusiasm.) By mid
month I was persuaded by lawyer Frommer to get a fax machine, to receive and to send the endless legal documents. It
was a good idea except that the boys started to use it to communicate with Dennis in Oxford and Jarrod in Atlanta, and
even Avram down in Cambridge. The place became a daily
beehive of fax rings and messages. The new electronic toy
was beginning to unite the group all over again, like a team
of the dispossessed. Somehow, the news of the fax number
got out—my phone was unlisted—and soon I too was receiving daily messages from the outside world, colleges, reporters,
pro clubs, agents, brother at Harvard and club owner in Rome.
Berger the Obscure was becoming a sulking Garbo.

While I waited in October for something to break legally,
like a young man waiting for his number to be called for the
army, I caught one break. Via the fax I was contacted by a
New York publisher, who offered me a six-figure advance
for a book about my Cinderella season, or, later, twenty-five

thousand for a book about teaching basketball. I was too confused, too wrought up, to try to write an account of the wild season with my players, Conway, the NCAAs. So I accepted the other offer and the lesser money. Twenty-five grand was still twenty-five grand. (Nike had written me a polite note, saying, "in view of the current unfortunate circumstance" I could not join their "team.") My Conway salary had ceased in September. So every fourth day I worked on *The Art of the Bounce Pass,* seeking to combine some of the strategy I'd developed over the past season with theories I'd been toying with for years.

The next day I'd shift gears and rejoin my anarchists at my desk. Over one shoulder I'd have Mama, Papa and Kropotkin, over the other Wooden, Iba, Newell, Clair Bee. And before me, Thoreau, Emerson, Whitman, Melville. Between basketball designing and society dismantling and literary protesting I was having myself a run.

Getting into *The Art of the Bounce Pass* gripped me, as I tried to articulate the lost art of passing in the game, beginning in the high schools and going up through the pros, but focusing on the college game. I spoke about the gradual erosion of beauty in the game, and the lack of full development of the players. Dunking and jumpshooting were weak replacements, I argued, since they encouraged individual moves, failed to inspire team play, and lost sight of a classic skill. No wonder there were so few competent pointguards left, and also why the nomenclature of "playmaker" had been dropped in favor of the narrower "pointguard." I wrote: "Without the exquisite skill of passing, a team is no more than five isolated atoms zigzagging on the floor together, wearing the same color jerseys. Consequently one of the highest beauties of the game, the timing of one player in conjunction with another with reference to foot and hand speed and the touch of the ball, is completely gone. Inevitably the high concept of the team is replaced by the schoolyard move, which signals the difference in an understanding of what the game is *in its essence* versus the perception of a glossy illusion."

Big problems arose trying to decide how, if at all, to describe what I felt a halftime speech should be. Though I recognized the importance my "Halftime Madness" (my tentative title for a short chapter) had had for my season, I was still at a loss to describe what had happened exactly. What had I been doing? Calming myself, educating them? Calming them, educating myself? Fooling them and making a fool of myself? Adding my own version of anarchy to the pretend order of the locker room at halftime? And how effective had those improvisational scenes really been? Could they be accurately measured? Or used as a model? Ridiculous!

Something else... Maybe my halftime readings had taken hold with Jack, Nurlan and the others because they were so unused to having an older man rant and rave unless he were telling them, with four-letter coarseness, what they had done wrong out on the court (and in life) and how they had embarrassed "the program"? Maybe they never had a father who was so intoxicated by certain sounds or certain narratives (or arias) that he grew lost in his own world and was now, bewitched himself, welcoming them to share in the enchantment? Maybe the stuff they got in the classroom was such thin dry gruel, so second-hand, watered-down and ideological-formulaic, that the boys were ravishingly open to the direct fresh voices of the great ones? (More likely, they were stunned by the ridiculous, vulnerable figure of their Coach, whom they cared for.) In any case there was more to those boys than Conway, or even I at the beginning, had imagined. More to their souls and sensibilities than SAT scores or GPAs or IQ tests could ever measure.... Yet how would I explain to a reader interested in the motion offense or the passing game, the unorthodox powers and healing use of high halftime rhetoric? A shot of Emerson or Whitman along with their biscuits and oranges? Indeed I was still at a loss for words, remembering only the boys' intent faces, flashes of marked text, a frenzied coach being dragged off at the buzzer by anxious assistants. So, reluctantly, I abandoned my chapter on halftime pep talks.

Though I was besieged with interview offers, I begged

off. That didn't deter *Sports Illustrated* from doing its cover story, which was three-quarters harmless and one-quarter foolish; bright coach, stupid acts. *The Journal of Higher Education* chipped in with a long piece by a philosophy professor from Northwestern, celebrating the intellectual "side" of my doings, questioning the wide moral territory of coaching nowadays, and closing by wondering whether this "half-baked, half-conman intellectual Coach" was to be the start of a new breed of college coach for the 90s? Was I "half-baked," and "half-conman"? I myself wondered. Further, inquired the prof, how had Conway acted in the affair? Not too well, on the whole; it had behaved like some giant corporate business run by lawyers, afraid of the possible glare of unpleasant publicity. Not at all like a serious university willing to look into its own house and make its own independent judgments, even to the extent of taking on the NCAA. It reinforced Professor Trimpi's growing skepticism of the moral credibility of universities in American life today. No match, he offered, for the subtlety and complication of Coach Berger's game, wayward as that was.

There appeared also typical "celebrity" pieces on Coach Berger in *Vanity Fair* and *Esquire*; not much meat. A long, damning political essay appeared in *Le Monde Hebdomadaire*, though I couldn't really follow it closely. The gist was, I had squandered a marvelous opportunity to really show up the new commercialism in American college sports. Probably right, I figured, though I didn't know that the French cared that much about basketball. Writing in the New York Times Magazine, Ira Berkow provided a long general account of the team, the season, the recruitment, coming down on my side because of my "pluralistic democratic humanism." Would he have said the same if my pointguard had been a white boy? Frank Deford spoke ambivalently about me on NPR, and George Will said I was the product of "failed secular humanism." Oh? I got hit from the Left, too. In *The Nation* their nasty lefty thrower, the wild Englishman with a penchant for beanballs, threw at me hard: "If any of you fans out there are feeling the least bit of sympathy for the so-called 'radical' coach of Conway College, forget it. The man is a liberal fraud, pure and simple. We have discovered, from our sources, the nature of those 'educational talks' at halftime, and they turn out to be the words of dead white wasp males. Nary a man or woman of color spoke forth in those halftime charades! Berger's poor boys would have been far better off listening to the rap wisdom of Ice-T or 2 Live Crew or Queen Latifah than the paternalistic pieties of Emerson, Parkman or Thoreau. The rules have changed, Coach, and we have seen through the deceitful veils of the cultural hegemony of the last 200 years. Where've you been?"

When the boys announced to me that they'd like to plan a real Thanksgiving, with Dennis and Jarrod and Avram joining us, I grew very nervous. What was going on? What was I being sucked into, enveloped by? What sort of house, or commune, was I running?

But something else happened in November that layered those nerves with a myelin sheath—except that the new membrane turned out to be yet another layer of anxiety stemming from a legal judgment handed down in the Grafton County Superior Court. The Superior Court judge, in a case brought by Jarrod's father against Conway College for its suspension—expulsion?—of the boys for a year, ordered me to turn over to the courts all my papers pertaining to the affairs of the season. Now, I knew that if I did that, the boys themselves were going to be tried, in one way or another, as accomplices, aware or unaware; the NCAA would mark them Wanted, prohibit them from playing for a year or two, and colleges like Michigan, Georgia Tech, UCLA would revoke their athletic scholarships. As for Oxford and the Rhodes people...? And who knew what any possible future clubs, NBA, CBA or European, would make of the judge's ruling? Turning myself in was one thing, but betraying the boys, via misdeeds, yet again?

What to do?

This latest dilemma weighed on me, attacking regularly

at 3:00 or 4:00 a.m., as in my divorce days, and keeping me up till dawn. I felt indecisive, torn, and so allowed the strange Thanksgiving to approach, to happen. Boys arrived in fits and starts, via air and bus and car, from Oxford and Brattleboro, from Cambridge and Atlanta. The weather was cold and grey, with snow trying to break out. From where I looked on, aloofness was the best mask for my steady ache.

I nodded to Dennis and made a remark about his new long English scarf, asking if he was "going Brit on us?"

He reddened, smiled, and said, "Coach, if you're still free later on, and care to visit, I'll take you over to the Bodley Head and show you the real thing—an original manuscript of *The Canterbury Tales*. Come in the spring, Mr. B, and you can watch me row against Cambridge in the Regatta. Now there's a taxing sport."

His phrase, "still free later on," stayed with me.

The boys did most of the cooking, and it was odd yet tender to see them fiddling about with the huge turkey. Jack and Robert were the chief chefs, making their own cranberry sauce and stuffing, and a special Lightfoot corn soup. The feast was tasty, too, as the kids joked, bantered, caught up. ("How's school?" Robert asked Avram. "MIT's no joke, huh?" Scooping sweet potato, Avram replied, "Classes no joke, but basketball is. Not worth trouble to go down for. Short on physical skills, short on... spiritual side.")

I stayed pretty quiet throughout, fading in and out with my attention, worrying about the judge's order, wondering who these boys really were, and what was their real or essential relationship with me? If I was not their Coach now, then who—what—was I?

Afterwards, about 4:00 p.m., we tried some touch football for a while, Roberto throwing long and lovely spirals, Jack and Antoine making some terrific catches, Jarrod running with deceptive hips. Until Eddie got the bright idea of trying a little hoop, and I was "encouraged" to take the gang down to the local high school, where the coach, a pal, had given me the key to the gym. And for forty-five minutes they scrimmaged, four on four, the ball rotating swiftly, the passing artful, the players moving in surprising rhythm. They still knew each other, and each other's moves, like a Swiss clockwork. The cones of light hit the floor, the sneakers squeaked in little squeals, the ball swished through the net like shots of honor, and Nurlan's laugh lit up the dim gym. In a flash it all came back, from the inept early scrimmages of a year ago, to the High Flow performance later on. The pleasure hurt now, however, and I called it quits by five.

Back home we had cider and tea with our pumpkin pie, and Eddie, across the long table, said to me, "Okay, Mr. B, a little surprise for you, sir."

I sat back in my Windsor chair, surprised and flattered.

"For your devotion, Coach," said Avram, brown eyes big.

Shuffling of bags and chairs around the long improvised table. What were they up to?

"We've practiced a little and will start with Jack here."

Jack took up a book, elbows on the wooden table, and began by saying, "This is Chief Joseph's account of the Nez Percé war, sir, printed in the... *North American Review*. Here are the Chief's words. 'I believe General Miles would have kept his word if he could have done so. I do not blame him for what we have suffered since the surrender. I do not know who is to blame. We gave up all our horses—over eleven hundred—and all our saddles—over one hundred—and we have not heard from them since. Somebody has got our horses.'"

I was dumbfounded. The audience of young men looked at me in anticipation, then back to Jack, who had paused to sip cider. The old dining room with the humpbacked floor was slanting crazily.

Jack started up again and read slowly in a flat voice. "'General Miles turned my people over to another soldier, and we were taken to Bismarck. Captain Johnson, who now had charge of us, received an order to take us to Fort Leavenworth. At Leavenworth we were placed on a low river bottom, with no water except river-water to drink and cook with. We had always lived in a healthy country, where the mountains were high and the water was cold and clear. Many of my people sickened and died, and we buried them in this strange land. I can not tell how much my heart suffered for my people while at Leavenworth. The Great Spirit Chief who rules above seemed to be looking some other way, and did not see what was being done to my people.'"

I listened to the slow careful reading, aware that the boys were periodically glancing at me. My heart, astir, thumped softly.

"'During the hot days we received notice that we were to be moved farther away from our own country. We were not asked if we were willing to go. We were ordered to get into the railroad cars. Three of my people died on the way to Baxter Springs. It was worse to die there than to die fighting in the mountains.

"'We were removed from Baxter Springs to the Indian Territory, and set down without our lodges. We had but little medicine, and we were nearly all sick. Seventy of my people have died since we moved there.'"

Jarrod remarked, "Man, with those railroad cars and shit it's a little like the Nazis doin' the Jews, huh?"

"What is 'lodges,' Jack?" asked Avram.

"Indian cabins, like wigwams or hogans," Jack replied, sipping cider. He caught my eye. "Mouth gets real dry reading, Coach." He turned back to his text. "'We have had a great many visitors who have talked many ways. Some of the chiefs from Washington came to see us, and selected land for us to live upon. We have not moved to that land, for it is not a good place to live. The Commissioner Chief came to see us. I told him, as I told everyone, that I expected General Miles's word would be carried out. He said it "could not be done";'" [voice overdramatic here] "'that white men now lived in my country and all the land was taken up; that, if I returned to Wallowa, I could not live in peace; that law-papers were out against young men who began the war, and that the Government could not protect my people. This talk fell like a heavy stone upon my heart. I saw that I could not gain anything by talking to him...'"

Jack read on slowly, almost painfully slow, yet it took hold, gradually, like the Chief himself speaking through the fog of years. At least that's how I began to take the words, the reading, after my initial shock. When I looked around just then, I saw something else: in front of each fellow, set on the table, was a book, paperback or hardcover. I was able to make out a title here, an author there; Frederick Douglass, William DuBois, *Classic Slave Narratives, Black Elk Speaks, Malcolm X.,Cheyenne Memories.* I nodded to myself, settled deeper into my chair, and sensed that it was going to be a long, long evening. My reward.

The Nez Percé chief via Jack continued slowly to lay out his painstaking tale, and it was a relief not to be the host but the guest; I had the freedom to drift, to inspect closely the enterprising lads. They had dressed for the occasion, I suddenly realized. Robert wore a riverboat vest over his wide-collar white-on-white shirt, and looked Brando-dreamy with those dark eyes and long slickbacked hair. Dennis, squarejawed and blue-eyed, sparkled as everyone's version of a young scholar, buttondown shirt and knit tie; only the mobile mouth expressed the mischievous mirth. Nurlan lounged about, fiddled with his maroon French beret, wore an oversized sport jacket and oversized grin. Brown matte face healthy again. Eddie the freckled Red leaned forward attentively, tartan check flannel shirt open at the white T-shirt neck, red hair combed and parted on the left side, the pure small-town bumpkin. Jarrod, absolutely preppy-spiffy in a cableknit white cardigan sweater with yellow GA Tech logo and piping, played an imaginary riff on the table, while listening. Antoine, with huge Afro, single earring and gold chain over a dark turtleneck, stared intently, an ebony Gasparilla. Avram sat bolt upright, attired in a formal navy blazer and dress shirt with cufflinks, Cross pen in hand for notes. And Jack, wearing his Final Four white cap and v-neck Conway pullover, jet-black hair flowing by his shoulders, appeared ready to break into chant at any moment, a shaman or cantor. Oh, it was a crew all right, an odd *minyan* (almost), and they were mine for better or worse.

"'Then the Inspector chief came to my camp and we had a long talk. He said I ought to have a home in the mountain country north, and that he would write a letter to the Great Chief at Washington. Again the hope of seeing the mountains of Idaho and Oregon grew up in my heart.

"'At last I was granted permission to come to Washington and bring my friend Yellow Bull and our interpreter with me. I am glad we came. I have shaken hands with a great many friends, but there are some things I want to know which no one seems able to explain. I can not understand how the Government sends a man out to fight us, as it did General Miles, and then breaks his word. Such a government has something wrong about it. I can not understand why so many chiefs are allowed to talk so many different ways, and promise so many different things. I have seen the Great Father Chief (the President), the next Great Chief (the Secretary of the Interior), the Commissioner Chief, the Law Chief (General Butler), and many other law chiefs (Congressmen), and they all say they are my friends, and that I shall have justice, but while their mouths all talk right I do not understand why nothing is done for my people. I have heard talk and talk, but nothing is done.

"'Good words do not last long unless they amount to something. Words do not pay for my dead people. Words do not pay for my country, now overrun by white men. They do not protect my father's grave. They do not pay for all my horses and cattle. Good words will not give me back my children. Good words will not make good the promise of your War Chief General Miles. Good words will not give my people good health and stop them from dying. Good words will not get my people a home where they can live in peace and take care of themselves. I am tired of talk that comes to nothing. It makes my heart sick when I remember all the good words and all the broken promises. There has been too much talking by men who had no right to talk.'"

As Jack paused here to moisten his throat again, I thought the Chief had a point—good talk was not going to solve my problems either. Good talk was not good play, in other words; yes, I saw his point.

Water looked over at me, and, with a glint in his eye, wondered, "Like halftime, Coach?"

I nodded. "A little like that."

And as Jack wound up the record again, his steady baritone voice going on, and on, and on, I thought it was going to be a long halftime, the whole night as well as evening, maybe even a long few days.

17 MY FELLOWSHIP YEAR

Having always aspired to a Guggenheim Fellowship for my work in U.S. History, I looked on my six months-to-a-year incarceration as my private version, a period of reading, writing and reflecting without large distractions or interruptions. Things could have been worse for a middle-aged fellow bent on finishing up two projects (one long-delayed), and bent too by events in his public life. Would Ahab have gone off in his mad pursuit—transforming Moby Dick into the general Evil of the world and his own personal enemy—had a Guggenheim arrived in the mail one March morning, offering him a year free to scribble his Memoirs?... So I interpreted my civil contempt charge not as penalty, but as reward. An idiosyncratic reward to fit my peculiar follies and ideals. After fifty, after all, weren't all objects and relationships of apparent solidity melted down and transformed by our fixed habits, whims, perceptions?

Of course no one wanted me to go to jail, or to stay in jail: not even me, at first. Not the law or lawyers, not the NCAA or Conway, not the parents (pursuing their class action suit) or the judge. It was all rather embarrassing, a public nuisance. No one believed I was a common criminal, a felon; no, I was a complicated rogue, a New-World sports scoundrel, a coach with sleazy scruples. Better to keep me roasting out there on the publicity spit—the pages of *Sports Illustrated* or the *New York Times* sports section. But once I got involved in the various suits—thanks to others' litigation and counselor Frommer—as defendant and as plaintiff, the judge wanted me to turn over all possible written documents which could explain and clarify matters: recruitment letters, admissions applications (and my "participation"), essays "reworked," receipts and checks for "personal aids" to the boys (bus tickets, gym bags, two pairs of Nike hightops, two Bean parkas, loans for clothes. How about Hallmark Notes of Good Cheer, Your Honor? Hot evidence also?) I thought: why get involved? By the letter of the rules and laws, I had done wrong, I knew. By the curve of the higher good, however, I had done well. (Double well, maybe: giving the kids a shot at a real higher education, and myself a shot at a real basketball squad.) More important, if I had turned over all my papers to the judge, the boys inevitably would have gone down the drain too, become implicated, lost out in the long run, with colleges, job opportunities, their good name. But in my book, they had been clean; and brave. How could I betray them again?

Stay put, I had figured, turn over nothing, accept the full-court press. "No, sir, I would prefer not to give you my papers," I had said quietly to the judge, not mentioning my borrowing from Bartleby. "And Your Honor, if I may say so, the State would have to hire an unusual team of investigators, headed by moral philosophers and serious thinkers, to look into all the rules and standards governing higher education and student athletes. A Moral Clean Air Act, sir, to check into the full pollution of the last few decades in higher education and NCAA sports."

Judge Powers nodded, smiled, said he thought I had a point, and sentenced me to the House of Corrections until I delivered the documents. As the guards came to lead me away, he added goodnaturedly, "I happen to be a hoop fan myself, Mr. Berger, and caught a few of your games last season. They were a pleasure to watch."

That was September. Then it was November. There I sat. Yes, I had my small chores and tasks to be sure. But that too was volitional on my part, since I only got to help out when one of the regular prisoners was sick and the dairy farm needed help. (Not that the labor was awful; shoveling hay or manure, milking cows or feeding chickens was more bracing than dealing with administrators.) For the most part I was free enough to get my work done there in minimum security, in the day room (like a library), except when some charming forger or bank embezzler (former president) insisted on engaging me in small talk; or else, to read, hear music on my CD (via earphones), or view my tapes. You see, doing time at the Grafton County House of Corrections in North Haverhill, New Hampshire, was not exactly a Gulag or Attica experience. The bed was fine, the three squares a day were filling, the guards were okay. (And Ronnie Smith, the head administrator, was human.) Though the library was modest, books and magazines were obtainable. The mail service delivered regularly, and once a week something of interest turned up. From my high window in the 1880s brick building I sighted families of barn swallows and evening grosbeaks, swooping and diving. And courtesy of my book advance, I had a smart new laptop to use, with 40 megs of memory to supplement my half-meg brain. The daylight hours were mostly quiet, long, even serene. What more could a reasonable man want?

Freedom, truth, values? Good talk? But where were you going to find those qualities—in society? At today's universities?

I had my share of visitors. For example, my lawyers. I now had a local one, added to my big-city one; shouldn't every respectable citizen, America 1991, be equipped with two, one for rights and one for suits? The local fellow, from a mountain hamlet, was a tall, loping, mustached Irishman in his late thirties, an exile from Los Angeles and Catholicism, who had settled here with his upper-class, true-grit New England wife. An avid reader and garrulous talker, Charles

McDonough had a wide range of interests (not sports), and a varied wit; every time he visited, he was like a fresh Irish tenor blowing in. Except when he exhorted me to give in and turn over the documents to the judge and get back out into the real world, so that pending suits could be dealt with, and charges against me dismissed. What could I do then but smile, tell a Yiddish joke or anarchist anecdote, and tune out. Get back out? For what, more hypocrisy, lies, calumny? (The college propaganda, in public pronouncements and alumni letters, had made me into the complete fall guy. So, simultaneously, the *Review* and Conway had the same common enemy. And maybe they were right? The *Review,* and *Wall Street Journal,* had had a field day, running editorials on the "pyrrhic victory of the Politically Correct Hoop Experiment" and its "ethnic PC Coach.") For more self-betrayal?...

My other lawyer, Marty Frommer, was much intrigued by my refusal to emerge, and had begun to see the "literary" side of things. Meaning, he was thinking of how to use the unusual situation to our benefit, first in his suit against the NCAA (i.e., the libel-damage figure) and secondly, in a subsequent related suit—joining Jarrod's original suit—against the college. Conway's lack of due process in suspending me in the first place added bias to the first case, and so on. If it sounds a bit tangled, more than I could understand, it was. Who knows, "Berger versus Conway College" and "Berger versus the NCAA" might have equaled Jarndyce versus Jarndyce in longevity and complexity. ("Jarndyce versus Jarndyce drones on. The scarecrow of a suit has, in the course of time, become so complicated that no man alive knows what it means. The parties to it understand it least...") Marty, dear Bronx soul, quietly drooled at the idea of taking on both venerable institutions—the national sports colossus and the prestigious Ivy college—taking them on, and upward, to the Supreme Court. Taking on the "big dicks" excited Marty, the way an Olivier might have been excited by a juicy modern Shakespearean role.

On another level, we'd already been offered several movie

"situations" by Hollywood producers, agents, and television. Naturally we'd accepted nothing, and taken the names down. To receive such offers in movieland America was standard operating procedure; would you please join in our long-running serial on euphemizing/phonying up history, and allow your life to be screen-dubbed into ninety minutes of sleazy celluloid myth? (Our refusals only jacked up the figures, Marty casually noted.)

Brother Robey deigned to BMW up from Cambridge and grinned over my "clever gig." Huffing with Cotton Mather wisdom and brotherly sarcasm ("You're not trying to play Thoreau, are you?") Robey wondered seriously if the "jail shtick" expressed a secret need to show Mom that I still wore "Red undershorts," or else, was it a ploy to up the ante for UCLA? Fascinated like a cobra facing a prairie dog Robey sat with his legs crossed, and tried to find out what was eating me. "I hope it's still not the sibling rivalry bit," he smiled, slipping me his latest imprint—his academic shiv—as he left, and reminding me that he was still my brother; if I needed anything... (Like a publisher for my literary monograph, bro? Robey was a reader for the Yale Press. For the past two years I had omitted mentioning to him that literary project of mine languishing on his turf.)

Claire came, begged me to come to my senses, told me she had a new "friend," then cried out, "No matter what you do to yourself I'll always respect you immensely!"

Little Dan visited a few times too, and considered me and the situation with a mixture of fear and thrill. He was eager to know Everything about the lurid side of jail, while I showed him the library, the crafts room, the cows. "Are there forgers and kidnappers here, Papa?" "Is that man a real thief?" and "Can we sit *in your cell* and talk there?" The harder queries then came. "Can you really leave whenever you want to? Then *why* don't you want to?" How could I answer my 7-year-old pal, when I was not fully sure myself? Maybe it was fear and thrill on my part, too?

The boys paid a couple of visits. They also seemed a little

confused, and even a little ashamed by my act. That was okay since I hadn't tried to explain my action to anyone, though the speculations had been rife. Anyway, the threesome of Jack and Roberto and Antoine showed up first, and strolled about, filling me in on the farmhouse (for which I was still paying a piece of the rent; only fair), and hesitantly asking me what was up, why was I staying in the joint this way? "Oh, it's just a retreat, to think things over a little, get some work done in seclusion." They stared at me with a fishy look. "Nurlan okay?" I asked, and they said he was still over at Stevens High, assisting the coach. "Good. I'll see you boys soon enough." I shook hands at the end. The next group arrived in snowy February: Avram, Nurlan, Eddie. "Are you stayin' here to protect us somehow, Coach?" asked Nurlan, sporting dreadlocks. "You shouldn't." Avram added. "We can accept all reality after what we go through." Yes, but could I? Actually, I was getting a lot of work done; my October rationalization had become a January truth.

"Thanks, friends. I'll remember that. In the long run, I think you fellas are protecting me. So, Water, how goes it, any more feelers from the pros or the European clubs?"

"Ya know, Coach, the thing that I really miss is your peculiar education talks. I mean they were real weird at first, but then we sorta got into the rhythm of it, and began to take something to heart out of em. Most classes are, you know, like Muzak, goin' in one ear and out the next, whereas those little lectures and readings of yours, Mr. B, well we got used to hearin' the *voices* of them different Americans even if sometimes they were hard to understand and stuff. Maybe it was your voice that sorta lullabied us too, huh? It's funny ain't it that the best class we had was one we didn't get no course credit for?"

A note arrived from Jarrod offering consolation and saying, "Man, now I know what a real athletic scholarship means. The perks would blow you away!" There was also a surprising note from Chip Bromley: "You did wrong for my school, but I'm genuinely sorry to lose you. You were the best coach ever. You had something special."

As I said, I was working hard, and *Bounce Pass* was coming. I had come to believe that while you could *see* the actual game on the court, you could only *understand* its full spiritual/mathematical beauty by writing about it. But trying to describe my zone of High Flow without having it sound like gibberish was daunting indeed. I wrote that by emphasizing the passing game and the playmaker, and by practicing thousands of repetitions and drills, you might finally hit seven or eight minutes of a game, maybe twenty percent, when the game was played the way it was designed; if you could move into that zone and get the flow going, you could win most games. In other words, play the game according to its internal harmony, with five players becoming one, that one becoming the sum of its own equation, and that sum becoming a new number, way beyond the total of its parts, and equalling play as perfection, motion as a form of transcendence.

(Naturally I realized the equation to be made between New England Transcendentalism and Berger High Flow—the team transcending the individual and playing the game in its *purity* for a short while equated with faculties that give man ideas and intuitions that "transcend" sensational experience; how the Team was Immanent in each player and offered spiritual energy much as the Oversoul did to man. But I wouldn't dare write down that stuff in such a book.)

Something else occurred to me, a spinoff from that idea: the notion that maybe my halftime half-baked superfluous readings may have been my attempt at getting into a personal coaching zone, my own High Flow of pure *Bergerisme:* a territory of rhetorical (and emotional) illusion that suggested my *eccentric* sense of native ground. But I didn't try to make too much of all that, since it really was an after-the-fact theory, a neat construction to shield against the sheer chaos of that experience.

Frankly, in looking back at my halftime excursions into compulsive reading and lecturing, I myself was filled with doubt and amazement, if not outright skepticism. What the hell had I put in my evening pastas, piss instead of pesto? Did those scenes really happen? I recalled a few sentences of Nurlan's after one halftime outburst: "Man, if I wasn't just sittin' here, witnessin' that, *I wouldn't a believed it.*" He laughed. "Though, come to think 'bout it, I 'spose I wouldn't a believed a lotta the scenes in my life, if I hadn't witnessed them myself." He had a point.

Something else. I knew too that many a speech I had heard in a locker room at halftime was not to be believed, for a different reason: the flow of vituperation and demeaning obscenity aimed at young athletes by adult men paid by universities as teacher-coaches was nothing short of hard-to-believe, amazing. Teacher-coaches or canines in heat? Any reasonable person or innocent professor hearing an uncensored tape of some college coaches' halftime talks, would be astounded and would wonder about their credibility. Was my own highbrow babble equally incredible but more dangerous, more injurious in the long run? Well, I couldn't quite judge all that. What I did know, from experience and from literature, was that some of our best moments were our least probable, and many of our worst, our most believable. Who knows, perhaps I was best when babbling in closed session, in full dramatic monologue heat? Maybe. I remained skeptical on all counts.

(I have forgotten to add here that during this past year I have consulted, on and off, with Dr. Emma Lichtman, a fortyish English therapist practicing in the north woods after marrying a Conway doctor, and used by the Grafton court as an "expert witness." Trained in London as a Kleinian, sporting vivid Liberty scarves and a trenchant wit, Emma grew interested in my "case," especially the halftime excursions. She tried out varying interpretations for my character, from MPD ("multiple personality disorder") to BP ("borderline personality"), before settling for a case of severe nerves and an obsessive need to succeed. I see... Since she had never seen a basketball game, or read our native literature, I showed her a few game tapes, adding commentary, and offered a reading list: Parkman, Whitman, Emerson... Noting that I was a "man of parts," she said it was a shame that my unresolved guilt and anger were keeping me from functioning well, and leaving the clink. I accepted her judgment, but also found that her clipped accent, sensible clothes and no-nonsense talks were consoling.)

One other notion sprang up, in writing. I came to conclude that a splendid coach is, in a certain crucial respect, a *superfluous fellow.* If you had taught the team very well; if your system was true and intelligent, and absorbed by the layers; if they ran the floor like a Swiss clockwork, trained by thousands of hours of repetition to make varying adjustments to any defensive pattern; then there was hardly any need for Coach to be present. I recalled the game I had kicked myself out of, and later the playoff game where I had been banned from the bench; the boys had played their parts fluently. So there was a perfect paradox in coaching well; *you could be superfluous.* Sitting in my jail, superfluous as a citizen too, I felt fond of that little philosophical irony, that novel way of looking at a coach's job. *(Bergerisme?)*

March came, bringing the season of hoop madness and memories of the year past, memories most vivid and therefore most painful. At the same time legal briefs were filed and it really looked like the season—or decade?—of litigation might also begin soon enough. Nurlan had sent me Piranesi-like charcoal sketches of the Powerhouse Mall in West Lebanon, and I hung them. Robert sent me a few of his own guitar tapes, and I listened. Dennis wrote amusing letters from Oxford, and I read. (Roberto had been contacted by Real Madrid, while Nurlan was periodically called by scouts from the Timberwolves and the Tel Aviv Maccabees. I advised them to go ahead, but they said no, they were waiting. For what, for me to come out of hiding, hibernation? Poor boys. And when UCLA finally wrote a nice note, saying they had decided to go in another direction after all, due to trustee pressure, and hire someone immediately, I felt relieved.

With fitting irony, I was asked by ESPN if I would consider being a guest analyst for the upcoming NCAA Tournament? Oh, that touched me. But did they know something I didn't? Were they going to wire me at the Grafton House of Corrections, and bring cameras in? I told Chris Berman that the offer was most uplifting, but I happened to be sitting tight for now in cell number 14. "No, no," the ESPN anchor explained, "you see, we've gotten permission to fly you out to the studio for the evening show and return you early the next morning." Indeed the prison was aflutter with the news, and I was encouraged to go. Confused, I checked in with Emma, and we discovered that I didn't really want that sort of celebrity outing. When I declined, Robin Roberts said, "It's a standing invitation, Coach, should you change your mind." A gutsy, honest station; why not an ESPN University?

The turn into March, and into painful memory, also brought a more pleasurable routine: the return to use of my precious video tapes. On the rented VCR I began to rerun my Cinderella season all over again, and became a newly devoted fan. In the evening, after the "feeding" hour (quaintly named), I watched, with careful controls set by Mr. Smith. (Frequently I had a cellmate or two who were sports fans, not to mention a few guards, and they viewed with me. And every so often this conman or that embezzler or burglar would notice the Conway Coach in his excited state on the sidelines, point a finger at me, and do a doubletake!) I would watch two, three times a week, following the schedule of the actual season, and sense the old rhythm. Ah, March, the swishes of March!

I'd view anew the magical ballhandling of Water, and his wide white smile as he wove his way through a tangle of bodies, dribbling through angles and openings like dribbling through the eye of the needle. Or slow the frame to see the subtle feel for the offensive board that Roberto possessed, timing the ball and his opponent perfectly, and sneaking himself into the inside position at the last moment. Freeze up close the defensive stance of Jack, the refined thief, as he feigned neutrality and anticipated a casual pass, springing forward to steal it and move downcourt. Instinct. I'd watch Eddie do all the boring things that a team needs and a fan misses—setting the picks and slipping off the screens, rebounding, throwing the outlet pass and hustling downcourt to be the scoring trailer. Focus anew on Avram's feathery jumper, delivered corkscrew from behind his ear, and watch it float up and up on that perfect arc, before beginning its exquisite descent into net. Admire all over the poise of young Jarrod when he was doubleteamed, the high post pick-and-go learned by stalwart Dennis, the blunt bodybanging of Antoine on the boards. Watching all that, I imagined it must have been like viewing reruns of old Astaire/Rogers films, where the stepping got better and better with each run as familiarity and leisurely repetition nudged you to take note of a new nuance of excellence, an unexpected gesture of subtlety. In all this play there was beauty, in all this motion there was poetic purpose and resolution; and as I observed my boys transformed into that block of Canadian geese timing their formations and flying with disciplined grace, it made my heart leap, my soul awaken. I wanted to honk too!

Jail? What jail?

Why leave these addictive repetitions, this subtle art, for distraction and disillusionment and imperfection out there?

18 THE PROMISED LAND

Flying across the wedged snow-capped mountains of the Continental Divide I felt as though I were flying into a a wider expanse of possibility; a new life or a new illusion? The thin stripe of pale blue horizon seemed just ahead, obtainable. Our big steel bird flew steadily, smoothly, balanced coolly above a cushion of white clouds. Self-illusion was as easy to come by up in the wild blue yonder at 38,000 feet, hermetically sealed by Boeing, as it was sitting in that New Hampshire cell for nearly a year. Listening to the news about the breakup of Russia, I wondered what Mom and Dad would have thought, and if that was to be my Humpty-Dumpty fate too?

Not entirely self-illusion, was it? I mean when I finally responded, out of prodding by the boys, to the BYU athletic director in mid-March during the NCAAs, Dr. Turnbull immediately perked up and said yes, of course he remembered his letter of interest last year, and he would be delighted to see me, just say the word. So I said it and there I was, a week later, flying high with suspended disbelief on my way to Provo. Looking for what—a coaching job, a second chance, a redemption among the Mormons?

The boys were in such a bedraggled condition, Nurlan, Jack and Roberto all drifting down there on "Hardscrabble

Farm," the others scribbling notes of puzzlement and uncertainty, and their parents moving from anger to deep disquiet and fears, that I gave in and turned over whatever papers I had to the judge (and let him make sense of them). My boys had gone out onto the floor for me, against their principles, so it was only fair for me to emerge from the clink for them. (Simple, Sydney, after nine months of not getting it.) Rereading my mail I came across the Brigham Young note: "If you're ever free, come see us. After what you did in the '90 NCAA Tournament, you're our man." Well, all that was fine and dandy to say when it didn't cost a plugged nickel, but how about when it would cost you real dollars and (maybe) professional status? Would they go for an ex-jailbird coach who was also facing possible probation with the almighty NCAA gods?

Get out and get moving for the sake of my boys, who still hung around my heart, no matter how hard I tried to release them (and myself). Get out and get moving, for this was America, I told myself, where the territory was trick or treat, you guess which. And just when you thought you had something figured out, poof! Anyway, good things had happened before for me in Salt Lake City, so why not hear the man out, enjoy the free ride and change of climate and temperament? Furthermore, wouldn't a good Jewish-Italian coach with a trim beard and anarchist wrinkles look just right against a Mormon backdrop?

Josiah Turnbull, A.D., was sixtyish, lean, lantern-jawed, white-haired, hawknosed, and looked like the son of stern Joe Smith, whose portrait hung above his desk. Greeting me as his present savior, Turnbull shook my hand hard and said, "We need a coach bad, to shake this place up, put the hoop game back on a par with the old days of '51 or '81, teach the kids and rekindle the fires. We need *a leader.* Judging from what Frank Layden and I saw in those NCAA's, you're our man."

I shook my head, dazzled and confused. I thought to remind him, "You realize that the NCAA investigation is still pending?"

357

"Look," he leaned across the desk, "an allegation is an allegation, as worthwhile as yesterday's newspaper, so far as I'm concerned. Mormons, you know," and he flashed a wicked grin, "are used to 'allegations.'" He waved a little green and white desk-flag. "Besides, from what I've heard from my spy in Kansas, there's never gonna be a final set of charges brought. Too damned risky, controversial, what with the ACLU hounds sniffing all around their turf. So if you want the job, you got it, son—beginning this July 1, when the interim man is done."

Chest heaving at the sudden news, I turned to my pipe, lit up and puffed deliberately. "I'm flattered, sir. Grateful." His zeal and charge was like some rhino digging in to let loose, and it scared me as much as excited me.

"Oh, yes, Sydney, one other item of interest—those boys of yours who got a raw deal and lost their scholarships, if you want any of 'em back in college, bring 'em back alive here!" He winked at his updated Frank Buck line. "Our Admissions Office is sympathetic to student athletes, we're proud to say. And the more *diverse* the better these days." He winked again. "Just as long as they can read a little, write a tad, say 'sir' once a week and tie a necktie for the alumni banquets. And maybe eke out some sort of a 2.1 in Hotel or Sports Management or Desert Landscaping or whatever!"

The boys back in college; oh that lifted my spirit! Back with me, back with schooling, back with a team—there's a homecoming! I got up and walked about and stared at the photos of the Mel Hutchins team of '51 and the Danny Ainge team of '81, and I imagined a photo for '92: Nurlan and my diverse ducklings beaming in their new uniforms and posed in a semi-circle with their mother duck Coach. *So what if that Coach would be forever tainted, marked with an asterisk like some Scarlet Letter, and probably banned for five years from The Big Dance. Coach deserved his banishment, unlike his innocent crew.*

"Come on over here and have a look out," he said, and I joined him at the picture window. "They're special, aren't they? That's Mt. Timpanagos, some 12,000 feet, and over there is Provo Peak, maybe 11,000. We got everything here, grand landscape, grand kids, grand tradition. But we've got *lousy* basketball teams. Syd, do you realize we haven't made a Final Four yet, ever? That's where you're going to take us, right up atop that Wasatch Range." He draped his arm around my shoulders. "That's your mission, my friend. We got the white boys, you'll bring in the colored boys, and you'll shake 'em and bake 'em and turn 'em into a team, by God! A Final Four team!" He squeezed me hard.

I stared out at the impressive range of mountains, looming like an unreal postcard, white-capped with snow in early June. I felt curious, indeed, as though he really were declaring my Mission. Oh, I had better read up on these Mormons, maybe start with the journals of Brigham Young, and get better acquainted with the place, people, traditions. Hadn't they too—like me—come in out of the cold, gathering themselves here to escape persecution and exile?

"What are your thoughts, son?" Turnbull still held me.

"Well, I guess I was just thinking about how to learn the ropes around here."

He clapped my shoulder. "That's the spirit! You know, son, you bring us to the Final Four, and maybe win one, and who knows, you may be listed up there as a modern Latter-Day Saint!"

His fierce blue eyes blazed, a madman with a transcendental vision. I felt Mom and Dad observing me as I studied the Mormons instead of their Anarchists, Brigham Young and Joe Smith for Bakunin and Kropotkin. Well, I rationalized, one group of outcasts for another, right? Besides, hadn't they taught me a healthy respect for rebels and exiles of any sort?... Why, there was an opera developing here, a *Berger of the Golden West*, say, with this life of mine.

Turnbull wasn't finished. "You bring us that Holy Grail and doggone, you may be nominated for the Council of Twelve. The Mormons are like that, rallying behind some leper or outcast who turns it around against all the odds with pride and honor!"

My leper's head was spinning from all the heady news, and Josiah took me by the arm and led me to a chair.

"Oh, Sydney, one last thing," he said, sitting on the edge of his desk and swinging his legs, Argyle socks showing. "Are those rumors half-true that you deliver a most unusual half-time preparation? Something about bluestocking lectures and readings?" He roared suddenly and slapped his knee hard. "My oh my, if that's true," he leaned forward his lake-blue eyes twinkling mischievously, "do you think we might work that up into a regular course and get the boys college credits for it? That'd be a first, huh?"

Halftime Neurosis as a course? Why not? On the other hand, I thought, why not indeed give the kids a real education instead of the pap and politics they received at colleges today? A little Emerson, a little Parkman, a bit of DuBois and Santayana. Before you know it a kid is hearing the right sentences, the right voices in his ears. Then even a gym rat is dangerous.

"Not a bad idea, eh?"

I eyed the curious angular creature. Was he teasing or provoking? A madman of perverse cunning or a truly innovative A.D. out to test me? Taking no chances I smiled and replied, "'Democratic Vistas, 1.1.' Why not?"

He bolted forward excitedly, again putting forth his hand, and I stood up to clasp it, half in fear and self-protection.

As we shook firmly on this new bargain, I improvised on the BYU nickname, "Berger's Cougars." For a moment the phrase had a kind of ring to it, before the dark asterisk by my name hit my heart. Could Joseph Smith, via Josiah Turnbull, transform that too?

After a moment his face tightened and he shot out, "Be forewarned: I can be a bulldog at times, often called by the media and faculty an 'impossible man.' What do you say to that?"

Well, it was one of those moments when the word or phrase fired out at you in challenge swiftly ricochets around your brain and lands in the most obscure pocket of childhood, only to emerge in the next instant in adult terms, fresh as yester-year: "'I shall continue to remain an impossible person,'" repeating one of the quotes from my mother's anarchist quiver, "'so long as those who are now possible remain possible.'"

Helpless, I smiled wanly and said, "Bakunin."

His gaunt face travelled from wonder to puzzlement to grin, grin turning into laughter, raucous laughter. "Well, I don't know who *that* fella is, but I do know *we* got the right one."